The
Acacia

Pantheon Books   New York

The
ACACIA

A Novel

Claude   Simon

Translated from the French by Richard Howard

All rights reserved under International and Pan-American Copyright Conventions. Published in the United States by Pantheon Books, a division of Random House, Inc., New York, and simultaneously in Canada by Random House of Canada Limited, Toronto. Originally published in France as *L'Acacia* by Les Editions de Minuit, Paris, in 1989. Copyright © 1989 by Les Éditions de Minuit.

Library of Congress Cataloging-in-Publication Data

Simon, Claude.
[L'Acacia. English]
The Acacia : a novel / Claude Simon ; translated from the French
by Richard Howard.
p.   cm.
Translation of: L'Acacia.
ISBN 0-394-58771-5
I. Title.
PQ2637.I547A6413   1991
843'.914—dc20   90-52554

Book Design by Fearn Cutler
Illustrations by Jenny Vandeventer

Manufactured in the United States of America
First American Edition

Time present and time past
Are both perhaps present in time future,
And time future contained in time past.
　　　　—*T. S. Eliot*, Four Quartets

The

Acacia

I

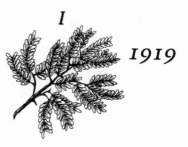 *1919*

*T*HEY went from village to village, and in each one (or at least in what was left of it) from house to house, sometimes to an isolated farm someone would tell them about, reached by stumbling along overgrown paths, their city shoes yellowed by the mud one of the two sisters repeatedly tried to wipe off with a wisp of grass, holding her black glove in the other hand, bent over like a servant, admonishing the widow who would reluctantly set her foot on a stone or a post and let it be wiped off while her eyes kept greedily scouring the countryside, the sopping fields no plow had turned for five years, the woods where there was still a touch of green, sometimes a whole tree, sometimes a single branch on which a few twigs had sprouted again, splitting the shredded bark.

Eventually people recognized them, got used to them. When it was possible, they would hire a taxi into which all three of them squeezed along with the child, over-charged by the driver with that pitiless rapacity of the poor cheating the poor (not that they were poor—at least not the widow—since they were rich enough to travel in this region where, at the time, the smallest hotel room—when there was a hotel—cost as much as a suite at the Ritz; it wasn't that kind of poverty which he (the driver) detected, but the other kind, the poverty of disaster), indifferent to the timid whispering of the two sisters while the widow paid him, counted out one after the next the limp, filthy bills (as if the money itself had been infected, contaminated by the same leprosy that seemed to have scourged the whole region, farms and farmers alike, leaving only stumps and shacks standing, walls here and there braced by beams stripped from other hovels, propping corrugated-iron roofs or just tar-paper patches like bandages), her face remote, somehow ghostly behind the black crape veil she folded back, pushing it over her shoulder, exposing her plump, flabby flesh, when they would stop to eat in some tavern or even some canteen, one of those American huts planted or actually stuck into the mud at the intersection of what had once been roads, now rutted so deeply that the trucks swayed and bounced, the drivers occasionally stopping to give them a ride, the two sisters standing behind the cab, joggled from side to side, clinging to the racks, the widow and child inside, the driver (a young recruit waiting for his discharge to come through) steering carefully to avoid nesting hens while he stole glances at the dim profile of the woman in mourning silhouetted against the transparent crape, at once imperious and outraged, stamped with that proud and inflexible determination recognizable on the medals of ancient empresses or, simply, in madwomen.

She was still young, under forty, judging from the full figure in those clothes whose choice (black shoes, black stockings, black coat, black toque over which the veil hung down) had for all its modesty—or perhaps even because of its austerity belied by the quality of the material, the cut, the accessories—something showy, stagey, like those outfits designed for nuns belonging to some worldly and lay order to be met with in salons or at official ceremonies, mingling with or directing groups of nurses, revealing, narrowly framed in veils like those masks of carved tomb figures, only the oval of faces affable yet severe, waxen, and remote. One night they slept in the dormitory of a convent (or of a seminary) where the beds were separated by white canvas curtains on rings. Once they slept in a café whose owner charged them the price of three rooms (he said he wouldn't count the child), the two women lying on banquettes or on chairs, the widow and the boy on the billiard table, right on the green cloth, the widow merely removing her hat, folding up the veil which she put on top of her bag as a pillow for the boy, who fell asleep on contact with the rough crape and its similarly rough smell and the heavy stone body lying beside his own. The billiard room was separated from the café by a wooden partition with ground-glass panels at the top over which late in the night came the clink of glasses and drunken voices. Once someone pushed open one of the swinging doors and a sheaf of yellow light spread into the room, and then while a voice stammered something, vanished, leaving on the retina of the child suddenly wakened the image of the plump Bourbonian profile, unmoved, calm, terrifying, eyes open on the empty darkness. Later (the lights were turned off by then, the drinkers gone), she carefully removed her coat, which she spread over the child. Once they slept in a hotel where the hallways were bricked up at one end, the mortar bulging against the plaster at the corners. From outside you could see the collapsed wing of the building, with wallpaper of different colors, yellow, pink, or pale blue, patterned with tiny flowers or garlands and hanging loose over the cone of rubble that half clogged the bed of a gray, nearly stagnant stream whose surface, like a sheet of tarnished pewter, drifted in silence among the wreckage, showing in a murky transparency, when a rare sunbeam pierced it, myriads of flecks of dust suspended, floating slowly with the stream, as if, from its very source, down its entire length and along all its meanders, it were draining the remains of some rain of ashes, some definitive, total cataclysm doomed to wash without hope of an end this earth consigned to sterility and these heaps of rubble among which the two women and the child followed the implacable odyssey of the widow who was dragging them behind her.

She did not complain, blamed no one. It was as if she met the discomfort, the carts, the trucks, the thieving taxi drivers, the food like gobs of burnt phlegm, the filthy toilets, and the mugs of bitter coffee with a sort of tragic satisfaction. She was the first one up in the morning, fully dressed at daybreak, as if, even during the nights when she had been able to sleep in a bed, she had not undressed, impatient (not that she didn't eat, but whether because she was in a hurry to be on her way again or because this was simply her habit, she did so very quickly: something fierce, a kind of voracity, a frenzy, a gluttony it might have seemed if, like the way she dressed or held herself, the way she managed to dispose of what was on her plate had not also possessed that character of rigor and lofty severity which emanated from her: simply from one moment to the next the plate (or the cup) was empty, the napkin which she seemed not to have touched already folded again, her hand gathering into a tiny heap the scattered crumbs, the face impassive), waiting in silence for the other two women (the two sisters) who hurriedly dipped their slices of stale bread into the mugs of coffee.

As if they had been her servants or, at best, ladies-in-waiting, though kissing each of them when they met in the morning or separated in the evening, speaking to them with that gentleness and that slightly vexed patience, as to persons of an inferior rank, poor relatives, old people, or children, though they were obviously older than she, differing not only by their square faces, their square—and creased—hands, but even by their garments which, though also dark, did not have that showy and somber uniformity, nor the look of coats or dresses cut to order by a seamstress, but sewn together from a pattern on an oilcloth-covered table, basted and tried on themselves, and finally stitched up once and for all, too tight or too loose, embellished with collars or scraps of worn fur.

The people she would question (the café owners, the nuns in the convent, the farmers' wives who cooked them omelettes in rancid grease) decided that they were sisters-in-law. While chalking the price of the omelettes on the scrap of paper torn out of a notebook, they tried to estimate the value of a diamond appearing when the widow had drawn off her gloves, would mumble something and vanish into the kitchen, returning with the bill revised. Even so, she would not ask the questions herself, using the two ill-dressed women as interpreters, as if she herself had not spoken the same language or as if some ceremony forbade her to speak to strangers directly, turning to her two companions, telling them the question they were to ask, waiting while they repeated it, listening to the explanations, the full Bourbonian face impassive still behind the crape veil, only the eyes (slightly globular, fixed, and black too, almost hard, a little like the eyes of a bird, or even of a bird of prey) gleaming in the shadow of the veil with a sort of wasted ardor, a charred luster, a fever.

Sometimes, letting the others continue the conversation, she would open her bag, search inside, withdrawing a thin wad of letters and postcards which she looked through for the hundredth time, removing one or another, rereading it carefully, then saying a few words to the closer of the two women and waiting in silence for her to repeat them. There were two letters on notepaper with headings and official seals, covered by some lines of spidery handwriting, also official-looking and laconic, like orders or military postings, and three or four of those postcards that the lovers or husbands of servants usually send. Once she dropped one of them, which the boy picked up. It showed in sepia, against a dark background, a 75 cannon in firing position and beside it a soldier wearing a képi, a red stripe running down the side of his trousers, one knee on the ground, one hand shading his eyes, the other pointing in the same direction as the cannon. In the left corner and a little behind the cannon, the smiling face of a blond woman above a bouquet of roses appeared in a bright halo. Written in big white letters on the upper part of the card could be read the words ON LES AURA followed by an exclamation point. On the back, in the part reserved for correspondence, wavered or rather staggered one of those clumsy and deliberate scripts, childish and chaotic, whose letters written in half-faded pencil clustered in disorder, the woman taking the card back from the boy, frowning now, leaning attentively over the loops and pothooks, and painfully formed letters, finally looking up, tapping the card with her forefinger, and saying something like: "This man mentioned the Jaulnay woods. Or maybe it's Gaulnay. Or Goulnoy. Ask them if they know where . . .," then, already standing, already adjusting the black toque, arranging the veil, the wad of letters back in the closed bag, saying: "Let's go now," saying: "Ask them if it's far. Ask them if we can find a car. Ask them if they know someone who has a car or a wagon. We'll leave our things here. Tell them . . ." Sometimes (that is, during the three days they spent in the hotel where there was nothing left of some of the rooms but rectangles of pale-colored paper still fastened to the wall that overhung the cone of debris) . . . sometimes she would set out with only one of the two sisters and be gone for the day, leaving the boy in the care of the younger one (or rather, of the one who was not so old—though actually she was not old at all, despite her wrinkled face that seemed like a cruel and parodic contradiction of her name, a goddess's name, just as her sister's mannish face with its prominent jaw and rheumy eyes seemed like a parodic contradiction of her name, the name of an empress or some flamboyant courtesan), and this woman, during the afternoon, brought him to the ancient fortified gate of the city with its monumental stone crest damaged in places and beyond which lay something vaguely like a promenade, with trees that still had leaves, a tiny carousel for children, and a shed whose open-air display offered vases made out of shell-casings, postcards, pink and yellow celluloid windmills, and wretched candies wrapped in waxed paper. Back at the hotel, the woman would try to make the boy read in a book with pictures of farm animals, then would give up, deciding then to tell him the remainder of a story that seemed to have no end, to which, tirelessly, her exhausted face stamped with a passive desolation, she would add new episodes every day.

Though the summer was hardly over, it rained a good deal. It rained on the walls of the ruined houses where the pastel wallpaper was gradually coming loose, it rained on the smooth, gray slow surface of the river where the drops produced tiny silvery circles, it rained on the grayish landscape, the circle of hills under which were rotting away the torn bodies of three hundred thousand soldiers, on the grayish fields, the grayish houses—or rather on what was left of them, that is, as if everything, hills, fields, woods, villages, had been demolished or rather flayed by some huge and jolting harrow with irregular teeth, leaving behind it nothing but a few patches of wall and some mutilated stumps, sometimes a house or a group of houses (or a tree, or a group of trees) intact, unexpected, around (or starting from) which seemed to well up a sort of gradual, larval or rather elemental life, dim and dazed, on either side of a zone where not one tree, not one plant, except for clusters of thistles, had grown back, where not one field had been sown again, where the stone existed only in the form of shapeless heaps and where the ground was no more than a series of larger or smaller pits, intersecting each other, filled with stagnant water and out of which rose clouds of mosquitoes.

Roads—or rather paths that were more or less paved—wound through the countryside or up the hills, but except for a few carts or rare wagons they were used only by the also rare trucks with canvas covers, painted the color of earth, sometimes singly, sometimes in slow convoys that swayed as they rolled along, driven by young, almost beardless soldiers who kept lighting their fat soggy cigarette butts with lighters also made of shell-casings, while there rolled across the floor of the cab, between the huge pedals and gear-shift levers, the bottles containing a purplish wine, its surface covered with bubbles in the green bottles that one of the two sisters would buy from them at the taverns or the canteens set up at the intersections. Once, the car in which the three women were riding had to pull over to let past three cars the same color of earth and mud but with polished chromium, in one of which, on the back-seat, was sitting an old man with a wan and frozen face, eyesockets hollow as those of invalids being pushed in their wheelchairs, still wearing a gold-trimmed képi, and the widow spoke a name, leaning toward the other two women who watched the three cars pass, and the man with the tubercular face, with that same blank, indifferent gaze that they met from the people they themselves saw passing or whom they would question, sometimes answering their questions with that voluble and incoherent goodwill of the humble, more often with that weariness, that impatience, or rather even that greedy hostility of people disturbed at their work, looking at the black veils, the hand where the diamond glistened, the child in its warm frieze coat, then turning away, back to their occupations. Another time, even, a woman addressed them in a kind of frenzy, insulting them and pursuing them with her curses as they drove off—or rather fled—the widow more impassive, more Bourbonian than ever beneath her veil, one of the two sisters leaning over the child and speaking to him hurriedly to keep him from hearing the insults screamed by the thin figure wearing a dark apron, standing in the doorway of a farmhouse roofed with tar paper. The night they slept in the convent (or the institution for young girls), the widow talked a long time, long after the child was put to bed, with the nuns who had taken them in, her companions remaining silent on their chairs, stiff, their wrinkled hands folded in their laps, their two mannish faces expressionless, listening, nothing more.

The hotel lobby was furnished with a couch and twisted ebony armchairs covered in garnet plush. Gradually, the voice that was telling the boy the endless story slowed down, occasionally breaking off at the sound of a car outside, of other voices at the door, while the woman glanced furtively at the clock, lost her place, was reminded by the child where they were, resumed the story, controlling the movements of her horny hands that kept fussing with the clasp of her bag or pointlessly smoothing the edge of her skirt, the story continuing in snatches, interrupted, abandoned again in the middle of a sentence, resumed again, until the voice would stop for good, the woman standing now, saying: "No. Tomorrow," saying: "I think that this time . . . ," saying: "Here they are!" her eyes fixed on the door, which would open, admitting the widow accompanied by the other woman, both looking harried, their shoes muddy, their skirts, too, occasionally mudstained, the widow heading without a word for the child, leaning over, drawing him to her, hugging him in her arms and always in her movements that something which was at once stiff, convulsive, emphatic, and gloomily tragic that seemed to control her gestures, while the sister who was following her would answer the questioning gaze fixed upon her with the same negative shake of the head, mute and resigned. One evening, in the dim dining room where three officers were also eating and some men who seemed to be businessmen or traveling salesmen (there was, one day, a noisy group of rather elderly American women, shoulders covered with fur stoles, accompanied by two persons who seemed to be officials), they would exchange almost in whispers between spoonfuls of soup a few words, as though ashamed, wretched, the two worn faces stamped with the same expression of calm and absolute despair, while according to her custom the widow remained motionless, imperturbable, in front of her empty plate. Occasionally, at dessert, she would take out of her bag and show the child the postcards that she had bought and that back in her room, the boy in bed, she would write and send to her relatives or her acquaintances.

To all intents and purposes, they could have been just alike, almost the same, that is, equally grayish, they too, poorly printed on rectangles of soft cardboard, monoto-

nous, like the hills, the ruins, or the shapeless stretches of
land they represented, the debris that lines the banks of a
swift river, at once silent and rustling, flowing between two
wakes of wreckage like those left behind by floods and
linked by one of those hastily built bridges the engineers
throw across a stream, starting from a mingled chaos of
planks, broken wheels, axles, and blocks of stone, ending
on the other bank in the same apocalyptic and tedious
confusion of car parts, beams, tiles, and broken machinery,
after which perhaps there would appear, reproduced on
another card, on either side of a road and spilling onto it,
two asymmetrical piles of bricks and rubble, and again
something shapeless, lumpy, where the only vegetation
seemed to consist of thorny bushes of rusty iron. Three
soldiers (two of them wearing police caps, the third in a
képi—probably the squad assigned to remove barbed wire)
posed for the photographer at the mouth of a sort of open
tunnel on the side of something that resembled not a hill
but those heaps of garbage dumped at the outskirts of
towns by the municipal trucks.

The back of the cards was a pale and apparently faded
green on which, as she wrote a few lines next to the recipient's address in a sloping, spidery hand, she pasted a
stamp of a similarly pale pinkish orange, representing a
woman dressed in a long tunic falling in loose pleats, her
hair escaping from a Phrygian cap, floating in the breeze,
one hand stretched behind her in the gesture of sowing.
One after the other, the little green rectangles stamped
with orange and covered with that script itself resembling
barbed wire accumulated on a corner of the table where,
while the child slept, she would sit, having at last taken off
her toque and carefully set it and the veil on a chair, severe,
her rather plump profile attentively tilted in the glow of a
little pleated lampshade, thoughtful, over the grimy or

grayish images which she studied a moment before turning them over to write across them in violet ink, mortally calm, monumental, black, mortally resolved, still filled with that unappeasable distress and that inflexible determination that forced her to wander under the rainy skies from one field of wreckage to another, from one charnel house to the next.

And in the end she found it. Or rather she found an end—or at least something she could consider (or that her exhaustion, the degree of fatigue she had attained, obliged her to consider) as able to put an end to what was making her scour, these ten days, the ruined roads, the half-abandoned farms, and the canteens stinking of drunken men. It was a very small, circular graveyard, about twenty yards in diameter at the most, bounded by a freestone wall like the kind you see around suburban villas, and the pillars on each side of the gate were surmounted by an iron cross painted black. Most of the graves were those of German soldiers, but she went straight to one of them lying a little apart from the others, which no doubt someone (someone who had taken pity on her—or rather on them—or perhaps had simply wished to get rid of them) had pointed out to her and on which, in German and on a metal tag, then in French on a wooden plaque more recently attached, was simply written that here lay the bodies of two unidentified French officers. It had finally stopped raining and a late-summer sun was glistening above the wall on the leaves of the little woods (the cemetery was located behind and to the east of the zone about ten kilometers wide which seemed to have followed a sort of gigantic tornado destroying everything in its path) of which certain branches were beginning to turn gold. She walked up to the inscription, read it, stepped back to the place where the dead men's feet would be, approximately, bent her knees, then stood up, rummaged in her bag, took out a handkerchief which she spread on the ground, then knelt, made the boy kneel beside her, crossed herself, and lowering her head, remained motionless, her lips stirring faintly under the shadowy veil. Somewhere in the still-wet leaves sparkling in the sun, a bird uttered its cry. There was no one else in the graveyard but the three women and the child, that is, the woman and the boy kneeling, and slightly behind, the other two women standing, holding their bags and their furled umbrellas, motionless, lips motionless in their motionless wrinkled faces, the flesh puffy and dark under eyes rimmed with pink the color of faience and now entirely dry.

May 17, 1940

For the exhausted cavalrymen whom he passed on his way to the head of the column, dejected, dirty (not the glorious and legendary mud of the trenches: simply dirty: as men can be who have had time neither to undress nor to wash for six days, who have alternately sweated and shivered—in early May the nights were still cold—in the same clothes, who have slept only a few hours—sometimes a few minutes—in the occasional barn, or abandoned house, or farmers' beds with red eiderdowns onto which they dropped without even unbuckling their spurs, or ditches), blinking with exhaustion in the morning light, slumped like bundles in their saddles, their shoulders hunched, humped rather, their helmets smeared with mud (those who, canteens empty, had found neither spring nor stream simply urinating on the ground in front of themselves before pulling off their helmets and smearing them with a layer of sopping brown earth, yellowing as it dried, flaking off, remaining caked in the grooves of the crest), their dirty cheeks bristling with a six-day beard, their eyes apparently dirty too, dusty, between burning lids, fixed (once and for all, while day was breaking, they had discovered, gauged, emerging out of the night, the huge, naked plain with no cover, few clumps of trees—and a little later every head tipped back with one impulse, watching approach, then deliberately circle above them, the little airplane no bigger than a boy's club model, and flying so slowly that it seemed impossible for air to support its weight, about to fall at any moment, the sound of its slowed engine like the buzzing of a wasp, and so low that they could see the black and white cross painted on its fuselage, itself painted a neutral gray (not tinted ochre or olive, like other military matériel and buildings: nothing but the mixture of black and white: iron gray, funereal), lazy, indolent (not insolent: indolent, not even seeming to defy them, and even probably without animosity), as if they could also see (watching them now, without any ill-will either, counting them, gauging them, the way a drover sitting on a wall or a hillock gauges the number and value of the cattle in his herd) the sleepy pilot even yawning, and still on his stomach the weight of the coffee and rolls (or the sausages) hurriedly swallowed at the mess table, and behind him the observer (or perhaps the pilot himself: they didn't know) tapping his Morse lever (or talking directly into a transmitter: they didn't know that either exactly: besides it made no difference: all they knew was that what was circling so lazily over their heads in the cloudless sky still vaguely tinged with the dawn's pink was the portent of their death), their eyes following it without slackening their gait, without trying to escape or scatter, their torsos still obediently swaying back and forth in the saddles, heads tipped back, turning as if on a single impulse, without a word, without a shout, not even a curse, not even a frown on the harassed, inexpressive faces, merely watching the fragile and funereal toy with a kind of passivity and yet a mute fascination, until after having circled one last time the pilot accelerated and flew off, then falling back into their lethargy); for the cavalrymen, then, suddenly starting up at the swift clatter of hooves, it was as if they had been caught up with, brushed past, and then left behind by a vague rustling, a rush of stirred air bearing with it a faint rattle of steel, futile and euphoric, as if horse and rider constituted one and the same mythical creature made of some metallic substance, sustained by invisible wings with metal feathers (and not touching the ground but moving slightly above it, barely striking or brushing it with its delicate oiled hooves, and not so much to gain support from it as to make it echo gaily like a ringing bronze dome under the light and rhythmic blows), passing (that is, not itself but the sort of invisible cloud at the heart of which it was borne) almost close enough to touch them, they on their exhausted mounts with galled spines (the only two times they had been able to unsaddle, the skin had stuck in strips to the saddle cloth, the first time the size of coins, the second, of their palms, exposing patches of raw, purplish, already purulent flesh), some leading by the bridle the horse of a cavalryman killed or missing (so that the squadron, the column of living men, was doubled by a second ghostly column of mounts with empty saddles from which the empty stirrups dangled gently, monotonously knocking the sopping flanks), their powerful chargers now no more than ghosts of horses, collections of heavy bones and muscles no longer cohering, no longer moving except by force of habit, still capable of galloping if the spurs dug once again into their bloodstained flanks: docile, doleful, tragic, continuing to advance until they balked a first time, spurred on, then a second, and finally, without warning, the hocks faltering, collapsing and no longer moving, lying on their sides, retaining nothing animate or rather nothing human but their huge nautch-girl's eyes, thoughtful, bottomless, and heartrending.

The horses which, like them (the cavalrymen), had eaten virtually nothing for six days (actually, five: on the first day, the cavalrymen had swallowed their rations cold and given the horses the hay in the saddlebags—eating without hunger (those who later on would know hunger to the point of rummaging in garbage heaps, flinging themselves on cabbage stems or rotten potatoes, bitterly disputing and even coming to blows over a few ounces of bread), concealed beneath the trees of some estate, and this: suddenly frozen, immobilized, the opened can held in one hand, the knife halfway to the lips, no longer chewing what was in their mouths, deafened, and immobilized right there, like statues of salt, and in the crook of one elbow the reins of their horses which had not even had time to rear or shy, paralyzed (like—half of them were not much more than twenty, with their stiff khaki uniforms barely weathered by the winter months, their boyish faces, their mahogany puttees carefully waxed the day before— some military school out on a picnic), as though petrified, while the maddening noise of the engine diminished, faded away, as quickly as it had burst over them, continuing, incredulous, to stare through the branches at the once again empty, unpolluted sky, simply gray that morning, as if the three cruciform shadows which had just roared overhead among the treetops had simply dissolved, no sooner materialized than absorbed, as if they had just observed some cosmic phenomenon creating screaming matter out of the air itself suddenly condensed into a noise of natural catastrophe like lightning or thunder, of mutations of inert molecules into a raging tempest; on the third (the third day) the field kitchen had come, bringing them a cold mixture of stew and sticky rice—and then they had not seen it again; later someone told this to the corporal— someone, that is, a ghost with a shaved head like him, dressed like him, in what had once been a uniform, with a face like all the other faces of the other ghosts marked with the stigmata of hunger, of bitterness and humiliation, who were strolling about after dark between the barracks inside a barbed wire fence, he and the corporal recognizing each other not from their features—in fact they had never met—but by the collar patches with their Marian colors (white on blue) of some religious institution still sewn on the collar of their tunics (the tunics they wore now without belts, simply hanging loose, covered with stains, like the smocks of workmen or farmers—or rather of tramps) and he (the ghost, the phantom) telling him this: the driver of the field-kitchen truck having taken refuge after a strafing in the cellar of the house (of the farm?) where the kitchens were posted, and not dead or wounded, but simply dead of fear: lying on his belly, head buried in his arms, and the sergeant in charge of the field kitchen being informed, going down into the cellar, ordering him to get up, and the driver still lying there, not moving, not answering, not even turning his head, not even groaning when the sergeant began kicking the inert body, merely jerking each time the hobnailed boot touched it, as a stuffed puppet or a sack of potatoes might have done, and finally the sergeant giving up, landing one last kick on the arms that were wound around the head, cursing him one more time and coming out of the cellar, so that it had been one of the cooks (or the sergeant himself) who had had to drive the field-kitchen truck—and the next morning the order to retreat, everything stuffed back into the truck, the engine already running, and the sergeant (or one of the cooks) running down the cellar steps four at a time where the

driver was still lying in the same position, arms still pro-
tecting his head, one hand ripped open by the sergeant's
last kick and not even wiped off, black with dried blood,
and the cook (or the sergeant) shouting: "We're clearing
out now. Beating it! Going home! Are you . . .," the driver
not letting him finish, standing up like a lunatic, pushing
aside the sergeant (or the cook), rushing up the stairs, out
of the house, still running, opening the truck door, climbing in, sitting at the wheel, and the man (the ghost) said
that when he heard the planes coming he had just time to
throw himself back and lie flat against the base of the wall,
and that when he could straighten up there was nothing
left of the truck but a pile of smoking scrap iron, crackling
still and stinking of burnt rubber) . . . the horses which,
like the cavalrymen, were drinking and eating only when
they happened on springs, streams, or troughs in the
squares of abandoned villages, or on barns of forage farms
with their doors battered down, or already pillaged stores
and kitchens which they furiously demolished by kicking
in the cupboards or the empty cabinets: and now he, the
man-horse, the aerial and muscular mount of copper as
highly polished, as gleaming as the inside of a cauldron,
the cavalryman helmeted not with mud but with gleaming
steel, and on the coatsleeves that seemed to come straight
from the tailor the five gold stripes gleaming too, like the
bronze fittings of the leather, the boots soldered to the
sweat-flaps of the saddle, the entire figure cast, it seemed,
once and for all in some metal alloy, the heels down, the
knees not even moving, while disdaining to rise in the
saddle, he let himself be carried forward, his bony torso,
his thin shoulders jerking with the quick rhythm of the
trot, as if he were attached to the horse by some hidden
mechanism: rising up on their left, not exactly brushing
against them but, so to speak, pushing past them, forcing

them to the side of the road (or they, suddenly wakened from their torpor, starting up, drawing back instinctively), the long column of cavalrymen curving imperceptibly, like the bottom of a swaying curtain gradually yielding to a gust of air, then resuming its alignment while he was already far ahead, leaving behind a persistent aristocratic wake of equine sweat, of polished leather, and of what seemed to the cavalrymen a scent of eau de cologne and was in fact merely the absence of stench, followed by a silent and furious murmur of smothered curses, of respect and execration.

Not a man: an entity, a symbol, the at-last visible incarnation (for half of the cavalrymen, those of the reserve echelon, who had not known him in quarters, only glimpsed him with other superior officers on the occasion of two dress parades, he was something of a myth, an abstraction), the materialized delegation of that occult and faceless omnipotence in which they included, pell-mell, generals, politicians, journalists, and whoever else was in any way related to that pandemonium to which they further added, themselves forgetting (they who had elected these politicians, promoted by their agency these generals, and believed what these journalists so eager to please them had written) the drivers of the automobiles of the generals and the colonels (at least they imagined them: they had never seen them either except at a distance), the officers of the general staff, the newspaper owners, the diplomats, the ministers, the private secretaries, the chancelleries, the gigantic savages with ritually scarred cheeks specially imported from Senegal to guard the gates of railroad stations on the arrival of trains filled with men on leave, the engineers ready to blow up bridges before they could get back across them, the motorcycle dispatch-riders bearing retreat orders already meaningless when they had been written and all the more so on arrival two hours later, delivered by dust-stained messengers, raging and cursing as they stamped on their starters and who all, from the general staff to the administrators of the mobilization centers ticking off their lists, had flung them here with the casualness of a gambler scattering over the green cloth a bundle of banknotes without concern for the numbers or the colors they cover (the one who had specifically given the order (the order to send them out into open country and on horseback to ride against tanks or airplanes) was a kind of dwarf, not much taller than the kind seen in circuses, with no neck and a sort of rat's head, with a pointed nose, and huge ears, who would pose for the photographers on the steps of the presidential palace, dressed in a jacket of the kind worn by floorwalkers in department stores, flashing, without unclenching his teeth, an unfailing smile that widened the tiny doll's face and submerged the squinting eyes in wrinkles, swelling his chest, straightening his back, the expression—with his center part like a waiter's, his flat skull, his plastered-down hair and his protruding ears—of an illicit street vendor who has just pulled a fast one), hurled into something that bore no resemblance whatever to what they (and doubtless with them the floorwalker) could have expected, that is, the shock, the confrontation of two armies of more or less equal—or even unequal—strength, but . . . what could it be called?: for they had absolutely no hope whatever: they had heard like everyone else some talk of units, of regiments or even of divisions sacrificed, of tactical ruses, of diversionary maneuvers; and at the start they believed him, thinking only: "That's it! No luck. We had to be the ones. That's the way it goes . . .," then they realized that it was not only the regiment, not the brigade, not the particular branch (the cavalry) to which they belonged, not the division, not the army corps, but the adjacent armies too, and that next it would be the reserve armies (if there were any), and after the reserves all those who could be collected in the depots, the factories, the smallest barracks, in the remotest parts of the country, whether they were cavalrymen, infantrymen, artillerymen, tank-corpsmen, truckdrivers, engineers, observers, medical orderlies, arms manufacturers (except, of course, the relatives of the minister, or even the relatives of the concierges and the mistresses of the minister who were strutting in designer uniforms in the garrison cafés of the Midi, protected by Senegalese imported by ship and for the habitués of which (victualers, merchants, makers of apéritifs, captains of industry or police departments) the war had always been something remote, vaguely exotic, reserved for the unfortunate populations of provinces created for precisely that, like Flanders, Artois, or Moselle), led to slaughter, flung in their turn, sacrificed (so that it was not only regiments, armies, the first reserves, then the second, and as a last resort—moreover, even if they had had any such intention, they did not have the time to begin—the captains of industry, like the proverbial story of the virgin or the explorer flinging one after the other over their shoulders some jewels or the last cans of food in order to slow down the advance of the monster gaining on their heels, just time enough for the monster to slow down and pick them up or digest them, time for the bankers, the businessmen, and the car manufacturers on another continent to decide on the best investment of their capital and then to begin making enough cannons, trucks, machine-guns, planes, ships, and bombs first to stop, then to crush the insatiable monster), all, one after the other, poured out, engulfed, vanished without leaving a trace, erased from the list of forces without even what was happening (what they (the cavalrymen) were now experiencing) resembling in any way shape or form something like a war, or at least like what they had vaguely imagined war must be: not even a setting, the minimum of a decor, of solemnity (or even of seriousness) which would at the very least have let them believe that they had been sent here to fight and not simply to be killed: no artillery barrages (every once in a while a few shells fell, as if they too were anachronistic, apparently fired at random, without any particular reason: in a field, an empty meadow where they suddenly saw spheres of dirty cotton form; once just one, incomprehensibly, of some monstrous caliber made to knock out blockhouses or steel gun turrets, and which raised the ground straight up in a gigantic pillar of smoke, remaining motionless in the calm air, black and tawny, slender as a feather and tall as a thirty-story building, lingering, useless and decorative, slowly drifting, dragging its tail of dust over the wheat-fields, the sprouting corn, and which turning around in their saddles, they could still see for a long time like an enigmatic exclamation point above the hills) and no trench to conquer or defend, no hand-to-hand or rather face-to-face combat where each man, brave or cowardly, could take the measure of his courage or his fear (with the exception of one day—just one: the day when the losses had been fewest; none in fact in the corporal's squad—where they had been posted on the outskirts of a village and where they had dug holes in the orchards, waited, then emptied their magazines on anything that moved or didn't move at the edge of a woods on the other side of a stream, ducking while the mortar shells exploded around them— but that evening, for no reason, they had received the order to fall back): nothing but the opulent meadows, the green hillsides, and no one in front of them, not on their left or on their right, not even the other squadrons of the regi-

ment, at least no one visible, except on two or three occasions and so suddenly and so far away (while they come
down the hillside in Indian file, figures jump out of sidecars
and motorcycles on a parallel road and without even bothering to take shelter shower them with bullets) that friends
or enemies themselves seemed to have strayed by mistake
among the woods and the meadows, and only now and
then, all of a sudden, those inconceivable explosions of
noise, of destruction, of violence, maddening, deafening,
paroxysmal, and over as suddenly as they had begun, the
last airplane already vanishing: a dot, a pigment, then nothing, sucked up, diluted into the empty sky which had engendered them, the roaring of the engines fading,
vanishing: and the silence; after which there was nothing
else to do, in the spring sunshine and the birds gradually
starting to sing again, but catch the riderless horses, try to
collect themselves (or to recognize themselves), and count
the missing: and no dead (only horses that no longer had
riders), and no wounded either, except those only slightly
hurt who could still stay on horseback more or less, clinging
to the pommel and shaken on their saddles, clenching their
teeth, eyes staring, feverish, as though anesthetized or
rather stunned, some already delirious now and then while
there gradually swelled on the torn cloth of their coats or
their trousers the patches of thick blood drying, coagulating during the five (or the ten, or the twelve) kilometers
covered at a trot (sometimes at a gallop) to the river, the
bridge crossed in disorder, the woods where the ambulances were waiting (then, like the field kitchens, it was no
longer a question of ambulances and, as though by syn-
chronicity, of the wounded: as if everything were going
too fast, as if (though no one had warned them, they knew
it, guessed it themselves, with that infallible prescience of
the victims of disasters) the absence of ambulances implied

the absence of wounded, or rather the uselessness of being wounded, or at least the uselessness of clinging onto a horse and suffering in the saddle), and from that moment there was no longer anything but cavalrymen missing, simply missing, vanished, as if the lush green countryside were gradually absorbing a ration, engulfed, digested with that greedy and imperturbable seemliness that permitted it in the fashion of those carnivorous flowers to ingurgitate animals and men (once, in a ditch—at the moment there must not have been more than four: the colonel, one of the two squadron chiefs, and two cavalrymen—they saw a horse almost entirely covered with a yellow mud like café-au-lait, as if it (nature) were secreting a sort of saliva, a sticky digestive fluid which had already begun to dissolve it while the slow process of swallowing had begun with the hindquarters) without anything in its organization, not a leaf, not even a blade of grass being affected, or if sometimes a tree or a few branches were knocked down, if the grass showed a few blackened places, sustaining its wounds (its scratches and scrapes) with that same sumptuous indifference, that perpetuity, absorbing in the same way the echoes of the explosions or the bursts of gunfire that echoed from hill to hill, lost in the woods, absurd, anecdotal, the opulent forests, the opulent meadowlands gradually swathed in the blue mists of evening, darkening, then slowly rising out of the night, unpolluted, a tender green, dangerous, perfidious, enigmatic, as if by its immutability the fresh decor of flowering fields, of hedges and groves, were participating in (it too generating, ironically attending) the sort of mutation which they (the cavalrymen) were actually undergoing, passing in the space of seven days (as if this time the Creator had employed this interval to perfect his work, then, facetiously, to destroy it) from their condition of docile and naive boy scouts (or students in some severe religious institution) with carefully polished puttees, with properly cleaned weapons, to that of inert things dangling on broken-down mounts (the morning of the alert they (the cavalrymen) were getting ready to take showers; in town, or in a nearby factory (they were never informed of anything: simply, the day before, at evening call, before lights out, the sergeant on duty had said: "To-morrow, showers. Ready at nine!"), a public place in any case, so that before going there under the command of the sergeants they would expect the captain (that is, the giant, the sort of lansquenet or reiter straight out of—minus the damascened armor, the slashed velvet, and the plumed helmet—a painting by Cranach or Dürer, in command of the squadron) to inspect them closely; in the clearing sur-rounded by tall oaks on which leaves were just beginning to show they had built a table and benches: and he (the corporal) remembered this: one of his feet set on a bench, having just spread the wax on his puttee, inattentively listening to (or rather hearing beside him) the senior ser-geant and two cavalrymen discussing the plowing and the sowing, when the officer of the day had run up, breathless, waving his arms, already screaming before he reached them; "On the alert! Muster in one hour! Alarm . . . ," the corporal suddenly motionless, brush raised, the gesture frozen, staring hard at the lid of the little round box set beside his foot on the bench, the black and red design (he could still see it: the lion, the letters with the elaborate flourishes, the metallic gleam of the background, rays like those of a sun fanning out around the mane), vaguely hear-ing the senior sergeant, while he was trying to put the lid back on the box, the words reaching him as though from a great distance, saying: "Alarm exercise?" the officer of the day trying to catch his breath, saying between two gasps: "No: alarm! Muster! Everyone ready in one hour!"

the senior sergeant already standing (the black and red box slipping in the clumsy hands: it closed or rather opened by means of a tiny eared key of gilded metal, probably broken, which the corporal's fingers fumbled, so that he had to give up, set the box on the table, and simply push the lid down with both thumbs), the senior sergeant, his face suddenly a little redder than usual perhaps (only perhaps: before signing up, ten years earlier, he had been something like a farmhand or a woodcutter in the mountains, his face always tanned by the open air, more purplish than red, brick-red precisely, bony, with protruding cheekbones, jawbones, and brow ridges), already screaming the order to the cavalrymen who stopped moving, stared at him a moment with a kind of amazement, then rushed back into the tents or came out of them, began striking them, running now in all directions, spruced up as though for a day's leave or on parade), and this (the mutation) passing through a succession of phases during which they would at first have suddenly grown older, have attained at great speed the stage of puberty (the evolution beginning with the first airplane attack), then of mature men (the one day when they had been able to fight), then (by one of those disturbing tricks of language which make it impossible to tell if it is based on what it says or the converse) immature men, in every sense of the word, that is, not only because they belonged (but did they still belong to something, or rather was there still something to which they could belong?) to a defeated army, but even as individuals: like those bundles, those sacks of which as soon as the cord tying them is undone or cut the contents spread, roll, and scatter in all directions, as if the invisible knot which somehow kept together that contradictory magma of passions, desires, constraints, brutality, tenderness, terror, pride, lust, and calculation which constitutes any human creature had suddenly given way: not disbanded then, not runaways, but worse still: having reached that stage where the idea of flight, the instinct of self-preservation, of safety in every-man-for-himself, could no longer even inhabit them, and not so much by the effect of discipline, of the reflexes that had been inculcated, as by that realization gradually come to in the course of these six days that there was nowhere to escape to, no safety to hope for anywhere nor from anyone, so that, when the colonel (the incarnation of that omnipotence composed of politicians, of pitiless militant pacifists, of generals in gold-embroidered képis who possessed over them an absolute power of life and death and had sent them here) passed along the long column of cavalrymen there was not even a silent shudder of rage that developed, ran from cavalryman to cavalryman, but a sort of shudder of stupor, of incredulity (some turning around on their saddles, staring after the automobile in which it was said that he traveled—and with it the van, the private bedroom, so to speak, which apparently transported along with him, to spare him any fatigue, like an accessory, a precious piece of furniture, the dazzling polished mahogany horse; but they had to acknowledge the evidence of their senses: aside from his orderly and the signals officer trotting in his wake, he was alone), the suddenly suspended or rather interrupted breathing resuming, the air spreading between their teeth with an imperceptible hiss or whistle not so much of anger as of something (just as they were beyond fatigue) beyond anger, hearing the high-pitched, irascible, and one-note voice that seemed to come out from under the helmet (or rather from behind a mask: as if he had spoken through cardboard or stamped tin, like the masterpieces of those master armorers of the Renaissance in the shape of a face: remote, inexpressive, the features frozen, the cheeks flat if not hollow, the mouth thin as a saber-slash, scarcely open, the lips scarcely stirring like those of a ventriloquist) spinning out an uninterrupted series of harsh rebukes about their appearance, the rust on their stirrups, the stains on their coats, the dust or the mud that was dirtying their shoes, their six-day beards; then already past, the bony and jerking body rapidly receding, until it had disappeared in the distance as it had come, doubtless carried back, returned to that remote and vague empyrean from which it seemed to have emerged (descended in a winged and clattering cloud) only to manifest itself to them in the raging and incredible form of a garrison sergeant-major. But they were mistaken: shortly afterwards, when for a moment the head of the column turned at right angles at an intersection, they could see him again, his horse walking now, solitary, unconquered, and outraged, a few yards ahead of the captain-lansquenet and followed by the file of tiny cavalrymen who thus, their mounts hidden up to the belly by a fold of the terrain, seemed to advance motionless, swept on by some mechanism, like those silhouettess cut out of zinc and mounted on a rail which parade, swaying faintly, between the walls of a decor also cut out of sheets of zinc in the shooting galleries of country fairs: the soft and successive undulations of the plain, the field of green wheat, the cardboard village and its pointed steeple emerging from a background where the road gradually vanished, the tiny figures vanishing at the same time, only the torsos visible now, planted behind the rounded croups of the horses, like chessmen, the whole squadron having collapsed again into its somnolence or rather its lethargy, exhausted, somnambulistic, so that when the shout rose, coming from the rear, passing from mouth to mouth, carried by the sergeants' hoarse voices, it (the shout) seemed to run, meaningless, like a simple vibration of the air or those incomprehensible cheepings of seabirds, of gulls, at once alarmed, hoarse, and plaintive, lacerating the indifferent silence without disturbing it, carried by each man with a sort of indifferent docility, a sullen lassitude, while they continued to advance, mechanically to urge on their exhausted mounts, each man barely raising his head to hurl at the body preceding him the monotonous, useless warning, repeated with that Cassandralike perseverance of all heralds of apocalypse and disaster: "Pass it on: the Germans are in the village! Pass it on: the Germans! Pass it on: German tanks are in the village! Halt! Tanks in the village! Pass it on! The Ger . . ."

August 27, 1914

THE journey lasted a night, a day, and one more whole night. Either because the operation had been poorly prepared or poorly conceived, or else because its plan had been elaborated with a view to possible obstructions and included a margin which allowed giving priority to the other units' advance, the convoy sometimes remained stalled on sidings for hours at a time. Whatever the reason, it took the regiment (the men jammed into cattle cars, the colonel and his officers in a first-class car with gray plush banquettes protected by mesh antimacassars) thirty-six hours to reach a tiny station in the department of the Meuse from which it set out toward Belgium by forced marches, each captain riding ahead of his company, the young lieutenants and second lieutenants bringing up the rear. The forces consisted for the most part of recruits from that department of the Midi, bordered on one side by the sea and extending inland to the first peaks of the Pyrenees, the birthplace of the commanding general himself (the corpulent—not obese: corpulent—man with the huge already white mustaches, dressed in a black uniform and a monkish cape, and whom the complicated intrigues of the general staff, masonic lodges, and the salons of the faubourg Saint-Germain had put at the head of an army, perhaps in consideration of a placidity and a capacity for sleep that were almost without limit), the bulk of these forces themselves consisting of round-headed, hard-muscled, short-haired farmers, gardeners, agricultural workers, woodcutters, or sometimes shepherds from the highlands, the majority of whom, except on the occasion of their military service, had never ventured outside the borders of their cantons or even of their communes, illiterate, speaking to each other in a local dialect and knowing just enough French to understand the orders of their sergeants with the same shaved skulls, with the black mustaches of prison guards, skins yellowed by tropical suns and livers corroded by absinthe.

While in their railroad car the colonel and his officers, having taken off their cross-belts and unbuttoned their tunics, leaned back on the upholstery and lit up their cigars, the men squatting or lying on boards in the cattle cars talked to each other in their harsh dialect about the harvests left standing in the fields, responded mechanically to the cheers that sometimes accompanied the train's passage, or slept dead drunk in their own vomit. This was a regiment of marine infantry, and if none of the officers had as yet been engaged in combat on a large scale, the colonel and some of the captains had nonetheless fought under difficult conditions rendered still more painful by terrible climates, sometimes surrounded, besieged, dying of hunger and thirst, in bamboo or cinderblock redoubts, some of their comrades massacred in ambushes or hideously tortured. Graduating from Saint-Cyr at the top of their class, they had chosen this much-envied corps, which was spoken of

as a seedbed for generals, because of the lure of adventure
and, for those born less well off, because of the retirement
benefits it offered. Like the young peasants they commanded, the shepherds or the illiterate men from the
mountains, their heads shaved like schoolboys, accustomed
from childhood to contend with the elements and the de-
manding soil, they were for the most part hardened men,
stubborn and single-minded, confident of their own courage, and in the case of the older men whose experience
had been acquired during remote expeditions where the
weakness of the forces engaged favored the use of rudi-
mentary tactics, had developed an unshakable assurance
based on study of the classics of warfare, still accredited
by analyses repeated for forty years on blackboards or in
mess-hall arguments. As for the younger men, assigned to
regions now pacified by occupation missions, public works,
or cartography units, if they had not yet had occasion to
prove themselves in combat, they had lived, sometimes
for years on end, entirely surrounded by native recruits
and by their prison-guard sergeants, something comparable
to those monastic askeses and those inhuman spiritual exercises imposed on the novices of certain religious orders
and upon leaving which the elect (or rather the survivors)
could pride themselves on the strength of mules and the
endurance of Trappists. Hence both groups harbored, with
regard to their fellow students who had graduated behind
them from the École Militaire and remained confined in
metropolitan garrisons, the same disdainful condescension
which professionals show to mere amateurs.

So that while gradually becoming aware as they moved
north (first in the train, then by road) of the first rumors
of combat (at least of what they had been permitted to
hear—or of what they could guess from the commu-
niqués), it was quite likely that in their conversation, their

way of sucking on their cigars (continuing to invoke memories of the opium dens of Hanoi, of governors' parties and the brothels of Colombo, admiring, as connoisseurs, their jade cigarette holders or their carved ivory watch charms—one of them owned a cloisonné cigarette case on which turquoise and pink birds fluttered among reeds and water lilies), it was quite likely that something in their behavior betrayed an imperceptible change: not yet anxious: simply attentive—and not for themselves, that is, for their lives, they for whom the ringing syllables that constituted the names Marengo, Malakoff, Bazeilles, or Lang Son signified nothing more, victories as well as defeats, than the one right way to live and die, who found it inconceivable to exercise any command whatever except standing, preferably in an exposed place, binoculars in hand and in plain sight—not for themselves, then, but as if, in their minds, something had just begun to bother them, to disturb the diagrams studied a hundred times on the blackboard, just as when they encountered the first remnants of retreating troops, the glum-faced officers and the exhausted, dazed-looking, dusty men, it was merely with that same attentive but reserved if not severe expression, scarcely concealing their professional disdain, that they listened to the officers' reports, disguising as best they could their irritation, their impatience, until the last wounded man had moved off, dragging his leg (the village street suddenly empty, deserted: not the way a village street can be empty or deserted on a Sunday afternoon or at worktime in the fields, but with that abandonment, that emptiness, that unaccustomed, threatening, and solemn aspect presented by a street, a hill, a bridge, a clump of trees before battle) and then almost immediately, without trumpets or shouting, something confronted them that bore no resemblance to a charge or to anything they could have learned in books or in the field, whether that had been in a cement blockhouse, on the dikes of the ricefields, or under the ramparts of some imperial palace; that is, simply a wall of fire slowly, even calmly, but inexorably advancing with only brief halts, if it encountered some obstacle, pausing for the time necessary to annihilate and digest it, then resuming its advance.

Having reached the Belgian village of Jamoigne-les-Belles on August 22, the regiment lost, on the single day of August 24, eleven officers and five hundred forty-six men out of a total force of forty-four officers and three thousand men. After having retreated on August 25 and 26, the regiment received orders to take up positions on the edge of the Jaulnay woods where, during combat on August 27, losses were increased by nine officers and five hundred fifty-two men. When four weeks later the corpulent general with the gardener's mustache managed to halt and even, in some places, to drive back the wall of fire (spending most of this time sleeping, waking only to listen to the dispatches, contemplating the map for a moment, inquiring about the reserves, giving his orders, and going back to sleep), there was scarcely a single man left, including the colonel himself, of those who, officers or troops, had on a stifling August afternoon and amid a cheering crowd crossed the town where the regiment was garrisoned to reach the station and climb into the train which was to take them to the front, emerging from the citadel, passing between the four stone giants at the gate in the wall built by Charles V, following the upper town's narrow streets, passing in front of the old brick mansions, the medieval market, the cafés with their terraces enclosed by boxes of hydrangeas and their interiors tiled with iris-women, the balcony of the club where the old gentlemen, distracted momentarily from their bridge tables and their lounge chairs, applauded with papery hands, their faint voices drowned out by the shrill cheers of the décolleté tarts leaning out of the windows beside them, offering as if in baskets their shining breasts, their lips open on their shining teeth and the moist pink caves of their mouths, and flinging flowers.

On the silk of the flag preserved through the battles (during one counterattack, a handful of daring men had even managed to capture an enemy flag) the head of state commanded that there be pinned the highest decoration he could award. The ceremony took place a little later, toward the end of October, just behind the front lines on the Valmy plateau, where against a gray sky loomed the black statue of the general who one hundred and twenty years before had routed an invading army on the same spot. A light rain was falling, and the gusts of autumn wind sweeping the bare parade ground rattled the wet silk flags of the other regiments mustered for the occasion, their slanting poles jerking back and forth, laboriously held in place by their bearers at attention, left hand resting on the saber guard whose rigid scabbard stuck out behind them, the superior officers also at attention, the gleaming blades of their unsheathed and vertical sabers at eye level, the képi straps cutting into their chins, their spurs on the heels of the black and glistening boots casting silvery reflections on the sopping grass, drawn up stiff and motionless like some kind of wading bird, at once arrogant, severe, and fragile. In the front ranks of the regiments in a formation, their dark lines barring the horizon, were the brigade and division generals, they too stiff, slightly slumped in their saddles, resembling—with their tall képis, their thickened bodies, and the thoroughbred with the white caparison and the long mane that one of the generals was crushing under his weight, their escort of aides and orderlies in Arab uni-

forms, rifles slung crosswise and mounted on reject
horses—some barbarian warlords out of the depths of History or the wilds of some remote steppes (they who, in
their youth, had fought their way across the continents of
Asia and Africa), mustachioed, stuffed into theatrical uniforms covered with gold braid. Above the group of horsemen, the bronze soldier continued to hold his sword up
to the heavens, impassive beneath the rain, mouth open,
uttering his bronze shout, frozen, with his bicorne and his
bronze frock coat, in an attitude of energy, enthusiasm,
and immortality. The wind, which was still rattling the flags,
gusted through a single little tree that had grown there for
no reason (or perhaps recently planted—which would explain why it had not been chopped down for the ceremony—by some patriotic committee), scarcely taller than
a man, like the kind to be seen in nurseries or bordering
empty lots, leafless already, culminating in a meager fork,
as though drawn with a squiggle of the pen, like a crack,
a fissure in the rainy sky. Beside it was silhouetted the
massive form of the general commanding the army. Having
got out of the automobile that had brought him, indifferent
to the rain, to the gusts that lifted his cape and burrowed
into its long black folds, he was standing in front of the
standard-bearers. Very upright, one of his white-gloved
hands resting on the pommel of his cane and his head
turned slightly to the right, he was staring, in the center
of the huge square formed by the troops, at the flag-bearer
of the annihilated regiment.

This man was a noncommissioned officer, very short
and fragile-looking in his isolation, his torso distorted by
the cartridge belts, his overcoat folded back in a swallowtail
behind him. Unlike the other flags that the wind continued
to twist fiercely, the one he was presenting hung motionless, either because the rainwater had weighed it down (it

had been a long time, long before the general's arrival, since this bearer had taken up his position), or because it had been weighted in some manner for the ceremony. Though he was shouting at the top of his lungs, the voice of the officer reading the citation to the army sounded weakened, faint through the gusts of wind and the rattle of the other flags, like a child's voice, remote, a little unreal. When it had fallen silent, a bugler stepped out of the square formed by the band in the first rows and advanced a few paces. With a sudden flash of brass, he turned his instrument with a deft, swift gesture that was fierce as well, and the notes of the Last Post rang out as though rusty, muffled, seeming to come from the same unreal Beyond, buried under the gray autumn rain. Then the flag-bearer slowly lowered the pole, and the general-staff officer, after having folded up the soaked proclamation, drew from a case the decoration which he began to pin under the tip on the bow and tassels, then stepping back four paces and saluting at the same time that the general raised his white-gloved hand to his képi and the officers with their naked sabers stiffened at attention. For a moment nothing was heard but the immaterial rustle of the rain that kept falling and the furious protest of the flags rattling in the wind like shots until suddenly the band began a stirring march, punctuated by cymbal crashes, sounding almost joyous, while one after the other, to commands, the detachments of the regiments, breaking their immobility, moved off. With a quick and cadenced gait, they paraded before the decorated flag, raised high now, fluttering faintly, still held by the short man with the fragile figure, the huge square of dark uniforms gradually shifting, the detachments following each other, the band stopping only when the last squad of the last section was gone. Two other noncommissioned officers then approached the bearer and with womanly gestures helped him fold up the flag which they slid into a sheath of black oilcloth, while the general commanding the army climbed back into his automobile which drove off jolting over the lumpy dirt of the plateau, and that was all.

Though it was not spared (entirely regrouped and replaced several times, rarely engaged, it is true, or sent into calm sectors like those seasoned troops, those old Pretorian guards or those elite corps kept in reserve for the most lethal actions), never afterwards, except on the occasion of a poorly prepared attack which cost it in a single morning nearly three-quarters of its officers and a good thousand men, did the regiment suffer such heavy losses as during those first four weeks when it left on the field more dead men than in the course of each of the four years that the war lasted. Among those who fell in the fighting on August 27 was a captain of forty whose still-warm body must have been abandoned at the foot of the tree against which he had been propped. This was a rather tall, heavily built man with regular features, his mustache waxed to points, his beard cut square, and whose pale, china-blue eyes, wide open in the calm, bloodstained face, stared up at the bullet-torn leaves through which the afternoon sun shone. The clotting blood made a bright red spot on his tunic, its drying edges already turning brown, almost completely disappearing under the swarm of flies with striped bodies and gray, black-tipped wings, shoving and crawling over each other like those which infest excrement in the fields. The bullet had knocked off his képi, leaving still visible in the blood-clotted hair the traces of the comb which that same morning had carefully made the center part between two waves. To the great disappointment of the enemy soldier who advanced cautiously, bent double, finger on the trigger of his weapon and who, lured by the sight of the gold braid, leaned over the body, brushing away the flies to search it, the tunic pockets were empty, and he found neither the gold repeater watch nor the wallet nor any other object of value. With the indemnity, everything was sent later on to the widow as well as half of the little grayish tag bearing the dead man's name and fastened by a slender chain to his wrist, the other half broken off along a line of tiny holes perforated for this purpose by a punch kept in the personnel offices. In the confusion there had not been time to slip the wedding ring from the third finger and no doubt the exhausted soldier, wearing a greenish uniform and boots covered with mud and dust, had severed that finger with the blade of his bayonet before being caught by a comrade or a superior officer. As for the enamel cigarette case decorated with pink-bellied indigo Chinese birds flying over water lilies, it had been put away before the battle in the narrow regulation chest painted dark green and strapped shut, carried in the vans with the company's baggage.

Thus concluded an adventure begun twenty or thirty years earlier, when the schoolteacher of a little mountain village (or rather doubtless the school principal of the neighboring town) came to find (or summoned to his office) the father of a young scholarship student still in the first years of high school (a peasant, a man just able to read, write, and fill with clumsy figures the sheets of an imitation-leather notebook, the gray figures laboriously formed in pencil—sometimes one of those indelible pencils moistened with saliva and whose mauve traces faded as the lead dried—the paper itself grayish, cross-ruled, speckled with tiny reddish flecks, like sawdust) and persuaded him to give up making his son a schoolteacher (his older sisters were already teaching in schools hidden by winter snows) and not to take him out of high school before graduating so that he would be in a position to continue his studies later on. It was perhaps on his return that evening, or after having taken the night to think it over, that the man who had spent his life digging up a few squares or rather a few strips of land scattered here and there in the valley and on the hillsides, so remote from each other that it took almost as much time to get from one to the other as was left to work, made his decision, or rather yielded to the decision he had already made, to put his children in a position to attain a situation that would permanently place the family name out of reach of the hailstorms, the droughts, the beetles, the ergot, or the cochylis moth which, periodically, wiped out in a few hours or a few days the fruit of a year's sweat and exhaustion. And what the principal had suggested to him was so far beyond everything he could have aspired to for his offspring that by comparison the condition of schoolteacher was more or less comparable to that of a peasant with regard to a schoolteacher's. This was doubtless what he explained to the two daughters who, during vacations, came from their schools, not to rest under the family roof, but to work ten hours a day in the potato patch, the cornfield, or the scanty vineyards. Or perhaps (he died soon afterwards, moreover) there was no need to explain anything to them nor to convince them, perhaps they made the decision themselves, spontaneously, perhaps they had even made it long before the school principal had shown an interest in their younger brother (the only son of the family, several years their junior), perhaps what they had already learned on their own of the pedagogue's condition in schools where they taught classes of young cowherds and girls in sabots had already inculcated in them the same determination to spare the boy a comparable fate, and this whatever it might cost to pay not only for his studies, his keep during the years of preparation for the examinations, or the competitions which he would face, but even, subsequently, the time necessary for his insertion into a social milieu where to cut a decent figure, at least at the beginning, what he could earn by himself would certainly be far from sufficient.

It was a family raised in a rigid and austere tradition. Not only that austerity natural to peasants obliged to reckon expenses with antlike care, wearing patched garments, eating in the kitchen, huddling together around a single fire whose smoking embers are doused in the evening, sleeping in icy bedrooms and scrimping on everything, but (the austerity) even emphasized or rather enforced by that proud thirst for justice, for decency and dignity, that spirit of intractable insubordination which, in that mountainous region so close to Switzerland, might have impelled it, a few centuries earlier, to follow the severe Genevan reformer and now found its power if not in the thought of bearded thinkers wearing their iron-rimmed spectacles, in the very heads of the schoolmasters or the typesetters (the father, at least, would have been incapable of reading their writings), in any case in a mingled but fierce adherence to ideas that the century now coming to an end had seen appear and develop. Though they were on good terms with their neighbors, using familiar forms of address and regarded with esteem, it was no more likely that a member of the family, man or woman, had ever been seen sitting on the benches of the tavern (if one could even give such a name to two tables thickly coated with brown paint in a corner of the single narrow shop in the village that functioned at one and the same time as grocery, tobacco shop, and taproom) than on one of the benches of the church, it too built during the preceding century as a rampart against the ideas of the thinkers in their iron-rimmed spectacles, built of cold and graceless gray stone, a kind of architectural symbol of that clergy in bands and surplice reappearing after the Restoration and who, in accord with the owners of the imitation-leather factory a little farther down the river, determined the employment, poor-relief, and votes of the inhabitants of the valley.

Of their education, of memories of figures reeling down the village street at evening, of screams of women being beaten, of heaps of stone out of which occasionally trickled a slender, twisting, iron-colored thong, of the years in the mountain schools around which the snow melted only to give way to rain, and of the loss of a cousin whom they remembered by her handkerchief speckled with blood, the two schoolteachers were to preserve till their dying day an almost superstitious sentiment derived both from fear and from a visceral repulsion which made them unite in one and the same terror (lowering their voices if they happened to speak of such things, as if the words themselves were obscenely suffused with a maleficent and corrupting power) drunkenness, vipers, mud, priests, and tuberculosis.

After the father died, they tried hiring a man to work the tiny fields and vineyards while they remained at their schools (leaving them Saturday evenings, once the last class was over, walking several miles through the snow or along the muddy roads, taking trains with wooden benches for seats, changing trains in the middle of the night in stations lit by lanterns, spending their Sundays laboring like mules, making the journey in the opposite direction during the night and once again, faultless and unpolluted in their long, carefully brushed skirts and their blouses buttoned up to the chin, a crocheted shawl around their shoulders, in front of their blackboard on Monday morning), but they were repeatedly swindled. Then they tried renting out the fields (it never even occurred to them that they might have sold them, the fields and the half-ruined, pretentious house which the father had acquired in town and which they were afterwards, board by board, ceiling by ceiling, and tile by tile, to spend years virtually rebuilding from cellar to attic), but most were so inaccessible and yielded so little that there were no takers, and even when they did manage to rent some of the fields, they were swindled still more, so that finally, despite the protests of the boy who also pulled on an old pair of trousers and worked beside them on Sundays, one of the sisters, the older one (there was also the mother, of course—or rather a thing (a lump) about as big around as a yellow fist, under a flounced cap, resting motionless on a pillow, the immaculate sheet pulled up to the chin, so flat that it seemed to cover nothing at all, and in the center of the wrinkles a mouth into which was poured, with the help of a tiny spoon, a little whitish gruel which emerged down below in the form of excrements which were carefully wiped up every day) . . . finally, then, the older sister resigned herself to returning to the condition from which the father had sought to release them forever, taking along with his tools the roads leading to the acres of corn, the vineyards, or the orchards whose trees produced pears wormy before they were even ripe and hard as wood.

Now that she was working alongside them, wearing heavy men's boots, her squarish face gradually changing into a man's face (later, on her upper lip with its withered skin ridged with tiny vertical wrinkles like incisions, appeared a faint mustache as well), she could supervise the day laborers who in spite of everything she was forced to hire for the heaviest work, at the same time as the pair of oxen (someone would have let her borrow them probably, but the sisters refused to owe anyone anything) which in autumn brought home the harvest of the vines she had so diligently spaded. The sole modification (the sole luxury) which she (the one who now took the father's place) allowed herself was the purchase of a secondhand bicycle on which, more often than not, hampered by her long skirts, she rode only downhill, content the rest of the time to push it along, leaning over the handlebars, the rack loaded with bulging sacks or tools, and pulling a wagon she had knocked together herself out of a few boards and some wheels found in a junk heap, just as she herself replaced a broken windowpane, repaired a wall or the loose door of the hencoop, knitted her black wool stockings on slender steel needles, cut and sewed their dresses, and mended the boy's clothes.

It was while this boy, still a scholarship student, was preparing for the polytechnic examinations at the lycée in the district capital that there occurred the event that was to determine the rest of his life, down to placing him, on an August day some twenty years later, at the edge of a woods in the trajectory of a bullet that would shatter his skull. Around the month of February, at the riding school (for despite his further protests, they also paid to have him taught how to ride), he had a fall and broke a leg. The break was a clean one, without dislocation, but though he continued to study in the bed where the plaster cast immobilized him, the time necessary for his recovery excluded any likelihood of his successfully undergoing, that year, the ordeals of a competition so severe, and when they visited him in the hospital he informed them that even if he were to recover in time, he had decided to apply, without waiting any longer, for admission to the military academy of Saint-Cyr.

Later they discussed this (this, that is, not the accident, the fall from the horse, but the decision which signified for them the collapse of their ambitions) the way the poor discuss natural catastrophes, diseases or infirmities,

droughts or hailstorms, which ineluctably mark any existence, speaking in their calm, even voices, eyes bleary in
the wrinkled faces of old maids stamped with that somehow
childlike innocence which neither years nor misfortunes
had been able to change, and listening to them you could
imagine the two of them in those coats exuding a faint
smell of camphor, in those hats (or rather those toques)
which the one who took the man's role sewed together
herself out of an old piece of silk or velvet carefully twisted,
embellished with a paste buckle or a feather saved from
somewhere, standing beside the hospital bed, brushed by
the comings and goings of the nuns in their rustling skirts
and starched coifs, whom they watched with that timorous
repulsion their father had inculcated for whatever had anything to do with religion, listening with consternation to
the patient explaining with a forced smile how lucky he
was to have enough time left to prepare for another competition, avoiding the sight of their frayed coats, their red
and chapped hands clumsily concealed in their muffs, the
older sister's mannish face or the fading face of the sister
who was already no longer of an age to find a husband, as
if his decision (to apply to Saint-Cyr) was perfectly natural,
represented no more than a negligible change of plans
resulting only from an unfortunate accident and not from
his incapacity to tolerate for another year the price they
were paying for his riding lessons.

Of course they did not tell it that way. They simply
said that having broken his leg during the winter he had
then decided to apply to Saint-Cyr. It was virtually impossible, hearing them, to be able to suspect not the disappointment (or rather the consternation) but something
like a timid mortification, a timid regret. As people say in
peasant families, without even cursing fate, that ever since
he fell from a ladder or the thresher the young brother

has been hunchbacked. A statement of fact. Nothing more. They for whom the blow (that is, the decision he informed them of) was at the time to appear as a sarcastic sneer of fate. As if had been brutally reduced to nothing, flouted, not only what they had sacrificed and renounced for, but even the very spirit, the proud tradition of this family in which was so proudly preserved the memory of a great-granduncle (they said they had known him in their child-hood, warming himself in the sun against the wall, sitting on a block of wood) who had gone into hiding for five years in the woods in order to escape the gendarmes scouring the countryside in search of young peasants whom an ogre was devouring by whole battalions or sending to die out on the frozen steppes. For no doubt, surmounting that superstitious aversion in which they included without distinction, like complementary personifications of evil, any man dressed in a cassock or a uniform, no doubt they had admitted only as an avatar without consequences (the obligatory transition of the butterfly's chrysalis before it spreads the apotheosis of its dazzling wings) the fact that their brother was putting on the famous bicorne and for a while the black uniform trimmed with red which, despite the absurd sword, they had probably come to regard as the attributes of some sort of lay order, the austere symbols of accession to the privileges of labor and of knowledge.

It was this perhaps that they tried to tell him in the whiteness of that hospital ward where they had rushed to see him, their prematurely withered faces tense, forcing themselves to ignore the silent and rustling passage of the starched, winged coifs fluttering around impassive wax masks (as if here were confronting, measuring each other in a mute, tacit, and instinctive hostility, the irreconcilable feminine incarnations of duty and virginity), their voices not much louder than a murmur, while he answered all

objections (or supplications) with an indulgent, slightly
recriminatory smile, the kind one addresses to children,
the patient who was almost ten years younger than the
younger sister, continuing to produce that same smile as
they finally withdrew, mingled with the other visitors
herded toward the door, one of the two sisters even turning
around perhaps, seeing him still smiling on his pillow, and
on the night table the oranges they had brought him, gaily
waving his hand, calculating not how he could get rid of
them but somehow rid them of him, without yet realizing
how mistaken he was, how little a man's will counts against
the fierce determination of two weak women, or rather of
two mules.

For nothing changed. Things were too far along now
(that is, too far along in the way the two sisters lived) for
them to be able to dream, even for an instant, that they
could do anything but remain old maids, continue to lead
their beast-of-burden existence, wearing clothes mended
over and over and economizing enough to be able to send
him the postal orders, which he returned and which they
imperturbably sent back again in the form of whatever they
imagined that a young man in his position (that is, the
position which he had reached: that of probationary officer,
then of officer in the marine infantry) ought to possess,
from kid gloves and the toilet kit with all its useless accessories down to the soft leather boots, accompanied by
a note saying, It has been arranged that if these are not a
perfect fit you can exchange them, adding in their copy-
book handwriting the fashionable bootmaker's address
which, from the depths of their valley by questioning someone or other, they had found the means to obtain.

Years had passed then and doubtless the whole affair
(the accident, the visits to the hospital, the decision taken)
had been forgotten (or at least tacitly erased from their

conversations, if not from their memory), laid, like the hailstorm or the floods that gullied the fields, to the account of profit and loss. For it was with the same blind and unconditional obstinacy that they had now transferred to what must for them have represented something like an apostasy that sort of incestuous and austere passion. Just as, had he been a murderer, they would have sold the last scraps of land and the last of the gold pieces hidden under a floor board in order to pay the best defense lawyer, would have gone to visit him in his prison, would have accompanied him, at a distance, to the wharf from which the ship would sail to the prison colony, so twenty-five years later they would wander, eyes red but dry, would try to calm a madwoman searching the fields and woods devastated by a sort of giant cyclone for his body (or at least what might be left of it), would try to bury him, like those relatives of a man who has been hanged, creeping under the scaffold by night, bribing the guards, in order to take down the corpse and carry it away, with this difference that now there would be neither scaffold nor guards to bribe, nor even any corpse with eyes pecked out by crows: only, among the uncultivated, ruined, somehow rotted fields (still so infested with shells that no plow dared to venture among them), a few ghostly figures sifting the rubbish for something that would cover with at least the effigy of a roof the patches of walls still standing, and who raised their eyes, starred with indifference (sometimes with pity, sometimes with irritation) at the three women dragging the boy with them, then went back to sorting the half-burned timbers sticking out of the heaps of bricks or rubble.

But that would be for later, to complete in a sense, to crown their destiny as mules. Meanwhile, it was doubtless enough for them just to know that he existed somewhere (as after his death they continued to live (to feed themselves) on his memory: not in that arrogant and in some sense rhetorical fashion of the widow with the crape veil who ordered masses said and in his memory lines from Ossian printed on black-bordered cards, but so to speak tranquilly—or rather out of habit, the way they continued to eat out of habit (not resignation: habit) the little worm-eaten pears with the consistency of pebbles that grew in their orchards), doubtless it was enough for them that in some place where they could send him money orders the same flesh as theirs underwent the phases of a mutation which, even if it opposed and shocked that severe intransigence which governed their own lives, nonetheless constituted a kind of social advancement—in any case the guarantee of an existence permanently secured from what their father, mother, grandfathers, grandmothers, great-grandfathers, great-grandmothers, and they themselves had endured, continued to endure.

And no doubt he had inherited, as they had, some of those faculties of endurance, of persistence, and of that unpersuadable way of being, laboring so that, at the same time that he was abusing his body, struggling to recover the flexibility of his leg stiffened by the plaster cast, he managed to mistreat his mind as well, preparing in two months the "second-chance" competition granting admission to that school which was actually no more than a barracks incidentally provided with classrooms and amphitheaters, reluctantly accepted, immediately applying himself to his studies in order to rise row by row to the first squad, finally graduating with a number that conferred the right to join that envied corps whose escutcheon was embroidered with an anchor, after having spent two years virtually in seclusion, cloistered (like the five or six—or perhaps nine or ten—of his kind included in the promotion, that is, if not poor, at least compelled to count and calculate, sons of administrators or of gendarmes who disciplined them with a military belt, or graduating from some military academy or reform school, and with whom, on Sundays, in the empty guardroom, between two rows of narrow cots lined up like coffins, brownish blankets folded according to regulations, gleaming parade uniforms replaced by fatigues, on the raw-wood table soaked with rifle oil and brass polish, he shared the packages that his sisters sent him, the tinned meat and pâté seemingly impregnated with the stale smells of steel and turpentine, and as hard, as cold as steel itself), leaving the place only for maneuvers or for brief leaves, running then, once out of the guardroom, to catch the first train so that the next day, sleeves rolled up and wearing sabots, binding the sheaves, carrying in the hay, chopping wood, he could manage to do the work of two men—which, added to that of the two sisters, made four—returning to find the unconcerned sons of good families or of generals whose dress tunics still seemed to show like decorations or rather like the pollen of delicate flowers the pastel traces of rice powder, the invisible pink and perfumed imprints, as though pressed upon them by breasts and bellies and thighs: boastful, happy, filling the guardroom with an obsessive and harsh smell of rut, full of stories of horses, races, actresses, champagne, brothels, and gossip of the faubourg Saint-Germain, listening to the tales of their drunken or priapic exploits with that same amused yet indulgent smile he had offered the two statues of desolation standing at the foot of his hospital bed and now receiving such boasting like an older brother indulging turbulent boys (he who was their age and whose entire experience of that kind had doubtless been with some goose girl thrown down behind a hedge—or more likely, given the austere family climate in which he had grown up, not even . . .), imposing silence upon the protests of his adolescent flesh no doubt as virginal, as intact, as that of the two lay sisters whose money orders, now that he was maintained at State expense, he could send back—or perhaps occasionally cashing one of them (conscientiously adding the amount to the column of what he already owed them) for the day when his turn came to stand drinks, doing it with that same amused, prudent smile behind which he continued to learn to conceal, gradually to erase, the country bumpkin, watching and knowing he was being watched, gradually uniting himself with that clan, that caste, that sect: something like a club, a private circle, a universe jealously closed and functioning quite apart, with its own ceremonial, its rites, like a residue of barbarism covered with a sort of varnish, as if, like the world of the stage, he had two faces: one to present to outsiders, flawless, the elegant and impeccable carapace of broadcloth, of carefully brushed mustaches, of meticulously waxed and polished leather, the stiff and respectable urbanity of façade, and the other, the opposite, for internal use, rigid, severe if not actually brutal, with harsh whiffs of creosote, of manure, of sweat, or rifle grease and latrines floating between the rectilinear whitewashed buildings, as if the State which supported him had somehow signed a contract at whose due date the only thing that would be asked of him in exchange, once he had become insensible to fatigue, accustomed to bearing arms and capable of reciting by heart the officer's manual, would be not so much to fight, nor even to die, as to do so in a certain way, that is (just as the acrobat or the ballerina wearing patched tights sweats and loosens up in the wings to the sound of an out-of-tune piano or in the ammoniac stench of the caged lions with a view to the brief and fugitive instant of unstable equilibrium, the orchestral apotheosis or the drumroll during which she becomes motionless, arms extended, covered with sequins, smiling, gracious, ephemeral, and weightless under the thunder of applause), only to stand twenty years later, in full view, the braid on his képi gleaming in the sun, his useless binoculars in one hand, patient until a piece of metal happens to blow his brains out.

Already long before the riding accident, the two women had moved to the town where the younger one had at last managed to be appointed—that is, had finished waiting for someone to be willing to answer the requests she made yearly on official stationery to some invisible omnipotence so that she might finally be reassigned from her inferno of mud and ice and entitled to live in a house of her own and to have, in order to reach her classroom, only a few streets to cover, sometimes icy too and covered with snow, but at least paved well enough for the melting snow or the rainwater to run off into the gutters instead of standing in puddles of icy mud. And as for the town, it was barely that, a few kilometers from the village, there where the slopes of the narrow valley opened out onto the plain, served by a single-track railroad whose line formed a long curve in order to reach it at the base of the last foothills of the mountain: silent, still medieval, with its long roofs of purplish brown, the ridge poles lined with zinc, its cold arcades, its tall steeple, and that empty over-size house or rather barn, where the sound of footsteps on the rough boards rang out as though in an echo chamber and which they spent years turning into something that resembled a real house, room by room, bringing to the task that same tireless obstinacy, until it was even provided with something that also resembled a bathroom (they who had never washed themselves except at sinks) with a galvanized iron tub, a rectangle of linoleum, a wood-burning heater, and about the size of a living room, arguing with the workmen, themselves doing all that their women's strength (or rather farm-girls' strength) allowed, finishing their task—or rather the ambitious dream of the dead father—only long after this son onto whom he had projected this ambition had been killed: years during which the only two really habitable rooms were for a long time the one in which lay the sort of living mummy (that is, the thing that breathed, scarcely lifting the sheet) and the one, the better one, closed most of the time and reserved for the few days when the person through whom they had chosen to live, so to speak, vicariously would make his brief appearances, relatively frequent at first, then more widely spaced, at the end separated by years during which they had no other image of him than the one afforded them by photographs taken infrequently and by means of which they could see transformed by a series of metamorphoses, or rather of abrupt mutations, the fragile boy who had resisted them on a hospital bed, as if he were now kept somewhere in the wings of those magicians' theaters or rather in a vague Beyond, that world, those unknown countries with no more reality for the sisters than the stretches of pink or yellow tinted paper on the maps of the geography textbooks out of which he would suddenly materialize, still keeping for a while that docile appearance of a studious schoolboy, the look of a simple soldier rather than of an officer, despite the sublieutenant's braid on his sleeve, awkwardly sitting on a garden chair arranged with others around a pedestal table for one of those groups people liked to compose in those days, the persons in it stiff, motionless in "natural" poses, one a lady in a silk dress, two other guests in uniform, and two girls serving refreshments, himself seeming, with his transparent china-blue gaze, his smooth face, his nascent goatee, and his immaculate trousers, a third girl in disguise who had playfully drawn a burnt-cork shadow of a beard and mustaches, not knowing what to do with his legs, his gloves, holding in one hand a tiny liqueur glass, on the back of the photograph the legend "Lorient 1897," then, without transition, suddenly a man, confident, even bold, standing stiff in that dark tunic tight as a corset, wearing boots (perhaps the ones they had ordered for him from that fashionable bootmaker), heels embellished with spurs, the twisted riding crop carelessly held, slanting across the riding breeches, a short goatee and waxed mustaches replacing the timid cork smears, the background of the photograph representing a pale vegetal scene of bamboo, date palms, and banana trees with huge notched leaves ("Martinique 1899"), then a blur of tree ferns, of giant boughs, shiny, fleshy, grooved, hanging in clusters, scattered, festooned, fringed, striped, tattered, aerial, mingling, intersecting, surrounding with an exuberant frame a wall of rock, a waterfall, a pool out of which emerges the milky torso of a man with a square beard, hands on his hips ("Madagascar"), then thornbushes, dry rusty weeds, a hillock where under an open parasol stands the same man with the square beard wearing an undershirt and duck trousers, tight at the ankles, and a pith helmet, his face sunburned even so, standing beside two of those tripods which are used to support instruments for topographical sightings and over which is fussing a Negro with cricketlike legs emerging from a ragged smock; and then the same man with the square beard, on horseback now, all in white, still protected by the same pith helmet, the horses shortlegged, sturdy, with thick wild manes, as though straight out of one of those cave paintings or the barbarous wastes of Asia, the riders on a plain out of which rises a high chalky protuberance like teeth, fragments of bone and jade, at the foot of which can be made out some huts, a slender pagoda with curled roofs ("Lang Son 1906"), the two women (the two old maids now) still busy calculating the price of a board, of a ceiling or a gutter, one leaning over her bicycle towing a wagon loaded with tools or potatoes, and other standing each morning in front of her blackboard facing rows of shaven-headed children, one or the other looking for her keys in the evening, opening the letterbox where, depending on the mails, depending on the schedules of the slow steamers of which he has also sent them photographs, she would find the envelope with its familiar writing, glancing at the exotic stamp, then slipping it among the bunches of leeks or the cabbages in the shopping net, waiting to take off her coat and put down the net in the kitchen before sitting at the table, putting on her glasses, then opening the envelope, spreading flat on the yellowish oilcloth the letter from which occasionally slipped the photograph of some more or less dark face, more or less slanting eyes, as delicate, as polished, as smooth as a pebble, wearing a scarf or just the braided black hair, emerging out of lace, out of collars, out of flounces, like those overdecorated dresses worn by Madonnas, showing only the two doll's hands, one of them resting on the back of a bamboo chair or the console of a photographer's studio, the statue with the childish face of gold or bronze as if it were starched, stiff, frozen, with that vaguely terrified expression of a gazelle or a captured bird, a wild animal, a disguised little girl, the sister who was holding the letter reading it to the end, taking off her glasses, rubbing her pink-rimmed lids with her forefinger, putting her glasses on again in order to examine the photograph, examining the flowerlike face with that same mute and proud satisfaction which illuminated it when she recognized the boots, the square beard, the transparent china-blue gaze, the two sisters in severe dark dresses, the impassive faces a little more worn each time, then putting

away as in the pages of an herbal the delicate tropical
flowers with the bodies hidden under the lace in the family
album, among the photographs of sickly little girls, of cousins or aunts in their stiff, whaleboned blouses, of fat children and vintners in their Sunday best; the way they would
put away, accumulated in the salon which they had managed to restore and to furnish (while they continued to
sleep in bedrooms where the plaster had fallen off the
walls), and in the center a mahogany table, armchairs with
ebony armrests, a piano which neither sister could play,
and a marble-topped vitrine, apparently to receive what
they unpacked out of the pried-open crates, the branches
of coral and the giant clamshells, the tigerskins, the spears
bought in native markets or in ports of call, ending up here
in a dimness distilled by the plush curtains and where there
glistened on the sides of the sooty bronze *cachepots* chased
with gold reliefs the plumes of herons pursuing each other
among winding rivers and hills like dragons, as if from
virtually everywhere, wrested from one place after another
on the surface of these continents which they journeyed
through vicariously (following on the map the routes of
the steamers whose trails of smoke lengthened and dissolved over oceans of pale blue paper, rounding the capes,
crossing the straits between islands, countries colored saffron or almond), there reached the two women in the form
of arrows, spears, porcelains, enamels, screens embroidered with birds-of-paradise and silky chrysanthemums,
and from a succession of smooth feminine faces, the heteroclite booty wrested from barbarous worlds at the same
time that gradually, photograph after photograph, they
could see the former little boy completing his metamorphosis, virtually barbarian himself now, with his eyes ever
brighter in his face scorched by the sun, his wild beard,
his piratical mustaches, like those conquerors gradually

assimilated by their conquests, his skin increasingly tanned, his beard increasingly bristly, until the day when, not from one of those remote countries with exotic names, with exuberant vegetation or sun-scorched sands, but from the Midi garrison where he was assigned between two tours of duty they received the letter in which he informed them that he had decided to marry.

IV

May 17, 1940

*T*HE shooting has stopped. Crouching now, he gazes around him at the bodies of slaughtered horses and cavalrymen scattered on the road and in the fields on either side, staring a moment at the man speaking to him (or perhaps screaming?), sitting on the edge of the ditch and cradling his bloody arm in his other hand, staring at him another moment without even trying to understand what this wounded man is trying to tell him (or not trying: speaking perhaps—or shouting—for himself alone, the mouth distorted by pain—or rage, as if he were screaming invectives), then, without remembering later having made the decision, leaping up, running now, bent double, his legs working furiously under him, toward the hedge bordering the field on the hillside. There is no shooting at first, and when it begins, the sound is casual, scattered, almost without conviction, as if the marksmen were firing by reflex, without really aiming (but aren't they shooting at him?), hearing no bullet whistling by him, hearing only the jerky, almost sluggish crackling of the machine-gun, it too merely a pointless formality, apparently a long ways off, at least as well as he can judge through the uproar of his blood and breath, then collapsing against the hedge, landing on his hands on the other side, pulling in his legs, all this in a fraction of a second, then flat on the ground without moving, deafened by the now tremendous sound of his breath coming and going, of the blood thundering in his ears.

Though the machine-gun has stopped firing he doesn't turn around, doesn't try to look behind him down the little slope strewn here and there with little brownish motionless heaps. What he is looking at is the next hedge. It might be around eight in the morning, but for a long while the notion of time has lost all meaning, whether for eating or sleeping, except that at night the planes don't attack. In any case, for three days he has eaten virtually nothing, and as for sleeping, he no longer really distinguishes sleep from waking, even in action, not only on horseback but even on foot, moving like a sleepwalker, muscles contracting and slackening on their own, governed by automatic reflexes, so that he could not say if it was his reason, his will, or some animal instinct that has made him straighten up and suddenly begin running. Just as he could no longer say how long he remained unconscious on what could not exactly be called a battlefield (the intersection of two local roads in the middle of sprouting wheatfields and flowering meadows): all he remembers (or rather does not remember—it will be only later, when he has time: for the moment he is solely occupied with studying the fields around him, estimating the distance that separates him from the next hedge, while he slides his rifle strap over his head, opens the breech and pulls it out) are the still pale and transparent shadows of horses on the ground a little ahead of him and to the right, so distended by the first sunbeams that they seem to move without advancing, as though on stilts, raising their long cricketlike legs and lowering them in apparently the same place like some fantastic animal mimicking the movements of walking where it stands, the long column of retreating cavalrymen still somnolent at daybreak, shoulders hunched, torsos swaying back and forth on the saddles, the head of the column making a right turn at the intersection, then suddenly the screams, the bursts of machine-gun fire, the head of the column falling back, then other machine-guns behind them, the rear of the column galloping up, the cavalrymen colliding, the confusion, the tumult, the chaos, more screaming, the explosions, the conflicting orders, then he himself becoming chaos, curses, preparing to remount the mare he had just leaped down from, his foot in the stirrup, the saddle slipping, and now straining, pushing and pulling with all his strength to put it back in place, struggling against the weight of the saber and the saddlebags, the reins sliding to the crook of his left elbow, then being jostled, tearing his palm on the tongue of the buckle, deafened by the explosions, the screams, the frantic galloping, or rather perceiving (hearing, seeing) something like fragments following one after the other, replacing each other, revealing each other, colliding, turning: flanks of horses, boots, hooves, rumps, falls, interrupted screams, sounds, the air, space itself apparently fragmented, chopped into tiny bits, torn by the crackling of the machine-guns—then giving up, beginning to run, still cursing, among the maddened horses, the screams, the racket, the mare he is holding by the bridle cantering off, the saddle under her belly, then suddenly nothing more (not even feeling the shock, no pain, not even the awareness of stumbling, of falling, nothing): darkness, no noise now (or perhaps a deafening uproar canceling itself out?), deaf, blind, nothing, until slowly, emerging gradually like bubbles rising to the surface of murky water, appear indeterminate spots that blur, fade out, then reappear, then grow clear: triangles, polygons, pebbles, tiny blades of grass, the stones of the road where he is now on all fours like a dog, his brain (or something swifter, more alive, and more intelligent) beginning to function again: something that doubtless, in agreement with his quadruped position, belongs to the animal kingdom, as if there were appearing in him what grants an animal (dog, wolf, or hare) intelligence and speed at the same time as indifference: complete indifference (while the animal part of him was functioning at top speed) with which he watched the wounded man screaming and quite close by, down the slope, head down, arms out, a stupid expression of surprise and incredulity on his frozen face, the lifeless body of the cavalryman who a moment before was riding beside him, beside whom he had lived, slept, and eaten for eight months, then suddenly no longer seeing him, seeing only the horizontal strip of hedge toward which, head pulled between his shoulders, he runs as fast as he can.

The breech of the rifle violently flung away somehow immobilized at the top of its trajectory glitters as it turns in the sun before falling some distance away, the rifle itself virtually buried in the grass at the foot of the hedge, his body again bent double like an ape, hands brushing the ground, one of them propping him when he stumbles, he already moves quickly (like those rats darting at the foot of a wall) along the hedge, then, having reached the end of the field, turns the corner, then in the same way following the hedge along the other side, then suddenly flat, the length of his body pressed against the ground, the air violently driven out of his lungs by the shock, then, without a moment's pause, like a rubber ball bouncing against a wall and ricocheting in the opposite direction, wriggling his hips, using his elbows and his knees, hurriedly crawling backward, then stopping, all movement stopping except for imperceptible lateral shifts, imperceptible contractions, as if he were trying to shrink, to diminish in size, huddling against the base of the hedge under the tiny hawthorn leaves, and at the end absolutely motionless.

He doesn't see the minute particles of diamond left by the dew on the part of the field still in the shade of the hedge, he doesn't smell the fresh earthy scent of the blades of grass crushed under his weight, nor does he smell the stench of his own body, his clothes, his underwear stiffened by accumulated filth, sweat, and fatigue, he hears neither the songs of birds nor the faint rustling of the leaves in the transparent air, he sees neither the flowers that stipple the field nor the young shoots of the hedge stirring faintly in the morning breeze, he doesn't even hear any longer the wild beating of his heart and the successive waves of blood in his ears. The only thing he now perceives (or at least that functional part of himself which knows no fear or rather which is beyond fear, only functional, practical) . . . the only thing he perceives is the dull, scarcely audible hum which comes to him on the right side, gradually growing louder, approaching, increasing, and all of a sudden he sees through the hedge the first one already very close: something all planes and angles, crudely made of riveted plates of steel, like a sort of crustacean, except that this is the size of a truck: blind, squat, dangerous, painted iron-gray, also vaguely resembling a coffin and moving along the road in a rumble of well-oiled engines, followed by a second then by a third, unexpected and unreal in the cool and calm spring morning, the three tanks about twenty yards apart advancing slowly, scarcely faster than a man walking, while he flattens himself still lower, snatches off his helmet, hides the bottom of his face in the crook of his elbow, then stares as though over a parapet at the first tank passing along the hedge, its turret open, a man's black-shirted torso emerging from the opening, one hand resting casually on its edge, the other periodically raising to his lips a cigarette whose smoke dissolves in tiny bluish clouds in the still air, the lozenges of sunlight shining through the leaves sliding over the metal plates, suddenly changing level, stretching or contracting at the joints in the armor, sliding up the turrets, sliding back down, as if each of the three tanks were crawling under an immaterial speckled carpet, an immaterial camouflage net which it raised in passing, stretched, distended, after which everything resumes its place, the rumble of the engines fading, the air no longer vibrating, the mineral smell of gasoline and burnt oil still floating, stinking, in the motionless air, then dissolving too, the momentarily disturbed world of nature calm once more as still lying at the base of the hedge he begins once more to perceive the murmur of his blood, his muscles gradually relaxing, then cautiously sitting up, first leaning on his hands, then on his knees, eyes turned in the direction where the last of the tanks has disappeared, still listening, then making up his mind, on his feet now, beginning to run again, moving again like a rat along the hedge, slowing as he approaches the road, stopping, listening again, leaning over the fence which encloses the field, examining the deserted road, then very quickly climbing the fence, dropping down the other side, and running on.

He doesn't try to locate the machine-gun that is firing when he crosses the road, jumps over the second ditch, and still running crosses a sprouting wheatfield and throws himself into the thick underbrush which borders it, no longer running (or rather prevented from running), stum-

bling, panting again, noisily, though he is now advancing
not much faster than a walk, slashed by the branches, pro-
tecting his eyes with his arm held in front of his face, careful
to lift his feet so as not to get caught in the brambles or
the dead branches breaking underfoot, thrown off balance
by the uneven terrain, advancing by a series of jerks rather
than any continuous impulse. The machine-gun has now
stopped firing, but in any case he is still not afraid. He
doesn't think. He doesn't feel tired any more either, nor
hungry. Later, trying to remember, he will not even manage to recall whether at one moment or another he needed
to squat behind some bush or in the ditch. As if during
this whole time his intestines had never had to be emptied,
as if what little food he has swallowed (things gone cold,
sticky, brought the first days by mess truck, then not even
sticky things, no more truck, only what they could find by
rifling the already pillaged kitchen cupboards in the houses
abandoned by their inhabitants) had been completely assimilated, without remainders or waste products, the body
at the exclusive service of what was being demanded of it,
that is, riding horseback, jumping down, lying prone under
the shelling, getting back on horseback, galloping, or, having dismounted, running, to the point where it seemed to
him he had run that way for days, never having stopped
galloping in a sense, and running, even in his sleep, sometimes forced (out of breath, lungs on fire, half-asphyxiated)
to resign himself to just walking, able to hear the bullets
looking for him, waiting for the impact that would plow
the flesh of his back, but still walking (or, mounted, simply
trotting: the exhausted mare, also asphyxiated, stumbling,
falling) until he feels once more the possibility in himself
to start running again (or, by using the spurs, to force the
mare to gallop), accustomed now to hear the loud raucous
hissing of the air coming and going in his throat (or the

mare's), drained of any kind of emotion, that is, no more than fear, feeling now neither rebellion, nor indignation, nor despair: perfectly calm, composing himself in order to reflect and decide in that cold part of himself capable of attention and cunning, not futilely occupied with the why but with the how to go on living, again suddenly frozen, still panting like an animal, cautiously parting the branches at the edge of the underbrush overhanging a road, studying with the same meticulous suspicion the road, the valley whose curve it follows, the stream at the bottom of the valley, listening to the silence (still hearing neither the songs of birds nor the rustling of leaves), estimating the distance that separates the road from the stream lined with reeds, then the stream from the woods on the opposite hillside, then, either because he has miscalculated his energy, his ankle held at the top of the slope as though by a hand (as if he had not only to fight against men, firearms, and explosives, but also against a conspiracy of underhand forces), everything (woods, valley, stream) collapsing while he falls head first, the hard and chalky surface of the road rushing toward him, rising up to strike him or rather to stun him, bumping his helmet with the metallic clash of an anvil, the chin strap half-strangling him, his larynx crushed, at the same time that his left shoulder seems to explode, the stones of the road driven into his body, the pitiless part of himself which governs his movements concerned with neither the pain nor the deafening racket of bells that surrounds his head while he runs, already hobbling, one hand on his wounded shoulder, reaches the reeds, the cold water suddenly in his boots, surrounding his ankles as the stream splashes up at him, then the cold water around his calves, then up to his knees: not a stream as he had supposed but, invisible under the reeds, the pool formed by a small dam downstream, his legs compelled now to struggle against the heavy resistance of the water, his feet shackled by the weeds, panicking for a moment, struggling, raising his thighs, his feet shoving violently against the muddy bottom, the water splashing noisily, each of his shoulders thrust forward in alternation, his arms thrust forward too, as if he were boxing, as defenseless, as vulnerable in this open space as a fly caught in the center of a spiderweb, then again on all fours, his heavy boots smeared with grayish mud sliding and skidding on the opposite bank, using his hands and knees to climb the moist slope, as if he were trying to wrest himself out of the earth, out of the primeval slime, then loose, running now, feet splayed to work his way up the slope, able to see now his heavy shadow wobbling ahead of him like a woman's, with his long coat dripping, finally reaching the edge of the woods, penetrating them, and then not running any more.

It is only a moment later that he hears the cuckoo. That is, the terrible racket of his breathing subsiding (now he is walking: at a regular pace but without hurrying, so that gradually his heart and his lungs recover their normal functioning), sheltered now, the awareness of the external world gradually returning otherwise than through the elementary alternative of cover and exposure; he can then perceive the tiny sounds that constitute the silence of the dense, motionless woods: the faint hissing of the air in the treetops, the rustle of the foliage, his footsteps muffled by the spongy ground, the elastic carpet of accumulated humus, and reaching him at regular intervals, the double cry of the bird, echoed between the vertical trunks, as if after having been uttered it continued to exist by its very absence, as if to underline the silence, to make it even more evident, sounded with the regularity of a clock not to disturb but to emphasize it, to release one accumulation of time and to permit another quantity to accumulate in its turn, to thicken, until the moment when it will be liberated by the cry, until he stops walking, stands there motionless under the stinking carapace of broadcloth and leather weighed down by water (but he doesn't feel it, merely constitutes with it one compact mass of filth and fatigue, of a substance, so to speak, undifferentiated, earthen, as if his brain itself, bewildered by lack of sleep, was filled with a sort of mud, his face separated from the external world, from the air, by a scorching film, a kind of mask stuck to the skin), listening, waiting till the cry of the cuckoo reaches him again, then hearing that silence flow back, peopled now by a tremendous uproar not that of the war (at one very remote moment, as though coming from another world, anachronistic as it were, at once absurd, scandalous, and savage, echoed a series of explosions: not a sound strictly speaking (or else something that would be to sound what gray is to color), not something human, that is, capable of being governed by man, cosmic rather, the air repeatedly shaken, brutally compressed and decompressed in some gigantic and furious convulsion, then nothing more), not the rustle of branches gently rocked or the faint hissing of the breeze in the vault of the foliage, but more secret, more enormous, surrounding him on all sides, continuous, indifferent, the invisible and triumphant impulse of the sap, the imperceptible and slow unfolding into daylight of the buds, the corollas, the leaves with their complicated folds opening, smoothing themselves out, spreading, palpitating, fragile, invincible, and tender green. Then he begins walking again (or rather, without his remembering having ordered them to do so, his legs move again beneath him, as though of their own accord, as though out of habit), his eyes (not he this time either: his eyes) seeing to it that his shadow keeps always in front of him and slightly to his right, his right hand holding the

wounded shoulder, the tear in the coat, then, after a moment, moving away, fumbling in his pocket while he is still
walking, taking out something which, without looking at
it, he takes a bite of and begins to chew, his jaws working
on a hard, peppery, and rancid substance, his thumb and
forefinger finally removing from his teeth the piece of
thread at the end of the casing, throwing it away, the hand
raising his canteen with the same movement while he is
still walking, never stopping, merely on the alert, listening
to the powerful vegetal silence, waiting for the cuckoo to
cry again, raising the canteen to his lips, tipping his head
back, his tongue barely moistened with a few iron-tasting
drops, the hand lowering the canteen, shaking it, turning
it, then corking it again and putting it back, without anger
or bitterness, still calm, still inhabited by that total absence
of feelings or impulses except for that something (he
doesn't even wonder what) that makes him go on walking,
his mouth simply on fire now, burned by the pepper, his
frustrated tongue mechanically moving back and forth over
his lips, the cuckoo behind him now, its cry fainter and
fainter, then gradually fading away, then relayed by another
cuckoo (later, he will calculate that he must have walked
this way for about an hour, covering about four kilometers
or rather, taking into account the slowness of his advance
in the underbrush, avoiding the thickets, three) until
through the trunks he glimpses again the light no longer
broken, patched, motley, but smooth, homogeneous, as if
the trees had suddenly stumbled, stopped against a sort of
wall which, from inside the woods where he still was, appeared to him as a concretion of sun—and now lying flat
on his belly, stretched out at full length, his hand pushing
away the tiny soft green crescents lying on the surface of
the water, then his face in its coolness at the same time
that he can feel on his tongue the taste of the mud while

clumsily, cursing himself for not being a dog, sometimes his mouth, his nose half-submerged, breathing, sometimes trying to collect the water in the palm of his hand, he drinks greedily without ceasing, like a dog lapping, to survey the surroundings, alert, listening to the sounds or rather to that new quality of silence, more porous, so to speak, still faintly punctuated behind him by the cuckoo call dominated now by a cacophonous and tenuous cheeping of birds through which, as though through a delicate embroidery, he can now hear quite close by and at regular intervals, like the cuckoo, as though governed by some absurd clock movement, meaningless, not even threatening, conscientious, tranquil as it were in a tranquil nature, like the labor of a lazy woodcutter, the widely spaced firing of a single cannon, while still lying on his belly, his torso now propped up on his arms, he stares in an incredulous stupor at the intact network of barbed wire glistening in the sun, following the curves of the empty landscape like a carpet of metal spikes being unrolled, vanishing into the little pool, reappearing on the other bank, interrupted only by the road along which are ranged as though for an inspection the *chevaux de frise*, the cool water he is drinking out of both hands now striking him, streaming over his face, splashing the front of his coat, his cartridge belts (now he has taken off his helmet, kneels, bending forward), his joined hands coming and going several times with a sort of frenzy, like those of an automaton, his hair, his forehead, his cheeks receiving the splashes of water without his ceasing to stare fixedly (still calm, scarcely touched by a tranquil and sarcastic indignation) at the barbed wire, the road, the blockhouse a little farther on, intact, unoccupied, finally no longer splashing himself, his forefinger rinsing his burning eyelids, then falling back, remaining crouched on his heels, now watching the heads of the little frogs reappear one after the other, breaking the green foam on the surface of the water smooth again, following one of them with his eyes while he wipes his hands carefully, deliberately, one finger after the next, with the grayish ragged handkerchief stiffened with mucus and filth, which he then carefully folds into a square, then folds the square in half, then puts it back in his pocket, raising his head at the faint hum of an engine, discerning, very high in the sky, only a silvery sparkle, following it for a second with his eyes, then no longer taking any interest in it, all his attention focused now on one of the frogs which is letting itself float with the faint current, inert, apparently dead, its delicate hands spread, while with a mechanical gesture he tears off the flap of one of his cartridge pouches (the frog quickly drawing in and spreading its legs, like a spring, once, twice, then vanishing), takes out a shapeless package of crumpled paper from which he removes a cigarette, also grayish and ragged, which he straightens as best he can, meticulously smooths with that same maniacal care, compelled to flick his lighter four times before a flame leaps up which he brings close to the tip of the cigarette, managing, before it goes out, to draw two or three puffs, then inhaling with no result but a faint sucking noise, continuing all this time without paying any further attention to it to hear in the succession of their lazy cadence the regular explosions of the single cannon, then pulling the cigarette away from his lips, examining it, discovering the tiny tear, smoothing it with saliva, this time holding the cigarette so that his forefinger blocks the hole, the grains of tobacco sizzling faintly in contact with the flame then going out again, examining the cigarette once more with the same placid, attentive, and serious expression, then not throwing it away but letting it drop, simply loosening his fingers and going back to observing the frogs, perfectly motionless, in that simian

crouching posture, unconscious of the passage of time, his
mind empty (not absent: empty) with the exception of that
part of himself always on the alert, vigilant, which makes
him suddenly flatten himself behind a bush, now carefully
watching the two cavalrymen who suddenly appear at the
turn of the road to his right, their horses coming down the
slope at a walk, as though they were casual promenaders
in the cool and glistening May morning, a third man leading
two more horses by the bridle appearing behind them, the
first two coming closer, stopping now, watching him in
their turn while frantically he runs the length of the pool,
deafening himself by the inarticulate screams coming out
of him, finding a culvert, crossing it, reaching the road in
a few strides, then standing, panting, at attention, listing
in a single breath one after the other his rank, his name,
the number of his unit, his division, his regiment, after
which he stands there, continuing to pant, under the almost
casual, apparently importunate, vaguely disapproving stare
which, under the shadow of the helmet, examines him—
or rather seems to pass through him, as if, still regularly
punctuated by the explosions of the same solitary cannon,
the scene were taking place in a sort of unreality, of re-
ciprocal incredibility: on the one side, he in his coat with
the torn shoulder, the sopping hems, the front spotted
with water, filthy, his helmet smeared with mud and
dented, his boots and puttees muddy too, his spurs rusty;
on the other, the cavalryman in a coat as impeccable as
though it had come an hour ago from the tailor, the boots
shining as if they had just been polished, the spurs gleaming, the sun glistening on the five gold-braid stripes on his
sleeve, the face bony, absolutely without expression save
for that of a total absence of interest (as if he were already
dead, he will think later: as if he had escaped that ambush
only to be compelled to get himself killed . . . Like some-

one whom a stranger, an intruder, might disturb by coming
into the room where he is already in the process of loading
his revolver after having carefully written out his will . . .),
to the point where there might be some question whether
the eyes transmit to the brain the image of the man who
is standing on the road, waiting, seeing finally the mouth
with the thin lips open to little more than a crack, a fissure,
the lips barely stirring, the voice dry, distant, annoyed if
not actually angry, saying only: "Fine," saying: "Take one
of the horses back there and follow me," the sparkling
boots imperceptibly pressing the flanks of the horse, the
horse moving, the two officers riding ahead without turning back, seen now from behind, elegant, as though corseted, the cut traces of the off horse ridden by the colonel
trailing behind it in the dust, then (without his being quite
conscious of the sequence of his gestures, that is, grasping
the reins handed to him, putting one foot in the stirrup,
hoisting himself up, straddling the saddle) mounted again,
still inhabited by that same somnambulistic sensation of
unreality, thinking that he would have to shorten the stirrups which were too long for him, still staring with astonishment at the two corseted backs swaying faintly with the
gait of their mounts, then hearing his own voice emerging
from him again, saying: "God damn!" saying: "But how
did he do it? He was at the head of the column when the
firing began . . . God damn: how . . . ," the man leading the
horses by the bridle (a cavalryman he had never seen before) turning his head a moment, he too fixing him with
that absent stare devoid of amenity, even hostile, the stare
fixed on a troublemaker or an idiot, and then taking no
further interest in him, turning away, abandoning him,
while he turns around in his saddle, looks behind him, sees
only two bicyclists pedaling slowly along, following them
at a distance of about fifty yards, describing curves on the

road in order to keep pace with the walking horses, again hearing (as if his own voice were reaching him through layers of glass, incongruous and remote) "And the rest, the rest? . . . Where are . . . This is all that's lef . . . ?" the man leading the horse by the bridle then giving him a quick look, as though outraged, furious, then beginning to swear, tugging brutally on the bridle of the horse which began to move sideways like a crab, dancing nervously on its hooves, the cavalryman tearing its mouth with violent tugs, shouting: "Hey there! Hoo! . . . Goddamn fucking bastard son of a bitch! Are you going to stop this shit or not? Are you, are you? Goddamn fucking son of a bitch . . ."

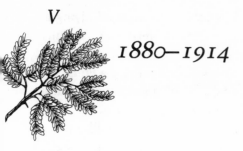

V

1880–1914

TWO of the three sisters (the oldest and the youngest) had already been married a long time (the youngest already dead, in fact, buried in an ostentatious mausoleum (that is, really ostentatious: not built in the form of an Egyptian tomb of black marble cut and polished by machine then engraved with gold letters, but consisting of a simple worn stone, over a century old in its present form, with no inscription, surrounded by a grill and cypresses, also over a century old, the kind that belonged to very old families), survived by a widower who, once a month, abandoned his club and his bridge parties to take dinner in the huge and lugubrious dining room with Venetian-red walls embellished with a frieze, where among the leafy tracery capered an endless sequence of jugglers, troubadours, monkeys, and trained bears hand-painted by the young lady's grandfather in the days when his dark romantic locks fell over the collar of an elegant mustard-colored frock coat, an old man now, with severe white mustaches, invariably dressed in somber clothes, who would not lose much time in joining the youngest sister in death, lying in his turn beneath a worn stone slab of comparable antiquity in the cemetery of the village where he owned not only two tons of granite to cover his bones but also a house, or rather an agglomeration of houses, inhabited by the oldest workmen and the bailiff of the estate around which, two or three times a year, leaving the city, he would make a tour of inspection in a barouche before driving on to spend the night, riding in that same barouche, under the roof of a second estate on the far side of the neighboring Department from which he would return the next morning) . . . her two sisters had already been married a long time, then, and she was nearly thirty herself when she met him.

Above the body beginning to thicken and in the face gradually losing its contours, the large calm eyes, to whose glory had been written on several occasions certain flattering and rhetorical quatrains on the backs of postcards representing views of the Alps, chateaux of the Loire, or chalky cliffs, still gave evidence of that brilliance which had been responsible for the receipt of so many snowy peaks, cathedrals, fishing boats, and peasant girls in regional costume accompanied by accounts of excursions, picnics, automobile trips, or complaints about the never-ending rain in Brittany. She was living with her mother now, an old lady with a plaintive countenance stamped by widowhood and the loss of the younger sister with an expression of chronic desolation, as old, it seemed, as the patriarch whose activity (he was now too old to paint jugglers, monkeys, and bears) consisted in being driven to his estates, not to supervise (the bailiff was there for that), but to ascertain that following his orders, the vines of his two hundred hectares ravaged around the end of the century by phylloxera had been torn out to be replanted, that is,

that after having imperturbably swallowed the six or seven
hors d'oeuvres followed by several dishes and desserts prepared by the bailiff's wife (this transpired around a stiff,
starched cloth so white as to seem blue, in a dining room
with walls stained by saltpeter, the floor covered with a
design of red and black tiles laid there two centuries earlier,
a huge fire blazing in the enormous marble fireplace also
dating back some two centuries, the old man's white-haired
head protected by a pale-gray felt with a round crown or,
if the cold was too intense, with an astrakhan toque, listening without hearing the voice of the old bailiff with the
pitiless slave-driver's face beneath the flat gray cap which
seemed to be a part of his body, to complete it (not like
some sartorial accessory but rather like a kind of consti-
tutive appendage, the visor like a beak, the skin of his bald
head, when he raised his cap for a moment upon the barouche's arrival, livid, vaguely obscene, vaguely pathetic
above the crackled earth-colored mask, like the fragile
membrane of some internal organ momentarily exposed,
then immediately covered up), now accounting to him for
the work under way, the two old men conferring in the
room the size of a reception chamber, the walls crumbling,
the tiling and the mantelpiece for which an antique dealer
would have offered a fortune, though neither man was
concerned, one because he had no intention of selling, the
other of buying, the bailiff's wife all in black standing near
the door, watching the table, leaning into the kitchen corridor to control the succession of dishes), then, from his
barouche halted at the edge of the drive, he (the patriarch)
stared in silence at the long parallel plumes of dust borne
horizontally by the wind, like the fumaroles on the slope
of a volcano, in the wake of the squad of laborers or rather
of tiny silhouettes (horse, plow, and man) no larger than
those of burrowing insects with many limbs apparently

pinned to the earth by the vinestocks above which occasionally shone a flash of sunlight, and that was all, until autumn when, returning to his summer property, he would arrive for the grape harvest, still in the same barouche, still dressed in the same frock coat and white cravat, would have himself driven to the vineyards, would stare, still without getting out of his vehicle, at the indecisive activity of the families of Spanish or Gypsy seasonal workers, vanishing at breast height in the thick foliage, the women mummified or elephantine, their faces gullied by the sun, the children staggering under the weight of the buckets, the men with cutthroat expressions, then would bark an order to the driver, a little later making the barouche stop in front of the gaping door of the cellar where, without entering, he watched the vague figures coming and going in the shadows, then again between the saltpeter-stained walls opposite the carved marble mantelpiece, alone now, sitting at the table in the cool penumbra and carefully peeling one fig after another which he chewed slowly down to the last one, not chosen from the fruit-bowl but from the pyramid arranged in front of him, then rinsing his fingers, drying them along with his mustache on the damask napkin embroidered with his initials, standing up, returning to the barouche waiting for him in front of the door, and having himself driven back to town.

A whole section of the commune land register bore the name made illustrious at the head of armies of the Revolution, then of the Empire, by the patriarch's grandfather, a sort of colossus, not only of gigantic size but of a weight so monstrous that it remained still recorded in the documents of the period: a man who unlike his grandson, unlike the dry and skinny old man with the beaky nose and the bony hands, had never lived except in and by violence, courage, boldness no longer attested to except by the interlaced initials engraved or embroidered on the tablecloths, the napkins or the sheets shut up in drawers or linen presses, as if since the Empire there had been patiently constituted (or rather amassed, accumulated) an inexhaustible booty, an inexhaustible store of silverware, of table or household linen whose sole reason for being now seemed to be the very accumulation and the filling of cupboards, wardrobes, and trunks.

As for the young lady with large eyes who was gradually running to fat as she approached her thirtieth birthday (the young sultana, as the authors of the quatrains scribbled on the back of glaciers and Brittany fishing ports were sometimes emboldened to call her), she had never (any more than her grandfather, any more than her cousins as well, one a young *député* by hereditary right, a poet on occasion, the other a cavalry officer), in her whole life, done anything except to learn, along with the Spanish language, to strum a few chords on the neck of a guitar and to develop, then to print the photographs that she tirelessly snapped of her family, of bullfights, or of the innocent charades performed, in order to amuse the ladies of the family, by the troupe of lively young men surrounding her, before they left to join at midnight their kept mistresses or the inmates of the fashionable brothel of the town.

Never, except perhaps at the ladies' sewing circle where persons of her condition produced layettes for the poor, never had she threaded a needle, sewn on a button, mended a stocking, put something on to cook, never had she even left the house for anything but promenades, visits, dinners, or parties, never (if occasionally she lingered in front of a shop window or a display) had she entered any store whatever, except perhaps that of a bootmaker: like the caterers and upholsterers, the dressmakers came to the house, showed their wares and models, offered to leaf through the heavy bundles of samples, returned and knelt, their mouths bristling with pins, for the fittings, bringing and carrying away dresses and coats in squares of black serge knotted at the four corners.

It was as if she had no desires, no regrets, no thoughts, no plans. She was neither sad, nor melancholy, nor dreamy. Rather gay, according to those who knew her at the time, greedy (and therefore doubtless sensual). From Spain, from Barcelona where she sometimes traveled for the holidays of La Merced—or from Figueras, closer to home—she had brought a taste for hot chocolate so thick that the tiny spoon thrust in the middle of the cup would remain standing and for the yellow photographs where on the deserted and saffron spaces of the arena could be seen the tiny silhouettes of horses and men around the massive shape of the bull. It was just possible to make out in her famous eyes a sudden brilliance which might have been either horror or excitement when she described the blind-folded horses, their bellies ripped open by the bull's horns and their guts hurriedly stuffed back in with straw before being sewn up and offered to the bull all over again. Apparently she was utterly unconscious that she possessed a body and what such a thing might be used for, aside from being fed with delicacies or dressed in laces and embroidered shawls in order to pose with one of her girlfriends, hips arched, arms raised, rump thrust out, one thigh half-raised, in postures of Gypsy dancers with castanets of whose lewdness she seemed quite unaware. Nor did she seem to envy her elder sister, married to a rich landowner (which made one more country house to visit during the summer, this one near the sea), whose four children, two boys and two girls, she treated as if they had been her own, with smiling and impenetrable affability, just as in reading the amorous quatrains or in listening to the com-

pliments of the young men she confined herself to tilting
her head to one side and stretching her lips into a vague
smile, her gaze, too, fixed on something inexpressible—
or nonexistent. Twice a year—in autumn and in early summer, the season of the races, of the Prix de Diane— she
would spend three weeks in Paris at the house of her uncle
the senator (the father of the *député* by hereditary right
and of the cavalry lieutenant by recommendation), or, accompanied by the patriarch and the old lady, at the Grand
Hotel, attending operas, horse shows, a performance at
the Comédie-Française, visiting department stores, after
which she would return to the huge house, the citadel of
silence and respectability at the heart of the labyrinth of
old streets of the old town, she herself like a kind of citadel
at the foot of the one built six hundred years earlier by a
king of Aragon, fortified by Charles V, later surrounded
by Vauban with impregnable and dizzying walls, which also
included the Gypsy neighborhoods, the streets of brothels,
the six or seven churches gleaming with the gold of baroque altarpieces, the convents, the mansions with Renaissance mullions, the ancient marketplace, the cafés tiled
with iris-women and exotic plants, the squares with bronze
statues, the courthouse with the Corinthian pediment,
cafés, squares, and courthouse linked by a tramway not
much larger than a child's toy passing, anachronistic and
rattling, in front of the gothic arcades, the terraces with
their boxes of hydrangeas, the hardware stores, the ribbon
shops, the advertisements for anise apéritifs, for choco-
lates, for soaps, for cigars, and the posters in violent colors
for the touring theatrical companies.

There was also (but outside the enclosure of the ramparts) a public garden planted with camellias, palms, shiny-
leaved magnolias, and huge plane trees, their smooth
trunks mottled with dark patches, under which, wearing

one of those long, camisole-like gowns whose flounces swept the dust, she walked with her elder sister and the latter's children, following or herself pushing the last-born's baby carriage, at the same time bearing in front of her like a mask under one of those extravagant hats like lampshades that imperturbable countenance with its serene gaze behind the long black lashes. She did not seem to be waiting for something, at least not in the immediate future. On one occasion, the old lady thought she discerned in her an inclination for one of the rich and idle young men who would send her verses on the backs of the picturesque banks of the Loing or views of Florence, but prudently questioned she simply observed with an amused smile that he had a silly name. She was in no hurry. As if, like those heifers kept from the bulls, actually unaware of their existence and lovingly fattened for some sacrifice (or like those bulls themselves whose death agony she attended, fanning herself and crunching salted almonds in the grandstand of the arena), she knew herself destined for something at once magnificent, swift, and cruel which would come in its time. She was pious. At least she accompanied her mother and her sister each Sunday to the cathedral, went to confession regularly—though it might be wondered what trifles she could admit to the invisible priest standing behind the wooden lattice—abstained from meat on Friday (which meant little enough, this day being the one when huge fish with delicate flesh were served, brought to the house by the fishmonger himself), and observed Lent, which doubtless, considering her gluttony, must have cost her more than anything else. She was not chaste but somehow asexual. As if it had never occurred to her that the alabaster belly concealed by her camisole-gowns and what was hidden by the silky fleece beneath which flared her pale thighs might serve for anything but

organic functions of digestion and evacuation, her breasts
for anything but nursing. Yet when one of her admirers
(or a practical joker) allowed himself to send her an unsigned postcard representing in the style of the posters of
the period a woman in black stockings, lace panties, and
only a corset astride a gilded chair, puffing her cigarette
at the ceiling, she kept it, too, along with the church portal
at Caudebec, a street in Limoges devastated by rioters, the
baths of Châtel-Guyon, and Trafalgar Square. As if the
enormous appetite which compelled her to swallow choc-
olates, goose liver, guinea hen, and sherbets during those
dinners whose terrifying menus she also greedily preserved
also permitted her to swallow and to digest without distinction, in the manner of a tranquil ruminant, the cathedrals, the shepherds of the Landes, the Stock Exchange,
the grotto of Lourdes, and the licentious little tarts in panties. Perhaps she helped her sister bathe the children before they went to sleep, but certainly no more than that.
For the rest, it would seem that her chief occupation was
to incarnate that sloth which the example of the patriarch
and of her own mother with the gullied face had doubtless
taught her to consider as not a privilege but somehow a
family virtue, an obligation constituting the distinctive sign
of her caste and of her social milieu. She would read. Or
rather (the false Montmartre painter had represented the
two of them: her sister busy with her embroidery frame,
and she sitting in an armchair, a book with a yellow cover
in her hand, open on a level with her face and within
reading distance) she turned the pages of books. In the
crates where, after her death, the contents of her library
had been piled, were found, without its being possible to
say at what period of her life she had read them, the works
of the Countess de Ségur, Hans Christian Andersen, several Balzacs, Verlaine, Albert Samain, Anatole France, and

two or three members of the Académie Française. With
her best friend she corresponded in Spanish. Perhaps because of the rhetoric natural to the language (or because
of her ineptness in using it) the tone sometimes appeared
impassioned, even suggestive, as for instance "*te beso*" instead of "*je t'embrasse*," and once, for a joke, they had
themselves photographed disguised as men. But, like her
sister, the best friend had married and gone to live in the
Camargue, and if they continued to write each other, the
tone changed. The friend who replaced her traveled a great
deal and began most of her cards with the same formula:
"To the laziest of friends, I send affectionate greetings from
Dieppe (or Vichy, or Florence, or Brighton) . . ." It appeared that nothing could perturb her mind, any more than
her body or her apparel. She played tennis (at least a photograph showed her on a court, a pear-shaped racket in
her hand) wearing those same long skirts sweeping the
dust and with flowers in her hair. Above their trousers
pegged at the knees, her partners wore a broad canvas belt
widening over the abdomen, like a sort of orthopedic bandage, vaguely obscene. Her laziness seemed to be equaled
only by her lack of curiosity, with the exception of the
gowns she could admire at the Opéra or in the paddock
at Chantilly. For the rest, she seemed to limit herself to
being there, confined in a static inertia, her face timidly
protected from the sun by parasols, milky and vegetative,
like the lethargic sovereign of some kingdom of absence
where she kept herself—not even in a state of expectation:
simply kept herself. Even with four children, her sister
spent several hours at the piano every day, capable of
deciphering with amazing virtuosity any sonata, trio, or
concerto, and the ebony music rack with the delicately
carved colonnettes could never hold all the scores bound
in red morocco. She abandoned the guitar. Yet she con-

tinued to photograph on the veranda, where the light allowed a good exposure, the family groups presided over by the severe patriarch, then, when he died, the old lady with the pendulous dewlaps surrounded by the older sister and the grandchildren who were growing up, dressed in sailor suits, then in jackets and neckties, the girls whose curls fell to their shoulders wearing enormous bows in their hair, their legs in dark stockings. She seemed to regret neither maternity nor her celibacy. It was as if she had known in advance that it was enough for her to accompany her sister's children on walks, to take photographs, to develop the plates in the red light of the laboratory, to make the sepia prints which she then dipped in hyposulphate baths, to make her two trips a year to Paris, to reveal her shoulders on the occasion of dinners or parties, to act in charades, to visit certain poor people recommended by her confessor. Nor did she seem to dread growing old. Several of those who had courted her married elsewhere. For her this was the occasion to have her clothes transformed by the dressmaker who circled her on her knees like a sort of amputee or dwarf, murmuring through the pins clenched between her lips, and to add another to her collection of menus which announced for a single meal turbot with hollandaise sauce, crayfish timbales, loin of venison, lobster quenelles, pigeon pie, asparagus *sauce mousseline* and a *bombe glacée*. She had (and had them still at forty) opulent shoulders which the seamstress exposed in shroudings and seethings of silk or tulle. Her older sister's husband had bought one of the first automobiles to be seen in the town, high on its axles, painted yellow, embellished with glistening brass trim, and resembling, with its headlamps, some enormous insect, and the day laborers who worked in the vineyards, bent over the vinestocks, backs to the wind, the collars of their patched overcoats turned up, would straighten to watch it pass on the narrow roads, trailing a cloud of dust behind it, a sort of giant beetle carrying its beetle young on its back in the form of passengers whose faces were devoured by enormous goggles or—the women's—protected by veils knotted under the chin and tying down hats resembling mushrooms. It was necessary to slow down and sound the klaxon at some length to waken the wagon drivers asleep on their sacking hammocks slung under the floor and to wait while they jumped down and ran to the bridle of the shaft horse to pull him to the side of the road. The horses wore heavy collars topped with a sort of tall horn glistening with nails and a brass plate. She photographed the teams resting while the tubs of grapes were unloaded and hoisted to the upper level of the cellar by a system of pulleys and chains. She also photographed bears from the Pyrenees exhibited by their trainers on the grounds of the summer estate. She photographed the parked automobile and the cloud of dust which hovered in the air a long while before falling back between the whitened laurels of the drive. Once, one of the men who worked in the cellar had his foot crushed by a tub and she gave him first aid, kneeling in front of a basin, the water in it quickly tinged with the blood flowing from the mangled flesh, untying the filthy espadrille, washing the wound, the knotty foot with its horny yellow nails, the trouser rolled up over a livid, hairy leg like that of some animal or mythological creature. She seemed no more concerned with the vacuity of her life than with seeing her waist thicken and her face lose its contours. She took photographs of the lively cousins and their friends, the poets published at their own expense, the eternal law students or phony artists from Montmartre with long hair and great looped *lavallières*. She took the last photograph of the patriarch in his eternal English pastor's frock coat,

with his immutable white cravat, his severe bony face, his
severe Buffalo Bill goatee, stiff, erect, in front of a curtain
of laurels, holding in one hand the invariable pearl-gray
hat and the ebony cane. And during all this time she continued to wait for nothing, as a traveler waits for the train
he knows will leave at the time established by the railroad
schedule and which he need only climb into a few seconds
before the locomotive's whistle, as if, without her even
formulating it, without her even becoming aware of it,
however vaguely—as if something were waiting for her
which would be a kind of levitation, some apotheosis in
which she would figure, transmogrified and swooning,
borne on a cloud supported by cherubs and from which
she would then be violently hurled into the void. To the
old lady who expressed some alarm, questioning her by
euphemistic formulas, staring at her with anxiety, she continued to reply by the same eternal and enigmatic smile
she bestowed on her admirers. There was neither disdain
nor scorn in it: she enjoyed seeing her cousins and their
noisy band of friends arrive in Carnival season or during
the summer vacation. She instantly, with neither hesitation
nor second thoughts, adopted the picturesque companions
whom they brought with them and who sometimes made
the patriarch frown, such as, one year, a little Turkish Jew
from Salonika, a millionaire who, to her great amusement,
paid court to her along with the others, or the violinist
from a café orchestra. She was frankly delighted when, for
her and the other young ladies, they transposed into innocent and silly masquerades the priapic saturnalia of the
Bal des Quat'z'Arts or of the Internat, and she acted in
tableaux vivants, disguised as a Druid priestess, chastely
swathed in a sheet, her brow garlanded, her long black
hair hanging to her waist. For a while she insisted that the
young *député*-poet write her a few witty lines on the back

of a postcard every day, but he lost interest. Others, less witty, replaced him. This was no more or less perverse coquetry, no more or less cruel flirtation. She loved them all. Simply, with regard to what the old lady was concerned about as the years passed, they did not exist.

It was, in fact, on the occasion of a wedding that she found herself placed at table next to a man like no one she had ever met before, had never even imagined could exist: one of the groomsmen, an officer wearing a midnight-blue tunic with red braid anchors embroidered on the collar, his expression (with his square beard, his mustaches waxed to points, his transparent, liquid, china-blue eyes in a sunburned face, his manners not so much taciturn as reserved, deliberate) rather like that of a disciplined barbarian, stamped with a tranquil assurance which, it too, was the contrary of what was betrayed by the little songs and quatrains scribbled on the backs of those postcards she was collecting less for the gratification of a much-courted young lady than in the way others collect stamps or match covers. Subsequently, when in his turn he sent postcards to her, mailed from almost everywhere in the world, he soberly confined himself to writing his name under three figures indicating the day, the month, and the year—as if he were already certain of the uselessness, if not even of the indecency, of any discourse, as if doubtless she as well as he had already reached that stage where a date and a name (the first ones, for form's sake, with the signature preceded by "warmest thoughts," then "best regards," then "faithfully," then nothing more than the name . . .) sufficed—just as no doubt they did not say much to each other that first time, talking about anything at all except themselves, neither one of them hearing, listening further to what they were saying, perhaps even avoiding looking at each other, while, deafened by the vague racket of the conversations and the clatter of crystal and silver that surrounded them, she could see the sinewy brown hands that emerged from the immaculate cuffs wielding the knife and fork, breaking the bread—and later lighting a cigarette—immediately understanding without his needing to tell her that aside from his uniform and his lieutenant's pay he had nothing, except perhaps debts—though even on this point she doubtless understood immediately that she could find no flaw in that sort of armor formed of urbanity and smiling propriety by which he kept himself at a kind of cautious distance (she who saw periodically appear from Paris, preceded by dramatic telegrams, the ostentatious senator who, for all his ostentatious parliamentary indemnity and the incomes of two factories and countless farms, did not hesitate to travel round-trip more than two thousand kilometers to extract from the outraged, protesting, and ultimately yielding patriarch a few hundred louis which he would never see again); something like this, then: an occasion where there were flowers on the table, champagne in the glasses, perfumes, silk gowns, dress suits, uniforms, laughter, mingled voices, perhaps an orchestra, perhaps a waltz, and perhaps not a rendezvous but several fortuitous meetings arranged for a promenade or the opening of some horse show by helpful friends, nothing more, nothing else afterwards, except four years during which from Port Saïd, from Aden, from Colombo, from Diégo-Suarez, from each port of call on the routes covered by the steamers serving Africa or Asia, she would receive the grayish or crudely colored postcards which took a month to reach her and which she carefully put away while she continued to lead the indolent existence of a decorative plant, wearing her gowns with lace inserts, and those incredible hats like bouquets or rather gardens beneath which was now installed, as behind the large black eyes, a determination of steel—not that she was not already inhabited by it, as might have been suspected from that interminable and stubborn celibacy, the smiling refusals which met all advances (as she was to evidence later on when, at the end of her life, she fell ill and, little by little, the surgeons began to cut her into pieces, very carefully, very gradually), but with this difference, that it (the steel) now knew what to rely on, that the "goal" in anticipation (or in hopes) of which she had preserved herself had assumed a real consistency, a body, a face, and then this: on one side the great-grandnephew of the rebel, of that peasant who had remained hidden four years in haylofts or in gamekeepers' huts in order to escape the recruiters of the man-eating ogre, on the other the great-granddaughter of the Empire general whose monumental marble bust with its leonine marble hair, its bushy marble eyebrows, its marble gaze, loomed, formidable, ironic, and severe, in a corner of the family salon, and how estimate what perseverance, what obstinacy they must both have evidenced, she loyal to that rigidity of principle in which she had been raised, that arrogant pride of class or rather of caste which she now actually turned against themselves, he who had dug up the soil, pushed wheelbarrows filled with manure, and did not hesitate (and even was pleased), when he visited his family on leave, to put on again the old trousers and the patched smock to help with the hardest jobs, at the same time circumspectly conducting the siege of that fortress of prejudice, of indolence, of futility and insolence in which, protected from the agitation of the external world, more closely guarded than she would have been by an army of eunuchs by the phantom of a patriarch and by a timorous old woman, there waited for him, passive and consenting, the inaccessible princess whose opulent and milky shoulders, whose complexion shielded from the sun,

whose figure that was beginning to thicken must doubtless
have seemed to him the antithesis not only of the harsh
and hard world where he had grown up but even of the
supple and docile naked girls with their coppery or golden
skins who slipped into bed beside him, opening themselves
to him beneath the mosquito netting in the humidity of
the tropical nights: something that resembled a wager, a
challenge that he had flung at himself at the same time as
at that order of things over which he had already triumphed
in raising himself by main force above the peasant condition—above, at best, the schoolmaster condition—or as
if, inhabited by a sort of premonition, pressed for time,
he had chosen before dying to deposit his seed and to
survive in one of those females destined to the reproduc-
tion of the species guaranteed by their faculties of inertia,
of opulence, and of fecundity: a need, a necessity, an ur-
gency doubtless confounded, as in that twilight of a world
which was going to die along with millions of young men
buried under the mud and in which mingled the paradoxical and caricatural images, frozen or jerky, of military
parades, of hobble skirts, of statesmen in barouches, of
flowered hats, of plumed helmets, of French cancans, of
intoxicated princes and comical old troopers.

Four years, then, during which he employed the only
weapon he possessed: patience, stubbornness, doubtless
unaware that he was benefitting from that other decisive
and glamorous trump card of seduction which is absence,
that enforced remoteness which he was probably cursing,
against which he found no other recourse, from port to
port, while the steamer trailing its sinuous plume of smoke
took him the entire length of the stifling equator, than
those postcards which offered (in alternation, in confusion,
like the testimony of a world of violence, of respectability,
and of rapacity) the images of Presbyterian churches, of

green lawns, of banks transported complete from their country of rain and fog, rebuilt (replanted) stone by stone (blade of grass by blade of grass) in the middle of deserts or jungles, and those of hairy, fierce, half-naked groups of warriors in rags, right out of prehistoric times with their parched skins, their arrows, their absurd bows, contemplated by their recipient with the same enigmatic, apparently indifferent gaze with which she considered the peasant girls in Limousin costumes, the views of Chambord or of Pornichet, still just as calm, smiling, imperturbable (though certainly, one time, something more between them than simple meetings on a walk, simple glances, simple banalities, must have happened, been exchanged, been spoken—something that had permitted him to replace the conventional formulas of politeness with only his laconic and eloquent signature), impassive when she saw on the tray brought in by the servant one of those stamped rectangles, pale green or pink, glancing at it, handing it almost immediately to the old lady sitting opposite her at the breakfast table, saying simply (the first cards sent from a green countryside, with waterfalls, rocks, old houses— then one from Marseilles—then, in succesion, from Port-Saïd, from Suez, from Aden, from Colombo) . . . saying at first simply: "It's from that lieutenant who was a groomsman at Marcel's wedding . . . ," then, "It's from the lieutenant . . ." and then adding the name, then adding the first name to the name, then leaving out the rank, then no longer saying anything but the first name: the old lady inattentive at the beginning, then intrigued, then alerted, thinking perhaps: "Finally! Finally! . . . ," nonetheless watching with alarm when one day an avalanche of cards arrived, all bearing the same date (12/7/08), all stamped with the same bald, bearded, and crowned profile framed with jade-green palms under the legend "Straits Settle-

ments," counting them in spite of herself (there were exactly nineteen—doubtless mailed at different hours of the
day and in different parts of the city for they did not take
the same steamer, arrived by two different posts, in two
lots, at first: Singapore: Boat Quay—Singapore: Club and
Post Office—Singapore: College Quay—Singapore: Presbyterian Church—Singapore: Group of Boyanese—Singapore: Botanical Gardens—Singapore: Battery Road—
Singapore: Indian Jugglers—Singapore: Botanical Gardens (another view)—Singapore: Raffles Place—Singapore: St. Andrew's Cathedral—Singapore: Malay
Women—Singapore: Hong Kong and Shanghai Bank;
then: Singapore: Botanical Gardens (still another view)—
Singapore: the Chinese Temple—Singapore: Street
Scene—Singapore: Tanyung Katong—Singapore: Group
of Sakais—Singapore: St. James), then (the old lady) even
more alarmed if not terrified, repressing a shudder (though
her daughter had done her best to prepare her) when after
a night on the train the two of them emerged (this was
about two years after the first meeting) on the platform of
a tiny station where he was waiting for them, dressed once
again in civilian clothes of no elegance whatever, trousers
stuffed into hunting boots laced to the knee, the man with
the square beard and the waxed mustache which she had
till then thought inseparable from a uniform (that is, guaranteed by the reassuring aspect of a decorative costume,
able, all things considered, to constitute the ornament of
a salon, whatever the head that topped it off), the unexpected personage himself seizing their suitcases, carrying
them to a rented carriage, a narrow wooden crate smelling
of mildew which started up with a jerk, driven by a leather-
capped coachman with a strange mountain accent, drawn
by a broken-down mare, jolting through the puddles (she
was to remember a country of rain, of slopes planted with

vines on wires, and of wooded mountains, with high chalky
cliffs), the skinny horse slowing down to a walk when it
began the uphill climb of the long street, while sitting on
a horsehair banquette and jolted by the cobbles she (the
old lady) watched file past through the deafening racket
of the panes in their frames the cold stone façades beneath
sloping roofs above which stuck out here and there the
branches of a rain-lashed tree, dripping, black, sopping,
the carriage (the crate) stopping at last, the man in the
gamekeeper's clothes who spoke so familiarly to the driver
helping them down, again carrying the suitcases, crossing
the sidewalk (it was he who had insisted, despite the ap-
prehensions he might have had about such a meeting, in-
flexibly demanded this journey, this visit), heading for a
threshold on which were standing two women well over
forty, their faces square, not exactly hard but worn, mannish, with square hands, wearing dresses they were evidently not in the habit of wearing (which is to say that they
(the dresses) seemed rather—so new were they, so stiff,
as if starched—to wear the bodies they were covering) and
whom for a moment, at the sight of their bearing, of that
stiffness, of those faces, the old lady took for servants until
she realized that they were the two sisters, then pressing
as if in a dream the callused hands, stammering, her countenance more than ever stamped with that expression of
panic, of haggard, dismayed consternation: women, people
who must probably seem to her not only beneath what she
had always considered (had been in the habit of considering) the level separating two social classes, but even two
different species of humanity: for he (the bearded man,
dressed now like a gamekeeper) insisted on showing them
not only the two old maids with their wrinkled hands, not
only the sort of mummy kept alive in a sort of closet
upstairs, the house which was just beginning to be no

longer merely the carcass of a house, but even the old half-blind aunt remaining in the village, walking along the paths and pushing the broken-down baby carriage in which she piled grass for her rabbits, eating a sort of yellowish gruel like what she fed her chickens. And after that two more years went by during which (perhaps this was the stipulation she (the old lady) had attached to her consent—or that he had imposed upon himself) he waited for that third strip of gold braid which would permit him to be assigned to a country where white women did not menstruate twenty-five days out of thirty and where without fear of disaster he could take the woman he had chosen to give him a son, the cards less frequent then (but doubtless they wrote each other letters now, for on some of the postcards, under the signature, the mere name, occurred the phrase "letter follows") coming from the far reaches of China: a place where civilization had flung a bridge with iron pontoons across a river in which water buffalo steeped, then some fifty houses and a stone barracks built alongside a few straw huts against a background of hills dominated by one higher hill in the shape of a sugarloaf, the text reading: "The Mao-Son is the large mountain in the background to the right marked with an X. Yours," and finally (the four years past now, the marriage celebrated: he in his uniform with heavy gold-fringed epaulettes, she in a gown entirely of lace, the photographs taken on that veranda where she herself had produced so many images of her family and of her life as a young lady, and both four years older than when they had met, the huge, lovely eyes which had inspired so many bad verses bulging a little now, the chin heavier, the torso heavier too, shimmering, or rather trembling, leaning on that arm which at last she was entitled to squeeze in public, he very tall, robust, with that face which was beginning to look worn, to bear traces of those climates he had endured, his beard carefully trimmed, his calm, china-blue stare a head higher than the group of cousins and friends in dress suits and white cravats surrounding them) . . . finally, then, it was she who in her turn sent them, she who had never been much farther than Barcelona, Paris, or Bordeaux, who, in matters of foreignness, of excitement, of exoticism, had known only the paddock at Chantilly, the bullfights, or a few evenings at the Opéra, she whose lips no man had probably ever kissed or even touched with his lips, suddenly wrested from her proper and vegetal existence, cast or rather catapulted, precipitated at the peak of her gluttonous thirties into a sort of dizzying maelstrom whose center was her own womb out of which broke in fierce waves something which was to the pleasures she had hitherto known what a glass of alcohol is to barley-sugar water, not even ceasing at the limits of her body, extending beyond it, if indeed she was still capable of distinguishing between within and without when, shaded by her parasol, still moist and panting, again leaning on that arm whose muscles she could feel through the thin linen cloth, exhausted (or rather satiated, cloyed, dazed), she walked down the gangway, went strolling through the ports (or rather gently drifting, as in a secondary, somnambulistic state), along the shop windows, the *souks,* or the native markets, perceiving as in a permanent orgasm those harbors, those cities, those pyramids, those camels, those ragged and barbarous crowds about which she wrote to the old lady: ". . . you wonder if these are human beings like ourselves; we have been ashore since six this morning, it is nine o'clock and the *Adour* sails at ten, we are in a café having something cold to drink. Kisses," the postcard representing three blacks, rather three skeletons (or three beanpoles or three scarecrows), three hybrid things, halfway between the human and the vegetal, that is, where it is impossible to distinguish what belonged to one or the other realm, or the place where one realm joined the other, or rather what distinguished the limbs like dry wood from the hanging fibers which half-covered them, revealing the swollen bellies, the conical navels, the protruding ribs (one of them hiding—or holding—his genitals with one hand), each of the three beanpoles surmounted by a shaved skull, with half-closed, oval eyes, enormous pudgy lips, a long wound open over one of the tibias, like a scar in the bark of a tree that had dried without having ever closed, or even like those openings made in the limbs of those statues of saints, of martyrs, revealing behind a pane of glass a fragment of bone: "Burogas"—the pink stamp, still embellished with the inevitable bald and crowned profile but this time above the legend "India Postage & Revenue," writing a little later (still apparently in the same state of confusion and indolent satiety) on the back of another card (several men now, still as black, as skeletal, the upper gums protruding like those of skulls or rodents, their hair crimped and swollen, draped as though by shrouds in a kind of biblical tunic, herding a few goats as skeletal as they: "Somalis"): "I don't have much to add to the long letter which" (here the name of the man on whom, by the effect of that fundamental incapacity for any effort, she now relied—as she had relied for thirty years on the patriarch and on the old lady—for everything that might constitute a demand or a responsibility) "wrote you yesterday. I only . . ."—for even for that, even for her relations with her own mother, she now relied on him, content to continue drifting over her orgiastic and lukewarm ocean of felicity, he with his close, precise handwriting, the letters distinct, made to specify orders or instructions, scrupulously filling the pages with those details likely to satisfy and reassure an old lady, such as, for

instance, the location and arrangement of the rooms in the
house, the number of servants, their references, information about the climate, the daytime and nighttime tem-
peratures, the quality of the water, the sanitary conditions
of the country (and, when the child was born, the quality
of the milk, the possibility of a nurse—or at least of a
servant especially assigned to the baby), making much the
same report he would have provided for a superior in the
hierarchy apropos of the installation of a camp, of a post
in the bush, or of a billeting, ending perhaps with "Your
son" or "Your respectful son," or "Respectfully yours," or
some other formula of the kind, the old lady gradually
forgetting the image of the gamekeeper standing on the
platform of a rainy little station somewhere or other, gradually substituting for it the one, at once ornamental (the
uniform, the epaulettes) and emotional, of the son she may
have wished to have, perhaps even favoring him over the
other sons-in-law because of that marriage she had almost
ceased to believe possible, adopting him, making him hers
like a belated Benjamin unhoped-for, just as the cousins
and the giddy band of friends adopted him too, not only
out of affection for her (impelled perhaps by a certain
curiosity, a certain respect, and a certain admiration for
someone who had been able to triumph over this impregnable fortress of inertia), but even with that unconditional
enthusiasm of an idle and gilded youth for whatever passes
for marginal, eccentric, like the Turkish Jew or the café
violinist, the way they would have enthusiastically adopted
in this same role of seducer of the inaccessible and slothful
sultana a baritone from Toulouse or a Polish count, without
considering that a man who owed his situation neither to
his birth nor to his fortune, nor to some accident or stroke
of luck, doubtless constituted in their eyes a particularly
astonishing and attractive specimen, these men among

whom the only one to wear a uniform (and the only uniform conceivable in their milieu, that is, that of the cavalry)
owed his stripes only to the powerful and senatorial influ-
ence of his father: an overweight young man (he shared
with his cousin the same tendency to indolence and plumpness) for whom, by common consent (including his own),
the entrance examinations at Saint-Cyr represented an obstacle so obviously insurmountable that he had finally been
enlisted by force, one might have said, if his repugnance
to any effort had not also forbade him to oppose any decision taken for him, then raised (still by force: by force
of dinners, by force of cigars, by force of letters to the
force of generals and ministers) from the condition of simple cavalryman to the rank of lieutenant after, for form's
sake, an interval at Saumur where, as elsewhere, he had
been content to wait passively, like those boys one sees
sitting in dentists' waiting rooms (with this difference, that
he was sitting on a horse and that instead of leafing through
dog-eared magazines he was standing his comrades to
champagne), while the paternal omnipotence continued by
parliamentary means to replace the corporal's stripes with
those of a sergeant-at-arms, then of a second lieutenant,
watching them succeed each other on the sleeves of his
tunics with the same indifference he showed for the money
he paid for the bottles of champagne and for the inmates
of the fancy brothels where his indolence (doubtless it was
that same indolence that made him one of the few who
had never addressed some rhymed compliment to his cousin: perhaps, for lack of wit, he was the one who had sent,
unsigned, the little woman in panties and black stockings
and blowing smoke rings) had led him to find the least
strenuous solution to the problems of a young stud, plac-
idly sitting on some upholstered banquette, allowing, with
the same placidity of a plump little boy raised by govern-

esses, the whores who sat on his lap shrieking with laughter to unhook the collar of his tunic, then one by one undo the gilded brass buttons, and finally release from its silky nest that stem emerging from him, its skin transparent and blue-veined, that swollen pink bud which he contemplated with the same placid and passive wonderment, that naive satisfaction, lying back on the cushions, wetting his thin blond mustache in the champagne, watching it grow even larger, amid the shrieks of laughter, under some expert tongue and finally vanish, engulfed, while the fingers of his free hand tightened a little in the head of brown, blond, or auburn hair slowly moving up and down: the same fragile bud, later, the same organ, and also the same phallic and ritual bottle with its neck swathed in gold foil (as if, for him, both incarnated complementarily the virile virtues he had made his credo: the latter (the champagne bottle) as an obligatory accessory to any ceremony, the former, depending on its state and the nature of the liquid expelled, priapic or flaccid, insolently exhibited, then, with that ignominious gesture ordinarily reflected by the varnished partitions of urinals) . . . the same organ, then, but retracted, shriveled, with difficulty extracted from the elegant riding breeches by his ungloved hand, the fingers swollen, frozen, the face stamped with the same impenetrable placidity, with the same puerile and animal satisfaction, the body three-quarters out of the narrow wood and canvas cockpit, one hand clinging to some bracing wire or longeron, the binoculars hanging over his chest, as he watched the rosary of golden drops carried away by the propeller wind disperse and disappear among the black puffs of the explosions, celebrating that evening his first mission and the exploit performed (the action not of bravura but of calm fury) before the sacramental bottles (he had previously ordered a case put on ice with the indica-

tion: "to be drunk even if I don't return"), with this difference: that the foil-wrapped necks emerged from a farm
bucket served by a mechanic with black and broken nails
and that, instead of reclining on a velvet banquette, he was
now sitting on a wooden bench (at best, on a chair with a
broken seat) in front of a crude table, the slender blond
mustache again moistened with bubbles that reflected the
light of the candles, his monocle again screwed into his
eye, the greedy lips again stretched in the same vague smile
of satisfaction and euphoria, except that in all the noise
and shouts of laughter that greeted the pilot's story, his
gaze, his canine or rather his pachydermatous stare now
veiled by something that no expert tongue, no skillful perfumed hand could ever again erase, as if he were both
present and absent in that smoky mess hall, sitting on that
old chair or perhaps on just a crate, with his boots stripped
of spurs now, his elegant custom-made riding breeches,
his cavalryman's tunic which he hadn't yet had time to
replace, his pachydermatous plumpness, having arrived
once again by senatorial recommendation except (during
a short leave he had had, with his father in deep mourning,
only a brief conversation following which the grief-stricken
senator had once again written the necessary letters)
. . . except, then, that this time there was no longer any
question of adding a stripe to those which embellished
the sleeves of his tunic but, there where it was worn then,
pinned over the old cavalry, artillery, or infantry uniforms,
the winged emblem the wearing of which was virtually
equivalent to a one-way ticket to death. As if something
that could never have been suspected in the placid plump
boy, in the habitué of brothels, something which, after all,
may have had its source as well in that erectile part of his
body, that organ for virtually all uses and functions (if it
is permissible to regard hatred and execration as a bodily

function), had made him compel his father to write the omnipotent letters and, a little later, made him buy that postcard, not one of the bright-colored, patriotic and sentimental ones produced at the time for mass consumption, but selected, not so much again by taste—as for beauties, the girls he found in the brothels were adequate to his needs—as because it was the kind of postcard he knew that she was accustomed to receive, or perhaps even more simply because the training camp where he was learning his new job as observer (he was already too old to become a pilot) was in the region, reproducing in sepia the famous and angelic smile from a damaged cathedral on the back of which he wrote his cousin's name and address and, on the left side reserved for correspondence, the simple words: "She will be avenged. Fondly," followed by his signature. For if finally death had no use for him (somehow his pilot managed to land in a field, riddled with shell splinters, the kind of bat or even dragonfly apparently fabricated out of brass wires and canvas on which (it was scarcely possible to say "in") he went up every day, armed with binoculars and a revolver, venturing among the shell-bursts—still managing to set his flares before the German field patrols arrived) . . . if death had no use for him (by one of those jokes of fate, he was not to die—or rather slowly to agonize, slowly strangle—until twenty years later, solitary, more walruslike and pachydermatous than ever, an elegant scarf concealing the monstrous edema that distended his neck, wracked by coughing fits like howls, hiding his physical collapse in the old family house surrounded by magnolias at the heart of the little city where people could see him pass, wearing a pearl-gray hat like his grandfather and suits cut by a master tailor to the measure of that obesity, doubtless inherited from the colossal Empire general, jauntily wielding a cane with an ivory handle and frequenting till the eve of his death the tearooms or pastry shops in the back rooms of which the obliging waitresses on their knees offered that phallic organ which had constituted the actual pivot of his existence their mercenary and buccal services, while he, slumped in an armchair and rummaging with one hand under their skirts, struggled painfully to wash down any number of cream puffs with sips of port) . . . if then death had no use for him, out of the three members of the family who had gone to war, two had already been killed, and less than a month apart, the first on a fine August day while soon afterwards another bullet passed through the carotid artery of the *député*-poet who, as a matter of fact, for some years already, had no longer been a *député,* had not been re-elected (had moreover done nothing to be re-elected, letting his constituents' letters pile up on his desk and confining himself to applauding the senator who spoke for him on public occasions), employing his newfound freedom in writing verses, climbing Mont Blanc, visiting New York, wintering in Majorca, painting watercolors, and continuing to send from almost everywhere those postcards on the backs of which, unlike his brother, the plump boy given to a modest military laconicism and bottles of champagne, he applied himself (perhaps in memory of the days when the capricious young lady ordered—challenged—him to make her laugh each morning by correspondence; perhaps too by the effect of another kind of modesty) to sustaining even under the threatening shadow which already fell over them all that tone of insouciant frivolity affected by the band of false Montmartre painters and high-spirited young heirs of their fathers' businesses, writing on the back of a card showing a barracks in front of which the guard and a few children had obligingly posed for the photographer: "Magnac-Laval, April 18, 1912—Dear Captain, I have the honor to inform you that, overcome by the liveliest desire to regain my regiment of which, on the reverse, I send you a magnificent representation, I have just reenlisted as adjutant. I hope we are going to war and that I shall have occasion to die for the flag. Devoted respects, Adjutant C . . . ," the card rapidly read, then held out with a gay (too gay?) burst of laughter over the table by the man with the sunburned face, the square beard, whose dazzling white tunic was embellished with gold epaulettes and opposite whom she now took her breakfasts served by the young black woman whom, at the same time that she decked her out in starched aprons, she had taught to make that thick hot chocolate which she continued to drink every morning, just as she continued to wear, under the tropical sun, the same hats that looked like lampshades or flower shows and the same severe high-necked blouses, the dining-room shutters already closed despite the early hour as though to keep out, to dam up, to contain the external thrust of something compact, solid, and incandescent which glided through the slats of the jalousies like laminated sheets of glowing metal in which the impalpable atoms of light circled slowly, the photograph on the back of which were written the explanations for the old lady (". . . at the bottom the dining-room window, then the railing around the terrace, then to the left the closed window of the sitting room where I am writing you and . . .") itself apparently devoured by light, faded, pale, of a uniform sulfur or saffron color, as if an implacable film of dust, a dusty and yellow layer of time were burying the house, the corner of the garden, the terrace from which now, leaning on the brick balustrade, she watched the white canvas tunic cross the garden, pass behind the clump of bamboo, cross-hatched by the silhouettes of the dry, pointed leaves, and vanish—the card still in her hands, her face suddenly pensive, strained, able to hear the rustle of the leaves being faintly stirred, making a momentary papery sound, then motionless again.

Or perhaps not. Perhaps continuing to drift, invulnerable, out of reach, in that sort of lethargy, of lukewarm nirvana, that orgiastic state of vegetal efflorescence, that vaguely fabulous world somehow set apart from the other one, and where the noise of arms, the rumors of war, arrived only muffled, remote, incredible. Later she would tell how people out there would keep a boa constrictor in the garden, like a dog or a cat in Europe, because it (the boa) was the best way of getting rid of rats, but that she hadn't wanted to, first of all from an instinctive repulsion, then, when she had gradually got used to seeing them, on account of the child. With the daily regularity of the rain during the wet season (she told how it came down every day exactly at five, how you could play tennis until a quarter to—for here too she would play tennis, or at least she kept photographs where she could still be seen carrying a racket, still wearing one of those huge hats and those skirts that swept the dust, silently watched from a distance, she and her masculine partners in their sportsman's outfits, by a motionless frieze of white-swathed figures with impassive ebony faces—after which there was just time enough to get indoors before the thick sheets of warm water transformed the streets into streams and the garden into a lake), and also the brevity of the twilights when, with virtually no transition, night replaced day, the litters in which she had herself carried about, gently swaying with the gait of the black bearers, the tame boas and the fabulous menus of the dinners at Government House seemed to constitute virtually all that she had retained, or rather all that, from the world outside, had reached her through the protective layers of that beatitude at the heart of which she drifted, weightless, in a sort of fetal state, herself soon bearing in the warm darkness of her womb a life in its embryonic or rather elementary stage. As if (though continuing to attend the mission church on Sundays, to wear a garnet cross on her severe blouses, mechanically to recite her prayers and to read novels with yellow covers) she had dizzily turned back time, transported into a primitive Eden, a primitive state of nature, beside the man with the fierce beard, surrounded by serpents and savages domesticated in either case: besides the orderly, she possessed three of the latter, two males and one female, whose black faces gleamed in the shadow of the gallery where they posed standing behind her rattan armchair, her hand on the neck of the family dog, smiling, as if the photographer had seized the fugitive instant of immobility, of equilibrium, in which having reached the apogee of her trajectory and before being once again subject to the laws of gravitation the trapeze artist finds herself in a sort of weightless state, liberated from the constraints of matter, able to believe for a second that she will never fall, that she will remain thus forever suspended in the blinding glare of the spotlights above the void, the abyss. And perhaps she believed it, managed to believe it, to convince herself, or perhaps he managed to make her believe it still, whereas already the curve of the trajectory was beginning to turn, then to shift direction, then actually to fall, casting her down with the same dizzying speed which had presided over her ascent, though everything continued for a moment longer as if nothing had changed: the same blouses, the same pale dresses encrusted with lace, the same hats now held in place by a veil tied under her chin as, accompanied by the black girl carrying the child, she swept her skirts across the promenade deck of the ship taking them back to Europe, the same flying fish, the same stale compliments at the captain's table, the same black children diving for pennies in the ports of call, the same reassuring smile at her side, the same ocean liner perhaps, riding low in the water, decks protected by canvas awnings, which four years earlier had carried her over the same ocean crossed now in the opposite direction, the ship whose last voyage this would be with women and children on board, and which, unless it was torpedoed, would for four long years carry, crammed like cattle in its steerage along with cannons, only men who were to die, soon threading between the scorched coasts of two wild continents, then re-entering that sea or rather that interior lake, that pond, that liquid matrix of alphabets, of numerals, of grooved columns and marble statues at the same time as the heat gradually lessened, as the names of islands, capes, straits, mountains glimpsed in the distance lost their strange or barbarous-sounding names, as already, in the cabins, the linen suits and the thin dresses were put away in the steamer trunks, as the dawns grew colder, as a scarf or a shawl was needed to go out on deck at night where they may have strolled, the two of them, walking slowly, stopping, leaning perhaps side by side on the rail, hearing the phosphorescent foam stream out from under the keel with a continuous hiss, swiftly fleeing beneath them, behind them, the muffled thumping of the engines, time fleeing too while day by day, hour by hour, there also diminished with each turn of the screw that expanse of water where she could still feel vaguely protected, out of harm's way, both of them silent, or perhaps whispering, he at least, while she kneaded in both hands the newspaper with its huge headlines bought at the last port, the tops of the masts swaying slowly under the indifferent stars, and he still leaning over, bringing close to her his wasted or emaciated eager face with that beard he had cut short now, black in the darkness, devouring his cheeks like the beard a sick man lets grow, his transparent china-blue stare already absent somehow, already elsewhere, a denial of his words, and occasionally a shower of red sparks coming out of the smokestack above them, circling, vanishing, swept away in the black spirals of smoke and always the muffled and implacable thump of the engines, the cold and motionless constellations, the eager and futile whispering which she doubtless ignores, just as she is doubtless unconscious of the nervous movements of her hands, which continue to knead the paper, doubtless no longer even aware that she is holding it, staring straight ahead into the darkness at the faint reflections playing over the shiny and shifting surface of the sea, rigid, erect, her pale profile blue as marble in the darkness, her eyes dry, fixed, and she does not even answer, does not even say: "A regiment like yours! Do you think I don't know, do you think I . . .": she falls silent, she thinks: But I knew, I knew, I've always known, I've always known what it was that I married . . . , the waves continuing to break rhythmically against the keel, exploding, falling back, the foam fleeing, twisting, swiftly vanishing, reappearing: as if she could feel the sheet of water shrinking, contracting like a magic skin, narrower and narrower, more and more precarious, ridiculous; then the last day, the last hours, the trunks packed now in the cabin, the straps of the service kit buckled now, the thin motionless line of land gradually, inexorably widening on the horizon, inexorably motionless, nearing, a lighthouse on the right, the calm foam throbbing at its base, gray rocks, a corniche road, carriages, houses, piers . . .

A crowd surges against the barrier of the customs office, hands wave handkerchiefs. She does not see the crowd. She sees a vague mass of multicolored particles, bright or dark, stuck together and moving. Around her the houses, the docks, the cranes drift more and more slowly now. She can hear a bell ringing and feel the frame of the ship trembling beneath the reversed thrust of the screw. She can see the churned water circling in great seething coils, and from it rises a faint smell of mud, of stagnation. She can feel the deck stop trembling. She watches the surface of the water forming an angle that still separates the side of the now motionless liner from the dock. She can see the weighted hawser thrown from the poop quickly secured, the curve of the rope plunging into the harbor, then re-emerging, gradually straightening, dripping, fringed with drops of water that shimmer in the sun while the winch motor hums. Slowly the long ship pivots, and the sides of the angle come closer together. For a moment the sunbeams are reflected on the black-painted hull where a bronze-colored area shifts position. Now she can see the shadow of the smokestack and of the upper decks falling across the pier. The shadow reaches the customs barrier and covers the crowd surging against it. She can feel a push against her elbow, and she raises her hand. She can make out the worn faces of the two women in the dark clothes who are waving their hand-kerchiefs. The water between the ship and the dock now forms an acute angle. Out of the corner of her eye she can see the child, held over its father's head, kicking its legs in the air. She continues to wave her hand. She tries to smile. She bursts into tears. The hum of the winch stops. Excited shouts break from the decks of the liner and from the crowd gathered behind the customs barrier. The tears run slowly down her cheeks. Between the now quite motionless black hull and the pier, all that remains at the bottom of the deep trench is a narrow strip of dirty water with garbage floating in it.

VI

August 27, 1939

ADVANCING slowly as though cloud-
borne, at once aerial and monumental, puffs of steam dissolving between pistons coated with yellowish oil, making
the ground shudder beneath it, towing a series of anti-
quated cars exhumed from stations where they had doubtless been preserved in anticipation of this day (wooden,
the dark-brown paint peeling, and with an open platform
at either end), the locomotive with a muffled din slid under
the glass roof of the station where, on the platform, a dense
crowd was waiting, the first row retreating as it approached,
not so much from fear of being scalded by the steam or
of slipping under the wheels as from a sort of instinctive
horror, an intuitive instinct of repulsion which made them
all keep as great a distance as possible between themselves
and the vertical side of the cars moving ever more slowly
past an illusory and final interval of space, a kind of ditch,
a narrow canyon, or rather an invisible wall, an invisible
rampart on the other side of which, once it was crossed,

would be sealed something irremediable, definitive, and terrible.

Leaning on the railing of the open platform at the end of their car, the mechanic and the stoker, goggles pushed up on their foreheads, clothes and cheeks black with soot, watched with red-rimmed eyes the crowd sliding beneath them, then with a long squeal the line of old cars stopped short at the same time as the swarm of men and women whose faces were raised toward them, whose arms were sometimes filled with babies and who, long after the train had stopped and instead of the usual assault, continued to stare at the brownish sides of the cars with a sort of incredulous stupor, of incredulous consternation. A moment longer, the two sides of the ditch (one formed of peeling wood and the other formed by bodies packed together on the platform) remained face to face in a silence broken only, at the far end, beyond the glass roof beneath which were dissolving the puffs of smoke, by the cadenced panting of the locomotive releasing at regular intervals its puffs of steam which rose toward the sun, grayish white, and dissolved. Then suddenly, at the same time that here and there some figures emerged from the crowd and began to climb the steps of the cars (doubtless these were men to whom the city was foreign, or who had no families, or who had refused to let anyone come with them), there rose under the glass roof a confused uproar not of shouts or protests, rather a kind of plaint, a moan, at once timid, discreet, and monumental, consisting of hundreds of prayers, hundreds of sobs, and hundreds of impotent curses. The station was that of a good-sized town in the Midi, built of pink brick which contrasted with the stone structure of the doorways to the platforms, to the waiting room, to the buffet, and to the offices. It was summer, and the women who were holding crumpled handkerchiefs under their eyes were for the most part wearing short-sleeved, bright-colored dresses, sometimes even, like several of the men, beach clothes. Like people surprised by a storm or some cataclysm during a wedding or a picnic, dressed up although informal, and among whom could be seen, anachronistic beside the light summer outfits and in the heat of the dying summer, a few old women from nearby villages or the poor neighborhoods of the city, fragile, mute, all covered up by their invariable black dresses, with black shawls tied under their chins framing their yellow, wrinkled faces, indifferent to the tears that flooded them, stamped with that permanent expression of hebetude, of dread and resignation, of the poor and the weak. Now, as if, even more than the train's entrance into the station, the sight of the first men who had made up their minds to climb into the cars had released the signal for the irremediable, far from diminishing in density, the crowd, or rather the human conglomeration out of which emerged one after the other new figures hoisting themselves up onto the train, seemed to contract into itself more compactly, as if it not only refused to come apart, to let itself be broken up, but even retracted, so to speak, into itself, the particles composing it somehow soldered to each other in a sort of crystallization, an inextricable multitude of embraces not, in most cases, of two bodies but of several, gathered into corollas around centers from which emerged the choked voices of women and the crying of babies, so that those who were wresting themselves from it and trying to climb into the train, most often followed by a diminishing group strung out in their wake, were still held back, prevented from progressing or occasionally even repulsed, kept away from the steps by some impulse, some convulsion or expansion of the motley incoherent swarm stirred by unpre-

dictable currents, unforeseeable surges. As if in mockery
finally, or to increase the confusion, a second train made
its way along the other side of the same platform, onto
which stepped down, immediately absorbed into the
crowd, the competitors in a *boules* championship match:
men of middle age, some obese, dressed like sportsmen
more or less, and wearing white caps that soon seemed to
float, scattered, drifting in their turn, immaculate, on the
surface of the human tide that, in the same way it had
pulled back a moment before, had now come by a converse
movement to press or rather to adhere with some furious,
stubborn, and viscous impulse against the sides of the cars
toward the windows of which arms were holding up babies,
extending rucksacks, baskets, sometimes merely a loaf of
bread, continuing to cling there despite whistle blasts and
the shouts of the trainmen, even when the locomotive
signal had sounded and while by a series of jolts, in a din
of couplings and hydraulic buffers, as though belching, the
traction spreading from car to car, as if it were trying to
shake off, like some animal covered with parasites, the
human clusters attached to its sides, the train started
moving.

So that for a moment it (the train) seemed unable to
free itself (either because they had begun following it on
the platform, walking first, then running, or because some
were still on the steps) of the kind of heteroclite conglomerate of men and women in paradoxical holiday clothes,
faces tense or wet with tears, dragging or rather carrying
in their wake, like wisps of straw or simple detritus on the
surface of a murky pond, the dried masks of the black-
clad old women the color of dead wood, like corpses, the
train gradually gaining speed, the human clusters releasing
it one after the other, until there remained on the steps
of one of the open platforms, not clinging but held round

the waist, closely embraced, only the slender arched body of a young woman, head and torso tipped back, arms round the shoulders of the man whose lips were glued to her mouth, her light summer dress of a cheap bright material printed with red flowers raised by the arm that encircled her waist, showing the back of her knees, beginning to pull free, then raised by the air, then flapping against her thighs, cries of alarm rising, and for a moment she seemed somehow suspended in the void, only still linked to the man as though by a suction cup at the place where the two mouths joined together, as if in a sort of aerial coitus, like those birds capable of coupling in flight, connected only by their genital organs and splitting the air like stones, a cluster of hands reaching toward her, pulling her (or receiving her), the train rolling now at about the speed of a man running, the slender figure breaking free, then herself beginning to run alongside the man still leaning out of the car, pushing aside the bodies in her way with the force of a wild beast, not even noticing them, the distance separating her from the man gradually increasing while she was running along the still-paved part of the platform beyond the glass roof, then twisting her ankle on the cinders, stumbling, losing one of her shoes, hopping on one leg, finally stopping and standing there among the tracks, still shouting, the occupants of the train leaning out the windows watching the slender form in the red dress diminish, quickly becoming remote, with the garishly painted whore's (or perhaps a clumsily made-up secretary's or salesgirl's) face still shouting, until she was no more than a silhouette lost in the August sunshine among the switches, the sparkling rails, tiny now beside the freight shed also diminishing faster and faster.

Then the train went around a curve and everything vanished: the woman, the gaping hole under the glass roof behind her, the lamp-shed, the signal-box, the river with its stony bed, it reedy banks: now the train was rolling over an embankment above truck gardens hedged by cypress or laurel, surrounding houses with tile roofs, with courtyards shaded by fig trees and filled with crates, with blue-caked fertilizer guns, with barrels and carts unhitched, as though hurriedly abandoned on the spot during the passage of some silent cyclone which had left behind it a world intact but empty, uninhabited with the exception here and there of a few chickens wandering at random, as though blind, busily pecking among the wagon shafts and the broken plows. Soon the orchards gave way to fields planted with vines where, as far as the eye could reach, lines of plane trees bordering the roads extended into the distance. A little farther on, the tracks ran between salt marshes not far from the sea, whose waves could be seen turning over, collapsing slowly, breaking, and sliding back in long scrolls beyond which a narrow band of silver sparkled in the morning air.

The train stopped at every station, even at level crossings, and again the regular panting of the locomotive could be heard releasing its jets of steam at intervals in the silence troubled only by the ringing of a little bell and the hissing of the wind in some pines along the sunny platform (platforms not even paved, stations no bigger than cottages, with only a double-faced clock, two benches, and a flowerbed) where little crowds were standing—sometimes only one or two groups, always somehow vaguely dressed up, it seemed, the immemorial black-clad old women now surrounded by men in shirtsleeves and women in smocks who were watching the clattering series of old cars knock against each other and stop and start again, standing there on the platform pressed against each other as if they could not bring themselves to leave, long after the peeling side of the last car had suddenly vanished, silently continuing to stare after the train while it vanished, the lined faces stamped with that same expression of consternation, of incredulity and despair—then no longer faces: patches—then not even patches: dots—then no longer dots: nothing but a vague and dark aggregation on the platform of the miniature station lost in the midst of the ocean of vines in the dazzling August light, sucked back, vanishing, shrinking still, then, in its turn, as a little earlier with the gaping glass roof, the girl in red shouting, the last houses of the city, disappearing.

After a while, in stations of a certain size covered again by glass roofs, the platforms overflowing with compact crowds from which rose (or rather above which hung suspended like an invisible mist) an invisible and distended moan, that same murmur, not of rebellion, of rage, but of plaintive stupor, the cars never stopped changing occupants, the newcomers with the same burdens of haversacks—sometimes of valises—with the same half-asleep faces (though it was now later in the day) replacing those who got off, struggled again to clear a way toward the exit beside which stood sentries, men carrying guns and wearing helmets.

Between stops, while the train was rolling again among the endless fields of vines, apart from a few drunkards who were singing and brandishing bottles at the windows, most of the passengers spoke very little. Sometimes, mechanically, one of them bent down, picked up from the floor some crumpled newspaper (with few variations, all displayed the same enormous headlines (a simple typographical expansion of words that the newspapers had already printed, or rather that were already postulated by the totality of words printed by the newspapers (but in smaller characters) for several weeks already—in fact, for several

months—in fact, for several years), as if, at the same time
as the rules of syntax which assigned them an order of, so
to speak, respectable and reassuring immunity, the others
(the other words: those by which they were habitually
surrounded) had suddenly lost all reason for being, the
syntax expelled too, the headlines (the headlines which in
days to come would be followed by several others increasing each time in size, until finally the letters filled half the
page) reduced to the assemblage of two or three nouns
isolated and excessively enlarged—the shapes of the letters
simplified too: thick, without serifs, simply massive, im-
mense—as though for myopic readers or for idiots), the
man for a moment passively shaken by the jolts, forearms
resting on his wide-spread thighs, the paper unfolded, his
eyes fixed, contemplating without seeing the printed characters and the photographs also excessively enlarged, then
dropping everything. One of the stations was built in the
middle of town on a viaduct, and when the train started
up, rolling slowly, the passengers could see in the shadows
of a boulevard below them a great number of horses standing together, their owners standing beside them, whip
under one arm, the other hand holding the bridle or the
halter of a huge percheron with its mottled rump or of a
piebald mare, sometimes carefully hanging over its ears a
feedbag out of which the horse ate steadily until it lipped
the last oats out of the bottom by tossing its head violently.
In the sunlight, this looked like some sort of fairground,
except that uniformed soldiers, wearing képis and carrying
clipboards, circulated between the groups of horses or
stood together comparing their lists. Then the train resumed its normal speed and everything (the tranquil horses
with their heads half buried in the feedbags, their owners
standing beside them, the men in képis with their lists)
also disappeared. Gradually, the kind of lethargic stupor

that reigned in the cars (they were cars without compartments or partitions, the wooden benches separated only
by their backs, the kind that were used only on local lines
serving remote country regions) grew still heavier, rarely
broken by some wine-clogged voice whose echoes fell into
a silence punctuated by the clatter of the wheels at the
joints in the rails. Delayed by its incessant stops, the train
made only slow progress, and night was beginning to fall.
With its onset the drunken songs also seemed to stop, while
the poignant twilight grew ever denser, until in the now-
closed windows (the air had suddenly grown cooler) began
to appear, interrupted at first by dark silhouettes of trees,
of houses, of hills succeeding each other, fleeing, returning
to paste themselves against the shiny surface, the shadowy
reflection of the cars' interior lit by yellowish lamps, as if
out there (finally, toward the east, everything was black)
were being swept along in parallel through the nocturnal
countryside where one or two lights occasionally floated
the immaterial and motionless doubles of the passengers
sitting or lying on the benches, the newspapers with huge
headlines torn and scattered beneath them.

* * *

And now he was going to die. It was already late when the
train stopped in Lyon. Trainmen walked along the platform
shouting that this was the end of the line and that passengers would have to change trains. The station lighting had
been hastily masked, and occasional faint gleams seemed
to make the darkness even thicker. Beneath the dim vault
of the vast smoke-blackened glass-and-iron roof echoed
the clashing buffers and the squeal of brakes reverberating
in a paradoxical silence in which drifted, as though contained by the sides of the trains in parallel rows, an indistinct din from which, unlike those which had filled every

station that morning, no cry, no shout was now discernible, only a faint murmur: merely the noise, the faint, inoffensive though vaguely disturbing rustle produced by hundreds of feet, by hundreds of men wandering as if at random, sent from one platform to the next, mingling, criss-crossing, turning back, hurrying, sometimes even running, bumping into each other, going back the way they came, in a sort of gloomy, mute, and docile tumult: no more women, no more tears, no more embraces, no more babies held out at arms' length: as if within a single day had occurred a sort of mutation, that is, as if, though surrounded by the sleeping city (or perhaps still awake, incapable of finding sleep behind the closed windows and blank house fronts), those who were here now had already been rejected, excluded, abandoned in the night peopled by that countless and invisible tramping like some furtive background noise above which, from everywhere and nowhere in the darkness, continued to reverberate, sporadically punctuated by the hammering of the buffers, the noises of locomotives maneuvering, the clatter of couplings and the hissing of steam.

Now he was stretched out at full length in the dark (perhaps the lighting system wasn't yet restored—or perhaps it was out of order—or perhaps it had been deliberately cut, though in principle the first-class cars were reserved for officers, but the other reservist (a young fellow wearing a cap and looking like a butcher's apprentice or a delivery boy) had said that no one gave a fuck about officers today and besides what could happen to them that would be worse than what lay ahead for all of them where they were anyway?), motionless, eyes open, slowly inhaling the acrid smell of dirt and dried sweat exuded by the upholstery on the first-class banquettes, the deleterious, anonymous, and carbuncular odor of all parting, all disaster, able to sense beneath him the inert and heavy assemblage of metal (wheels, axles, bogies) motionless, too, as if soldered, but threatening, as if he had been granted one more moment for the first time since morning, a sort of halt, an uncertain respite (the trainman who had indicated the dim line of cars beside the platform had not said any particular time, simply shrugged his shoulders and turned away, exasperated) during which he could contemplate in a telescopic perspective (just as, his head raised a little, the nape of his neck resting on his folded hands, he could see his whole body lying flat on the banquette, from his shoes gleaming in the darkness to the creases of his jacket rising and falling with the rhythm of his breathing) the twenty-six years that were now in all likelihood coming to an end: twenty-six years during which, since even as a child he had been dragged through an apocalyptic landscape in search of an elusive skeleton, he had with the same calm and docile amazement, without really understanding, first seen the woman always dressed in dark clothes who was his mother gradually dissolve, waste away, exchanging her Bourbonian countenance for that of a waterfowl, then of a mummy, thanks to the scalpels that kept cutting away her body, a sort of living scarecrow, the fleshless bird's head emerging from shawls that covered something flat lying first on armchairs, then on divans, then in a bed, flatter and flatter, scarcely raising the sheet, then disappearing altogether, leaving nothing behind but a varnished oak box under a heap of flowers whose violent odor mingled with that of the candles, and nothing else, just as, he thought, lying as though in a box inside a train compartment on a banquette stinking of coal dust, there now remained nothing more than the insignificant residue of not even some violent chemical reaction, some sulfurous seething of antagonistic and contradictory substances, but of twenty-six years of idleness and unconcerned inertia—at best, of anticipatory impulse, of frustrated expectation of something which had never happened (or which, perhaps, he thought again, was going to happen now), which couldn't have been provoked (or deceived) by any of the disguises successively imposed or attempted, from the stiff uniform with its military cut in which, once the oak box had vanished, they had dressed the boy of eleven, with its collar like a carcan, its gilt buttons, and its cap with a shiny leather visor, down to the latest one which included as accessories the brushes and palette of a cubist painter, having meanwhile tried an anarchist's belted blouse, then, still with the same incredulous indolence, the same incredulous amazement, wearing tweed and flannel, having followed all across a sick old continent echoing to the sound of boots and firing squads the trunk on which hotel porters had pasted many-colored stickers one after the other, while all he had to do was to scrawl his signature at the bottom of little rectangles of paper bearing along with the date the amount to be paid and walk out of the bank or the agency with, in his pocket, the coined sweat of the men and horses that worked for him on acres of vines of which he knew only the approximate whereabouts (the old steward with the slave-trader's face was dead, replaced by another, younger man who, when he pulled off his cap, revealed the same bald skull, white or rather livid, contrasting with his sunburned face), having visited (the acres of vines) according to the immutable family custom four or five times a year, remote, distracted somehow, actually bored (and now he could hear a suitcase knocking against the sides of the corridor, coming closer, then someone pushed open the compartment door, groped for the light switch, gave that up, at the same time that a dry, hard voice said Who are you what are you doing here first-class is reserved for officers get out! the other boy saying without getting up No kidding? the dry voice repeating Who are you show me your papers where are you going? the other boy answering still without getting up We're all going to the same place: to hell, the dry voice saying Get out of here right now or . . . , the boy saying Or what? the dry voice saying I'm an officer I'm ordering you to get up and get out of here at once that's an order, the boy saying You couldn't let us sleep, huh? the dry, furious, outraged voice saying Sleep . . . Sl . . . That's it, that's all I . . . We'll see about that we'll see . . . , the sliding door remaining open, the raging voice and the banging suitcases fading down the corridor, the furious voice reaching them a moment later but from outside now, shouting Guards! Guards! . . . , the boy saying Keep going! while the two of them stood up, lowered the window, leaned out, watched vanishing down the platform, pushing his way into the dark and gloomy confusion of shadows, the slender figure wearing a felt hat and a short gabardine raincoat showing the leggings wrapped around the calves: in the distance they saw reflections glistening on a group of helmets, Guards! the voice shouted again fainter and fainter: they saw him stop near the post of men in black uniforms and speak to them pointing to their car, but no one moved: Fucker! said the boy in the cap; he closed the window again and lay down again on the banquette)—and he too lying down again, inert again in the train plunged into darkness and silent (except for the intrusion of the officer whose suitcase, once again, they heard banging down the corridor with something outraged, something furious in the sound, passing without stopping where they were, then a little farther along in the train the noise of a door sliding open and banging shut violently, the train apparently empty, unoccupied, as if it were abandoned on a siding, forgotten,

withdrawn from the outside world by the thickness of the
closed windows through which nothing penetrated any
more but the vague and unreal shuffling of feet), unable
(or refusing) to fall asleep (in the darkness he could now
hear the regular, slightly clogged breathing of the sleeping
soldier)—and at one point there was a shock, or rather the
brief repercussion of a shock (as if the entire train had
been traversed by a hiccough spreading from car to car)
very far away, at the head of the train no doubt, and after
that, though the train was still motionless and plunged into
darkness, it seemed to have been somehow reattached to
the outside world, thinking then that twenty-six years of
something which had not yet really begun to exist would
now definitely cease to exist, so that all he could reasonably
wonder was after how many zeros after the decimal point
to the right of the first zero would be written the number
by which he should multiply (that is, divide, reduce to its
true dimensions) what had happened to him during these
twenty-six years, thinking (the train was moving now, that
is, at first a few livid lights fanned slowly then faster and
faster across the interior of the compartment, so that he
could see that the soldier had kept his cap on to sleep, the
visor pulled down over his eyes, then everything was dark
again) . . . thinking of all the trains moving at that same
moment in the night, dragging their freight of fear (now
it was as if he could feel himself retract: like an oyster
under lemon juice, he thought, as he frantically tried to
shrink down, to withdraw into himself, to diminish his
vulnerable surface, shuddering with a joyless laugh), thinking (still furiously inert, his horizontal body faintly shaken
by slight jolts) that if he pressed his ear against the upholstery of the banquette (but he did not move: stubbornly
keeping that same position in which he was frozen by the
impossibility—or the denial—of sleep, hands still folded

behind the nape of his neck, eyes wide open) he could doubtless hear through the noisy racket of the wheels under him and their regular shocks at each joint of the rails something like a huge and dim rumble that would be rising from the ground itself, as if from one end of Europe to the other the dark earth were trembling beneath the countless trains chugging through the night, filling the silence with a single, inaudible, and dismaying thunder, keeping similarly awakened in their beds, eyes similarly open on the darkness, staring into the night with the same anxious hebetude, the same apathetic terror, the inhabitants of farms scattered through the countryside, of villages, of darkened cities: as if the tears, the faces bathed with tears turning away, abandoning the stations, had flowed back, at first in sad groups, then separating, dividing, ramifying like a river flowing back toward its sources, then strung out, then each one taking refuge in the rooms with cold beds empty (the tears dried by now, the eyes dry, merely reddened), and he cursing again in silence, thinking: It's that paper; if she just hadn't wrapped them in that damn tissue paper or rice paper or whatever the fuck it's called! . . . still feeling it weigh on his stomach like a stone, the half-sandwich he had taken a bite of, chewing interminably before managing to swallow it, then quickly folding up the other half (and the other two which he hadn't touched) in that semitransparent paper the woman had carefully wrapped them in: the woman—almost a girl still—who slept beside him, lay beside him, reading a book—or docilely took off her clothes, lying naked, patient, and motionless, with her pink and white breasts, her pearly belly, her semitransparent skin—while according to the lessons of the teacher in the cubist academy he tried to spread colors over what he called (or tried to convince himself could be called) paintings, converting into inept triangles, inept squares, or inept pyramids (or cones, or spheres, or cylinders) the sails, the boats, and the rocks of the fishing village where they were spending the summer (or the breasts, the thighs, the belly, the tender breathing flesh)—then, later, taking (the woman) secretarial courses to type the pages of what he supposed must be a novel, and now she too no doubt listening to the trains on the plain—and again he swore under his breath, thinking: Tissue paper, what the fuck does she think . . . , the sticky mass of bread and ham chewed now to the consistency of wet cement refusing to go down: even if I stuck my fingers down my throat, he thought, cursing still, as if rage (or rather the facsimiles of rage and vulgarity) now constituted his sole recourse, nonetheless deciding to move, unclasping his hands, lowering them to his belly, unbuckling his belt, realizing that the train had stopped again but not even getting up to see the name of the station, thinking then to think hard about something else . . .

In Poland they were all built of wood, suddenly looming up, apparently without reason (the train simply moving slower and slower, then motionless without there having been anything else: neither suburbs nor trace of any habitation) in the endless plain (or it too without reason—that is, there seemed to be no reason for a plain as absolutely bare as this one to surround a station or for a station to be planted in the middle of an absolutely bare plain), solitary beside a birch grove, the leaves ceaselessly stirring, as though of their own accord, this too without reason, since the smoke from the locomotive rose straight up in the air, and only a few blond, barefoot children, the girls with braids, and some low carriages harnessed to three horses abreast, which trotted off one after the other in various directions, raising huge clouds of dust on the flat expanse, where as far as the eye could see there was no house, and nothing else: the children with blond hair, the shivering birches, the wooden station, the clouds of dust raised by the troikas and slowly settling through the motionless air, the troikas growing smaller until they were no more than dots on the horizon, then not even a dot, all this before the train came to a complete stop, or rather no: leaning out the window in the cool air (evening was falling), he first saw the stoker and the engineer get down from the locomotive, now motionless in the continuation of what seemed to be the same endless plain (or the same steppe), except that straddling the track rose a triumphal arch (or rather the skeleton of such a thing) bearing on its pediment an inscription in tall Cyrillic letters cut out of brass (or else inlaid) surmounted by a crossed hammer and sickle themselves surmounted by a five-pointed star, the whole thing (Cyrillic letters, tools, and star) painted red (and he could remember this: the gray steppe at the day's end, the triumphal skeleton, the inscription, the emblem, and the blood-red star), the plumes of steam escaping regularly from the locomotive, toward which two figures exactly like the ones who had just got out of it were advancing with an armed escort, starting from the triumphal skeleton raised in the middle of the bare steppe, the two figures climbing the ladder of the tender, a whistle sounding, the train almost empty of passengers beginning to move, slowly passing under the rhetorical text, stared after by the four men of the guard wearing long gray overcoats, then slowing again almost immediately, this time coming to a permanent stop in what looked more like a little shunting station than a real station (for again there was neither village nor town to be seen: only a few low buildings—or rather sheds—looking like warehouses, or lamp-sheds, or barracks) and where, this time, they were requested to get off, he and his traveling companion (a student of cubism

as well, who not only spoke English too but even Spanish—
and without having had to bother to study them because
he spoke them as it were from birth in Mexico City, so
that aside from cubism he had even had time to study (or
at least so he claimed) the principles of dialectical materialism in German which, combined with those of geometrical painting and an extensive knowledge of various
brands of whiskey, permitted him to make long and un-
challengeable speeches): beside the platform where the
train came to a halt stood a sort of shack inside which was
seated behind a table the interchangeable official employed
at frontiers the world over, possessing the same interchangeable countenance, at once bored, restrained, and
expressive by dint of inexpressiveness, who, while his sub-
alterns were inventorying the contents of their luggage,
carefully studied the papers and the photographs which
the two students presented him, the latter (that is, the last
series of photographs: a good dozen were required which
he (the official) stapled one after the next to successive
documents) taken by an artist-photographer with long hair,
dressed in a long frock coat, working with a bellows camera
and a black hood over his head in a studio embellished
with portraits of other personages with the same tonsorial
system and the same clothes, like those who were strolling
in the neighborhood where the studio was located, inhabited (old men, grown men, or adolescents) by a multitude
of replicas of the same type: dressed in black, bearded if
adult, the face framed by little wisps of hair escaping from
under a black hat, an expression, already at twelve, thirteen, or fourteen years of age (even running, playing soc-
cer, or chasing each other in the squares, uniformly dressed
in that sort of gown or rather sheath which flapped against
their heels), of something like seminarians, priests with
pensive, sad, and sweet faces, as though in mourning, as

though condemned to wear eternally along with their own mourning that of some remote Eden, some promised land eternally denied them, subsequently dedicated to prayer, to the ritual viands, to the commerce of furs and lamentations—a neighborhood (or refuge, or conservatory, or reservation, or phalanstery) which seemed like a city inside the city itself, the last capital where they (the two students) had stopped before catching the train which was to take them to the triumphal arch and which had been pointed out to them with disgust (it was a religious holiday—that is, a holiday of the porter's religion) by the festooned giant who was standing at the entrance of the hotel where a plaque recorded that the Emperor Napoleon I had lodged here (between two battles, two of those indestructible treaties of indestructible friendship by which he parceled out Europe the way one might tear up a paper map), had received in his bed, naked and rosy-fleshed, the blond countesses or the brazen intriguers who were brought to him by his plumed chamberlains, the porter's disgust (he could barely keep himself from spitting on the ground, from handing back the tip over which his fist had closed) growing still greater when he learned the use to which the photographs were to be put, because an honest Polish hotel porter, festooned to the elbow with gold-braid stripes and bemedaled up to the chin, could without humbling himself slip a card bearing the address of a brothel (which he had just done the moment before), and if it came to that could indicate the whereabouts of a Jewish photograher working on the virginal Feast of the Assumption (which apparently the Polish whores did not scorn to do as well—and the Mexican had said that they certainly ought to pay them a visit, just to see if they do it with a little cross hanging round their necks . . .), but could hardly endure that two rich students of cubism, one of whom moreover had the face of some wild Indian, should take the train across the barbed-wire line attached to a skeletal arch of triumph surmounted by a red star—and before that the cities with the names of iron, coal, steel, of sledge hammers, the horizon bristling with factory chimneys like the trees of a forest, the platforms of the carefully swept stations iron gray (that is, made of cement like all the others, but no doubt a special cement that resembled iron) where there waited, getting off the train, getting on it without any particular disorder, travelers, men or women not exactly starched, or stiff, or severe, or sad, but carved (overcoats, raincoats, hats, faces, suitcases or briefcases) out of wood (or perhaps out of steel too), and among them sometimes, they too wooden (or perhaps steel), men with faces of steel—or of pigs—squeezed into black or brown uniforms, wearing riding breeches, gleaming boots, one sleeve sporting a red armband with, in the center of a white circle, something that looked like a big black spider—and that capital somehow swollen, its museums filled with Greek temples transported stone by stone to the linden-lined avenues, with its heavy domes, its baroque palaces, its philosophers stuffed with Greek philosophy, its columns and its triumphal arches surmounted by iron beasts, its Opera, its philharmonic orchestra, the nocturnal terraces of its restaurants lit by tiny pink lampshades where women like iron flowers were delicately eating those—whatever they're called—rather soft, gelatinous pastries made of tremulous superimposed layers, pink, cream, mauve, "Bavaroises," the Mexican had said—"Just the word I was looking for! . . . What a thing it is, after all, to know philosophy the way you do! Thanks! The Berlinoises enjoying Bavaroises. Ha, ha! . . . No, sorry, not so good. Excuse me. Actually wretched. I'm just trying to be funny. Because these guys with the spiders on their sleeves really scare

the shit out of me . . ." (thinking, lying in that car stinking
of cold sweat that was rolling through the night—the night
in which were rolling at the same moment with a threatening and inaudible rumble all the trains of old Europe
filled with young flesh: Good God, how young we were,
how young! . . . as if not only two years but something like
an invisible wall, an irremediable scission, separated him
now from that spring—it was almost summer—when they
had been sitting on that terrace illuminated by tiny pink
lampshades, populated by ravishing women made of pink
steel, in that city at once severe and frivolous which looked
something like the product of a series of complicated cop-
ulations between the rococo style, the Doric order, philosophy in frock coats, and Wagnerian opera: "An old
lady," he had said: "an old dame, obese, and starched to
the . . ." ("An old trout, yes!" the Mexican had said,
"stuffed like a sausage!") "Right: an old trout stuffed like
a sausage, covered wih jewels, domes, pediments, and with
a swarm of ravishing *lectrices,* or soubrettes, or heiresses,
the kind you find in novels: the old widow of an iron
general who has today fallen a victim to the charm . . ."
("You might use another word," said the Mexican) " . . . of
her first *valet de chambre* or of the second coachman . . ."—
"Rather of the gamekeeper," the Mexican had said: "something more like a Lady Chatterley seduced by her chief
groom, or rather her master of hounds, at once terrified
and enchanted . . ." (thinking again: But how young we
were, how young! . . .) "And now," he had said a little
later (at this moment the official with the face expressive
by dint of being neutral had returned their passports, his
subordinates had closed their suitcases, and the two of
them were back in the train about to start) ". . . now we
have just had the privilege of seeing the philosophy of
materialism materialized in the form of a skeletal arch of

triumph raised in the middle of the steppe . . . Don't make such a face: I'm still trying to be funny. That photograph-collector also scares the shit out of me . . ." (remembering the impassive Indian countenace with eyes like coffee beans, half-closed, turning away, pretending to look out the window where there was nothing to see (night had fallen) but his own reflection, with that expression simultaneously fierce and sleepy, his aquiline nose with its broad nostrils, his shiny black hair that women liked) and then he, continuing: "Sorry again, forgive me. All right: that one was a Jew. But even so, he was a German too, no? . . ." saying again: "Good. Fine. It's probably because I haven't studied philosophy. In any case, you have to admit they all seem to have the same frantic passion for boots, for uniforms, and that same shit-color aesthetic. Not to mention their common and equally frantic passion for red. Except that here they wear cute little blue and green caps. Probably that's what makes the difference. But since you know philosophy, tell me: the ones the police wear, are they the blue ones or the green ones? . . ." still thinking now: Good God! Good God! How young we were! . . . as if years and years had passed since he had teased his traveling companion in a train rolling through the darkness of that endless plain where nothing except the skeletal triumphal arch which they had left behind them marked the frontier between Europe and Asia, or rather what was already no longer quite Europe but not yet quite Asia.

In the Russian trains all the passengers lay down at night, even in third class where the wooden benches were turned into berths. They were old cars dating back to tsarist days, but they were infinitely more comfortable than their French equivalents. By paying a little more, you were entitled to a skimpy mattress and a pillow. The compartments were not closed off, and in the daytime people kept coming and going, visiting the end of the car where there was a samovar, returning holding huge glasses of hot tea which they took a long time to drink, chatting and sipping, then going back to refill their glasses. He could remember the long bony fingers of an old man clumsily trying to rake a slice of brownish tea-soaked lemon out of the bottom of an empty glass and slide it into his mouth. As they drank their tea, the passengers kept staring at the two foreigners, one of whom looked like some kind of savage with his oily hair and that face resembling a terra-cotta mask emerging above a bow tie and an immaculate collar. By sign language, counting on their fingers, and still staring at the tweed jackets and flannel trousers, they informed them that the old man was over a hundred. Even more than their jackets and their trousers—some of the passengers tested the material with their fingers—it was their shoes that seemed to interest the Russians. Still by sign language, one of their neighbors informed them that it would be wise to put such things under their pillows when they lay down to sleep. But it was not only the language—though the Mexican (or rather the Indian) apparently possessed a sixth sense (he claimed to have European parents—but someone (another of the students of cubism, someone else also attending the expensive school ("academy") where an ingenious professor taught how to transform the tender pale nudes sitting or languorously stretched out on the model's platform into steel tubes, cones, and spheres) had said one day that then his honorable European mother must belong to the category of fanatic museum-goers and that his appearance was doubtless a case of mimicry—what might be called, he had said, archaeological mimicry) . . . a sense inherited from his ideogrammatic ancestors which despite his sleepy expression seemed to allow him to speak at length without needing words to any stranger in any country; but there was something else: something like an opacity, something that resisted everything, something passive, patient, apparently naive, and which did not permit (even by the dextrous use of that ideographic idiom) getting more than certain elementary and picturesque information concerning the age of a centenarian or the precautions to take to avoid having your shoes stolen, as if with their clothes which were not exactly wretched but (it was hard to describe) uniformly dim, uniformly threadbare (even when they were evidently new), which always seemed either too tight or too loose or too short or too long (what came out of the stores—the state stores—where they had been bought seemed already threadbare and wrinkled (and irremediably un-wrinkleable, incapable of showing wear) even before having been put on), as if the obliging and communicative passengers they had met in the trains (or the less communicative people in the streets—yet they too insistently stared at their shoes) were not only condemned to live inside a barbed-wire enclosure which they were forbidden to escape and which stokers and engineers on trains from neighboring countries had no right to approach closer than twenty yards, but as if this were a normal state of affairs which did not change them from what their fathers, their grandfathers, and the grandfathers of their grandfathers had always known: an opacity, then, a screen, like the saleswoman in the store—in the state store—where they had wanted to buy embroidered caps worn by certain people in the streets (people with wrinkled yellow faces the color of deserts, with the squinting eyes and impenetrable faces of mountaineers or shepherds, they too dressed, except for the bright cap, in the same shapeless threadbare and unwrinkleable clothes, coming from some remote province, from some remote philosophical republic, it too wrinkled, yellow, and, like them, impenetrable: and sometimes there were people wearing gowns and slender mandarin goatees, sitting like idols, like those paintings on silk, imperturbable, waiting, in the armchairs of the hotel lobby, or actually of the caravansary: a long gallery with Oriental hangings, filled with the incessant clatter of abacuses), the saleswoman merely setting a single cap on the counter at the same time as she adroitly removed the previous one, all quite mechanically, unconcernedly, showing neither irritation nor impatience nor interest either for what she was doing or for the buyers, any more than could have been shown by a slot machine or an automatic vending machine, merely careful not to let go of the cap she was showing and to watch the hands of the two customers until two men (young men actually, more or less their own age) appearing somehow out of nowhere, suddenly materializing, whispered a few words in their mysterious language, after which she consented to allow a choice among several caps lined up on the counter now, though still within reach of her hand, and still watching with intensified vigilance the hands of the men on the other side of the counter, the two newcomers presenting themselves in French, smiling, cordial: students, they had said, happy to be able to speak a little French, looking about as much like students as a fox looks like a hen, wearing clothes that if not luxurious were at least not as threadbare as those of the people in the streets or the trains, increasingly obliging, courteous, amusing, eager, as they had just been with regard to the purchase of the embroidered caps, to arrange matters for their new friends, to help them with other purchases, since it was easy to imagine that two students, even dressed in comfortable tweeds, even wearing bow ties, could not buy many souvenirs at the discouraging (this could be said among friends, that is, since the Mexican had confided to them his desire to bring home to other friends in his country a red flag with hammer and sickle, star and Cyrillic characters embroidered in gold) official rate of exchange while by selling for example even just one of their wristwatches (they—the new friends materialized out of nowhere—knew where this could be done) it would be possible for them to invert by four (thereby multiplying by sixteen) their purchasing power—which was accomplished a little later, one of the two friendly strangers disappearing a few moments with the Mexican's watch and returning almost immediately with a bundle of filthy notes, the pink, orange, or green paper of a downy texture, and so thick (the bundle) that they (the two cubists) didn't know where to stuff it, even by dividing it in half, the Mexican saying: "I told you, they're neither thieves nor police—if they were police, they'd have had us arrested," and he: "And if they were thieves they'd have vanished. All right! Apparently there's an advantageous moneychanger on every street corner. Because he merely went around the block and came back. As for that helpful saleswoman, all they had to do was whisper something in her ear for her to show us her complete line of caps. Very useful fellows, really nice guys! . . . ," the Mexican not answering, staring determinedly elsewhere, with his face of a sleeping god, his thick lips, his mask with half-closed eyes which more than ever resembled one of those terra-cottas to be seen in the museums: the clock over the vast door in the brick wall had then begun striking and three guards had appeared, very young, blond, dressed in gray with yellow belts, holding their rifles vertical in their left hands, walking in step like mechanical toys, flinging their stiff and high-booted left legs very high into the air, and he: "Don't make such a face. Everyone knows there aren't any police in this country. Just a lot of pretty little toy soldiers that you wind up in the back with a key. That bearded Jewish philosopher

of theirs, he certainly had a solid basis of German culture
too! . . . All right, let's go, our charming guide is calling
us . . ." (it was an old woman, or rather an old lady—and
perhaps, as a matter of fact, not so old—with a gray and
exhausted face, her dignity exhausted too, speaking in a
dim, also mechanical voice): since they were strangers rich
enough to do no more than sign little squares of paper,
she moved them to the head of the long line of men and
women which was winding without making any progress
at the base of the red marble cube, to the door framed by
the two new guards with weapons polished like mirrors,
as motionless as if they had been molded out of wax, with
this difference, that wax imperceptibly breathed whereas
what they were guarding seemed nothing but a dried-up
mummy, with a tiny yellow head with Mongol cheekbones,
a short beard doubtless combed every morning by the
embalmers, looking like a high school headmaster and
some barbarian Oriental satrap, pedantic and pitiless, lying
under a spotlight as though inside a reliquary in a cryptlike
silence made still more silent by the religious shuffle of
feet across the marble floor while there filed through the
penumbra, ectoplasmic, fascinated, and fearful, the broad
faces with prominent cheekbones, wearing caps or shawls,
the potato-colored, wrinkled masks out of the depths of
Asia, the blond heads of babies, following each other
slowly, as though strung on an invisible thread, trailing
warm and asphyxiating whiffs of sour cabbage, of rancid
oil and dirty bodies, and he remembered that coming out
into the fresh air and the light he had said: "But it must
be because I haven't studied philosophy. Now, please, just
stop making faces once and for all! Tonight we'll have
ourselves a time! Now that we've got all this money, we'll
do our grand-duke number! . . .": and their new friends
had come for them at the hotel, accompanied by two girls

in skirts and freshly ironed blouses, they too, though
young, not withered but faded, with already tiny, almost
invisible wrinkles, but wrinkles even so, at the corners of
their mouths: rather like secretaries or typists, the kind
who must lunch on a sandwich on a bench in the square,
"granting," he had thought, "that there might be a little
smear of grease between the two slices of bread. Don't
even mention ham. Granting that there are slices of bread.
Like the famous knife without a handle with the blade
missing . . . ," saying aloud (and almost immediately disgusted with himself for having said it): "Because they might
whisper to them the same things they whispered to the
saleswoman and then they would show us their wares? . . ."
and the Mexican saying: "Shut up for once, you shit!" and
he had said: "Right, this time I'm sorry. Really, I'm
sorry . . ."; but not grand dukes, not gambling, not even,
apparently, any fun (only some other diners whose clothes
were not threadbare, whose faces were a little broad, a
little heavy, a little stiff, accompanied by women of a certain uneasy elegance, or not accompanied: sitting several
together around a champagne bucket, like those men leaving a committee, a business meeting, silent or exchanging
infrequent remarks) in that restaurant where they ate spicy
shashniki with little raw onions, as in all the Russian restaurants or Caucasian taverns in the world, with here and
there Oriental hangings, candelabra and lit candles on the
tables, a balalaika orchestra, and a dancer in Cossack costume with an astrakhan toque, soft boots, and a black tunic
whose skirts flew around him when he whirled and leaped
amazingly high, two torches (or were they flaming skewers
of meat?) in his hands, the balalaikas playing louder and
louder and faster and faster, the Russian (or Cossack or
Gypsy) voices of the singers louder and louder (bass voices
and one woman), deep, penetrating, the voices of some of

the diners (the ones wearing clothes that were not threadbare, luxurious rather, even those who were not wearing
neckties, whose shirt collars were simply fastened by a
button) accompanying them, several clapping in time faster
and faster, the Mexican clapping too, ordering another
bottle of vodka, filling the glasses (and at the same time,
that same evening—but they found out about this only
when they got back to Europe—the commander-in-chief
of the whole army was being shot by a firing squad (or
disposed of by a revolver in some cellar), and as every day,
every night, in hundreds of houses, apartments, or on simple farms, blows (kicks) rang out against the panels of
doors—and perhaps the doors of some of the diners with
stiff faces or of the Cossack dancer or of one of the waiters
or of anyone), and a little later the four men and the two
girls squeezed into a taxi which jolted through the ruts of
the unpaved streets, then not even streets: muddy stretches
too long, too wide (like building sites) which stretched into
the mean light of a few streetlamps between the apartment
blocks, some quite new, of raw cement, others brand-new,
no doubt built the year before but already dilapidated, as
though crumbling, peeling, then getting out of the taxi,
stumbling across the ruts of a muddy space, then passing
under a portico, stumbling again in a dark courtyard, then
passing under another portico, then all six of them sitting
in a room: but no doubt he was already drunk by then and
he couldn't remember anything but yellowish walls, as in
a barracks (or perhaps it was the yellowish light in the
kitchen which they had passed through and of which the
door was open, so that they could hear what sounded like
pots being moved around on a stove), a divan covered with
a brown cloth, chairs—in any case seats—but not enough
of them because they now seemed to be not six but ten,
or twelve, or fifteen, and never the same ones: unknown

faces which appeared at the door, staring with a kind of childish curiosity at the bow ties and the shoes, changing then, the door to the kitchen apparently shared by several lodgings, as apparently not only the tenants of the same floor but those of the whole building, men, women, and children, seemed to replace each other, to come into the room, to leave it again, to reappear without this seeming to disturb its occupants, as if this too were a normal state of affairs, as if it were normal that no one was asleep at this hour of the night and that someone was cooking things in the kitchen (things that smelled like cabbage and rancid grease), the Mexican still holding the vodka bottle he had bought as they left the restaurant, arguing philosophical problems with the two ("All right, let's call them agents of exchange," he had said: "since it seems that police employees deal with such matters—all right, let's call them agents of providence, but for God's sake stop making that face once and for all!"), he for now sitting on the divan that was too low, overcome by a terrible desire to sleep, trying as best he could to wedge two cushions that were too small between his back and the wall behind him, staring with perplexity at the face of one of the two girls who was pouring out her words, hearing the voice of one of the two Russians momentarily interrupting the philosophical argument to say to him: "She's asking you if you want to marry her," and he: "Marry her? But . . ." and too drunk, too tired, still trying to wedge the two pillows behind his back, and later, alone with the girl who had asked him to marry her and the two Russians, the tenants of the house still coming and going, staring at him curiously, the girl now at the other end of the divan smoking one of the cigarettes out of the pack he had given her and having apparently forgotten him, for now she seemed interested in the argument which was continuing in Russian between those whom he was calling the agents of exchange, the Mexican having vanished with the other girl into the next room the door of which she had locked behind them, which suggested that certain rooms of the building—or of the apartment—could be locked, in any case that one where she didn't want to be disturbed while she was sewing in the lining of the jacket the Mexican was wearing the famous red flag embroidered with gold (he had given up buying one with a (gold) fringe whose bulk inside the lining might have caught the attention of the customs officers (or of the police) at the borders of the hostile countries which the Mexican would still have to cross before returning home), the ones whom he had called agents of exchange being listened to by the girl smoking cigarettes (long cigarettes half of which consisted of a cardboard tube you made into a filter by flattening it twice in opposite directions), the taller of the two, who claimed to be Lithuanian, glancing more and more frequently at the locked door, people still coming in and going out of the room as if they were at home (and perhaps they were, as a matter of fact), the Lithuanian's face hardening, gradually changing, the conversation itself becoming pitted with silences, blanks, the Lithuanian's face tenser and tenser, tragic now, and now he no longer on the wretched divan but lying on the banquette of a railroad car, in one of those trains which all together, at the same moment, were roaring over bridges, racing through tunnels, crossing rivers, whistling lugubriously, panting across the plains of a continent seamed with scars, somehow or other stitched together again the way they sew up the belly of a horse gored by the bull in order to offer it to the animal once again, thinking: Of course they were in the police! Of course! . . . And probably the girls too. But that wasn't all . . . No. Something else. Something much more complicated, much more . . . ,

then thinking: But we were so young! God, we were young,
how young we were! . . .

* * *

And now all that was far away, over and done with, and
he was going to die: though it was scarcely more than two
years ago—two years of trying to believe that what you
could read between the lines of the newspaper articles
would not happen, and knowing that it had to happen—
scarcely more than two years since he had been there, in
the depths of a night that was itself in the depths of a
ruined suburb itself almost in the depths of Europe, almost
at the limits of another continent, uncomfortably sitting
inside a peeling concrete block on an uncomfortable couch
beside a woman—a faded girl—whom he had uninten-
tionally offended, and half-drunk, half-asleep, hearing the
arguments (or the fake arguments) of two (but what? in-
formers, police spies?—but to inform on whom? spy on
whom?: two idlers, two students of cubism, having come
there with their bow ties, their tweed jackets, and their
calf shoes the way someone might go to a zoo to look at
the strange animals, and with no more shame than visitors
to a zoo, they who had only to sell their wristwatches at
four times what they had paid for them in order to buy at
sixteen times less than the cost shashniki with onions and
bottles of vodka, watching a dancer dressed up as a Cossack
whirling in front of them)—and not even three years since
that day when this time without a bow tie or a tweed jacket
but wearing (or rather disguised with the help of) an old
lumberjacket—the jacket he put on when he was going
fishing: the same one, in fact, that he was wearing now,
stretched out like a corpse, but his eyes wide open, sliding
horizontally into the night, on that upholstered banquette
in a compartment reserved for officers and where he had

no right to be lying, the bench then of wood, the compartment a third-class one but one where he had in truth
(or morally, or decently) no more right to be lying either,
exhibiting, in order to get in, what once again could be
called a forged document, that is, the fraudulent conjunc-
tion of his name (the same one which appeared on the
little rectangles of paper on which he needed only to scrawl
his signature for some obliging cashier to count out a bundle of banknotes for him) and the card of a political party
whose avowed goal was to suppress the banks and their
clients at the same time, the card (covered with stamps
testifying to his conviction with regard to ideas (notably
that of suppressing the banks) of which he himself was not
any too sure he approved) obtained (he had paid for the
stamps all at the same time—though not by check—and
just the day before) so to speak by trickery, by skillful
persuasion, by parading his adherence to those projects of
closing the banks then popular (if not obligatory) among
students of cubism, tricking himself as well then (that is
to say, half-tricking, that is, to the degree to which that
philosophical program of suppressing the banks only half-
seduced him), and then standing there, while those who
were examining it (the fake document) on the platform (or
was it in an office?) of the frontier station were examining
him as well: there were two of them, paradoxically two
foreigners to the country he was trying to enter (or rather
sneak into): an American in shirtsleeves, with a pistol as
big as a cannon stuck into his belt, looking just like a bank
robber (which he was, moreover, in all likelihood—or had
been—or wanted to be, in accordance with his convictions)
and an Italian wearing nothing but overalls, carrying a rifle
bigger than he was; the American sullen, suspicious, anything but friendly, scornful even, for whom the card and
the stamps covering it did not particularly seem to con-

stitute a good reference (if not even an execrable one—
not that he was suspecting a fake, but precisely because it
seemed to him to present all the signs of authenticity), the
Italian, on the contrary, cordial, fraternal: a killer, or rather
a *pistolero,* who in the middle of Paris, at a restaurant table,
had shot one of the political leaders of his country (he told
the story between the frontier and Barcelona in the train
which the American had finally let himself be persuaded
by him to let the newcomer take and which he had taken
with him—a train where they were apparently the only
two passengers, so that, though it was composed exclusively of third-class cars with brown wooden benches and
though it was leaving almost on time (or perhaps on the
orders of the Italian going home—if in fact he had a
home—his day's work over) it seemed to be operating as
a special train, like the kind chartered for chiefs of state:
night had fallen and while he was talking you could see his
head reflected in the dark compartment window: a face
not much bigger than a fist surmounted (or surrounded,
as though by a halo) by a voluminous sphere of kinky black
hair, the kind associated with virtuouso violinists and Zulu
warriors), the Italian, then, prolix, fraternal, and endowed
with the mind of a twelve-year-old child—then again (it
had taken the traveler armed with his real fake passport
only a few days to see what he wanted to see, to know
what he wanted to know: it was at once pathetic, naive,
furious, deplorable), again by cunning, at the price of a
new so to speak moral subornation (this time effected on
the person of an Austrian with a swollen, terrible countenance (he had been savagely beaten in his country), he
in nothing but overalls, owning nothing more than a
Basque beret, a pair of broken-down shoes, a rifle, and
certain police connections), again, then, in a train of the
same kind which was taking him back where he had come

from, stopping also at the smallest stations, the merest level crossings, poorly lit sheds scrawled with graffiti and emblems of victory, and where, on the platforms, aside from a few figures in the brown overalls of mechanics, armed with long rifles, all you could see were scattered groups of people dressed like peasants grouped around vague heaps of luggage and waiting for no one knew what since virtually no one (unless furnished with the necessary papers) had the right to take the train: in one of the stations, at the end of the platform, virtually facing the place where the car had come to a stop, hung a rain-soaked flag; it might have been one of those red flags which signalmen carry rolled up under one arm and which they wave when the train leaves, but it was under no one's arm, waved by no one, it simply hung there, at the corner of the roof of a lamp-shed, its wooden pole curved by the weight of the material, not red but (insofar as the colors could be made out now, soaked as it was and hanging heavily) half red and half black, the rectangle divided diagonally (the black for mourning, for despair, for death); in the light from the nearby lamppost it was only a dark rag around which the continuously falling raindrops sparkled in tiny weals; the flag was too soaked for the wind, occasionally driving the rain against the car window, to do much more than make it sway faintly, and at its tip huge drops formed which would gradually distend, stretching into a pear shape, glistening in the light of the lamppost, and falling one after the other quite regularly; before starting up, the locomotive produced a sort of plaintive, lugubrious wail, repeated twice, suggesting the sound emitted by locomotives in westerns.

Three years. And eventually he must have managed to fall asleep somehow, for he started up when the door was suddenly and noisily slid open, the fierce light flooding the

compartment as they pushed into the narrow space one
after the other (but this happened so abruptly that they all
seemed to enter at once, already to have been there when
the light had come on, seeming enormous (perhaps because of the cramped space) in their black uniforms, their
leather equipment), as though engendered by the night
and the war, bringing with them at the same time as the
cool air from outside a smell of disasters (the smell of
grease and shoe polish and of well-fed bodies), talking
loud, the harsh voices questioning each other as they tossed
hard objects into the luggage nets with a clash of metal,
unbuckled their belts, tossing them up with their helmets
and guns (the train having stopped, the whole car now
filled with the sound of boots, of things thrown into the
nets and bumping against the partitions), then already sitting, their tunics unbuttoned (the train now moving again),
taking out of their haversacks chalky cheeses which crum-
bled as they spread them on the slices of bread before
beginning to chew—the whole episode (bursting in, taking
off equipment, settling down, opening packages of cheese,
chewing) concatenated with a sort of calm, innate, somehow mechanical violence, that is, the violence natural to
former farmhands, plowmen, or laborers (same round, reddish faces, same protruding muscles of chewing jaws, same
square-nailed hands, same way of holding the pieces of
cheese on the blade of the knife with one thumb as they
raised them to their mouths) somehow domesticated, the
way the gunpowder packed into the cartridge casing is
domesticated so long as the firing-pin doesn't hit the cap-
sule, and as pacific, as harmless as an unloaded pistol or
rifle—the butt nonetheless reinforced with that metal plate
meant to break a rib or crush a foot (or a face)—the two
reservists suddenly wakened, blinking painfully in the
light, slumped now in a corner of the benches on which

they had stretched out a little earlier—but none of the newcomers seemed to pay attention to them, nor seemed to want them out of there, nor even seemed to see them (simply, there were two seats less in the compartment they had been told to take), any more than they seemed particularly interested in or concerned by events (the anguished crowds, the weeping women, the tense faces, the huge headlines of the newspapers in which their food was wrapped), except that they (events) were making them get into trains in the middle of the night to get out (probably again in the middle of the night) when they were ordered to do so, taking advantage of the first favorable moment to take out their cheese, their bread, or their sausage, exchanging with their mouths full the jokes not of soldiers but of schoolboys, playing schoolboy tricks on each other, calling each other Toto or Charlot, as if there existed among them a language not so much of initiates as specific, elementary, consisting of a limited number of words and jokes, as if they belonged to a world apart, marginal to the groaning and fearful human race, like (with their unbuttoned field jackets revealing between the dark lapels paradoxically pastel shirts with mauve stripes or polka dots, with handkerchiefs of the same pastel colors knotted around their bull necks) creatures halfway between man (or rather stevedore, horse trader) and those spiny shellfish with a purplish interior consisting of an elementary digestive system and an elementary network of neurons: on an order from the corridor and with that same violence, that same savage docility, they stopped eating, made the cheeses vanish, buttoned up their tunics, pulled on their belts, and fully equipped all over again, helmeted now, chin strap like a sort of muzzle, rifles shouldered, hurrying after each other with a new clanking of metal, they left the compartment in Indian file while the train braked and once again came to a complete stop.

Soon after, he heard them lining up on the cinders of the deserted platform, stamping and pounding their gun butts. The faint light from a lamppost glistened on their black helmets as though on a formation of tortoises. It was another little station, and from the place where the car had stopped he could see nothing but gleaming rails and freight cars. After a moment the train started up again, slowly gaining speed, and on an enamel plaque nailed to a post the reservist (his companion in the leather jacket had already stretched out again on the bench) could read: CUL-MONT-CHALINDREY, the name suddenly looming out of the night, passing rapidly before their eyes and again swallowed up, as if, like the soldiers, it had been engendered, fabricated expressly by the darkness, vaguely menacing with its heavy consonance and steamlike hiss, to emerge here, far from everything (from light, from seas, from inhabited regions) in the depths of this time without dimensions in which the train continued to advance. No matter how hard he (the reservist) stared, he could see neither houses nor river nor hills nor sky. As if fields, woods, hills, and sky were indiscriminately soldered into a single and impenetrable blackness in which slowly drifted, illuminated by a few yellowish bulbs, a star-shaped structure whose arms extended into sheds where he could just make out, as though in some dark den, the locomotives. Two or three were half outside. From under the wheels of another, motionless on the turntable in the center of the star, emerged jets of gray steam. Then, the way a constellation or the lights of a harbor vanish, everything disappeared and it was dark again. As if, having stopped in accordance with the prescriptions of the signboard, the train thrust ahead into a world where night would never end, merely lit here and there by the unexpected glow of forges or of locomotive depots of which the Mobile Guard with their pale shirts, their chalky cheeses shoved into their cartridge belts, their shiny helmets, their shiny belts, their heavy boots, and their weapons with dark steel barrels were the vaguely mythic and fabulous guardians, dressed in black and harnessed like horses.

At the next stop they were replaced by something which in the darkness (they did not turn on the light, left the door open, calling to those who, still standing in the corridor, had found no seats) resembled one of those flights of tiny cheeping birds suddenly landing on a roof or in the corner of a garden, except that they were not cheeping, merely shouting like boys to keep up their spirits in the dark, suffusing their young, provincial voices with a forced gaiety and crudity, boasting, cursing the heads of State and the station workers who had dumped them into this dark- ness where they were wandering like blind men from one branch line to the next, taking trains in the wrong direction, exhausted, still half-drunk, in the dark handing each other bottles three-quarters empty, protesting, swearing, then all rushing out together at the next stop and vanishing, en- gendered by the night and swallowed up by it as the Mobile Guard had been. He heard their harsh voices fading at the end of a dimly lit platform. In the restored silence he noticed, between the jets of steam from the locomotive, the cool sound of an overflowing sluice and, invisible, quite close, like a shudder, the majestic rustle of a curtain of trees like some huge frantic murmur, unappeasable and threatening. He closed the window and then stretched out again.

When he awakened he was alone in the compartment and day was breaking. That is, beyond the window he could see a pale gray mist through which vague shapes passed. Outside, when he got off the train, he suddenly began to shiver. Over his shirt he was wearing only a light summer jacket, and he went back into the little station to pull on a sweater, then stood there, motionless, looking around him at the cold, empty room that seemed already devastated, although nothing in it was broken or destroyed, the woman at the newspaper stall rolling up the black shades that had covered the windows, already by habit apparently, as if in less than twenty-four hours he had abruptly passed not only from sunshine into cold but from a normal universe (including the crowds and the women in tears) to a severe, mourning, categorical world, the outside door opening, admitting with a clatter of boots two infantry soldiers, two men already middle-aged, wearing old sky-blue overcoats, helmets, and carrying gas masks strapped over their shoulders. At the sight of them, one of the two shapes lying on the wooden bench sat up and shook his companion. Like the new arrivals, these two were also wearing old military overcoats and they yawned as they strapped on their helmets. These men were also middle-aged and one man's face was furrowed with a deep, bright-pink scar across the middle of his nose. He rubbed his nose and his eyes and said: "Not too early, let's go for it," readjusted his gas mask on its shoulder strap, while his companion exchanged a few words with the men who had just relieved them, and they left the room. There were also conical black cardboard shades that had recently been put over the lamps. Some dirty crumpled papers were lying on the floor. The reservist went over to the newspaper stall, now that the woman had rolled up the shutter, and looked at the headlines, but they were the same ones as the day before. He went out onto the platform then and stood there a moment while two half-empty express trains passed without stopping. Finally a bus arrived and he got in. The bus too was almost empty. In a few minutes the mist dissolved completely. On the horizon, against a white sky, were silhouetted tall gray blast furnaces, factory chimneys, and an occasional steeple bedecked with baroque ornaments.

VII

1982–1914

*H*E had driven slowly the whole way, even stopping once, parking the car on the shoulder, turning off the ignition, lighting one of his little cigars and sitting there, hands resting on the wheel, watching the last rays of the sun gradually vanish behind the chain of icy peaks already covered by the first snows, until in a notch there remained, as in a crucible, no more than a tiny effervescence of melted gold, contracting or rather retracting, seeming to grow doubly bright, then nothing, his momentarily blinded eyes still staring at the darkening peaks, now a violent blue against the absinthe-colored sky, already gray toward the sea, while one after the next (as in a theater where the technicians have turned on and dimmed successive rows of spotlights, as if the whole sky were gradually catching fire) the scattered clouds now touched from below by the last rays were tinged blond, then bronze, then copper, then, in a continually darkening periwinkle sky, turning into long oblique streaks dangling their pink gauzelike fringes above the plain where the vines had dropped their last leaves, leaving the winter soil bare, stripped, wasted, abandoned to night, to silence, and to sleep.

One streak of light still persisted between the dark banks of the canal when he crossed it, shimmering, silver, tinged with jade, contrasting with the inert glow of the electric lights which came on now, strung out along the quays, spattering the scaly trunks of the plane trees with yellow, stagnant over the dazzling and aggressive roundabout of headlights, of red lights, the inert and impotent conglomerate of interlacing cars pursuing itself without advancing around the decorative palm trees, under the neon of the movie theaters and the stores, like a blind, sterile, and incoherent agitation while above the roofs, scarcely visible in the darkening sky, the flights of starlings circled in extended skeins, drew closer and condensed into blackened suns, then seemed to explode, spreading once again into a myriad of tiny and palpitating particles.

Then silence again, peace. As if at the heart of the old town (with its narrow streets now clogged by cars, stinking of gasoline, the ground floors of its old mansions gutted to give way to illuminated store windows inhabited by glittering mannequins as artificial as the palm trees, they too imported to match the fake-Riviera tinsel, the tinsel canned music drifting out the doors, the tinsel salesmen and saleswomen emerging fully dressed from their cars too, decked out in American surplus, hunters' jackets, or furs imported from Hong Kong or Chicago along with the tempting travel posters for Hong Kong or Chicago) the house constituted a kind of island, a sort of redeemed interval, preserved in space and time (the house where she had lived as a girl, the woman who was later to bear him in her womb, where he himself had lived as a child and grown up under ceilings fifteen feet high, between two widows, one always stubbornly dressed in black, the other, a very old lady with a ruined face, a permanent mask of affliction made, seemingly, of solidified wax tears, the two women (daughter and mother) merged so to speak in their widowed condition, watching over the child with a sort of fierce and possessive passion until the daughter (the widowed daughter) had joined her mother under the stone surrounded by cypresses, after which (first dressed in the strict uniform of the strict religious institution, then in jackets and trousers that aggressively defied any sense of a uniform: the carefully studied informality (tweed and flannel) of a fake Oxford student or an apprentice cubist) he had returned only occasionally, occupying in passing, almost as a stranger, the half of the house he had inherited (that is, the half of about a thousand square yards of structures (shed, stable, cellars, staircase, veranda, salons, dining rooms, bedrooms, corridors, kitchens, pantries, closets, attics) surrounding a courtyard, a garden, and a terrace)— and now he was an old man in his turn, had sold his half of the mausoleum, had fled the irresistible tide of juke boxes and vendors of American clothes to go live in the country, in another of the houses he had inherited, this one entirely his: the house with the pavements decorated with red and black flowers and the carved marble mantelpiece in front of which once sat the old patriarch slowly ingesting the pyramids of figs), and now, of all who had lived here once, there remained only two old ladies, two more widows with ivory faces and white hair, and who, in the days when he could not yet walk, when he was still carried by a black woman brought back from the island of boa constrictors, were already dressed in gowns with pleated skirts, in middy blouses over which tumbled their adolescent curls, their knees still bare, their calves sheathed in dark socks, but old enough at the time to remember (and not only they: it was as if the house itself, the enormous mass of masonry, the room (the one where almost two hundred years before, on the night of a lost battle, a remote ancestor had come to blow his brains out) where the three of them were now, he sitting in a stiff tapestried armchair beside the pedestal table where they had put the crystal wine cooler and the plate of biscuits, the four walls, bricks, mortar, gravel, the white marble mantel against which, it was said, the defeated general had leaned in order to prop the pistol against his temple, the hexagonal tiles, also preserved, in the fashion of those heavy mahogany boxes, those cases that show the empty shapes of the weapons or of the jewels that have been removed from them, the memory) what had happened sixty-eight years ago: the scene, the tableau which had served as a prelude to the brutal intrusion, among the laughter, the outbursts of joy and the odors of the bouquets, of that violence from outside, breaking into their adolescent lives, the lives of young women for whom, till now, death removed, gently, even stealthily, only the sick or the very old: that thing which in its crudity, its brutality, had come to attack them, had driven the youngest of them out of the house, running down the beach, suffering from a child's unconsolable grief, her face in her hands, her shoulders shaken by sobs.

And they told that story, sometimes making him repeat his questions, straining to hear, their ivory faces attentive, wrinkled by reflection while they tried to remember, their dreamy voices speaking in turn, a little absently, as though from a great distance, filled no longer with grief—it was too long ago, now—but with compassion, with pity: scarcely three weeks after they had witnessed, in this same room, the definitive departure of the man who had entered the family so to speak by breaking and entering, by ravishing if such might be called, in both senses of the word, what had been a sort of rape, an abduction: suddenly appearing with his beard, his dark uniform, and his boots from faraway, vaguely fabulous countries in order to seduce an idle heifer of a woman, to marry her, to carry her off over the oceans, the warm seas, to an island inhabited by black savages, to bring her back with the child he had given her, to restore her to this citadel, this fortress of somnolent respectability, and to abandon her there, to go off somewhere into the woods or the beetfields to a rendezvous with a piece of metal; this, then: the sweltering summer afternoon coming to an end, the beach (he had still known it more or less as it was then, that is, not bordered—it too—with deafening juke boxes, with concrete apartment buildings, with fast-food stores, with tame palm trees, with shops offering gold lamé bikinis and yachting accessories, with neon lights and gaudy signs, with parking lots and bars: nothing but a long stretch of sand where the waves rolled up and died, and, protected by low dunes, their terraces and ground floors invaded by sand, some twenty or thirty villas with whimsical gables and turrets, lined up on either side of a tramway terminus, a simple plank shed like the kind used for warehouses, brownish, the paint peeling in the salt air, the rails ending against a buffer, it too half buried in the sand, a plank road leading to a bathhouse or rather a group of wooden sheds forming the three sides of a square from which, on Sundays, when the wind carried, came the echoes of a band to the sound of which the counterjumpers and shopgirls of the town would dance, but empty the rest of week) . . . the beach that summer (or rather at the end of that summer) not empty but deserted, just as most of the villas had been abandoned in a state of emergency, and only six or seven groups on the huge expanse, as well as five or six boats drawn up on the sand and in the shadow of which women in black were mending nets, and they (the two old ladies who were talking now) in those bathing costumes that in those days were like dresses, severely buttoned up to the neck, with loose tunics and knickers fastened tightly below the knee, wearing bonnets festooned with flowers, holding hands, jumping with each of the waves that rolled toward them, unrolled, broke over their shoulders, sometimes knocking them down, half-drowning them, so that deafened by the huge rumble of the sea, all they saw at first (perhaps one of them capsized by a wave, managing to regain her footing, coughing, dazed) was, above the line of the dunes, between two villa roofs, the parasol, then the hat, itself like a parasol or a lampshade, then the head, the torso, then the whole woman, walking as fast as her city shoes would allow, having just got off the tram, twisting her heels in the sand, growing larger and clearer as she crossed the width of the beach, struggling with something that made her gesticulate like a clown or a doll, raising and lowering her parasol like a signal, already shouting perhaps (but her voice lost in the racket of the waves, the cascades of foam, the immensity), and having reached the water's edge, still holding her parasol, hopping on one leg, removing her shoes, throwing them behind her one after the other, and without even taking off her stockings entering the water herself, her long skirt tucked up, ignoring the splashing water, the bottom of her dress already drenched, and despite this continuing to come toward them, still shouting, while the bathers drew closer, until they could understand what she had already doubtless been shouting since she had climbed the dune, what she had not ceased shouting during the whole time it had taken her to cross the beach with that limping gait, those wild gesticulations, the movements of a puppet, the voice hoarse from shouting now dominating the indifferent racket of the breakers, of the foam, of the wind, repeating for perhaps the hundredth time the news with something terrified, excited, and at the same time funereal in her voice, the sentence that sixty-eight years later the ones who had been playing then in the water still seemed to hear: "They say in town that Captain . . ." (and in the uproar of the breaking waves, of the harsh cries of the gulls, they had had no need to hear the name, knew it already, already understood what was to follow) ". . . has been killed!"

The same room, then, the same bedroom where they were now sitting, the three of them (and one of them saying: You want a little more wine? Take another biscuit, and he: A bisc . . . ? No, I'm fine. No. I . . . Then you . . . And the younger one saying: It was the next day that Papa received the telegram. And he: The telegram? From where? and she: From the town hall. Or somewhere. Or maybe he went there and they told him about it there. Everyone in town was already talking about it. Your mother and our grandmother had taken you to the mountains. You used to have trouble with the heat, you suffered from . . . , and he: And then? and she: Then Papa took the car and went to tell them . . .) the same bedroom, the same mantelpiece, and at a hundred and twenty years' interval the triple agony, that of the woman who on that day already realized she was dead, and that of the two men: the first in a wig (or perhaps without a wig, without the extravagant plumed bicorne, his hair uncombed, dirty, his face unshaven, his uniform filthy with mud or dust), the other with his square beard, his waxed mustache, his short hair carefully brushed, his china-blue eyes, already prepared, doubtless needing only to buckle on his cross-belt, adjust his pistol, slip his binoculars and his map case over his shoulder, and, in the courtyard, the first broken-down, similarly muddy or dusty horse, its flanks torn by spurs, the reins flung to a groom (the scene lit perhaps by a lantern, the booted figure already vanishing up the stairs without turning around, then the vague light of a torch (perhaps of a simple candle) behind the windows, coming and going, suddenly stopping, then a little later on that night no doubt (the time it took to scribble a few lines on a scrap of paper—or to burn papers—or simply to stand there motionless beside the cold fireplace staring perhaps into empty air, the void—or almost immediately perhaps, in the same movement, the time it takes to load the weapon, the action decided upon, already begun while he was still galloping, already almost performed) the explosion, then other gleams of light, doors slammed, shouts . . .), the second horse (the horse which three weeks later would scarcely drag itself, skeletal, filthy, exhausted, buckling under the load not of its rider but of equipment, rucksacks, weapons of dead soldiers—or perhaps dead itself) still fresh, just out of the stable, the leather saddle gleaming and at his side the glistening saber guard: and on the two occasions the ringing of the horseshoes on the pavement echoed by the vault of the portico, a spattering of sparks, the noise which a handful of marbles can make falling on a sheet of metal, and which, they said, when it reached them (that is, when it reached the occupants of the bedroom gathered around the couple and the child: they told how it was just like what they had read in those Russian families where, before one of the members undertakes a journey, all the relatives and even the servants—at least, the house servants, as this time the black woman—gather together and sit down in a room, waiting for the moment of the departure) made them start, shiver, he already standing, simply saying in a hoarse, calm voice, as if he were going to catch the train or the bus: "Well, now it's time, let's go," handing to the black woman the child he had been holding on his knee, buckling on his equipment, perhaps assisted by the woman with whom he had spent this last night—or perhaps only a few hours: returning late from the barracks after a last inspection, undressing, stretching out beside her, pulling her to him, and she stiff, silent, frozen—or perhaps drawing him to her one last time with a kind of fierce avidity, opening herself to him, receiving him, clinging, already mad, gasping, in a furious protest, a furious, lacerating, and ultimate embrace, and now stiff again, eyes dry, taking from the bed and handing them to him one after the other that shoulder strap, the weapon, the binoculars, without taking her eyes off that face, those lips, then following him while he passed through that same glass door in front of which she had stood four years earlier, fainting with happiness, almost intoxicated, leaning on his arm, posing for the photographer in her bridal gown, among her happy cousins in their white cravats, in the uproar of voices and the clatter of champagne flutes from the salon, all the others passing through the door too, then stopping as he turned around, kissed them in turn, leaned over, saying in a voice half-reproachful, half-joking, to the youngest of the two little girls (of the two old ladies now) in their middy blouses: "You, you're green!" caressing her cheek, smiling, crossing the whole length of the veranda, then coming to a halt in front of the stiff ghost with the bloodless face standing between him and the door of the landing, who said only: "The last one for me."

Perhaps he simply made a sign. Or perhaps there was not even any need for that. Doubtless the black woman was still quite close to that kind of thing, that is, she came from a part of the world or rather of a universe where combat, death, disaster are as familiar as pleasure, hunger, or sleep. In any case, when he went out into the courtyard, then reappeared (now they had opened both of the French doors in the center of the veranda, all standing there in their pale summer clothes, the suntanned children with their serious, alarmed expressions, the women in their complicated chignons, the man too old to go, pressed against the balcony with its elegant cast-iron scrolls), the black woman was walking right behind him, with the same rapid, decisive, supple, animal gait, like, with her mysterious ebony face, her ebony hands holding the child, and her long draped toga floating over her heels at each step, some statue from the depths of time, from the very womb of the world, and they (the two old ladies who were talking now) told how she stopped at the same time that he did, motionless, standing there, hands empty now, arms hanging alongside her body, the open palms showing the paler, brownish-pink skin, while the man in uniform took the child, held it close a moment before relinquishing it to her again, the arms, the apparently wooden hands closing over the child, then remaining there, still resembling in the long vertical folds of that garment a column of marble; and this: the group: the orderly still standing at the horse's head, holding it by the bridle under the bit, the horse nervous perhaps, pawing the ground, raising and replacing its hooves one after the other, the iron shoes ringing on the pavement in the silence, and a brief moment (two seconds, perhaps three—and no one can see if in the beard or the shadowy face the lips of either one have stirred) the man decked out for war, barbarous in his dark tunic, booted, belted, resting one hand on the shoulder of that statue, that column surmounted by an impassive ritual mask and which seemed delegated here, at this precise moment when his own life was collapsing, by those lands, those fierce, remote continents, from which he had brought her back, as though to preside, mute, at once docile, ancillary, and funereal, over some ceremonial: the falling-due, the point of arrival of those twenty years during which the former little peasant who would dig up potatoes, lead the cattle to water (or rather the cow: they (his family) had never possessed more than the one cow), later wielding the scythe, pushing the barrows of manure, splitting the wood between two nights spent over books, had run not after the fortune (wearing under his uniform those coarse linen shirts which his sisters sewed for him, sleeping under the stifling mosquito nets in those pajamas which they also cut to his measurements—or naked, clasping in his arms the body of some native girl—getting himself assigned for some meager supplemental pay to remote posts in the bush, cut off, severed for months from the civilized world, confronting fevers, drinking filthy water, economizing every sou—borrowing perhaps—until at the end of this askesis (he knew that it was not a question of money, that nothing other than this long ordeal could permit him to penetrate to the interior of this caste, this citadel) he could buy the ring, the diamond, the magic pebble), but in some sense after the password, the introduction in the form of fringed epaulettes, of spurs, and of the dress uniform which would grant him access to the inaccessible princess, the indolent and idle sultana in whom he could deposit his seed, drawing from her a son, and once this was done, like those male insects which, having performed their function, go off somewhere and die: and then detaching his hand from her shoulder, turning away (there was now something almost violent in his gestures, something hasty, though still precise), putting his foot in the stirrup, then mounting, gathering up the reins in one hand, quickly adjusting the folds of his tunic while the orderly released the bridle, stepped back, the pavement of the courtyard already ringing under the horse's hooves, the broad back striped by the two overlapping straps moving away, then, at the moment of passing through the gate, the torso pivoting in a three-quarters turn in the saddle, and all that could still be seen for a fraction of a second was the profile, the square beard, the arm raised in a final gesture, after which the horse and its rider turned right, and then simply the empty street from which some passers-by, pausing, cast a curious glance through the gate still open as though for a party, a wedding, as long ago after the departure of the carriage in which the old man with the goatee, the last male descendant of a colossal Empire general, went four times a year to visit his properties: the empty courtyard with its two dwarf palm trees in their boxes, its magnolias, its two rows of decorative plants, the fringe of ivy which hung from the veranda, and in the middle, where he had left her, the strange and barbaric divinity draped in immaculate linen, holding a child in her black hands.

Then she moved, vanished, reappeared an instant later to the left of the veranda, rejoined the group surrounding the woman who had also remained standing, her hands clutching the balcony railing, still staring sightlessly at the open gate, the street, the curious onlookers, until someone of the group leaned over, shouting something, and the concierge moved toward the gate. This was a thin woman with a goiter half concealed beneath a black serge scarf, a yellow birdlike face (a nose like a beak), lusterless, reptilian eyes between folds of pink flesh. She crossed the courtyard deliberately, arched her sickly body to push closed one after the other the enormous leaves of the gate, and fastened the heavy hasp which bolted them, after which she closed the smaller door inset in the left-hand leaf of the gate. The whole structure was massive, painted dark green, reinforced with thick chevrons and iron bars. The small door locked by means of a swing-bolt. Pushed by the woman and under the momentum of its mass, it slammed with the sound of a hammer on an anvil. Turning back toward her lodge, the concierge could see that up on the veranda they were trying to lead into her room the woman who had taken the bundle of lace from the black woman's arms. The veranda remained empty for a moment. A little later someone came out of the bedroom, moved from right to left toward the middle of the gallery, the left arm grasping in passing one of the still-open French doors, the right arm extending to grasp the other door, the silhouette for a fraction of a second appearing crucified, the arms spread wide, then the doors closed.

VIII

1939–1940

A small crowd pressed against the gates of
the abandoned factory, a little beyond the brothels, where
the cavalry mobilization center had been set up: about two
hundred men carrying valises or rucksacks, most of them
young but bearing no resemblance to the ones who had
got on the train the day before or during the night; as if—
just like the little station with its black-curtained windows—the dawn mist, the sopping woods, the melancholy
rolling landscape somehow implied these already bloated,
already worn faces, almost all wearing the same caps under
which their coarsely cut hair stuck out, their bodies stuffed
into the same tight jackets, with the same shirts buttoned
up to the severe collars, or even in their Sunday best, with
the same loud neckties and the same vaguely anxious,
vaguely miserable expressions, like the crowds that gather
in a village square after some natural catastrophe, hailstorm
or flood, or in front of the church for a funeral, silent or
murmuring in low, inaudible voices.

Occasionally a uniformed orderly opened the gate and

let in about twenty men at a time, the rest advancing a few yards, shuffling their feet, picking up their valises or pushing them ahead with one foot along the black cinders, then resuming their conversations, the humble and passive murmur, the humble and passive calculations of the harvests still in the field, of tillage, of beets to be dug and cattle requisitioned.

The fog had set in again, deposited now with an inaudible rustle in tiny grayish droplets, like a mildew, on the clothes, the caps, the farmers' shirts, the jackets of a few city slickers venturing a joke from time to time, noisily calling to an acquaintance, the shouts broken off, stifled as though swallowed up by the fog, the susurration of the patient, anxious voices. The strong smell of the nearby gas factory filled the air. Inside the shed long trestle tables had been set up, covered with files, records, and ledgers, behind which sat uniformed officers, their gloves sticking out under their képis set beside the files.

Twenty-four hours later (the weather was fine now—the setting sun of late summer glistened on the grass, on the still-green leaves, a bluish mist blurred the soft contours of the distant hills) the reservist, or rather the corporal (since, wearing a new uniform—everything was new: clothes, shoes, the just-tanned leather leggings, the oily black guns unpacked from the crates, the frozen sides of beef bearing the violet seal the Argentine health service had stamped on them three or four years before, the thousands of tons of gummy rice doubtless stockpiled for years as well in anticipation of what was now happening), was sewing onto the sleeves of his tunic the two blue chevrons which he had just been forcibly awarded and which entitled (or rather obliged) him to organize forage parties, stable watch, and mess duty—in other words, to negotiate (with the five cavalrymen he was supposed to command, with whom he slept in the haylofts, shared the gummy rice, went drinking in the taverns) the prosaic distribution of everyday tasks, and nothing more: three, then, sitting in the orchard grass, he and two others (a puny Jew, errand boy (or clerk or bookkeeper) in a dry-goods shop in the rue des Franc-Bourgeois, and a jockey: an Italian—or at least with an Italian name though he was mobilized in the French army—who rose through hell and high water: that is, not one of those dwarfs, one of those little monkeys pickled in steam, the kind you can see crouching, tiny and wan, on the back of some broken-down nag, but a boy of normal size, with the square face and melancholy gaze of a *condottiere* or a bravo, right out of the frame of an old master, flesh pitted with smallpox, the thin lips of some duke or count painted in profile and dressed in red against a background of pearly hills bristling with bushes) watching him try over and over (breaking the thread or losing it, moistening it, squinting as he worked it through the needle's eye, losing it again, starting over) to sew on the fallacious chevrons, all three wearing the same earth-colored uniforms in which the Jew (he was so puny that a stranger coming upon the group would have taken him for the jockey), with his cropped hair, his prominent ears, his skinny neck emerging from the loose collar of his tunic like a plucked chicken or a mouse costumed as a soldier in absurdly oversized boots, nonetheless deemed qualified for service after a final examination, that is, after having waited in the line of conscripts, then being moved forward in his turn, knees shackled by his lowered trousers, suspenders dangling, in the tiny country *mairie* where the medical officer successively hefted the testicles of farmboys and beet growers (the favorable judgment rendered, not without hesitation perhaps, almost reluctantly, assignment to such a branch (the cavalry) of a Jew (as the medical officer had realized not only from the sound of the name called out by the nurse holding the file but also *de visu,* under the shirttail brutally pulled aside) being the result (the officer doubtless thought) only of some aberration, if not of some sardonic and facetious malevolence (that is, malevolence with regard to the branch, to the whole cavalry corps), if not even of a deliberate outrage on the part of the mobilization center): the only one of the three reservists (or rather already cavalrymen, one of whom was to find himself raised to the rank of corporal as soon as he had completed the delicate demands of his sewing), the only one of the three, actually, who did not seem to be in costume (that is, who wore his riding breeches with a certain naturalness, even the poorly cut variety issued by the quartermaster, as if he had emerged booted and spurred from his mother's womb, or rather as if he belonged to a species, a special race, halfway between horse and man, furnished instead of legs with something, like fauns or satyrs, on the order of pasterns and hooves) being the Italian who was telling, while attentively watching the clumsy oscillations of the needle, how he had been rewarded for his first win at the age of thirteen by a couple of stinging slaps and a kick that almost broke his coccyx, bestowed by the trainer who had run the (unfortunately winning) horse only to lower its odds in some future race: he spoke without raising his voice (a slightly husky voice with just a hint of coarseness in the accent) and only when someone insisted: the insistence of the corporal at grips not only with his laborious sewing but also with the awareness of the void, not actually of his twenty-six years, since from them would have to be subtracted those of his early childhood and those he had spent in the religious institution requiring the severe and already military uniform, but counting accurately, ten good years, or, differently calculated, one hundred and twenty months of idleness, of impostures and ineptitudes accumulated in order to conceal from himself his nonexistence (and he could recall: Berlin, the Friedrichstrasse station, the evening or rather already the night, the Mexican and himself already installed in their sleeping car, their train to Warsaw still in the station, and on another platform a swarming crowd of men, women, and children loaded with bundles, waiting to get into a train consisting of third-class cars, and the two of them, the two casual tourists, watching with at first just the curiosity of tourists in a foreign country, then with a growing feeling of discomfort, then (when they saw the several uniformed figures walking among the bundles, the suitcases, and the children, pushing them—without any special brutality, in fact with patience, but inexorably, tranquilly, as machines might have done it—even sometimes helping them hoist themselves up, themselves and their bundles, into the cars, and finally closing the doors, remaining on the empty platform) understanding, the Mexican then breaking into profanity, both of them lowering the shade with the same impulse and sitting there, incapable of exchanging a word, side by side on the already made-up lower berth in the compartment with the little pink lampshades and the mahogany woodwork, incapable even of looking at each other)—ten years, then (added to the sixteen more spent in that upholstered cocoon of childhood), which now found their fulfillment (their sanction? he thought: but the jockey and the puny little Jew were also similarly furnished) in the form of an oval brass tag attached to his wrist by a tiny chain, perforated lengthwise and bearing, on each side of this easily broken median line, similarly perforated, his registration number and his name: "So that," the jockey said, "they can keep one half to bring their losses up to date, and send the other half to your

family. Of course," he added, "they may throw in a decoration. I would guess it's automatic, when it comes posthumously. Some people have them framed. Which the
horses are not entitled to. Besides, you'd have to take an
axe to the horseshoe engraved with each registration number and send it in a bag to the auditing department. So
they could be sure the horse wasn't stolen. But who'd want
to steal anyone like you and me? Or a Yid who rides a
horse like a prick on a cake of soap? Don't get mad, Levy:
we're all in the same boat." He didn't say "boat," but another word. "My name isn't Levy," said the little Jew. "And
mine isn't Macaroni. But that's what the neighbors' kids
called me when I was little. That hasn't kept me from
wasting my time for a year's service and ending up here
today. And as for where they're sending us, Levy, Isaac,
Abraham, Blum, Macaroni, or Mohammed, it's all the
same; we're all grist for the same mill. Of course, thanks
to the little chain, they won't need to cut off our hands at
the wrist. Damn lucky they didn't think of tattooing those
numbers on the back of our hand, like the plugs. Hell!
You see the bureau of audits filled with chopped-off hands?
Not to mention the effect on the bereaved to receive a
nice little box with one of those things wrapped up in
cotton . . ." He never said "the horses" or "that horse,"
but "the plugs" or "that plug" (sometimes "that nag" when
he meant a mare), always talking without raising his voice,
as though he were speaking to a nervous horse (or the way
he would have spoken to a nervous trainer—or owner),
that is, the way he had learned to talk to anyone since the
age of eleven when he had been placed as an apprentice
by his mason father who had brought his countless family
from Italy: that slightly husky voice which he owed to the
brutal and meretricious world where he had been raised
by thrashings with stirrup leather, sleeping in the straw

alongside the horses, waking with them, and, so to speak, eating with them too (or more exactly, after he had fed them), with this difference, that instead of substantial rations of oats, he devoured wretched scraps gone cold in the tin mess kits, so that it was in the same tone of voice, neither mocking nor aggressive, without any special cordiality either, simply the way he would have indicated to an owner that his horse was limping or wouldn't go the distance (the owner not a maharajah or some press or music-hall magnate in a pearl-gray top hat and wearing a frock coat like the ones you can see in the fashion pages of the newspapers: butchers, cattle dealers, or seedy provincial landowners, in Brittany or the southwest where he rode in stadiums with wooden galleries or sometimes without galleries and sometimes not even stadiums: simply tracks mown in a field, indicated by ribbons or ropes attached to stakes, with a wooden booth for placing bets, a public of cattle merchants pulling out of their pockets thick bundles of banknotes secured with red rubber bands, money they had made just that morning at the local horse fair; and sometimes obliged to escape cross-country, pursued by furious bettors, when he wasn't carried out on a stretcher with a wrist, an arm, or a leg broken—at twenty-six he already counted five fractures whose calluses you could feel under the hard muscles), the monotonous, placid voice, without even a jeering intonation, saying to the Jewish clerk from the rue des Francs-Bourgeois: "With a name like yours and the way they are on the other side, you'd better not make any mistake about trying to get yourself taken prisoner," the sort of mouse dressed up as a cavalryman saying: "I know. Thanks. I'll watch out for that" (as it turned out, he was to be taken prisoner, and in the most ridiculous way: the train bringing the men returning from leave reaching its destination, and the doors of the cars wrenched open by laughing giants in round helmets and willow-green uniforms, machine-guns under their arms, shouting in their guttural and laughing voices: *"Halé! Raus! Efferyvone aus . . . Loos, loos! . . ."*—and then this: the dark, stifling car for eight horses and forty men, in which for two hours already, with seventy-five others like himself, the corporal was imprisoned (it was night, on a siding of the station of a tiny Belgian town where all the balconies were gaily flying the obsessive red flame stamped with the obsessive black emblem and where he had arrived the day before after having for the first time crossed the southern half of Belgium on horseback, then having crossed it in the other direction, still on horseback (but sometimes at a gallop, pursued by bombs or machine-gun fire), then crossing once again (following almost the same itinerary as in the opposite direction, but this time on foot, under armed escort, dying of thirst and his stomach lacerated by cramps), then following (eating grass, one evening, in a meadow where they had been dumped for the night) the trajectory he hadn't been able to continue on horseback the first time, then one whole day shut up in the school of the little town all hung with the scarlet flags, and now in this car and the virtual impossibility of moving a limb without ten or twelve other limbs belonging to other bodies being obliged to move in a chain reaction in a concert of swearing, obscenities, and curses, and suddenly the sliding door wrenched open from outside, and at the same time that the cool night air penetrated, struggled with the viscous stench of the crushed bodies, a shape looming black against the black of the opening, and something like a struggle then, as if in a sort of gesticulating pantomime of human shadows the confrontation was repeated, the conflict, the combat between the suffocating interior stench and the cool purity of the outside air, a voice which he (the corporal) immediately recognized, and more exhausted than resigned, more outraged than plaintive, still quite sonorous, saying without their knowing whether it was addressing the silhouettes who were pushing from outside or the furious shadows struggling in the opposite direction, saying: "You don't have to hit me! I . . . You don't . . . ," the concert of shouting voices submerging it, smothering it, screaming: "There are already seventy-five of us in here, it's murder, there are already . . . ," the racket of the sliding door closing again, the dark, the clang of the bolt outside, the guttural voices fading, the silence again inside although a muffled noise of blows and oaths continued to come from the direction of the door, and then the corporal shouting the Christian name (only the Christian name), shouting his own name, shouting "Over here! Over here! Let him through, for God's sake! Let him through, shit, we're in the same regi . . . We're together, we . . ." still shouting and struggling at the same time while the blows rained down on him, thinking in a flash Good God but these aren't men this is a load of mules! . . . then without either one or the other being able to say how they managed it, next to each other now, touching each other, embracing, the corporal repeating "Good God! Good God! How did you . . . Good God . . . !" something warm and sticky streaming over the two bodies, the two panting respirations trying to find air, the two invisible faces in the darkness coated by something liquid and salty . . .).

But that hadn't happened yet; for the moment he (the corporal) held up, dangling it by the collar, the tunic on the sleeves of which he had finished sewing the double chevrons, brushing off the cloth and smoothing out the stripes, the jockey saying: "Congratulations! I don't know how you did it! . . ." then lying back on the grass, stretching, straightening out one arm to pick up one of the plums

that strewed the ground around them without anyone's
having come to the orchard to harvest them (the first day,
the woman and the children still on the farm had brought
their baskets from town—baskets the size of laundry baskets—as full as when they had left and had dumped out
the contents at the foot of a tree), while the corporal,
standing now, pulled on his tunic, buckled his cross-belt,
and said: "Let's go see if that fine woman in the bistro can
make an omelette for us, or something edible, I'm paying . . ."

And four days after that, he (the corporal) was standing,
one shoulder leaning against the open door of a freight
car, the jockey having remained with the squadron's horses
in the last car where they had been loaded, the Jew squatting beside him on the floor, leaning against the side of
the car, silent, occasionally glancing outside through the
corporal's legs and between the bodies of the four or five
cavalrymen sitting, legs dangling, in the doorway and who,
since morning, since the train had started, hadn't stopped
shouting and singing, calling out to men working in the
fields (the train wasn't moving much faster than a galloping
horse), railroad workmen, girls, or anybody who happened
to be watching them (standing motionless at level crossings
or on the platforms of stations they passed through), brandishing bottles and if not really getting drunk, drowning
out everything with their songs and their shouts. As if, in
the space of four days (the four days they had spent billeted
in the village where the orchards were strewn with un-
harvested plums, fingering their equipment and their weapons, getting used to orders and to the horses all over again),
the timid and peaceable beet-growers or the peaceable
salesmen who had docilely crowded at the gate of the gas
factory with their little valises, like refugees from some
disaster, some cosmic cataclysm, speaking in low voices,

anxious and glancing around them uneasily, had, in putting on the uniform and fastening their spurs, put on at the same time a sort of anonymous and virile disguise in which they could now give free rein to an aggressive rage, an aggressive rancor, challenging this world which less than a week before was still theirs and which now excluded them, condemned them, transported them like cattle toward some ineluctable fate of cattle against which they raised, in the form of filthy language and obscene songs, an ultimate and impotent protest.

Evening was falling and low clouds of a cold metallic gray were streaming above the pines around the station where for a moment the interminable convoy of dirty-pink cars had come to a halt beside a platform where a civilian train had stopped on the other side, an express with long green cars of which the windows framed the faces of travelers contemplating with mute consternation the slovenly groups of men crowded in the openings of the sliding doors and whose gesticulations and songs, which had begun to grow listless and quiet down, seemed reanimated, fired up or rather exacerbated by that very consternation, redoubling as if under the effect of a challenge, of a provocation, of a festive and intolerable parody, at the sight of the gas masks worn over their shoulders—the way they might have worn landing nets or fly rods—by the members of a little family just getting off the express and hurrying toward the underground passage as though pursued, tracked step by step by a series of fierce shouts, the father and mother burdened with suitcases pushing ahead of them in a desperate flight, as though to protect them from a shocking and painful scene, two little girls who kept turning around, and then this: one of the travelers who had also got off the express and who was heading for the exit stopping suddenly in front of the opening where the corporal stood, leaning on the doorjamb above the drunken group stirring at his feet, and then spreading with both hands, the front page turned toward the shouters, a newspaper of which the headline showed this time in letters so huge that each of the two words filled the whole width of the page (and the two together its height as well): GENERAL MOBI-LIZATION.

For a long time afterwards he (the corporal) would remember that man standing, the spread newspaper concealing his face of which he could see above the headline only two eyes staring at him with a kind of rage, reproach, and vindictive spite. In a few moments the civilian train and the military convoy started up almost simultaneously and in opposite directions. Soon it had grown dark, and with the darkness, though it was only early September, a sudden chill, as if there had been a storm somewhere. In the car, excitement had given way to sullen silence and one after the other those who had been at the door all day, legs dangling, withdrew to the interior of the car and sat down like the others, backs leaning against the wall of the car, knees bent, taciturn. Someone had lit a lantern set on the floor which illuminated from below the thirty men now motionless and silent. In the rectangle of the door, which after a while they had slid halfway shut because of the chill, they could see undulating against an almost black sky the jagged and now completely dark line of the tree-tops.

*   *
*   *

A light rain was falling when the train stopped, late at night, in the middle of a field apparently, for they saw neither buildings nor any lights but those of storm lanterns or fainter flashlights fluttering here and there like fireflies, furtive in the darkness, according to the comings and goings of their invisible bearers. For a moment there were only brief commands, calls, then the rattle of the sliding doors being pushed shut, then the shouts and cries of the men bent under the weight of the heavy planks leading up to the doors, then one after the other appeared the fantastic and whinnying silhouettes of the horses, looming black for a second against the shimmering background of the rain around a lantern, resisting at first, pulling back on the bridle, hindquarters braced, then suddenly springing forward, cantering down the inclined plane in a brief drumming of hooves on the planks, surrounded for a moment by the shafts of light turning like the spokes of a wheel, and then again engulfed by darkness. Groping their way, the cavalrymen began saddling the horses again, adding the heavy packs and the swords. They worked in silence now, sometimes smothering an oath when one of them got tangled in the straps or skinned a finger on the tongue of a buckle.

When everything was done, they lined up at the head of their mounts in the cindery mud, gradually beginning to stink of the sweat cooling on their shoulders and down their backs. With the visors of their helmets gleaming faintly under the rain that kept falling, their faces invisible, their dim silhouettes huddled in their long overcoats and their spurs occasionally flashing, they resembled some kind of birds with sopping plumage, iron beaks and claws, set there at regular intervals as though on a chessboard beside their apocalyptic steeds with their long necks hanging as though overwhelmed by the weight of the rain which gradually stuck the hair together in dark patches slowly spreading on either side of their clipped manes and on their hindquarters. Now and again the light from a lantern revealed the tiny circles of silver which seemed repeatedly

to blossom, vanish, and reappear on the surface of the
puddles of black water.

Hitherto, busy getting the horses out of the cars, lining
them up and saddling them, they (the cavalrymen) had not
noticed the rain. Or at least they had paid no attention to
it. Now, in the silent dark, they could hear it falling continuously on the roofs of the empty cars, on the helmets,
on the leather saddles and saddlebags. Not that it constituted, strictly speaking, a problem: they simply became
aware of it. But, like the rest, they accepted it. As if, for
them, it inevitably participated in what they had already
consented to from the moment they left their houses and
their farms, then stripped off their clothes, putting on at
the same time as those furnished by the army (itemized
down to the most intimate—undershirts and shorts—in
contact now with their flesh and their sweat (as though to
indicate that starting from this moment their flesh, their
sweat itself, would no longer belong to them) with a med-
dling and maniacal concern for detail in the quartermaster's
records along with the rations necessary for feeding these
same bodies and the cartridges destined to tear others
apart), something which had succeeded the anxiety, the
stupor, and which was now nothing more than a passive
indignation, the mere registering of the ineluctable and of
the accomplished fact, just as they had registered, vaguely
bewildered but not really surprised, perhaps without even
quite understanding its meaning, the enormous headline
in huge black letters, like a funeral announcement (of their
own death) which was spread out over the whole length
and breadth of the front page of the newspaper unfolded
a few hours earlier before their eyes.

And now it was simply as if the rain had to be there
too, at this rendezvous to which, so that everything would

be in order, it had been summoned along with the night, that is, not the rain you watch falling on the other side of a pane of glass or that you hear drumming on a roof, but the rain beneath which you remain motionless, standing or sitting on a horse, as long as it chooses to fall and exactly as if it were not falling. After a brief whistle from its locomotive lacerating the shadows (somehow spiteful, ironic, and contemptuous) and in the racket of its shifting couplings, the empty train had left, irremediably abandoning them, solitary and wretched, as if they had been released from the last link of the chain (or rather of the umbilical cord) still connecting them to their past life, and it now seemed to them as if they had been here for hours, condemned by all appearances to remain here forever, to melt and slowly dissolve, still standing (it would doubtless be, starting with the feet, only a question of time, he thought; he must have had to learn this: that henceforth time was a notion without meaning, that you could sleep, remain awake or motionless, walk or eat at any hour of the day or night and under any conditions: in the dark, under the sun, in the snow, at dawn, at twilight, dry or soaked—or frozen—to the bone), until the moment when there would be no more of them and their anachronistic steeds left but little heaps that had returned to the original mud, rising here and there on the cinder track among the puddles of water.

Then finally mounted all the same, the rain still as heavy, constant, pitiless, but in spite of everything now (the corporal thought) his feet dry (though he would soon learn how the perverse and cunning rain would once again attack, that is, a little higher: at the knee, jammed between the feedbags and the saddle, at the corner of the groove where a tiny trickle worked its way in, so that very quickly the spongy material of the riding breeches became soaked and icy in its turn), and no sooner had they begun to move than the corporal heard the sound: immemorial, as though rising out of the depths of History, faint to begin with, insidious, like a faint nibbling of rats, a pattering which, at first, when the first horses (those at the head of the column) turned onto the paved road, was simply added to that of the rain, then growing louder, amplified as one after the other the cavalrymen ahead of him took the paved road in their turn, then very close by, then he could hear the four shoes of his own horse pounding the asphalt beneath him, the sound, the pattering which he could now decompose into a quantity of near or remote shocks, not only ahead of him but all around him, continuing to swell, to grow, so that at the end he found himself completely drowned, preceded and followed by that alarming and tranquil murmur, consisting of hundreds of hooves to which were nailed hundreds of iron shoes, rising and falling, striking the ground in a continuous hard and multiple pattering which seemed to fill the whole night, to spread everywhere, formidable, disastrous, and static.

For in the thick darkness that enveloped them, the sound implied neither displacement nor progression at any speed in any direction. The cavalrymen (passive, backs hunched under the rain and their fatigue) could just as well have been riding on those artificial mounts, screwed to a plank and imitating by an ingenious mechanism the swaying and rather stiff movements of a walking horse. No wind, no movement of the air (only the rain kept on, vertical, dense, not even stubborn or insistent, merely content to fall), no perceptible modification of their surroundings (the dark was opaque, impenetrable, with nothing permitting them to hope that sooner or later daylight would once again return) making apparent an advance, or even a plan of advance. Simply, they were there, virtually motionless, sitting or rather mounted on invisible animals, making no effort themselves (save that of enduring exhaustion and fighting off sleep), surrounded by what was perhaps meadows, plowed fields, or woods (sometimes the echo of the pattering altered slightly, as if they were crossing something narrow, constricted (a hamlet, a copse?), then returned to normal, spread out again) uniformly engulfed by those inky shadows filled with that vast trampling or crackling or pattering like (with occasionally some clattering, some rattling, faint echoes of clanging metal, like the rustling of wing cases, the clatter of mandibles) the vague murmur of a myriad of insects landing in dim clouds, devouring the fields or, the corporal thought, climbing on top of each other, clustered around some already stinking carrion: not the womb but (as if such a thing contained at once its origin and its end) the black corpse of History. Then he thought that it was the contrary, that it was History which was in the process of devouring them, engulfing, alive and pell-mell, horses and riders, not to mention harnesses, saddles, weapons, even spurs, in its impassive and imperforable ostrich stomach where the digestive juices and rust would manage to reduce everything, including the sharp-toothed rowels of the spurs, to a viscous and yellowish magma of the same color as their uniforms, gradually assimilated and finally rejected by its wrinkled anus, like that of some ancient ogress, in the form of excrement.

Later the rain stopped, but he couldn't have said at what moment nor for how long (he had ceased paying any attention to it; no doubt it had gradually slackened), and in fact, a little later still, the moon appeared, not very bright, misted over, without relief or luster, a disk slightly flattened on one side, simply livid, as though covered with ground glass, which was enough however for the cavalrymen now to make out the vague and black shapes (bushes, hedges, clumps of trees?) which drifted slowly on each side of the road, scattered on the dim, milky reaches of the countryside, and to distinguish as well the silhouette of the rider in front of them and a froth of pale reflections on the two rows of helmets, suddenly becoming aware that they were now restored to movement and to action. Still another hour or so passed in this way during which, it seemed, the same stocky silhouettes of trees and bushes continued to slide past almost imperceptibly, concealing and revealing each other, isolated or in groups, as if they were floating weightlessly, borne by some indolent current, on the surface of a sleeping body of water, or like bizarre mineral concretions on the grayish and lifeless crust of some dead star. Later still, orders were shouted up ahead, approaching by degrees: orders that, no doubt, the horses understood even before the somnambulistic shadows riding them; they (the horses) pressed of their own accord to the right and, though they were still walking, it suddenly seemed to the riders that their speed doubled, for what now went past in the opposite direction, on the other side of the road, was not only the vague silhouettes of trees and bushes but, as though cut out of black paper, a procession of cars, of animals, of men and women, some walking, leading teams by the bridle, others crouching on wagons bristling with what seemed to be heaps of vague objects, sideboards, tables, chairs, pieces of beds, mattresses, chicken coops (or hens and roosters simply tied by the feet, flung pell-mell among the bundles and mute with terror), or even those swollen bundles like enormous tomatoes or enormous pumpkins surmounted, as if bunches of leaves were still attached to them, by the four knotted corners of a bedspread.

Now the clatter of the hooves mingled with the creaking of ill-greased axles and the faint patter of gravel under the wheels. And nothing more, nothing but this double current, this double procession moving in opposite directions, the heads of the cavalrymen all turning with the same impulse toward the left, their sleepy eyes watching pass beneath them, with that grim abjection of the protagonists of a disaster (earthquake, tornado, flood), what constituted so to speak something like both the negative and the complement of themselves: on one side, then, the long dark column of horses and armed men advancing surrounded, or rather haloed, as though by a malefic aura, by the apocalyptic clatter of hooves and the clicking of bayonets—on the other, the slow procession of heteroclite vehicles (hay wagons, manure carts) the color of earth (it was something which even in the half-darkness they could see, as they could smell an odor in the shadows; something which was inherent in the carts, in the heaped-up bundles, in the clothes: the dim brown of the blankets, of the mud stuck to the wheels, of the crusts of mud peeling off the hocks of the cows and calves—only sometimes a black patch betrayed the red of an eiderdown quilt), their tied-up bundles overflowing, the cattle attached by a rope behind, the women sitting among the bundles, themselves like bundles (they—the cavalrymen—could sometimes glimpse a hard, rigid profile carved out of some inert substance, like misery), the men leading the cattle and they too in profile, also staring with a kind of fierce stubbornness straight ahead in the dark, the men, women, and children grim— at least those who were not sleeping, buried under the blankets among the bundles and pots and pans hurriedly tied together—cast, you could have said, in the same stupor, under that same malediction which drove them from their houses and flung them in the middle of the night onto the roads, dragging with them their piles of furniture, eiderdowns, sewing machines, and coffee mills, crowned

with old bicycles lying on their sides, like skeletons, car-
casses of insects possessing a complex morphology, arach-
nean and horned.

And at one moment (as if there mingled in their misery
everything which, one way or another, had driven them
away, armed with papers, wearing a képi or a helmet: the
secretaries of some *mairie* or the gendarmes who, a few
hours earlier, at the same time that the newspapers were
printing their enormous headlines, had knocked at their
doors), without stopping or even slowing down, a man who
was driving one of the carts began shouting something at
the cavalrymen, his head raised, articulating with violence
in a raucous, guttural language words they did not understand. It could have been a warning, threats, or insults, or
all three at once. Then, in the same language, one of those
following also shouted—but this time at the first man—
still in that same fierce, violent language, and he (the first
man) fell silent, driving his cart back into line. As a matter
of fact, at the speed at which the two columns passed each
other (that is, twice the speed of a walking horse) it was
unlikely that any of the cavalrymen could grasp any words,
or rather any articulated sounds which also resembled
something muddy, primitive, heavy, that is, resembling a
rough draft of a language, one of those dialects by which
the populations on either side of a frontier understand each
other, not exactly the same on each side but retaining
enough of their original mud and clay so that the cousins
can sit on Sundays in front of a bottle, or in the village
dance halls the boys and girls can understand what they
both want, with or without frontiers. There was no cow
tied to the last cart, nothing but a dog attached under the
footboard by a string, walking in silence, his vulpine silhouette sliced by the spokes of the wheels. A skillet must
have been dangling from the cart, badly packed and bang-

ing with each jolt, setting up a tintinnabulation that approached, grew louder, passed, faded. For a moment they could still hear it clanging, like a bell, while the creaking of axles gradually diminished, like a last protest, a stubborn groan, weaker and weaker, faint now, finally covered, drowned out by the monotonous patter of hooves, once again the only sound to fill the night.

As if they (the cavalrymen) had once again been abandoned, denied (the first time by the locomotive with its derisive whistle, the symbol of the mechanical and civilized world bearing with it the cars from which they had been extracted in the middle of the night and under the rain to be deposited in a place of which they did not even know the name, the second time by the inhabitants driven from a place toward which they themselves were heading and of which they once again did not know the name), and even accursed (for, from all appearances, it was certainly something stamped with hatred which the driver of the cart had just shouted at them), which (after the man in the station who had shown them the unfolded newspaper, staring at them above the enormous headlines with eyes that were both somber and furious) constituted the second malediction of the day, or rather (for another day, judging by the position of the moon, had already begun) of their journey.

As if the community which had designated them (as cattle or draft horses are chosen, and according to the same criteria: for their youth and their vigor) had already cut itself off from them, torn them away from itself with horror, excluding them, ostracizing them to its periphery on some extreme fringe of the tribal territory from which populations were driven at their approach; the last cart moving irrevocably away and leaving behind it, just as the air goes on vibrating long after the bell tolls (for a long

time now the furious voice had fallen silent, for a long
time the cavalrymen had ceased to hear the creaking of
the axles, the patter of the gravel beneath the wheels, and
even the clanging of the skillet), its wake of passive execration. Now, fighting off sleep, loins and knees aching,
they could feel at each step their horses took that chasm
spreading behind them (or that wall: just as the man with
the newspaper had spread between them and himself, like
a sentence to signify their banishment, the thin sheet of
paper with the monumental letters so to speak mortared
in, without cracks or interstices) which henceforth would
isolate them from the rest of the civilized world, relegating
them, they and their geldings and their mares condemned
to celibacy, to a universe of helmeted eunuchs confined
to the limits of depopulated lands, watched from a distance
by gendarmes and gigantic black men brought on purpose
from the depths of Africa, with their brilliant teeth, their
cheeks marked with ritual scars, their bayonets, to close
behind them a second defensive curtain (or rather a sort
of *cordon sanitaire*) meant to protect the world from which
they were irremediably cut off at present, not so much
against improbable impulses of mutiny as from its own
culpability. Then the moon vanished. In any case they lost
sight of it, for a moment uncertain, since the light (or rather
the vague whitish glow spread over the countryside where
the same black forms still seemed to drift past) subsisted,
for a moment itself uncertain, it seemed, as to its prove-
nance, then growing stronger, no longer by the effect of
the moon but in and of itself, the fields now seemingly
covered with hoarfrost, then (at the same time that they
were beginning to make out the color of the horse in front
of them) they realized that it was not hoarfrost, also gradually distinguishing tilled fields, fallow fields, and harvested
fields—and no longer black shapes but hedges, bushes,

trees which gradually seemed to shake themselves (though there was no wind), to quiver faintly, as though to disentangle themselves, to extirpate themselves from the shadows which, at the same time that the leaves shook off the night rain, withdrew from them like a tide, a dim mist still caught in patches, persisting under the branches, at the heart of a grove, the countryside grayish for a moment, then gradually diversifying (as if colored pigments were rising to the surface of a muddied liquid, were separating and resuming their proper places), the meadows a tender green enlivened by the rain, the tilled fields brown, the hedges a darker green with, here and there, precociously touched by autumn, a bush or a tree already tawny, then, at a turn in the road, they could see ahead of them, preceded by the formidable captain on his formidable ebony horse, with its waving ebony tail, its ebony mane, the long column of cavalrymen in their mud-colored uniforms, the long repetition of the same back, obliquely striped by the same rifle belt, surmounted by the same helmet, the long repetition of the same leather-wrapped leg sticking out of the same fanning overcoat, falling almost to the foot thrust into the same stirrup at the heel of which glistened like a tiny flash of silver the same spur, and, beneath, the indefatigable oscillation of hundreds of indefatigable legs coming and going as though under some long caterpillar with an ochre back, a mahogany belly, crossing, separating, crossing again, like compasses, slender, light, elegant above their reflections on the asphalt of the wet road, filling the countryside with that pattering which had not stopped though they had ceased to hear it (or at least to pay it any attention), but now different, no longer diffuse, threatening, but as though triumphant, bright in the rain-washed air, faster too it seemed, as if the horses themselves had perceived, caught between two hills beyond the hedges

and groves, the high mauve-tiled roofs, the steeple, the
first houses of the village where on the doors of the barns
would be chalked the numbers of the platoons, the groups,
the squadrons: it was day.

*
* *

And the day after the next, morning call was not much
different from the others: the squadron mustered on three
sides of a square, the captain standing in the middle of the
fourth, empty side, with just behind him, the four lieutenants, and somewhat to the side and still farther behind,
the medical officer, the sergeant-at-arms in all his leather
straps, the helmet strap cutting his chin in two, his saber
guard in the crook of his elbow, listening (or pretending
to listen) to the brief reports of stables, mess, and sickbay
from the noncommissioned officers of each platoon, then
making (the sergeant-at-arms) a half-turn, walking to the
captain, stopping three steps from him, clicking his heels,
a maneuver which in this farmyard enclosed by sheds
echoed with a faint clang from the spurs drowned by the
gentle murmur of the dripping trees. It had rained more
during the night; now it was only drizzling or rather, suspended in the cool morning air, there drifted a veil of tiny
droplets which did not even wet anything, merely sustained
the luster of the leaves and deposited a gray effervescence,
like impalpable drops of mercury, on the cloth of the uniforms—and from the mouths of the noncoms, then from
the sergeant-at-arms, then from the captain when he spoke,
escaped each time a faint mist, not even of the consistency
of a puff of cigarette smoke, immediately dissolving, as if
the brief exchange of official formulas were occurring in
a sort of aquarium where the mouths of the fish open and
close noiselessly, sometimes releasing silvery strings of
bubbles, with no more reality and signification than any

ritual determined once and for all and from which none
of the participants expected anything except that one after
the other the mouths should open to release tiny clouds
of immediately vanishing mist; the captain thanking the
sergeant-at-arms, raising his arm to his cap, but the sergeant, being under arms, did not salute, simply made a
quarter-turn, advanced three steps, made a second quarter-
turn, and came to stand on the captain's right, then, after
a complete half-turn, remained motionless, frozen, heels
together, the polished saber guard still shining in the crook
of his elbow, remaining that way even after the captain's
voice had uttered the syllables "At ease," a vague relaxation
then occurring on three sides of the square, then the cavalrymen once again motionless while he (the captain)
cleared his throat, his blotched, fleshy, and sanguine face
merely becoming a little deeper red when he began speaking, his voice rising then with great distinctness in the
silence, pushing in front of it, at each articulation of vowels,
of diphthongs or of consonants, the tiny clouds of immediately dissolving mist, so that it seemed to the cavalrymen that what they could now hear (that is, simply that
the war had begun) had no more signification and concrete
reality than a little earlier the exchange of official formulas
between the captain and the sergeant-at-arms, concluded
by the inevitable clatter of spurs. For several seconds after
he had finished speaking, he (the captain) stood in the same
position, his thick fleshy face even redder now, crimson,
frowning, his expression anxious or rather embarrassed,
either because the fact of having himself uttered the several
words which, at the same time, were spread across the
headlines of the newspapers of the entire world in gigantic
letters had made him even more violently conscious of
their signification, or because he had prepared to accompany them some long-calculated formula which, now, in

front of the motionless and mute squadron, suddenly seemed to him either insufficiently (or excessively) virile or insufficiently (or excessively) paternal, hesitating, his face purplish now, then all of a sudden, in his distress, as though impatiently (or helplessly) turning his head toward the sergeant-at-arms, and without the sergeant-at-arms even seeming to have noticed not the command but the request expressed, the voice (that of the sergeant-at-arms) shouting now: once again an inarticulate, brief, raucous shout, the kind animals make, though implying neither fear nor anger (the kind that might have been produced by some clockwork mechanism endowed with a voice), answered by the silvery clatter of three hundred spurs clashing at once, the three sides of the square formed by the mustered cavalrymen suddenly immobile again, the captain raising his hand to his helmet, saluting, then, even before the voice (the shout) had echoed a second time, turning his back abruptly, already walking with long strides toward the open door at the rear of the house to which the courtyard belonged and into which he vanished, the doorway for a second almost completely obstructed by his broad back, followed one after the next by the four lieutenants behind whom, for a moment, like the cap of the chauffeur carrying packages and passing through a revolving door, the garnet velvet képi of the medical officer leaving last of the four was still visible, after which the door (one of those doors of which the glass top-half was curtained by netting and protected by decorative ironwork) closed.

And nothing more: the cavalrymen broke ranks, returned to the barns and stables where their horses were waiting for them, two or three (of those from cities: shopkeepers or office workers) making a stab at boastful or macabre jokes, their bantering and ill-assured voices lost in the void, falling silent, and during the whole morning

no longer speaking, eyes fixed elsewhere, absorbed with
an unusual, meticulous, and fierce concentration, sweeping
their already swept billets, cleaning their equipment, in-
tently polishing an already polished stirrup, oiling an already oiled bridle, waiting for orders until there came
simply, exactly like that of the day before, the order to
saddle the horses, and again exactly like that of the day
before, the order to exercise the horses, and then trotting
fast on the muddy paths, through the still-sopping underbrush, still managing not to talk or look at each other,
mechanically rising and sinking in the saddles, sometimes
turning their heads toward the east, but except for the
close breathing of the horses or the impact of a shoe on a
stone, hearing only a monumental unaccustomed silence,
and nothing else, and the same thing the next day, and the
same thing again the day after, and the week after, and the
month after as well, and the months which were to follow:
only the empty melancholy countryside, the melancholy
woods where the leaves were gradually yellowing, falling,
gradually vanishing in the glowing splendor of autumn, the
moist and vaporous light, under the rains, the increasingly
cold winds, then really cold, then glacial, then no longer
the perfidious trickles of water which insinuated themselves between the saddlebags and the cloth of the riding
breeches at knee level, but the melting snow, the countryside and apparently the whole world somehow buried,
paralyzed under a uniform and silent layer of white, the
woods and hedges now a brownish mauve, or black, and
they (the cavalrymen) still mounted on their anachronistic
horses: the chestnut, the elegant thoroughbred which he
(the corporal) had been assigned died after a month, skeletal, so exhausted by the interminable marches that it didn't
even think of protesting, of rearing and kicking when he
set foot in the stirrup (and, like that horse, the jockey with

the Italian name disappeared too: by accident, the day after
the day the captain had announced to the mustered squadron the declaration of war, catching his ankle between the
rungs of the ladder which led up to the barn where they
(the six men of the squad) slept, but, as he had said himself,
he didn't actually have a fracture, and lying on the stretcher
while they slid it into the ambulance which would take
him away and making a last gesture of farewell, he (the
corporal) couldn't have said if in the impassive *condottiere*
face one of the two eyes which returned his farewell hadn't
just winked) and the corporal had replaced the chestnut
by a clumsy but robust mare capable (as she proved when
compelled, the spurs lacerating her flanks, the sword-knot
which had come loose from the saber lashing her rump)
of galloping almost without having to catch her breath for
fifteen kilometers—after which he had had to abandon her
as well.

Gradually, in the same way, they saw the solid peasants,
the Herculean beet growers shrivel, then report sick, then
disappear, while the puny little Jew with his prominent
ears, his skinny neck, and his sickly expression seemed
daily more indestructible, enduring with the same imperturbable expression the kilometers covered on foot or on
horseback, as well as the stable duty and the rations based
on rice from the Banque d'Indochine and beef furnished
by Argentine billionaires: usually they slept in barns, sometimes, when they were lucky, in houses evacuated by farmers and where they stole firewood or chopped up the
furniture; on horseback or riding in trains (no one gestic-
ulated or sang now, legs dangling from the open doors:
these were mostly or completely closed because of the
cold, and it was a rare thing if at the stops one of them
managed to slide the heavy panel open, trying to see the
name of a station, of a town (most often discovering only

a tangle of sidings and interminable rows of cattle cars like their own, or tarpaulined platforms, or of those odd ore cars which looked like coffins, the rails, the cars, the tarpaulins glistening under the rain), uttering it (the name of the station) over his shoulder to the thirty or forty silent, indifferent, and sullen men huddled in their overcoats), they first headed south, riding at night through the mountains, billeted in hamlets inhabited by fierce peasants, leaving the next day, following gorges, crossing invisible bridges over which the clatter of the hooves became more sonorous, following milky rivers vaguely phosphorescent in the darkness, then turning north again, halting in a melancholy gray-roofed town with barracks and little squares strewn with the yellow leaves of chestnut trees (and this was Sedan: to the east ran like a wall as far as the eye could see the formidable edge of a formidable forest gilded by autumn; in the course of an exercise, they passed a whitewashed cottage at the foot of a slope as they rode out of town: there was a plaque on the house, the place was called Bazeilles, and on the marble plaque set in the grayish stucco was written "The Last Cartridges"). After the first serious cold spells they finally stopped: it was a village from which almost all the inhabitants had been evacuated, with a watering trough in the center of a muddy square, piles of dung in front of the houses, and a tavern. At Christmas the officers arranged a celebration: they were served pâté and chicken and sparkling wine. A lottery was organized in which everyone won something: a pen, a lighter, or a watch that immediately stopped. Soon after, when he (the corporal) came back from a leave, he found the squadron in a state of alert in the middle of the night, the horses already saddled, the flames of two burning haylofts reflected in the leather, the saddlebags, the gleaming rumps of the horses: they made a bucket chain to put out the fires, then left in the night and reached a woods where they were ordered to dismount but keep their weapons; it was twenty degrees below freezing and they slept as well as they could in the snow, huddling against each other, after tying the horses. But it would not be this time: in the morning the order came to return to their billet.

When the winter came to an end, they bivouacked on the frontier in a forest bordering a pond. At one end there was a tiny beach with cabins, a diving board, and wooden tables under a trellis. The cabins with their gaping doors, the trellis with its peeling paint, had that habitual look of dilapidation and abandonment such establishments acquire during the off-season, except that everything seemed to have been hurriedly abandoned, as if in a panic, as if during the first raindrops of a summer storm, mothers calling their children, packing their food and dishes, the proprietor emptying his till into a sack and leaving without even bothering to turn the key in the kitchen door, everything just as the fugitives had left it, further corroded by the winter months during which the rain, the cold, the wind had gradually attacked the paint, dismantled the doors blowing back and forth in the dark.

The pond was usually a dull, metallic gray. Between this gray and that of the sky stretched a horizontal strip of yellow reeds which grew along the banks and another strip of a purplish-brown which was the forest. The winter had just ended, but the trees were still bare and swayed their clawlike branches stiffly against the sky. Between their trunks the little khaki rectangles of the tents were terraced on the sloping ground, matched by the mahogany patches of the blankets of the horses attached by their halters to ropes stretched between the tree trunks. Occasionally the notes of a bugle sounded, echoing through the woods. After a week, the horses' hooves had so pulverized the sopping earth that in some places the men sank in the mud to their ankles. Discipline was greatly relaxed and work confined to the indispensable tasks of the bivouac. Every day the horses were exercised in the woods and in the afternoons the cavalrymen watered them at the pond, riding bareback, galloping happily through the mud and leading one or two horses by the bridle. At the edge of the pond, where there had been a little beach with cabins and a peeling white-painted trellis, the blackish and trampled mud was marked by the deep overlapping prints of the crescent-shaped shoes half-filled with gray water. During the day they could see in the distance, on the hill which rose beyond the pond, the men of a native regiment dressed in bright fatigues digging and pushing wheelbarrows, coming and going like ants, busy digging a wide trench and setting barbed-wire entanglements.

Gradually the underbrush is imperceptibly covered with tiny green points, like a dust at first, a mist, then with leaves. Those of the hornbeam are striped with delicate folds from their scalloped edges on either side of the central vein. The weather becomes increasingly fine and the mud begins to dry up. Later, he (the corporal) will remember the bareback rides, the echoes of the bugle sounding lights out, the campfires orange in the darkening woods, the smells of humus, the irresistible and invisible rising of the sap all around them in the darkness as if they could hear it, the whinnying of horses fighting in the middle of the night, the shouts of the guards rushing to separate them, the milder air. The men of the group have built (or stolen from the beach?) a table and wooden benches in the little clearing where they sit to take their meals. One morning, as the platoon is preparing to go to the showers, the horses already saddled but without their packs, the corporal is busy polishing his leggings and listening to three men of the squad arguing about plowing and farmwork with the sergeant-at-arms when the alert sounds. It is beautiful weather and the sun is playing among the already broad leaves, warm green, emerald, lemon, sparkling. Airplanes pass occasionally, very high in the sky, almost invisible. The corporal stands motionless for a minute, his brush in his hand, staring at the reddish wax in the round box, the lid of which shows a lion's head, black against a red background, the rim of the lid decorated with tiny rays, alternately red and black. He thinks Now, now . . . He doesn't hear the bugle notes repeated several times, short, dry, hurried, he doesn't hear the orders already shouted by the sergeant-at-arms standing in the middle of the clearing, he is vaguely aware of the sudden agitation of the bivouac, the comings and goings of the cavalrymen busy with their tasks. His heart may beat a little faster. He feels light, excited. He thinks of death but he is too excited: there is too much to do and he too begins running toward his tent.

IX

1914

*T*HIS was the period when summer begins to withdraw, to topple, to collapse so to speak under its own weight, with that heavy and inexorable gravity weary of itself, and that year, as the days grew shorter, each evening carried with it a little more of that nostalgic deprivation of the light, the warmth gradually abating, leaving behind it (the summer) that monstrous something with which it was swollen, which it had borne to term like a pregnant woman, with that same stupor, that same dazed pride, delivering it to the sound of bugle calls and the shouts of drunkards, already preparing to abandon it, horrified, in order to rediscover it a year later, adult now, covered with mud and itself changed into mud, buried alive up to the neck or rotting under the returning sun in a stench of excitement, of purulence, and of decomposing carrion.

But they were only at the very beginning. It was not even a month since the thing had begun, the stooping *maîtres d'hôtel* mournfully strolling now between the abandoned tables (virtually no more diners, no more tennis players, no more tourists with hobnailed boots crossing the lobby so noisily in the evenings, no one crowding around the silent music kiosk, no more gamblers, no more bare shoulders, taffetas, or white carnations around the green felt tables now under their canvas dust covers), and between the young bellboys (youths from the nearby village hastily recruited, useless, decked out in uniforms too big for them and clumsily taken in) and the gardeners who continued to maintain the urns of flowers decorating the lawns, there had virtually been created a sort of caesura, a gap, as if the masculine world was now uniquely composed of children and old men.

You might have supposed that nothing had changed in the little spa at the foot of the mountains where rich people from the city escaped the stifling summers: the same coolness under the shade trees in the park, the same omnipresent murmurs of the streams, the same August storms gathering on certain afternoons, high up, around the peaks, then breaking, the calm and majestic echoes of the thunder rolling and echoing through the valleys, against the bald slopes studded with stumps, with rocky splinters, gradually wooded as your eye descended to the opulent vegetation of chestnuts and plane trees, their opulent foliage dripping onto the lawns among which rose, like a wedding cake on a cushion of giant hydrangeas, the strange and giant construction of which the signboard (HOTEL IBRAHIM PASHA) in gilded letters, following the curves of the fan-shaped canopy with its glass and iron panels, heightening still further the incongruous, paradoxical character, as if, with its consistency of whipped cream, its whiteness so to speak beribboned with pale blue and pink by the beds of hydrangeas, like those sugar decorations embellishing the pastry cook's masterpieces, it had been constructed here, in the depths of this Pyrenean valley, by the whim of (or in homage to) some adipose baccarat player with an olive-hued face surmounted by a fez, with pudgy hands glistening with rings, come from the banks of the Nile or the Bosporus to honor it with his custom, with his tips and his vaguely adulterated pomp, or simply to figure (perhaps simply a vague supercilious crook with a card up his sleeve in some casino and brought here by force, contract in hand, his mission to toss each evening onto the felt the counters and tokens he restored to the management each evening) as some sort of attraction, so that the scene, the ensemble might be complete, as if the respectability of the heavy construction, the lobby decked with cactuses and palms, required the spice of an exotic and vaguely dissolute note: the red patch of the fez, the black and artificially curled mustache, the round and oily face, intended to confer on the place the indispensable cosmopolitan and vaguely suspect status requisite for every spa (the wedding cake where, twenty-six years later, the child whom the black woman, the old lady with the Victorian jowls, and the woman who was still young accompanied along the deserted paths of the park—the child having subsequently become a young boy, then an adult, then again a creature or rather a living organism exclusively inhabited by animal preoccupations, the sole concern of eating and drinking, and who was to learn by the voice of a loudspeaker set up in the middle of a prison camp that it (the wedding cake) had vanished all at once, in the space of a single night, as though by the effect of a magic ring, effaced from the surface of the earth, as if at twenty-six years' interval disaster and desolation were to return to strike in the same places, and this time not to aggrieve, to lacerate, to wound to death a simple stroller walking behind a baby carriage pushed by a black woman, but the place itself (and still more radically than

could have been accomplished by the shells or the bombs
exploding a thousand kilometers to the north), the murmuring streams changed from one minute to the next into
a furious, roaring torrent, sparing in its wake (this lasted
only a few hours), of the terraces, of the canopy, of the
balconies, of the lawns, of the beds of hydrangeas, and of
the memory of the Oriental pasha, only a desert of gravel
two hundred yards wide, which the inhabitants of the village built on a shoulder of the mountain discovered with
astonishment when the sun rose once again).

And perhaps, after the first days (the three or four
necessary for their installation, busy unpacking trunks,
hanging gowns in closets, and arranging furniture to their
taste in the apartment rented by the old lady on the first
floor of the hotel, installing the black woman and the cook
brought with them—for there was also a cook, either because ultimately the establishment had given up paying the
old *maîtres d'hôtel* just for standing around, wrinkled,
stooping, and mournful in their black suits between the
rows of tables without diners, or because the old lady and
her daughter preferred not to show themselves, dreading
at their meals the inconvenient proximity of young people
or of indifferent strangers, living quite sequestered, emerging only to take the child for walks), perhaps it was then
she sent that childhood friend (to whom she continued,
by an inert and trivial coquetry, in memory of their virginal
years, to write in Spanish) a card showing the strange structure with, lined up under the canopy made of glass panels,
the director surrounded by his staff of chefs and their
assistants, and on the back of which (beginning with the
usual *"Niñita querida"*) she simply gave her new address,
justifying it merely by the child's health, modestly (or
proudly) keeping silent about the rest, what had preceded,
the true motive for this installation—or rather for this

flight, for this deliberate, arrogant, severe retreat from the
world: the separation, the departure, the horse in the courtyard, the man decked out for war, the family on the veranda—and she in the center of the front row, as if in a
box at the theater, as when she would attend in Barcelona
those bloody and cruel spectacles she was so fond of,
watching this time, pale but without tears, her jaws tight,
the warrior take the child held out to him by the black
woman, kiss it, press it for a second against his transversely
strapped chest, hand it back to the black woman, mount
his horse, spur it forward, and vanish while she remained
there, clutching the railing, her fingers whitening, still staring through the gaping opening of the *porte-cochère,* which
for a last second had framed the equestrian silhouette, the
man she had waited for until her twenty-fifth year, then
waited for again throughout that interminable and secret
engagement of four more years, standing fast against prejudice, scandal, the old lady's aggrieved countenance (her
remonstrances, her objurgations perhaps), meeting all objections with that passive tenacity of a statue, that affable,
smiling, but inflexible inertia; four years during which all
that she had possessed of him were those cards sent from
faraway countries, representing pagodas, rice paddies,
steamships, pyramids, camels, savages armed with assegais,
lava-topped or jungle-clad mountains, and on the back of
which was written, in a fine hand, a simple name followed
by a date, the indefectible determination finally triumphing: then, those four light-years on the tropical island populated by peplum-clad blacks and tame boas, that nuptial
flight, that liberation, that ravishment; at the same time
that her long-imprisoned flesh opened, dilated, welcomed
into itself the man who had so to speak carried her off by
a legal rape, the sudden revelation or rather irruption into
her life of the multifarious, inexhaustible, motley, swarm-

ing world of crowds, of wild animals, of unknown flowers, and into which she penetrated dazed, exhausted perhaps (in that moment when the chrysalis having become a butterfly and managed to extract itself by successive spasms from its sheath catches its breath, still viscous with nutritive juices, still bewildered by its own metamorphosis, before spreading its wings and taking its flight), not yet rid of that protective sheath of silliness, of insipid affectations in which she had wrapped herself (or in which her birth, her milieu, her education had so to speak corseted her), marveling now when she watched the little black boys diving, tossing them coins, when she was carried on the shoulders of black slaves, greedily copying out, in order to send them to her mother, the endless lists of consommés, of timbales, of *foies gras,* of guinea hens, of *bombes glacées* which constituted the menus of the governor's dinners, sending photographs in which she appeared radiant, obstinately hatted with extravagant creations, wearing hobble skirts (as if women shared with architects that faculty of imperturbably carrying with them in any latitude the fashions of Chantilly or the architectural styles of the cafés of Agen and the casinos of cosmopolitan spas), sitting under the gallery of their bungalow and surrounded by her household of servants at the side of the man who, without képi or sun helmet, in his white linen uniform, seemed to figure there as a fifth servant (or the majordomo), with on his face that enigmatic expression, at once indulgent and amused, of the first *maître d'hôtel* or the master of the hounds for the intolerable heiress with the childish whims and the childish amazements—he having emerged from his years in the brush, from his geodesic surveys, from his swamps and marshes, exhausted if not saturated with women, with those docile and tender bodies with copper or saffron skins who had embraced him, the exquisite faces with slanting eyes beneath Madras scarves of whom sometimes (when it was not merely the casual encounter of a port of call, of a stopover, when the exotic orchid did not occupy only his nights but also his days, served him his meals, perhaps gave orders to the other servants, distracted him with her birdlike chatter) he would send the photograph to his sisters—the austere mountain-dwelling virgins back there, in their country of snow and rain, divided between their lives as schoolmistresses and farm women, putting away Madras and flower-maidens in the family album with its cardboard pages where, framed in a gold wire, the rigid portraits of cousins and aunts with their hair severely drawn back from their temples, with their whaleboned blouses buttoned up to the chin, of men in their Sunday best, alternated with the portraits of Creoles or of savage children led half-naked to the photographer who, before making them lean on some console table in front of a *trompe-l'oeil* balustrade, devised for them (at least facing the camera) out of pins and a few yards of taffeta a gown worthy of some Indian empress or the Countess of Castiglione.

Now, each Sunday (she also sent the photograph of the mission church, a hideous pseudo-Gothic brick building, surprising and almost indecent under the tropical sun) he would accompany her to mass, she wearing one of her Chantilly hats, he carrying under his arm one of those colonial helmets like bowler hats, he who hitherto had never set foot in a church, whose family from father to son and from mother to daughter, by that highland and rigorist tradition, had entrenched itself in a fierce, an inflexible rejection of everything that resembled a priest or a prayer, for whom to enter such a place was simply regarded as a sign of dishonesty. And this must have been the only time he directly contradicted those women who had raised him in every sense of the word, had effaced themselves, deliberately expunged themselves from the world for him the way the younger sisters of the male heir destined to make his way at court or under arms were once shut up by force in convents: the only divergence, the sole occasion when he was to confront that puritan intransigence, the first time when one of them (the elder, no doubt, of the sisters who had quite naturally adopted, integrated into the family album the mulattresses in Madras scarves and the childish black women) allowed herself to raise her voice to say: "She is not from our circle!", the same objection though differently formulated ("He is not from our world") made to her daughter by the old lady for whom the world was limited to those who like herself could presume an interminable sequence of costumed ancestors, she too conventually sequestered in her prejudices and the old family mansion, that mausoleum of past glories; but perhaps they would even have accepted that (the difference in social situation, in milieu) if that difference had not postulated or rather implied what was for them an insurmountable obstacle, the word ("believer") which in itself constituted an offense to their dignity, which between themselves, when they received the letter in which he told them of his intentions, the sister who read it (not to the mother: that something (rather than someone) shrunken, earthen, reduced to the dimension of an apple under a winged cap, sticking out of the sheets drawn up to her chin, and who night and day occupied the same place on the pillow, except when they moved, in order to pour a little sugared milk into the mouth or to wipe up its evacuations, the body which did not even raise the covers) doubtless hesitated to articulate, lowering her voice, doubtless finally uttering the word with consternation as when speaking of a vice, a taint, a shameful disease, an object of scandal, as if all the hopes they had placed in

him (that delegating of themselves, vicariously empower-
ing him with their pride, their ambition, by means of which
they would accede not so much to any social elevation of
the family as to its escape, its release from a condition
of beast of burden) collapsed all at once, as if in denial of
everything they had been taught to regard as the struggle
of good against evil by their peasant lineage, pit sawyers
and vine growers, where the Bible was replaced by those
grayish brochures decorated with allegorical designs representing a plowman or a blacksmith against a background
of a rising sun, it grayish as well.

And perhaps one of them (the elder sister again?) could
not endure it, told him—or wrote him—what between
themselves, in their distress, avoiding each other's eyes,
they had not dared formulate louder than a whisper,
emerging from her reserve, doing violence to her modesty,
her pride, her tenderness, then waiting (and if it was a
letter, through the sheet of paper and the careful schoolteacher's handwriting, it must have been as if he could see
her face or rather their faces, both of them rather square
and already worn, the flesh beginning to wrinkle and collapse, contemplating him with an anxious, dismayed, almost frightened expression), and he answering them,
cajoling them with that indulgent jocularity, that same
smile which since his school days, then preparatory school
in his worn scholarship uniforms, then at Saint-Cyr, he had
learned to offer to all obstacles, the same patient and un-
alterable smile with which he must have answered the teasing of his fellow students with their titles of marquis or
baron (those for whom wearing a plumed képi, white
gloves, and a sword represented not a social promotion
but a right, a due, simple accessories already laid in their
cradles), always answering their objections, their obstinate
silences, with that same playful, cajoling expression, as if

he had been speaking to children (the younger of the sisters was ten years older than he), emphasizing his words perhaps with a wink, as though to make them into accomplices, dismissing with a gesture (explaining to them that it was merely a formality, a polite pretense, a concession to an absurd custom) the excessively intolerable words or images (for he had certainly had to be baptized, to bow down, to kneel before one of those men in robes who, for them, incarnated iniquity and crime), and finally triumphing over them too, obtaining, seizing their consent without which (even though it were given with no more than lip service, tears trembling in their eyelashes) he might have given over, broken his engagement, set out for another part of the world, the depths of some jungle, some desert, or some lava-covered mountains.

And on the other side (while for four years he set about conquering the austere and superstitious predisposition of the two sisters, the two sisters wearing dresses like cardboard made for them out of old ones by the sister who took the man's role—for she knew how to do that too—and even hats, out of birds with onyx wings, draped velvet, a little tulle, and some cheap beads), that other symmetrical confrontation: the old lady who saw arriving regularly, sometimes from Cairo, sometimes from Ceylon, from Aden, from Singapore, from places whose guttural names she had never heard, like Lang Song or Loc Binh, like (the names) jade stones or gobs of opium, the postcards which she handed without a word, perhaps repressing a sigh, to the young girl, already not so young, still as imperturbably serene, docile, secret, taking them with a casual gesture, contemplating for a moment the camel market, the beach lined with coconut palms, or the village of straw huts, putting them down, perhaps without even reading what was written on the back, on the table where they would

breakfast together without seeming to pay any more attention to them than to the rest of the mail (another card,
perhaps, which the old lady had handed to her at the
same time with a secret hope, bearing, scribbled on the
back, one of those high-spirited and suggestive gallan-
tries—sometimes in verse—which were the specialty
of some friend of the cousins vacationing in the Alps,
trying out a new car, or on maneuvers with his cavalry
regiment), always with that same negligent, absent expression behind which was hidden a passive and formidable determination, until in the end, seven hundred
kilometers away from each other, the two lay sisters
in their much-economized dresses and the Victorian
old lady in the bedroom embellished with a crucifix sur-
render, resign themselves, acknowledge themselves defeated.

So, those four years, that island, that piece of Africa
lying in an ocean inhabited by sharks and flying fish, those
biblical crowds with black faces under straw hats, their
bodies draped with togas, those markets where, languid,
her flesh fulfilled (and soon heavier, feeling a new life stir
within it), sheltered by a parasol, leaning on the arm of
the man she had waited for for four years, she would buy
strange-shaped and strange-tasting fruit, embroidery, useless baskets, and where she would attend those prefecture
functions at once provincial, stiff, and vaguely corrupt
where, among the wives of administrators, of civil servants
and planters, wearing one of those gowns copied by skillful
black hands from the latest newspapers from the mainland,
she came into contact for the first time in her life with
people to whom the old lady would never in the world
have opened her door, stupefied, listening with an amused
indulgence to the would-be worldly remarks, more or less
suggestive or more or less crude, of that mixed company

peculiar to such climates and where there mingled, in the mahogany setting of the Grand Café decorated with mirrors or in the gardens of the Residence with its façade of some thermal spa, freemason governors, mission brothers, greedy merchants, and, in their white duck uniforms with gold braid slightly tarnished by the desert sands or the humidity of the swamps, those men with severe faces, with feverish eyes, with bodies fed on quinine and absinthe bowing to kiss the hands of ladies who, protected by flower-colored parasols, watched them, on parade days, stifling in their dark linen tunics, brushed, polished, motionless under the terrible tropical sun, in geometrical formations, sabers drawn, mastering their mounts tormented by flies, and blind under those sun helmets just revealing the tips of stiff mustaches or of goatees.

Four years, then (and before, the twenty-nine others— or rather the fourteen others (or sixteen) if it is counting from the age of fifteen or thirteen that young ladies begin to dream of the man who will unbutton their blouse, will touch and penetrate those parts of their body glanced at askance in the bathroom mirrors), and suddenly, as if everything had been merely an interlude without reality, one of those ephemeral butterfly flights (or rather moth flights, the moth dazed, blinded, burning its wings in the chimney of some lamp, some night lantern), brutally, without transition (for perhaps he still managed to deceive her, to elude her, to preserve her till the last minute, suddenly interrupting the anxious (or, who knows: impetuous, impatient?) confabulations held among three or four men (still in their white-duck uniforms, while the steamer was slowly drawing its wake over the waters of warm oceans, heading north through the narrow sea lined with scorched mountains) in the corner of a corridor, or lingering in the smoking room, suddenly changing the subject, walking

toward her and offering her that same smiling, reassuring
face; or perhaps, by a tacit agreement, a tacit modesty,
each of them—she and he—playing that game (even if at
the ports of call she flung herself too nervously upon the
newspapers—or perhaps, behind his back, deploying the
resources of her coquetry, joking, displaying a false in-
souciance, attempting to extort what she wanted to know
from the telegraph officer on board), and then, once
again—the last time, in reverse so to speak—the captain's
table, the coins mechanically tossed to the little black boys,
the Oriental stalls of the bazaars, the purchase of useless
knickknacks, giving each other (or already giving each other's ghosts) useless smoking sets or useless toilet sets destined to remain in the boxes, the crates which she would
not open, would only bring herself to unpack ten years
later, on the eve of her own death, her face ravaged, contemplating dry-eyed the cloisonné enamels, the tobacco
jars decorated with pink- and blue-winged birds, the ham-
mered trays), without transition, then, once again plunged,
or rather precipitated, back into that apathetic state, returned to the waiting, in the slumberous refuge of that spa
deserted in catastrophe, with its immutable decor of peaks,
of forests, of lawns, its old gardeners with sleepwalking
gestures bending over the pots of hydrangeas, the omnipresent murmur of the streams cascading down the moun-
tainside, the cool shade beneath which you could see her,
still wearing as though in bravado one of her astonishing
hats and dressed (again in bravado against fate, against
destiny, stubbornly) in one of those bright dresses she had
worn under the tropical suns, walking slowly, as if her gaze
were fixed, absent in her slightly plump, masklike face,
bearing upright, above her long skirts, one of those naively
sculptured busts, mounted on litters and borne on votive
feast days on the shoulders of penitents, crowned with

golden rays and between the breasts of which, in the hollowed-out bosom, you can see through a tiny pane of glass some relic, some splinter of darkened bone—she who would not be able to recover, later on, even the tiniest fragment of bone, a vertebra, a rib, and who, as a tombstone for the man who had held her in his arms, had mingled his limbs with hers, could merely have printed up a discreetly black-bordered cardboard rectangle embellished with a slender black cross above the name, the date (that of one of those days when regularly, at the same hour, she would accompany the black woman pushing in a baby carriage the child who less than a year before she was still bearing in her womb), with the brief verses of Job or Isaiah and with the phrase (the cry) which perhaps filled her throat, stifling, smothering her, while under the long skirt sweeping the gravel path, her legs giving way beneath her, she continued nonetheless to advance, eyes fixed on the automobile, the sort of monstrous beetle with iron wings, with exophthalmic eyes, with shining brass mandibles, parked in front of the hotel with its driver still in a duster, his huge goggles in his hand, watching her advance toward him, standing beside the old lady sitting beside a garden table and who was also watching her—if it can be said that through her tears, through the shining film that covered the old, suddenly collapsed cheeks like a varnish, the silent screen of tears, she (the old lady) could distinguish anything but two bright shapes blending into the shadowy background of foliage, growing larger, managing (the old lady) to stand up, to walk in the direction of that dead woman with huge eyes whose mute lips were stirring mechanically, incapable of articulating a sound, opening and closing on words whose meaning the woman trying to utter them (or not even trying: murmuring mechanically, the way a fish out of water, half asphyxiated, continues to open and close its mouth on the void) no longer (or not yet) managed to understand, words inaudible among similarly meaningless noises (the rustle of wind in the swaying branches, the gurgle of leaping water, the chirping of birds): merely assemblages of letters separated by blanks, as they would figure later not engraved in marble or stone but simply printed on the back of that grayish announcement no bigger and no heavier than a playing card, her lips still moving of their own accord, faintly, agitated as though by a nervous tic, a tremor, endlessly forming over and over the same phrase, the same mute lacerating howl, with no other echo than the indifferent stir of the branches, the monotonous cry of the same bird, the monotonous scraping of the hoe wielded by one of the lethargic gardeners, as if the whole lethargic universe, the earth which was continuing its slow turning, the shaggy cloud which was continuing to disintegrate, to coagulate, to disintegrate again around the jagged peaks, the mountains, the valley, were gradually diluting, absorbing, erasing, annihilating the series of words powerless to escape her throat, stammering, disintegrating, returning again, like a litany, a madwoman's mumbled phrase: Thy will be . . . Thy will be . . . Thy will . . .

X

1940

IT all happened suddenly, starting from the moment when he was back on that horse (the one whose reins the raging cavalryman had handed him), as if that warm and viscous film he had tried to remove from his face by sprinkling it with cold water had immediately formed again, even more impermeable, separating him from the external world by the thickness of a pane of window glass more or less, he guessed, if such a thing is possible as to estimate fatigue and filth and lack of sleep by reference to a pane of glass: in any case he tried, which is to say that at a given moment he raised one hand to his face and brought it close, but without managing to touch it, as if between the skin of his fingers and that of his cheek which they were trying to reach was interposed a layer of invisible substance or as if the two skins (that of his fingers and that of his face) had become numb: at most his fingers perceived that they were encountering something compact which might just as well have been the material of his tunic or the strap of his helmet, and his cheek a vague sensation of pressure, but remote—and a moment later it occurred to him that he wanted to shorten his stirrups (thinking at the same time that after all this was only the second time in four days that he was riding a dead man's horse, in other words that he had lost two horses in four days, or that conversely the two horses during the same period had lost their riders, or again that he was apparently destined to take the place of the dead on successive horses, the first with too loose a saddle girth (or rather the saddle he had transferred from his exhausted mare to the first replacement horse had too long a saddle girth for the latter, so that when he put his foot in the stirrup amid all the explosions, shouts, whinnying, swearing, chaos, the whole pack—saddle, saber, rolled blanket, and saddlebags—turned upside down, and that was about all he remembered before being knocked out as though by a bludgeon, then coming to surrounded by bodies of men and slaughtered horses and then beginning to run), the second with stirrups that were too long now, thinking that all they had done was to substitute one horse for another or, conversely again and if you took the horses' viewpoint, that for them one weight had been replaced by another, like those toy cavalrymen molded once and for all in the same position, legs arched, so they could be transferred just as they were, helmet, equipment, and spurs (except, he thought again, that now I'm rid of that damn rifle), from one lead horse to another, again in that state of passive somnolence from which he had been roused by the shouts of alarm followed almost at once by the first gunfire, surprising the squadron (as if his later dash for the shelter of the hedges, passing between the armored units, his crossing the forest, had somehow constituted only a sort of parenthesis, already closed again, already no longer quite real, if not imaginary, entirely negligible in any case in the colonel's eyes, judging by the way he had looked at him (or not even looked at: looked through, his expression even slightly offended if not irritated, importuned) when he had reported himself present), and now finding himself sitting on a horse exactly as he had been a few hours earlier and lulled by the monotonous sound of the hooves), the length of the dead rider's stirrups now constituting his chief preoccupation, but he would have had to raise each of his thighs one after the other and lean over in order to shorten the stirrup straps and merely imagining the series of gestures he would have to make was already too tiring, so he rode on just as he was, his heels barely touching the stirrups, and that was enough, since all he needed to do (now that he no longer had to make any decision but only to follow the two officers whose dim figures he saw swaying elegantly against the blinding daylight a few yards ahead of him above the twin hindquarters) was to keep his own body virtually upright on the saddle, swaying back and forth like a dummy, entirely encased in that sort of filthy glass or rather yellow cellophane (like those bonbons wrapped in waxed paper, banana or lemon, he thought) whose creases he could feel in each wrinkle of his skin, just as each time he blinked something scorching and painful passed before his eyes, trying nonetheless to keep them open, his eyelids fluttering, the effect of which was to wrinkle the cellophane into fan shapes with razor-sharp folds on each side of his temples, the whole phenomenon (yellow wrapping, creases in the glass, and warm viscosity) pivoting along with him on the saddle in a twisting effort which gave his waist and ribs the sharpened creases of waxed paper, while he watched slowly withdrawing behind them between the flowering meadows the winding and empty ribbon of the road on which he discovered nothing else following them but the two couriers lazily pedaling, making S-curves in order to

keep riding at the same speed as the walking horses, like
two drunken bicyclists, as though they too were somnolent, as if everything were happening in slow motion, so
that later on, when he tried to tell these things, he realized
that he had fabricated instead of something shapeless, in-
vertebrate, a relation of events that a normal mind (that
is, the mind of someone who has slept in a bed, has got
up, washed, dressed, eaten) might constitute after the fact,
according to an established usage of sights and sounds
accepted and agreed upon, that is, giving rise to more or
less clear and orderly images, distinct from each other,
while in truth this had neither definite shapes nor names
nor adjectives nor subjects nor complements nor punc-
tuation (in any case no periods), nor exact temporality, nor
meaning, nor consistency if not that—viscous, murky, soft,
indeterminate—of what reached him through that more
or less transparent glass bell under which he was imprisoned, the cannon fire (he couldn't have said at what moment it began or rather at what moment he began hearing
it or rather when he became conscious that he was conscious of it: simply, starting at a specific moment, the guns
began firing regularly) as though it too were in slow motion,
without haste, one solitary cannon (or the explosion of a
shell: he also couldn't have said whether the sound meant
the firing or the landing of the shells) making itself heard
at fixed, rather wide intervals, and apparently without reason or precise goal in the smiling springtime nature, with
the regularity of a metronome, like those solemn salvos
of honor which salute the accession of a king or the funeral
of some statesman, his attention at the same time distracted
by the swearing of the man leading the last horse (while
he was instinctively trying to estimate the length of the
stirrups hanging alongside the empty saddle: but considering that the colonel would certainly not have tolerated

a halt, even for just the time to change mounts, that too represented a sum of efforts beyond his means) whose mouth the man was unnecessarily lacerating by repeatedly yanking at the reins, the distracted animal now dancing sideways like a crab, moving nervously on its hooves, a grayish slobber faintly tinged with pink foaming at its lips, sometimes forming long strings that sparkled in the sun—and then, as though disturbed, importuned by the racket, the colonel turned his head slightly, frowning, looking annoyed, in profile for a second, his dry cheek striped obliquely by the dark line of his helmet strap; but he said nothing—or perhaps simply something like: "All right, all right! . . . ," the sound of his voice coming, like the images, from a great distance, just as tenuous, as dubious, through the thick wall of yellow and dusty glass (or cellophane), then again nothing more was to be seen than the back of his helmet: in any case the man leading the horse stopped tormenting it, doubtless humiliated by this call to order either in his conceit as a cavalryman (he did not belong to the squadron—at least insofar as through the wall of dirty glass it was possible to identify him: a prematurely wrinkled face not much bigger than a fist under the oversized helmet, with eyes like marbles and an expression at once scornful and disgusted: doubtless that jockey whom the colonel had taken on as his orderly, with tiny hands and legs so short that they seemed added onto each side of the saddle, like those booted and artificial legs that hang on each side of the hole through which emerges the torso of a child astride a hobbyhorse, like, if it hadn't been for the pitiless hardness that emanated from him, a child dressed up in a soldier's outfit), or (humiliated) at being caught out scared, and eager to take it out on the lead horse by nastily lacerating its mouth two or three times more, but without swearing, then turning his rage, the backlash of his fear, on the new companion now riding beside him, saying: "All right, what did you expect to see back there? The whole regiment, bugles and all?" (or perhaps not: too outraged, too scornful, perhaps assuming, because he was the colonel's orderly, a sort of aristocracy, a caste too far above men in the ranks to address a word to one of them—or perhaps the sounds (at least the articulated sounds) arrested by the glass bell, the furious expression of the face speaking for itself), or again because the aspect of this companion whom fate was now imposing on him (his helmet smeared with mud and dented, his coat torn, his trousers and leggings still sopping wet) was felt by him to be insulting, outrageous, he who was as impeccably brushed and polished as the colonel himself (as if, following the colonel, he had traversed immaculate and intact the four days during which the other cavalrymen of the regiment, pursued and starving, had beaten a retreat as well as they could), he inspiring, like the animal on which he was taking revenge for his fear, a compensatory rage, so that, no more than he would have dared allow himself to question the colonel, the corporal enclosed in his yellow glass bell did not venture (moreover, he felt no curiosity whatever) to ask him how he and the colonel had managed to survive that ambush into which he (the colonel) had led the squadron at daybreak aureoled with his magnificence and his air of lofty invulnerability: even so, instead of the smart thoroughbred polished like a piece of mahogany on which he had made his appearance a few hours earlier, moving up to the head of the column at a trot, bullying and hectoring the exhausted riders, he (the colonel) was now riding bareback on a heavy and clumsy off-horse of a machine-gun team, its speckled wine-colored hide pasted down by sweat and its severed (or disengaged—or broken) traces dangling on the ground, making a faint rattle (that of a loose buckle?) on each side

of the hindquarters and leaving a double track in the dust;
yet, at this moment, it did not immediately occur to the
corporal chiefly preoccupied with the length of his stirrups
that he (the colonel) had from all appearances gone mad,
so that without asking himself why, despite the two saddled
mounts the jockey (his orderly) was leading, the colonel
persisted in riding bareback on the heavy off-horse, he
confined himself (without amazement, or rather as if an
additional amazement had been added to such a succession
of amazements that the very notion of amazement had
vanished from his mind) to registering this: the heavy hindquarters and the stiff gait of the Percheron, the long tow-
like tail, as though it too were faded, mounted by the bony
and in some sense graceful torso, that is, not exactly rigid
but as if by some internal flexion he was absorbing, trans-
forming into an elegant and almost imperceptible undu-
lation, the heavy movements of the animal, the naked blade
of the saber glistening on the flank of the plow horse, the
two elegant figures of the two officers silhouetted now by
the blinding shimmer of the thousands of splinters of glass
that covered the ground like a carpet, crunching, pulver-
izing sometimes with a sound of glass crushed under the
hoof, the corporal enveloped in the somnambulistic
warmth of his cellophane cape realizing now (perhaps he
had slept, had closed his eyes a moment on that black and
burning thing which lowered along with his eyelids) that
they were advancing no longer surrounded by fields,
woods, and hedges but between a double wall of brick
house fronts—or rather (for everything continued to un-
fold with the same viscous deliberation) that they (the four
cavalrymen and the five horses) were marking time where
they stood, not advancing, while there paraded past to the
right and left house fronts without glass in their windows,
as if these had been blown out from inside intact houses,

the severed traces of the off-horse occasionally catching
on a piece of glass, dragging it a few yards with a silvery
clatter, then abandoning it, the horses of the two officers
and their black shadows overwhelmed by the sun, now
high in the sky, so that the helmet and the long cavalry
overcoat (they hadn't yet been given orders to take them
off, and in fact they weren't at all too warm during the
night but, at this moment, terribly heavy) seemed to unite
with the stifling bell under which the corporal now found
himself imprisoned, thinking At least it isn't like in polo
when they change horses at each halt in the game so now
a Percheron, thinking again Or perhaps he keeps it as the
irrefutable testimony of his rescued honor (the street—or
rather the carpet of glass—widened: they were crossing a
paved square where only a few splinters glittered here and
there, then the house fronts drew closer again, street and
square equally deserted under the brilliant sun; it was just
as if between each of the regular explosions (now they
were coming very close, though there was no puff of smoke
to be seen, nor any wall crumbling, and it seemed that the
firing of the invisible cannon was aimed at the city) you
saw creeping along the walls a sort of procession of cockroaches, dragging or carrying vague things, vanishing into
the recesses of the doors or under the porches, into invisible holes, at each explosion, then reappearing, progressing a few more yards: the firing was so regular that
they (the cockroaches) seemed to know exactly how much
time they had between each shell), thinking again But
maybe he keeps it with the intention of presenting himself
like that at headquarters in all his glory, triumphantly dragging with him a Percheron, two cavalrymen, and two bicyclists, the notion that the colonel was simply mad not
yet having occurred to him: later (that is, when he was
once again capable of using his reason to think about such

things) he was to remember that the first suspicion came
to him when he heard the colonel's dry and metallic voice
shouting for the third time: "I'm asking you to open this
barbed-wire barrier right now and let me through! I don't
need any advice from you. I'm going where I have orders
to go and that's all! Open this barrier at once!" the territorial guard standing, head raised toward him, arms spread
as though to bar his passage, staring in alarm at the four
riders, the plow horse, the caricatural jockey, repeating
something inaudible, the sound blocked by the glass bell,
then lowering his head and his arms, making a sign to the
second territorial guard and beginning, with his help, to
pivot the long beam resting on the struts and wrapped with
barbed wire which was blocking half the road leading out
of the town, the colonel not even glancing at them, tranquil
again, busy making his horse step around the wide crater
made by a bomb, apparently an old one since there had
been time to clear one side of a fallen telegraph pole and
its tangle of wires, the heavy Percheron maneuvered by
the gloved hand executing an elegant half-circle exactly as
in the riding ring: there was a little woods where the
barbed-wire barrier was set up, but soon afterwards the
sun began pounding again on the corporal's helmet, stupe-
fying him, casting him again into that state of semilethargic
resignation which had come over him as soon as he had
found himself back on that horse, sitting on a saddle where
his feet barely touched the stirrups, thinking later But for
the role they wanted us to play it didn't matter I could just
as well have found myself tied backwards on a donkey in
a shirt with a candle in my hands like those criminals they
derisively parade through the streets or those clowns who
make their entrance into the ring during bursts of laughter
staggering on the back of some tiny pony held by the
ringmaster only he needed something more martial to ac-

company him where he had decided to go, like those Oriental potentates accompanied to the other world by their servants and their favorite horses which was why the commander and that jockey would doubtless have been enough for him, doubtless why he hasn't even been worried about the disappearance of the two bicyclists when they rode off God knows where and also why perhaps he hasn't been able to keep that expression of vexation when he saw me all muddy and with this torn overcoat as little presentable for this kind of parade duty as a shitty dog compared to a greyhound the only thing that would be bothering him now being no doubt the prospect of having to sniff beside him my filthy and stinking ghost to the end of time, but for the moment incapable (the corporal) of thinking anything coherent, if not even of thinking at all (if by thought is meant a somewhat structured ensemble of judgments, reasonings, or ideas, in which case he would have done the only thing there was to do, that is, turn his horse into the first cross-street and get away from this road with all possible speed), as if all logic and all coherence were going counter to what he was in the process of experiencing, although he was less and less in a position to be amazed, still less to rebel against a state of fact which he was even inclined now to judge normal in its incoherent appearance (gradually led in five days to admit that it was granted him to see in action the forces habitually concealed by some artifice (or in sleep, by pure indolence on their part) and resuming their imprescriptible rights, animated by their formidable ferocity at once blind, negligent, and summary, obeying that irrefutable logic, that irrefutable coherence proper to the elements and to natural laws) so that imprisoned under his stifling glass bell, cut off from the outer world by that filthy glass partition, he now indifferently stared from his saddle at the procession still in slow motion

below him, strung out to the right and left of the road no
longer winding through fields and woods but quite straight
now in the faintly rolling countryside flooded by the sparkling May sunshine, the double rosary of wrecks which
seemed to have been left on its banks by the withdrawal
of some flooded river, bearing pell-mell vehicles, animals,
and people pushed to the sides, sometimes isolated, at
other times agglutinated, as though halted by some obstacle tangled amid the wan and scattered contents (sheets,
blankets, crumpled newspapers) of split bundles and broken-down suitcases, as if some giant snowplow had driv-
en through one of those automobile graveyards you can
see outside cities or occasionally in the countryside, pushing to either side trucks, carts, baby carriages, wheelbarrows, or gleaming limousines, some belly up, collapsed in
the ditch, elsewhere apparently intact, sometimes still sinking into the dust, gradually consumed in a stench of burnt
rubber, of indolent vapors rising here and there, as though
from those public dumps where fires are continually smol-
dering, then he was there himself, prone, face pressed
against the harsh, rubbish-soiled grass, deafened by the
thunder of motors in the middle of which the crackling of
machine-guns also seemed to be strung out in slow motion,
then up, torn from the ground like a puppet, his shoulder,
his arm half disjointed, his hand still clutching the reins of
the horse whinnying in terror, eyes wild, rearing, then
bucking, the jockey too struggling with the other two
horses, the thunder of the motors already diminishing,
gone now, the calm and indifferent countryside still under
the springtime sun, the colonel planted in the middle of
the road on his halted Percheron, saying simply: "All right,
are you ready?" while the corporal's foot was groping for
the stirrup, hopping clumsily, finally hoisting himself into
the saddle once again, staring in bewilderment at the truck

enveloped in crackling, joyous flames; then again the monotonous swaying to the monotonous gait of his mount,
able now to feel in himself that thing which in the coherent
and logical vocabulary must have fear for its name, except
that it was manifested by nothing logical or coherent like
getting away as fast as your legs could carry you but was
expressed on the contrary under the blazing sun by a name-
less sensation of vacancy, of cold, of helplessness, and if
that had a color it was the color of iron, grayish, as if he
had now entered into something like a state of virtual
death, sitting (or rather swaying) on that oversized horse
which continued to walk on behind the two elegant officers, thinking (or perhaps saying aloud: in any case the
jockey—or at least the one he was imagining to be a
jockey—seemed to hear nothing: he now had given up
tormenting the lead horse and sat hunched in his saddle
like a little monkey, frowning, still furious, which was perhaps for him, now that he was not relieving himself by
brutalities, his way of enduring his own fear), saying then
(or thinking aloud): So he hasn't even got off his . . . He
hasn't even tried to . . . He's stayed there right in the middle of that road, in broad daylight, and the other one too,
while I, while we, while those planes . . . ; but it wasn't
only that, not just the sudden attack of planes trying to
kill them (and not, to tell the truth, the four horsemen in
particular: machine-gunning the road and everything that
was moving on it—or was even not moving (to tell the
truth again, they (the four horsemen) seemed the only ones
to be using the road), so in a sense machine-gunning as a
matter of routine, negligently so to speak; furthermore,
after six days they were used to it: to jump off their horses,
to run to the nearest ditch and lie down in it had become
a series of reflexes so familiar that they did not even need
to give orders to their muscles; again the colonel had

turned around to watch them get up, had raised that voice impregnated with a contained irritation, impatient, arrogant, yet somehow indulgent, cordial in his way), whereas what he (the corporal, back in the saddle now) had been able to see, continued to keep printed on his retina with a terrifying fascination, as clearly as he might have read his own condemnation to death, was the perfectly motionless back of the other officer silhouetted (polished helmet glistening in the sun, the shoulders, the waist slender as though laced into a corset, the booted legs framing the horse's rump (it too perfectly motionless, as if everything had been cut out of a sheet of zinc), not just disdaining to turn around but not even thinking of it, simply waiting until the colonel had arrived beside him, then imperceptibly squeezing the flanks of his horse and continuing on their way, the two officers peacefully moving on again side by side, having resumed their tranquil conversation, as indifferent to the burned trucks, the baby carriages, and the overturned cars as to the regular firing of the solitary cannon, futile and stubborn, which continued to echo behind them, shaking the sunny air, gradually fading, deaf (the two officers) to the voices that occasionally rose toward them from the road's edge, sometimes whining, sometimes begging, sometimes alarmed (and at one moment, through the sides of his bell, from a group standing around an overturned cart (or around a corpse lying there—but that was something he forbade himself to look at—and, when there was one, it simply crossed his field of vision from left to right, then vanished from it, neither more nor less apparent than the other wrecks, mechanical or otherwise) the corporal could see a man, a civilian, separate himself, clutching to his chest a red blanket which hung down to his knees and making broad gestures with his free arm, indicating the road, the hedges, the bushes, trotting over to the colonel's boot, shouting something, mouth wide open, then running, passing the horse, turning around, facing it, then walking backwards, gesturing with his arm, as the territorial soldier had done, to bar the way, the colonel and the other officer, still without ceasing to talk to each other, delicately turning their horses and walking around him, exactly as they had done with the bomb crater), and later (but doubtless he had dozed off again: the glass bell thicker and thicker, the external world as though viscous, gummy, more and more dubious, while inside was now installed, rigid and inexorable, that grayish icy thing) the two officers still continuing to talk, but dismounted now, both with their backs arched, their weight on one leg, the other set slightly ahead, in the courtyard of a sort of tavern (or of a farm since there was a trough where they (the corporal and the jockey dismounted too) watered the five horses, their nostrils blowing noisily into the water), and the bewildered, alarmed face of the serving-girl in her smock (more of a farm-girl than a waitress) bringing a tray with four bottles of beer, the colonel taking one, filling a glass, handing it to the other officer, then holding two other bottles by the neck in one hand, turning toward the trough, raising them toward the two cavalrymen, the jockey stuffing the bundle of reins into the corporal's hand, running up, then coming back, taking back the reins, the two cavalrymen drinking from the bottle something warm and bitter, the cannon fire distant now but continuing with the same stubborn and soothing regularity, the colonel filling the second glass, wetting his lips, then setting it down on one of the crates of bottled water piled up against the wall, thrusting one hand into one of his pockets, extracting from it (still with that meticulous, terrifying calm, that absence of haste, of sleepwalkers or madmen) a cigarette case on which the sun flashed a moment, opening it, offering it to the other officer, then placing a thin cigar between his own lips, lighting it, sending out of his nostrils a stream of blue smoke, still not interrupting his conversation with the other officer nor seeming to pay any attention to what the woman with the haggard face was trying to say to him so volubly (the same thing that the territorial guard had told him, which had been repeated to him by the gesticulating man with the red blanket: "Yes, madame. Thank you. How much do I owe you, please?", taking out a wallet and beginning to count out the coins when the woman's face convulsed, her eyes suddenly raised toward the sky, then, without paying any attention to the coin which the colonel was handing her, uttering a groan, turning her back, beginning to run toward the house and vanishing into the door, the two cavalrymen brutally dragging the horses from the trough, trying as best they could to lead them into the shelter of the shed, the hum of the motors and the staccato of the machine-guns approaching rapidly, a shadow passing like a dark flash over the courtyard, breaking, scaling the wall, gone, the colonel and the other officer still standing in the same place, their glasses in their hands, simply raising their heads to stare after the three planes flying higher this time, machine-gunning something on the other side of the road, already vanished, the colonel finishing his beer, wiping his lips with an immaculate handkerchief, returning it to his pocket, dropping the little half-smoked cigar, crushing it carefully under his sole, then signaling to the jockey, turning, his left leg already raised, knee bent, resting it on the jockey's hands—the jockey had run up—then back in the saddle on the massive Percheron the color of wine lees, still dragging in its wake the double lines of its severed traces, the five horses again walking along the straight road still bordered here and there with wrecks, and later (or almost immediately afterwards: the houses of a village were now lining the road: low brick façades, almost all alike, sometimes joined together, sometimes separated by little gardens) the corporal heard the jockey swear, turned his head, saw an arm passed over the withers of the lead horse, a terrified, reddish face crowned with reddish hair and a leg trying to mount the animal, rushing into the void, the colonel at that moment turning on his saddle, shouting: "Get off that horse! Right now! Get-off-that-horse, do you hear me? Immediately!" while the jockey, one stirrup loose, sending kicks into the lead horse's flank, trying to reach the body now lying flat on the pommel of the saddle, shaken like a sack by the hysterical horse which had begun trotting where it stood, head raised high, the mouth again savagely tugged by the bit on which the jockey was pulling hard again and again, the colonel's rigid torso not even twisting around, still very straight, blind so to speak: "As if," the corporal described it (at that moment, six months later, he was lying in the bedroom of a brothel, his body naked, thinner but intact, lying beside the body of a whore who was pretending to listen to him, her expression vaguely alarmed or simply bored, the way you listen to an old man or a sick man ramble on) . . . "as if that was some tiresome thing which a colonel has nothing to do with, something too alien to what was concerning him at that moment, as if he had simply interrupted his elegant conversation with the commander to say quite incidentally out of the corner of his mouth: 'Get that man off that horse,' the way you say 'Get that dog out of here,' and nothing more, as if he had no need to lower himself to speak directly to an infantryman, as if that would have been a contravention of what was suitable to his rank, a sort of derogation. Because if he could at most condescend to let two cavalrymen, a jockey and a corporal—the latter even filthy, ill-shaven or rather unshaved for eight days, with

rusty spurs and a helmet smeared with mud—follow him
and keep him company—or polish his boots—in the empyrean of colonels killed on their mounts, he could still
not tolerate finding himself there with a mere infantryman,
but why am I telling you all this, what the fuck can it matter
to you, what the fuck can it matter to anyone? . . ." the
girl saying: "No, no, I'm listening to you. What was that
word you said: empyrean?" and he: "Empyrean? . . . Oh,
something like paradise . . . But special. Not just anyone's
paradise, a superior corner. Like a sort of exclusive club.
Reserved just for cavalry colonels. A private club where
they are entitled to walk in with their boots on, with their
horse, with their spurs and their damn ass screwed onto
their saddle. Though that idiot had decided to get there
on a Percheron, a plow horse. Just to show, no doubt, that
his supergroomed thoroughbred had been killed under
him. So I imagine that his entrance must have made quite
a sensation, among all the fine folks who were waiting for
him (or at least whom he must have imagined were waiting
for him) to give him his medal of honor. The ones from
Agincourt, from Pavia, and from Waterloo. Except that it
wasn't exactly the Reichshoffen charge. Rather the contrary: walking on that damned slaughterhouse of a road.
Because, I suppose, 'The French cavalry never runs
away' . . . Wouldn't have made his horse trot or taken a
shortcut for a cannonball. As it turned out. And the hell
with him! Good God, that's a nice pair of knockers you've
got there! . . . ," looking at the slender and naked body
still mingled with his own, the silky transparent skin under
which ran the blue or jade-green veins, one of the milky
legs over one of his, thinking: Good God! thinking: But
no more than a fish passing through the water. Me just as
much as her. What has passed through her. What we have
all passed through. Or rather what hasn't passed through

me . . . , trying to remember (but it was already impossible), to be again the way he had been on that oversized horse, or rather with the stirrups that were too long in the dazzling May sunlight, already no longer a living being, waiting passively for that brief, brutal, gray-black thing which was going to happen to him from one moment to the next, strike him violently, fling him off his horse, thinking that when he fell to the ground he wouldn't even feel the shock, any more than a sack of sawdust or of grain feels the cement or the pavement onto which it is thrown, because he would be dead, and exactly like a sack of sawdust or wheat under the sun, dusty, limp, except that through the holes, the tears in the cloth of his already earth-colored uniform it wouldn't be sawdust or wheat that would be flowing, but (only he wouldn't be feeling that either) his blood which would be slowly draining, red and shiny at first, then coagulating, congealing, absorbed as though by a blotter by the cloth where a dark-brown patch would gradually widen, thinking vaguely with that same macabre, despairing irony: And if it's in the belly it will be that damn beer, able to feel in that state which was like a transcendence of fear (something like a lacerating melancholy, a lacerating agony) the compact ball formed by the beer swallowed too quickly jiggling heavily in his stomach, his wasted body slowly shaken back and forth on that saddle with its hard armature, as if through it he could also feel between his thighs the powerful bones, the skeleton of the similarly wasted animal which was carrying him, perceiving the monotonous clatter of ten pairs of hooves on the surface of the road, the majestic echo of the cannon which regularly continued shaking the air, but very distant now, the black and telescoped shadows of the two officers distorted as they passed along the ground, undulating over the roadside, the wrecks, then at the same time that he

heard the gunfire crackling (and compared to the roaring
of the planes and the sound of the heavy machine-guns,
this was merely something like a faint, tenuous cough, like
the noise of a cap gun, of a child's toy) he saw him raise
the sparkling saber in his outstretched arm, everything,
rider, horse, and saber slowly collapsing to one side, exactly
like one of those lead soldiers whose base, the legs, would
begin to melt, still seeing him collapse, sink down endlessly, the saber raised in the sun, while, without his even
being aware of having made his own horse turn or of having
dug in his spurs, he was galloping alongside (or rather his
horse was galloping alongside that of) the jockey, the ambushed sniper behind the hedge continuing to fire, sprinkling them now with wasted bullets (though the jockey
claimed to have been grazed: but it was only a rip on the
side of his riding breeches), the three loaded horses struggling to gain speed, the lead horse slightly ahead, pulling
on its bridle, now covering again at top speed and in the
opposite direction the way they had just come, until they
managed to master their mounts and to get them walking,
the horses snorting noisily, the corporal busy trying to get
his foot back into the stirrup he had lost, the jockey saying
in that still furious, outraged voice: "For God's sake, shit,
the bugger! The goddamn cocksucker . . . ," then gathering
the reins in one hand, passing the other hand over his
thigh, looking at it, then touching his thigh several times
(but there was no blood), repeating: "The cocksucker, did
you see that? The goddamn cocksucker! A little more and
he . . . Jesus, the goddamn cocksucker! . . . ," then the
three horses halted, continuing to snort, their flanks rising
and falling, while they (the corporal and the jockey)
watched two soldiers lying side by side on their backs on
the other side of a slope, perpendicular to the road, in a
strange and identical position, legs and arms outstretched

and half-bent, like two frogs, moaning vaguely, the jockey saying: "Look at those two assholes, would you!" the corporal saying: "What assholes?" the jockey saying, still in that same furious, outraged voice: "Those two assholes on their bikes! They thought they were so smart. And they got theirs! . . ." the world, the things still behind the thick bell of sleep in the blinding sun, yellow and black, the distended shapes telescoped by the walls of glass, and at that moment he could see, distorted, alternately stretching and shrinking, the silhouette of a soldier running out of a house, without a gun, without a helmet, tunic unbuttoned, as if he had been suddenly wakened in the middle of a nap or of a meal, waving his arm, shouting: "Are you crazy standing out there in the middle of the road on those nags? Who do you think you are? Are you crazy? They're all over the place? There's one over there, just behind the corner of the barn! He's already got one guy! You . . . ," then stumbling, bending down, picking up one of his leggings that had unrolled like a snake or an orange peel, crouching a moment, but his head still raised, shouting: "But don't stay there, don't just stay there! Are you completely crazy or what? Hey, don't you see him? There! Now he's gone again! They shoot and then they change positions. They . . . ," then no longer trying to attach his legging, making another furious gesture with his arm, limping away, half bent over, holding his leg, toward the house out of which he had come and vanishing inside. A narrow path opened between two orchards to the left. "Goddamn shithole!" swore the jockey: "All right, get in there! Hey, gee up . . ." They thrust their spurs into their horses' bellies and galloped into the opening.

*T*HE two sisters, the two women who had somehow served as a mother to this brother several years their junior, not nursing him with their breasts which no man had ever touched but so to speak nursing him on their own flesh (or rather on the refusal of the desires of their own flesh) as that flesh withered into a virginity not sterile but sacrificed or rather preserved as an offering to that incestuous and austere passion; the one who took the man's part spaded the kitchen garden, pruned the plum trees, sawed the wood, cut the grass for the rabbits—and the other who, while her brother was sailing the oceans, the tropical seas (for that was about all they knew about it: not the fevers, the mosquitoes, the torrid or stifling climates: only the postcards where they could see palm trees by moonlight, pyramids, or the photographs of docile Antillean girls), came home each Sunday to help with the work, leaving again in the evening on a freezing train, waiting in a freezing station for another freezing train which deposited her in the middle of the night in the stone-cold mountains (she described how after having walked between two walls of snow she pushed open the door of the school where the stove had been cold since Saturday, how she had the impression as she crossed the threshold of penetrating into something hard, mineral, dense, which she could even smell (not the smell of wet floorboards, but the smell of something hard and metallic which also thrust into her lungs), taking off only her dress to slide between sheets stiff with cold, waiting without being able to sleep for the time to get up, to wrap a shawl around herself, to go into the classroom, to light the stove and stay there, incapable of moving, until the iron-colored daylight should gradually whiten the windowpanes): the two sisters, then— one not yet an old woman, still pretty, and even beautiful, if beauty is the contrary of coquetry and triviality, with her regular, straight, rather square countenance, and the other (the one with the almost masculine features), both still offering their brother the sacrifice of enduring the ordeal which it must have been for them of that wedding, not only a religious ceremony but one pompously celebrated in a cathedral—they who for nothing in the world would have even set foot in their village church forced to attend the service, to stand up, to kneel—followed by that pompous reception in a house compared with which the one they lived in had at most the look of a heap of attics furnished with those pieces you find only in attics, though they were waxed and polished with that sort of intensity that the poor lavish upon the maintenance of whatever they possess—and this then: the monumental stone staircase, the monumental salon where stood enthroned, carved in a ton of marble, the bust, draped in Roman fashion, of an Empire general, the walls embellished with copious portraits of male and female ancestors, in oil, in pastel, in watercolor, the framed miniatures, the potted palms, the forest of cactuses and other plants decorating the veranda where they had to sit for photographs among groups of austere old ladies, of men in uniforms decorated with gold braid, or wearing white ties, raising cigars to their lips, cavalierly seated on gilt chairs, mustachioed, with the faces of revelers or idlers, young or old *rentiers,* living on debts (not that anyone told the sisters this, but they could feel it, they for whom money was a thing with which you could no more play than with the air you breathed or the bread you ate, as they could feel the decorous indulgence of the glances cast upon them or of the words addressed to them, they in those rigid gowns overembellished with embroidery, with bows, with ruffles, which he (their brother) had insisted on buying for them just as he had insisted (pleaded) on their presence or rather demanded it, threatening them with his anger, telling them the name and the address of the Parisian dressmaker where they had finally consented to go on the one condition that they themselves pay for those dresses whose price was about the equivalent of what they could have saved in two years, unless (which was more likely) he had made an agreement in advance with the dressmaker or the shop in which the salesman (a man with curled mustaches, in a frock coat, striped trousers, and wing collar) showed them models without seeming to notice their clothes, which were too carefully brushed, too scrupulously neat, any more than their chapped and wrinkled hands): that winter all the rivers and streams overflowed, so that they had to wait in damp and drafty stations for the trains to be authorized to proceed at a snail's pace through landscapes that looked like pewter out of which emerged the dotted lines of trees and fences, as if it was necessary that even before being celebrated this marriage

which was to last only four years, of which the principal
actor (the man with the square beard and the face marked
by terrible climates) and several of the carefree supernu-
meraries with golden epaulettes and cigars similarly gold-
banded had no more than four years to live, be announced
premonitorily by a natural disaster (if it could be said that
the one which was to occur four years later was not in
essence as natural as the rain, the drought, the epidemics,
or the frost), in the same way that thirty years later, as if
nothing were to remain, neither the bodies (the one which
the widow sought in vain through the ravaged fields) nor
the sites, a torrent emerging from a mountain of the Pyrenees (or rather what had never been anything but a peaceful stream), suddenly furious, inexplicably swollen to the
dimensions of a cataract, leaving extant only a desert of
stones like some field of bones in the place where there
once stood the hotel placed under the patronage of the
Egyptian (or of the Turk, or of the Levantine) wearing a
fez and addicted to baccarat, amid the lawns, the flower-
beds, and the park with the cool shade trees under which
the bride of scarcely four years promenaded, in a baby
carriage pushed by the black woman, a child already father-
less.

Nonetheless, in the sepia-toned, slightly faded photograph, among the ephemeral and joyous grouping of the
ephemeral, vaguely unreal figures, they (the two women,
the two sisters with the names of an empress and a goddess)
are still there, surrounded by dwarf palms, by aspidistras,
by the forest of potted plants, tormented, rigid, sitting on
the gilt chairs, dressed as though derisively in their heavily
embroidered gowns of the kind worn, in documents of the
period, by actresses or *demi-mondaines,* their unsmiling
faces crushed under their heavy chignons, embarrassed by
their mannish hands, encased in those whaleboned blouses,

those skirts of heavy fabrics which swathed them like carapaces, like elytra, like armor.

*   *   *

There is nothing special about the man's face in the center of the group. Rough-hewn and tanned by the open air of maneuvers or by hunts, this might be the face of a workman or of a peasant from which it is distinguished only by its waxed mustaches, the tips curled upward, then the fashion in a certain society, as frequent in Germany as in the faubourg Saint-Germain, and the pointed helmet which surmounts it, of some dark metal, ornamented with polished brass. He is surrounded by other figures like himself, with similar waxed mustaches, some in long overcoats, others in uniforms with gold braid, and they too wearing pointed or plumed helmets, the wind sometimes pushing the white feathers to one side. The feathers, the metal helmets, the shiny boots, the sudden and unforeseeable changes of position of the figures make them resemble some sort of birds, plumed and beaked and steel-taloned, moving abruptly, at once fierce, anxious, trivial, and irresponsible. From time to time they turn toward one another, pivoting with a vehement movement, tilting their heads to hear the way old men do, exchanging a few words, pivoting again in the opposite direction and becoming motionless again. The one in the center has rested on his saber guard the tiny hand of a tiny, atrophied arm, an arm like a doll's arm. They remain like this for a certain time, stiff, cut out of metal, dressed in dark cloth, spasmodically stirred by brief movements, eyes vacant. At the end, an open automobile arrives. That is, all at once, without anything having announced it, it is there, suddenly materialized out of nothing, taking up almost the entire width of the screen striped by swift scratches, like a black rain. As if he too did not so much move as successively shift from one fixed attitude to another, the officer sitting beside the driver leaps from his seat and opens the rear door beside which he stands at attention, motionless. Still holding his tiny arm against his side as if he were embracing a swaddled doll, the man with the waxed mustaches hops forward toward the car and gets in. For a moment (while the officer closes the door (that is, stands motionless for a fraction of a second in the pose of a man closing a door), then resumes his place beside the driver; that is, appears successively in the middle of a half turn, then half-leaning, then seated), for a moment then we see the man with the waxed mustaches standing on the floor of the car, his doll's arm pressed close to his body, then, suddenly, sitting on the backseat, and the automobile starts up. As a matter of fact he does not sit down, seems brutally drawn in the opposite direction by the sudden start of the automobile, the backs of his knees bumping against the seat, his knees giving way beneath the shock, his back making immediate contact with the quilted leather of the seat back, yet his torso keeps straight, stiff, with his stiff-pointed mustache pointing upward, his tiny stiff arm still pressed against the saber guard as though sewn against his side, staring straight ahead and vanishing while a second automobile already occupies (not advancing: already occupying) the place of the first, and while its passengers resembling herons or cranes take their places in it in their turn, the tails of their long overcoats fluttering around their shining spurs, their plumes or the brass points of their helmets tilting and straightening again, the automobile immediately replaced by one just like it, each one suddenly drawn after the next to the left like those images that the operator of a magic lantern causes to succeed each other horizontally, swept away (cars, birds, plumes, and helmets) and effaced.

* *
*

Toward the middle of the night, the train started up. With frequent and long stops, it ran the whole following day, the whole night after that and again the greater part of the next night as well. At the stops, the four or five men whose heads virtually blocked the frame of the narrow windows at the ends of the car vainly begged for a little water from the sentries pacing the tracks (or the cinders) alongside the locked cars. Day or night, their pleading voices could be heard repeating in a monotonous lament the only three German words they seemed to know, while behind and beneath them rose the chorus of curses and insults from the confused tangle of sweating bodies, breathing with difficulty, gasping for air, suffocating.

Sometimes a quarrel broke out somewhere in the dark or by day in the dim light among the indistinct huddle of bodies in filthy earth-colored uniforms, their limbs tangled and their earth-colored faces filthy too, with their fifteen-day beards and their red-rimmed eyes. As if some ill-banked fire of violence flickered up suddenly here and there, in an outburst of voices, of oaths, as if the shapeless and vague aggregate composed by the prisoners was shaken in places by impotent convulsions, quickly wearing themselves out, exhausted, falling back, inertia returning, merely troubled by some insult, some curse still rising, the voices answering each other another moment, vehemently accusing each other of cowardice, of treachery, then tiring of the insults, then nothing more, merely silence, merely the sound of choked breathing.

This time it was in open country that the train had stopped. Here and there they could hear the outside locks of the doors being opened until the guttural voices and the crunching of the gravel under boots reached them, quite close now, right against the wall of their own car, the panel suddenly sliding open, the air from outside suddenly penetrating at the same time as the voices, suddenly distinct, as though they too were stamped with that violence of the finally breathable air in which, staggering as though drunk, they clumsily let themselves drop onto the ground, able to see the long motionless train with its gaping doors from which, like excrement, clusters of men in earth-colored uniforms kept dropping out, sliding down the gravel slopes, and huddling at the bottom.

The day is ending, calm and cool. The tracks border a field sloping down from the cinders and then rising again to the edge of a thick pine woods. On the road that skirts it is walking a couple preceded by a little girl in a bright dress, with long hair, who runs ahead, playing with a dog with a coat of the same color as her hair. These people are too far away to be able to make out their features. They advance calmly without seeming to notice the train and the fringe of crouching men lining the tracks. The blond hair of the little girl floats behind her when she runs. The dog prances, seems to snap up something the child throws to it, runs back to her, runs away again. The dog prances backward in front of the little girl, yapping. It is too far away for them to see its mouth opening, but its whole body leaps up at each bark of which the joyous sound reaches the prisoners an instant later in the evening's calm, as through an opaque density of time.

*　*　*

It had already been a long time since the battery had stopped firing and under the big trees it was completely dark. From far away, they could see the column arriving. Only the first of the vehicles had turned on its lights which illuminated little more than four or five yards ahead of it, and they could see them for a long while, suspended in the darkness like two pale moons trembling faintly, not seeming to advance, imperceptibly growing larger as they approached along the forest path. Having come up to the battery, the first truck stopped and, behind it, the row of vehicles became motionless. Two officers got out and while unfolding their maps headed toward the artillerymen's radio truck. The trucks of the convoy were canvas-topped and nothing was moving inside. The canvas flaps were open at the rear of each one, and as they approached, the artillerymen and the cavalrymen saw two rows of soldiers sitting opposite each other on benches set lengthwise in the truck. As a matter of fact, they could make out only the first men in each row, those closest to the rear of the vehicle, with behind them, in the dark, motionless and silent shapes whose presence they could divine—their breathing and something else that emanated from them, more silent than silence itself or rather as if silence and darkness had themselves been something tangible, something that enveloped the two rows of soldiers or rather emerged from them and remained there, stagnant, compact and unbreathable, enclosed under the dark canvas. Packed against each other like children, docilely sitting face to face, their rifles vertical between their knees which touched each other, they seemed like those little frightened animals which huddle in the back of a cage and keep perfectly still, like rabbits, merely breathing. The cavalrymen asked them if they belonged to that North African infantry division whose arrival as reinforcements had been repeatedly announced, but they continued to keep silent. Perhaps they did not understand French, or perhaps they had been forbidden to answer questions from strangers. The darkness made it impossible to determine whether they were North Africans or Frenchmen. Somehow all they could tell was that they were very young, and they could feel that thing which emerged from them and kept them squeezed together as in a case. It also seemed that they could see their eyes shining, floating in the darkness, suspended there, all turned toward the rear of the vehicle. After a moment the officers got back in the first truck, after which the whole column started up, slowly driving into the night and bearing its cargo of wretched little frightened animals jolting in the ruts of the forest path, and soon they could no longer even hear the noise of the motors.

The following night the cavalrymen who were covering the retreat passed a convoy immobilized on a road by a bombardment—some of the cars were still burning. By the light of the flames they could see the charred bodies of the drivers still sitting behind their steering wheels. Some of the trucks were tipped over on their sides, their canvas tops half consumed, and inside they could vaguely make out tangled heaps. There was also a motorcyclist— or rather the charred form of a motorcyclist—still straddling his machine which was lying on its side, his hands still holding the grips. One of the cavalrymen said that these were the trucks that had been trying to find their way the night before, but someone objected that there had been no motorcyclist with them. No one answered. The lead car had been blocked by a bomb which had hollowed an enormous crater in the center of an intersection where several houses were still burning, crackling slightly. The cavalrymen had to ride single file to get their horses around the crater. Tiny yellow and blue sawtooth flames were chasing each other along the beams of the fallen structures.

* * *

Some that had doubtless hit a pebble or a splinter of rock had their tips broken or twisted, like a hook or even a nightcap, a horn, like those limbs of sawdust-filled dolls, with a soft fold of yellow metal, faintly rusted, now a grayish ochre, except for thin striations resulting from the contact of some hard particle where the brass glistened, as though from gold scratches.

It wasn't he (the four-year-old boy) who had discovered the place, still less the two women with runny eyes, with precociously wrinkled faces, one of whom, wearing sabots or heavy boots above which her thick wool stockings formed accordion folds, accompanied him, holding in one of her hands the shaft of a spade (the one she used to dig up the potatoes) and in the other, with its callused palm, its callused fingers, the boy's hand—at least until the two of them had come out of the village and away from the road where the cars were passing, or at least as long as she could keep him from escaping and running ahead.

And if they (the two women in the invariably dark clothes) knew the place (actually everyone knew it, there was nothing secret about it: a month earlier, a regiment of young recruits in training had been billeted in the neighboring village school and twice a week the high rocky cliffs overlooking the valley had echoed with shots), they had said nothing about it, either because of some superstitious horror, or because by some decision of the military authorities, approaching the place (and with all the more reason, digging there) was forbidden, or else because they feared being blamed by the other woman (the one who paid them a visit each summer, accompanied by the child, after an interminable journey during which they had to change trains four times in the middle of the night, once in a huge station (this was Lyon) with a high glass roof vanishing into the dark and where the child with sleep-swollen eyes awakened to contemplate with excitement, on the platforms and even in the buffet, the animated racket of armed soldiers of all races (some were wearing a red chechia, there were sailors, too, with pompoms on their caps, huge Senegalese with cheeks striped with ritual scars, Arabs) wandering or strolling from one platform to the next, sometimes lying on the ground, using sacks, rolled-up blankets, or rucksacks as pillows, sound asleep amid the vast and vague tumult punctuated by the whistles of the locomotives or the impact of the buffers, the woman with the black veils sitting imperturbable beside him on the imitation-leather bench, with that simultaneously royal and outraged expression, her inflexible Bourbon profile, her globular and dry eyes staring proudly ahead, beyond the noisy buffet, the noisy troop of men in artillery uniforms, sailors, gendarmes, at the ghost of an incommunicable, sublime, and ruined dream).

To reach the place where you could dig up the bullets (he—the child—had all the same managed to get himself taken there), you had to follow a path climbing up to a ridge where the ground formed a steep slope which had served as a target for the firing exercises. The bullets were more or less deeply buried depending on the obstacles they had encountered. When she had found one, the woman wiped off the earth that had remained stuck to it before handing it to the child. The spade clanged and sometimes brought up bone-shaped pebbles which the moisture of the ground had yellowed. Drying, they would not take long to turn white. When a bullet had hit one of them, it had twisted as it broke the pebble into pieces.

In the evening after dinner, he took out of his pocket the tiny cones warmed by the heat of his body and lined them up on the table where they glistened faintly under the light from the oil lamp, hooked, flattened, or twisted, while the three women, knitting or embroidering, talked among themselves in their calm, low, despairing voices.

Sometimes one of them glanced at the table where he was clumsily trying to make one or two balance on their bases which the shock of impact had not deformed and which nonetheless fell over like ninepins, rolling in arcs on the surface of the table. For a second the red-rimmed eyes remained fixed on the pieces of metal, as if from them emanated something fascinating, obscene, intolerable, and venomous.

* * *

(Perhaps, after all, the legend according to which he refused to read orders or documents if mention was not made, not only of his rank, but of his title as baron, was not so preposterous, perhaps he was crazy even before having seen his regiment melt away in the course of days without even having had occasion to fight, perhaps he had his horse brought up and came to lead the first squadron only out of some sort of furious defiance, of scorn, in order to show, for instance, to his men and his officers how the cavalry tradition meant that a man should behave in case of a surprise attack, and perhaps it was that intimate and absurd conviction of the absolute superiority of his courage which allowed him to emerge unscathed from that ambush he had got himself caught in? Perhaps he was convinced that with enough audacity and *sang-froid* you could emerge unscathed from any situation, or perhaps, after all, he wasn't crazy, only maintained still on that road strewn with dead men the serene assurance that his title and his contempt for danger rendered him invulnerable?)

* * *

The available testimony was vague: it was impossible to know where the first bullet had hit him. Perhaps in the legs, since afterwards it wasn't possible for him to stand up as the officers were accustomed to do in maneuvers at this early stage of the war, observing through his binoculars the enemy's movements, and since his men had to carry him to the edge of the woods, setting him down at the foot of a tree where, leaning against the trunk, he continued to give his orders. Or perhaps he was hit in the chest, or even in the belly. Hurt badly enough in any case to resign himself to that position from which the view he could have over the battlefield (the faintly rolling landscape, the beetfields, the cut straw, the little groves, the depression where the river flowed) was necessarily reduced.

The second bullet hit him in the forehead. At that time, wearing helmets was not yet regulation and the combatants wore only a soft képi decorated, for officers, with gold braid sewn into a four-knot cross. The regimental number was embroidered in gold threads on the front part of the lining. The visor was made of molded leather. The witnesses did not specify whether the projectile made of an alloy of tungsten and brass hit his forehead above or below the visor. Nonetheless his captain's binoculars, which were later sent to the widow, were intact, which suggests that the bullet struck rather high, unless he was not using them at that moment, simply holding them in one hand resting on his thigh or hanging at his side. In any case it can be presumed that in carrying with it fragments of leather and cloth the burning metal cone splintered the frontal bone and, slightly twisted by the impact, lodged itself with several splinters in the brain. Death was certainly instantaneous. The army was then in full retreat after the defeat of Charleroi and the body was abandoned without burial at the very place where it was lying, perhaps still leaning against the tree, face concealed by a sheet of sticky blood which gradually thickened, filling the eye sockets, accumulating on the mustache, dripping more and more slowly over the thick square beard, the dark tunic. Before leaving him behind, his orderly, or the one of his officers to whom the command of the company had fallen, was nonetheless careful to remove the grayish zinc tag attached to his wrist and bearing his name as well as his serial number. This tag was later sent to the widow at the same time as the binoculars and a death notice, followed a little later by the attribution of the cross of the Legion of Honor awarded posthumously.

That was all. The regiment subsequently suffered such losses (it had to be entirely reconstituted several times in the course of the war) that it was virtually impossible to find and to interrogate the direct witnesses of this event regarding which details are lacking, so that there continues to be uncertainty concerning the exact nature of the first wound as well as concerning that of the second, the account given to the widow and the sisters (or the account which they made of the episode subsequently), though doubtless in good faith, perhaps somewhat embellishing the matter or rather theatricalizing it according to a stereotype impressed upon their imagination by the illustrations in history books or the paintings representing the death of more or less legendary warriors, almost always dying in a semi-recumbent position on the grass, head and torso more or less leaning against a tree trunk, surrounded by knights wearing coats of mail (or holding a plumed bicorne in once hand) and represented in attitudes of affliction, one knee in the dirt, concealing with one iron-gloved hand their face turned toward the ground.

Nothing else, then, but these vague accounts (perhaps at second hand, perhaps poeticizing the facts, either out

of pity or kindness, in order to flatter or rather, insofar as
was possible, to comfort the widow, or again because the
witnesses—those who had been there or those who had
repeated their accounts—were themselves deceived, glo-
rifying the episode, obeying that need to transcend the
events in which they had more or less directly participated:
hence we have seen the performers of brilliant actions
distort the facts, though these were to their advantage,
with the sole unconscious goal of making them agree with
pre-established models), hence nothing confirms that when
they reached the scene the enemy soldiers (these too were
exhausted men, filthy, covered with dust or mud, who for
three weeks had unceasingly marched and fought without
rest, eyes red-rimmed from lack of sleep, eyelids smarting,
and feet bleeding in their short boots) found him just that
way, which is to say, as described to the widow later on,
still leaning against that tree like a medieval knight or an
Empire colonel (even the stereotyped expression of the
bullet "received full in the forehead" makes the matter
uncertain), and not, as is more likely, in the imprecise form
these shapeless heaps offer to the eye, more or less soiled
with mud and blood, and where the first thing that strikes
the eye is most often the excessive size of the shoes, forming a V when the body is lying on its back, or else parallel,
showing their hobnailed soles to which still adhere clots
of earth and grass if the dead man is lying face down, or
stuck together, drawn up toward the buttocks by the bent
legs, the body itself entirely huddled in a fetal position,
distractedly turned over with one foot by the man arriving
on the scene whose attention is suddenly alerted at the
sight of the gold braid, leaning down then perhaps to unbutton the sticky tunic in search of some general-staff
paper or marching orders, some inadvertently forgotten
map, or, simply, a gold watch.

*
*   *

It was not mistakenly or out of teasing malice that the Italian jockey derided the way the little Jew rode his horse—not that he was so inept at any physical exercise as his sickly appearance led one to believe (he belonged to a basketball club in his neighborhood), but as for keeping his seat on a saddle, he had once and for all shown a categorical, visceral opposition to that, preferring to suffer, to let himself be painfully shaken up, whether at a trot or a gallop (finding a way, even at a walk, even wedged in by the saddlebags, to look like what the jockey had said in his figurative way apropos of a man's member and a cake of soap), as though by a sort of passive, furious protest—or rather execration—and just as in certain Oriental countries a man kills himself to dishonor his enemy, he showed by this proud resistance, this scornful disgust, his refusal of what he was forced to do not only by the noncommissioned officers and the officers themselves but, beyond them, by a system at once military and social that had been able to conceive forcing a man to be shamefully, as in circuses, paraded on the back of an animal.

*
*   *

. . . as a matter of fact—but they didn't know it—it was a whole armored column that had passed through here, the general leading it, standing in his command car, one cheek striped with a bloody bandage, bouncing in the ruts, clinging to the windshield, imperturbable, incapable (he would say later on), in the racket of the engines and the explosions, of halting the firing which was vomited in all directions by all the weapons of his armored vehicles launched at top speed into the red-striped night—the general (he was later to be made a marshal) who for four years would formidably drive ahead in the same manner, sweeping aside everything in his passage, in deserts, under even hotter suns, still continuing to drive ahead on other roads, between other ruins, other smoking wreckage, other dead men—and later retreating in his turn, still impassive, calm, dangerous, still striking, chin high, close-shaven, erect as a mannequin, with those eyes of a bird of prey, that leathery face, and instead of the traditional monocle those motorcyclist's goggles pushed up onto his forehead or above the visor of his marshal's cap, so that, on orders (those orders which for four years he was to obey with that same impetuous audacity, rigid, distant, arrogant), he himself would aim at his temple the barrel of a pistol and press the trigger—but on that May morning the cavalrymen knew nothing: they did not know that for some ten hours the order of battle had been so to speak inverted, turned around, which caused the regiment (or rather what was left of it) to have ceased to beat a retreat and for its remains (or rather its wreckage) to wander now behind the enemy on which it believed it was turning its back, ridiculous, abandoned, good only for drawing the indolent gunfire of some roving plane or of some sniper ambushed behind a hedge.

*　*　*

By dint of boiling the water for sterilizing the syringe in it every night, the bottom and sides of the little aluminum pan with the dented rim are covered with a deposit of chalky scale. Its handle, ending in a loop by which to hang it on the wall, is surrounded by a gently bulging unvarnished sheath of wood (or from which, in any case, any trace of varnish has long since vanished), which has gradually come loose.

The still-warm pan is now empty. The syringe and the

needle have been removed from it and the water thrown away, and a just-perceptible damp crescent, rapidly shrinking, remains on one side, on the bottom of its inner wall. The pan is resting on a narrow tabletop of gray-veined marble between the bathroom sink and the door, now closed, of the bedroom. Above the piece of marble the wall is papered with a shiny paper, an imitation of squares of pottery, divided into regular squares by two narrow pale-blue bands strewn with tiny round disks like beads. The inside of each of the squares is embellished with a flower, also pale blue, the center surrounded by a crown of open petals. This crown is alternately oriented toward the left or the right. Behind the bands forming the squares and the flowers is a cream-colored background. At the height of the little gas stove on which the pan is resting, the decorative imitation-pottery wallpaper shows a slightly brownish trace, fading toward the top.

Since the door to the bedroom is closed, the boy stares hard at the empty pan, the piece of marble, and the ampule of morphine, orangish-yellow at the broken tips, which is still lying there on its side. When a faint cry, like that which might emerge from a mouse's throat, reaches him through the door, the boy violently presses his hands over his ears and can hear the throbbing of his blood. Almost immediately the door opens and he drops his hands. Now he can see the bed illuminated by a night-light, the vague shadows, and can hear indistinct voices. On the wall, to the right of the bed where the sheets are now pulled up, hangs a sepia photographic enlargement framed by a broad strip of brown wood. In a faded halo can be seen the face of a man with a square beard, with waxed mustaches and a bold, gay expression, wearing a soft képi with gold braid on it.

* * *

The two soldiers are lying side by side on their backs, on the side of a hill, as though on the raked plane of a stage or a sort of showcase. One man's knees are parted and his heels together, so that his legs form a lozenge, like those of a frog. The second man's right leg is bent back and his heel almost touches the calf of his left leg, stiff and extended. From this angle you can see the soles of the hobnail boots. Both men seem wounded in the belly, covered (but perhaps this is an accident?) in each case by one of their hands. One of the men has lost his helmet. The only apparent signs of life are the slow movements of their heads tipped back and rolling from right to left, the occiput in contact with the ground, at least in the case of the man who is bare-headed, the other's helmet, its rear visor wedged between the nape of his neck and the slope, is pushed back above the forehead, held on only by his chin strap which has slipped off the chin and is now under it, at its junction with the neck, stretched in a V and doubtless slightly choking the wounded man. They have their eyes closed (or perhaps not: perhaps this is merely an impression resulting from the fixity of their stare which, obviously, sees nothing). Faint moans and incoherent sounds emerge from their open mouths. Yet you can distinguish, repeated in a whining voice, the words "Ambulance . . . ambulance . . . where's the ambulance? . . ." At each of the movements of the head still wearing the helmet, the sun flashes for a second on the helmet's crest. Like the heads, the hands too are perhaps agitated by faint movements or faint spasmodic clenchings, but of a very limited extent and scarcely perceptible (for example, one hand alternately clenches and spreads its fingers). There is no apparent wound (at least from here: at a distance of three or four yards and in passing), no trace of blood.

*
* *

The ceremony was over. However, long after the departure of the emperor with the withered arm, the troops continued to parade. Between the gray and severe façades the columns of men followed each other, passing infrequent automobiles with delicate wheels, with globular headlights, with fenders like coleopteran elytra, and high square bodies like those of fiacres. The rows of men also advanced with that same hopping gait, as though they were pushing each other, moved by a kind of incomprehensible haste, rifle at the ready, carrying knapsacks, their pointed helmets covered with a sort of sheath which made folds above their inexpressive faces inhabited only, it seemed, by that incomprehensible precipitation, one of them occasionally, on the flank of the column, gesturing with one arm toward the cameraman and vanishing, replaced by the next, exactly the same, while from time to time a woman in a hobble skirt and a bright blouse and wearing a huge hat approached (sprang from the left side of the screen), ran hopping down the flank of the column, and flung bouquets of flowers to the soldiers with an abrupt, almost hostile gesture, as if she were striking them, as if she were flinging in their faces something like stones or handfuls of dust, or sometimes taking a man's arm, embracing him, accompanying him for a few steps while he smiled with an embarrassed expression, still keeping for a while in one hand the bouquet the woman had thrust into it, then, not knowing what to do with it, letting it drop, the petals and the stems scattering on the ground, crushed by the trampling of the mechanical boots, and soon gray.

*
*   *

Like those exotic birds with huge beaks, with naked necks, perched on some guano-encrusted branch in the cage of a zoo, the four persons are sitting on a bench, torsos upright, on the side of a barracks. The wall of crudely planed horizontal planks, clearly showing the veins and knots of the wood, is of a dark, tarry brown. The skinny torso of one of the figures is wearing a torn olive-green undershirt. The other three are wearing the remains or rather the vestiges of khaki uniforms, tattered and stained, the tunics unbuttoned over khaki-green undershirts stiff with dirt. From their inexpressive faces tilted backward, from their globular and half-closed eyes which show only a thin bluish slit, like the eyes of blind men, emanates something terrifying and macabre, as if from those scarecrows sewn together out of rags and furnished with a slanting plank at the top of a pole instead of a head. On the bony and close-sheared skulls the cheekbones, the hollow cheeks, the tight skin resembles a kind of tanned leather whose initial color has given way to a grayish or ashen hue. With their narrow and receding foreheads, their flat noses that seem to be devoured by some sort of disease, the lower part of their faces drawn excessively tight on each side of the lips in thick folds, they suggest those products of hybrid breeding, mules or hinnies, passive, somnambulistic, and cunning, docilely drowsing between the shafts of carts. When they part, the palms of the man who is striking a tin can with the flat of his hand can briefly be seen, a dirty pink, as though faded, as if here too the initial color of the skin had been diluted, had disappeared as a consequence of sweat or continual rubbing. On his skull apparently suffering from alopecia, the hairs are beginning to grow back in patches, in short, woolly curls. Sometimes he replaces the tin can with an aluminum mess kit of which the outside is covered with a layer of black paint (or of smoke?) scratched in places, exposing the shiny metal. The other instruments consist of a reed flute with a hoarse timbre and two pieces of wood whose impact produces a dry, hollow sound, contrasting with the rattle of a box of nails. Except for the mess kit, the whole scene (the side of the barracks, the musicians, their clothes, their faces) is entirely composed of a range of earth colors, and the only bright notes are provided by the collar tabs still attached to the tunics, one showing a black number on a red background, the other a red number on a green background.

The torsos of the four musicians with their scarecrow heads are absolutely erect, the four faces absolutely parallel too, their sleepy blind-man's stares directed straight ahead. They would seem to be dozing if the movements of their hands shaking or striking the instruments did not spread in brief vibrations faintly agitating their shoulders and their heads. Just as much as the world outside they seem to be ignoring each other, making no sign of concerted effort, absent, fierce, patient, changing rhythm spontaneously when the flutist attacks, without warning it seems, another of those repetitive melodies whose very monotony serves as a support for the various percussion combinations. The hands with the dirty-pink palms which are hitting the can have long bony fingers with knotty joints and pale pink nails that seem stuck on, like patches. At each movement of the skinny wrist a thread of wool hanging in a spiral from the ragged sleeve twists in tiny convulsions.

No more than from the four frozen faces there emanates from the hoarse notes strung out by the flute and sustained by the cadences with which the other instruments accompany them neither melancholy nor mirth. A ghostly crowd of other persons with skinny bodies, also wearing ragged and filthy uniforms much too large for them, wander slowly in little groups down the row on either side of which the barracks are aligned. On the backs of their mustard-colored tunics can be read the two letters K and G, drawn in red paint and about a foot high. Most stop as they pass and stand for a moment dourly contemplating the four musicians, sometimes gathering round in a group, then resuming their stroll. Sometimes a guard stops too. He is wearing a pale-green uniform, a cap, and low, carefully polished black boots. The shoulder tabs of his tunic are bordered with silver braid. He too contemplates the four mulattos sitting on the bench, then walks on, turning back several times, casting incredulous glances over his shoulder. Indifferent to the spectators, eyes still half-closed, dark, fierce, their heads tilted back, the musicians continue to play. The regular and syncopated impacts of the two pieces of wood can still be heard for a long while as you walk away. Through a gap between the black sides of the two barracks you can see, beyond the barbed-wire fence, the orange disk of the sun setting on the horizon. As it descends it seems to grow larger and the orange gradually turns to red. The sky is a delicate silky gray above the sandy plain where a skimpy grove of pines is silhouetted here and there. Sinking farther, the disk touches the treetops. At the end it is pink.

XII

1940

*I*T was only three days later that he thought about it. Or rather that his body remembered: already in bed, the lamp out (he went to bed early; he undressed, slid between the sheets, without even a book or a magazine), once he was prone he turned the switch, then lay there without even waiting, without impatience, knowing that sleep would come almost immediately, swallowing him up not in but under its thick black cape, remaining for a moment like that, perfectly motionless, eyes open on the darkness where the wan rectangle of the window gradually appeared, floating suspended, imponderable, while slowly the night's milky light picked out a reflection on the curve of a piece of furniture, the convexities of a picture frame, then the pale portions (the shirt of the man with a rifle, the slashed sleeves of the woman's court dress) of the clothes in which remote male and female ancestors had posed for a painter, frozen there for two hundred years, the solemn gold-framed portraits which, after distribution among the heirs, had ended up in this bedroom of the apartment which, after distribution as well, he occupied (or rather did not occupy: where he slept two or three weeks a year when he returned, at the period of the grape harvests, to the vast provincial building where he had lived as a child, which he had left, still a child, never to return except like this, only in passing), and into which (the apartment) had been moved the furniture and the paintings which the distribution had allotted to him, which he had not touched, and where, alone since the last spring, lived the two old women who had arrived by one of the last trains that had still run south, pursued in the distance by the muffled explosions of bombs which seemed to advance as rapidly as the broken-down convoy consisting of cattle cars and first-class sleepers in which were indiscriminately crammed women, children, grown men, and dead-drunk deserters: the two women whose faces he had never known except furrowed, with red-rimmed eyes from which something shiny, silvery, had silently begun flowing, mixing with that grayish powder that old ladies use, when they had opened the door and had seen him on the landing where he stood, with his eight-day beard, his broken fingernails, filthy, shivering without even realizing it, dressed those first days of November only in the overalls and espadrilles given him by the farmer whose door he and his fellow fugitive had pushed open (or rather, forced) in the middle of the night, watching them change in the barn while he weighed in his hand the gold wedding ring and the wrist-watch, examined the boots, the warm riding breeches, rolled into a ball the tunics marked with red, all the time repeating, Hurry up! Make it quick! Hurry up! And now get out of here, get out, get out, get out of here! . . .

And even before he had time to distinguish, emerging in their turn from the darkness, the vague patches of faces and hands (the almost feminine, carefully manicured hand resting on the trigger guard of the rifle, the other (the woman's) hand holding between its fingers a mask which itself was masked with a carnival mask), he fell asleep. That is, sleep fell upon him, absolutely black, opaque, almost palpable, leaving room for neither dreams nor even for mere reflexes: sometimes, if he wakened, there was only time to realize that he had not moved, was still lying on his back in the position where sleep had seized him, then to roll over onto his belly with a bestial groan and fall asleep again. And this had been so ever since the first night, when for the first time he had slipped his clean body between clean sheets, the body he had looked at with a kind of amazement, as if it did not belong to him, floating weightless in the green transparent water of the tub, not fleshless nor even gaunt, simply thin, intact, the same body in which he had slept for five months, stretched out each night on the thin mattress of a bunk not much wider than a coffin in the dense, unbreathable air of the barracks among other bodies piled up on three levels, feeling, each night with the same horror, the same insurmountable disgust, the numberless swarming, the minuscule and numberless nibbling, desperate and voracious, of numberless lice moving over his body.

And now he was here, lying stiff and naked in the smooth sheets, merely calm, merely inhabited by that sort of silent, furious, cold laughter which was the opposite of gaiety and which had lodged in him four days earlier, specifically on the morning when they had left the farm where, despite the assurances of the sergeant commanding the post, he had tossed and turned all night in the hay, waking with a start, soaked with sweat despite the cold under his thin overalls, believing he heard outside the footsteps and the guttural voices of their pursuers (or perhaps not waking, dreaming that he was waking, or perhaps awakened while sleeping, or perhaps sleeping wide awake, in that secondary state where exhaustion and action bring a man to the condition of a wild animal capable of passing from sleep to movement or the converse in a second . . .).

For months he had forgotten their very existence. That is, their existence in flesh and blood, limbs, skin, moisture, breath, saliva, odor. For months, each Sunday, sitting on his bunk, he had made pencil drawings which, through a Jewish pimp from Oran, he sold to their guards for the packages of tobacco that constituted the camp currency. Patiently, each Sunday, he repeated the images of the same couple or of the same woman (he had learned to give them a childish face framed by silky hair) in the postures of coitus, of sodomization or fellatio (and at the end—this was the one that was most successful—the same posture: the woman kneeling, her body arched, offering her rump): something which was to drawing more or less what a cake of soap is to a stone or a root, gradually learning with a grim perversity to heighten the details, the shadows, to draw the hair very carefully, doing this mechanically, as he might have polished lenses or raked a courtyard, leaning back to judge the shading and to determine the whole effect the way a pruner or a plasterer might do, wondering sometimes—then ceasing even to wonder—how anyone could actually pay sums so enormous as three or four packages of tobacco (which, in the universe where he was living, represented a small fortune) for things as totally lacking in interest to his eyes as to those of the Oran pimp who judged thoughtfully, solemnly, mentally converting buttocks, vulvas, tongues, and cocks into their equivalents of "Porto-Rico" (this was the brand of the best tobacco, printed in red letters above palm trees silhouetted against a yellow sky) or rations of bread.

Then the Oran pimp was sent on a commando mission

(not as a punishment, not as Jew either though he made no secret of it, even prided himself on it, he who had never in his life set foot in a synagogue, never observed Yom Kippur except, for the first time, yielding to a reflex of dignity and defiance inspired by some obscure and ancestral consciousness and his pride as a swindler, in that camp where they were guarded by child-murderers: simply they had been lined up in the central square with at their feet the rucksack which contained all they possessed, and foremen or farmers in rubber boots and caps with leather visors had passed slowly down the lines, inspecting them, feeling their muscles, and doubtless the Oran pimp had seemed to them better equipped for the work than they had expected) and it was over—that is, drawing rumps, vulvas, and childish faces framed in silky hair (he had learned to produce the effects particular to blond hair, had also learned to create a certain disorder, so that the hair fell in clusters, partly masking the delicate faces, without either the vulvas, the breasts, or the bellies which the sharpened pencil shaded so carefully representing for him anything but the odor of "Porto Rico" tobacco and what he could exchange it for: luckily (luckily for his stomach), almost immediately he was assigned (two electricians had been called for and another of his friends, another Oran pimp who had also worked as a mechanic in a music hall or as a man-of-all-work in a brothel, knew more or less how to connect wires and replace a fuse, had taken him with him) to the German camp and there, with the same sharpened point of the same pencil, he now drew with the same mechanical care, the same total lack of interest, the tiny intersecting swords that embellished certain decorations on the chests of the *Feldwebeln* whose portraits he was making, dispensed not only from the electrician's tasks (the Oran pimp had been assigned another helper) but from

any kind of work at all, so that no sooner had the tender
bodies offered to penetration, the tender swollen vulvas,
the childish faces with greedy lips been summoned for the
needs of his stomach than they ceased to exist, not only
on sheets of paper but apparently even in his memory, his
consciousness, banished to the outer darkness in that total
absence of reality in which was erased, annihilated, everything outside the quadrilateral delimited by the triple barrier of barbed wire inside which subsisted concretely only
two exclusive and furious obsessions: to eat and to escape.

And this was only the third day. And it still took him
a moment (still lying in the dark as on the preceding nights,
without any desire it seemed to him but the one which can
be felt not even by an animal but by a machine, something
like an automobile after a long race or a locomotive
brought back to the depot, listening in the silence to its
metal organs cooling one after the other with faint ticking
sounds, relaxing by degrees, fading by degrees to the memory of sound and movement, aspiring to nothing but the
mere inertia of matter) . . . it took him a moment then to
realize what was keeping him awake in the dark, keeping
the shadowy cape of sleep from engulfing him (now his
eyes had had time enough to manage to make out, like
marbles in the darkness, the dim glow of eyeballs in the
remote, proper, vaguely reproving faces of the man with
the gun and the unmasked woman, the two remote fore-
bears who two hundred years before had coupled in a
rustling of tucked-up linens, panting breath, and the whiteness of bent thighs so that a minuscule amount of the
semen expelled, a minuscule element of the blood which
had circulated in their veins might circulate in the veins
of the man who without being able to fall asleep now was
lying beneath them): what he felt now, what kept his eyes
open, was no longer that glee, that vindictive sentiment of

triumph and that vindictive indignation at the thought of what they had done to him ("The nanny goat!" he called it later (only later: when he had more or less become a normal man again—that is, a man capable of granting (or of imagining) some power to speech, some interest for others and himself in a narrative, in trying with words to make the unspeakable exist; but later: for the moment he contented himself with telling the two old women and those who questioned him that his regiment had been annihilated and that it all (the battle—though he hesitated to use the word, wondering whether the name could be given to that thing which had happened in the bright spring greenery (that—but how to put it? battue, pursuit, route, farce, mort?) and in which he had played the role of game— and what had followed after: the interminable and humiliating procession of captives winding over woods and hills, the train, the cattle cars with the tangled bodies, the piercing hunger and thirst, the stench of rotten potatoes which floated permanently above the lines of barracks . . .), saying only that it had all been tough): "Yes: the nanny goat," he told them later with that brief, joyless laugh that was like the opposite of laughter: "The nanny goat which the hunter ties to a stake to make the wolf come out of the woods. Or in the hope that once the nanny goat is eaten the wolf will decide to stop—at least long enough to digest it. And to make the thing funnier, wearing that carnival disguise and straddling a broken-down horse. With this difference, that the nanny goat all the same has two horns to defend herself with and the disguise included as accessories only a tin saber and a five-shot popgun. And with this further difference, that the wolf had already come out of the woods and that after the nanny goat was swallowed he had also eaten the hunter. Except that according to what I understand, there wasn't even a hunter. And then that

fucking imbecile with his fucking combat saber . . ."), goat,
wolf, and hunter now out of his mind: then throwing back
the sheets, his body moved now by something as furious,
as elementary, and as imperious as hunger or thirst, re-
gaining that impetuosity (or rather than animality) that had
permitted or rather had forced him, in broad daylight, as
soon as the sentry had turned his back, to fling himself on
the ground, to slide under the barbed wire, to dash out,
to race on all fours into the woods like a dog, hands lacerated, indifferent to the pain, hearing nothing above what
seemed to him a terrible racket of leaves and broken
branches but the formidable roar of his breath scorching
his lungs, his throat, the roar of the blood in his ears, until
blood, muscles, lungs, heart, arms, and legs refused to
circulate or to function, that is, refused all on their own:
not his reason, his will, which were already protesting even
before they (his muscles, his body) began moving, continued to protest, waiting with terror while the arms and legs
struggled wildly for the echo of the shot, the impact, the
pain of the bullet that would pass through him: then motionless in the underbrush, still on all fours, out of breath,
thinking then that this was a good postion for vomiting,
thinking that if he vomited now it could only be something
like a piece of lung, or heart, in any case blood, thinking
at the same time Now they don't need to hurry: they can
take their time, calmly slip a leash around my neck and
afterwards lead me back, still on all fours, while gradually
the dreadful racket of his organs diminished by degrees,
and he once again began to hear the tiny sounds of the
forest, the calm hiss of the wind in the pines, and nothing
else, while gradually too his body and his reason were
reconciled, the latter resuming command, at least with
enough authority now to oblige his arms and legs to continue with great circumspection their quadruped's progress

for another moment until he straightened up cautiously, examining the silent forest around him, then standing and walking away taking great strides. And then three days walking through the underbrush, he and another fellow he had met up with later, a sort of knife-edged beanpole of a man, a *pied-noir* (he said he was from Constantine), he too having managed to thread his way into one of the cars of the convoy filled with Arabs which had crawled for two days and two nights from the Elbe, from the sandy Saxon plain to the shores of the Atlantic: still later they saw some distance away a black man still wearing the uniform marked on the back with the huge letters K G in red paint, who was walking in the same direction they were and who stopped stock-still when they made signs to him, watching them gradually approach through the ferns until they could discern what made the flashes of light appear in the hand he merely held out to them at chest height, stopping at the sight of the steel blade, the black man and the two other fugitives staring at each other for a moment over the ferns, the round, glistening, teak-colored, perfectly inexpressive face merely staring at them over the knife blade that glittered in the sun, then the black man turning without a word and walking away, leaving them, solitary, wild, bestial, his tawny outline cross-hatched by the pink and parallel trunks of the pines as straight as ship masts, until he vanished altogether, the Constantine fellow swearing angrily while they went on their way (saying That asshole, did you see that? saying He would have done for both of us, him and his knife, shit! He was ... All right the hell with that let him go fuck himself ... saying All right but look where the sun is now over to the left, saying Shit on the Senegalese! him and his chocolate friends that used to be on guard duty with their bayonets when we were on leave Shit! Send them all up to the front that's what I say, and a bullet right through the head of the first one who runs away then we wouldn't be in this shithole . . . , saying But where the fuck are we! These fucking ditches! Try and figure it out under these fucking ferns! What the hell good are they . . . Wait till one of us breaks a leg in this shit let me have a look at that fucking map . . .), forcing a path through the high and inextricable vegetation which the autumn was beginning to yellow: they were in it up to the chest, sometimes even up to the shoulders, and they had to push the ferns aside with their arms, like a man swimming, forcing his way, taking turns leading the way. The first night (the one when they reached the farmer's place, put on their thin overalls, and before leaving tore the department map off the back of the postal calendar) they covered nearly forty kilometers on a deserted road, not so much to put as much distance as possible between themselves and the camp as simply to walk, as though drunk, light-headed, as indifferent to exhaustion, though they had eaten practically nothing for three days (the farmer had given them a hunk of bread which they chewed on while they were walking), as to the cold, to the white frost which, as dawn approached, gradually made the legs of their overalls heavier around their ankles, finally forming a thin crust: nor did they feel it when it melted in the barn where, in the morning, another farmer let them sleep, but after that they avoided the roads, guided by the sun, walking or rather swimming in the sea of tall autumnal ferns that seemed to stretch as far as they could see over the absolutely flat ground while above them lazily hissed the long gusts of wind slowly swaying the tops of the pines (they could hear them coming from far away, like a huge murmur at first, approaching, widening, as if the vast motionless forest were waking from its somnolence, shaking itself, beginning to live, then it came, passed over their heads with a muffled roar, deep, majestic, fading, giving way to a few rustles here and there, then everything dying down until in the west a new and slow swell started up again). The sun was shining. During the day (at least while they were walking) the air was gentle: they could have been the first men in the first forest at the beginning of the world. Except for the black man, they met no living creature, no forester, no woodcutter, and except for that low and powerful rustling of the wind they heard no sound except, occasionally, the song of an invisible bird they could not identify. Later they stumbled into a bog it took them a long time to get out of without daring to call for help toward a farm whose chimney smoke they could see; toward the middle of the second day the forest thinned out a little, dwindling, giving way to fields, then to vines when the ground began to form valleys, and they were forced to take paths, creeping along the hedges or walking bent over in the vines. They still didn't feel how tired they were—or rather their fatigue had for months constituted so much a part of themselves that they no longer perceived it, any more than they felt the cold—any more, even, during those days, than they felt hunger or thirst, stealing overripe tomatoes from an overgrown garden, sharing the bread a woman brought them on the sly, drinking water in the streams and once the water mixed with the black mud of a swamp. Sometimes the farmers drove them off, sometimes allowed them to sleep in their barns, another woman served them a real meal, hot dishes they swallowed, like the tomatoes, without realizing what they were eating, ears cocked for the outside noises, continuing by habit to shiver without even realizing, again, that the stove was lit and that it was warm in the kitchen, they way they shivered calmly the whole afternoon they spent hidden in the vines, a hundred yards from the road which was now a frontier within the same country, waiting for the clouds to begin turning pink in the west, above the pine woods which bordered the vines and in the branches of which the soft wind kept raising its slow hiss, patient, continuous, solemn, while first the thickets, then the treetops gradually darkened under the orgy of gold that appeared in the west, the highest clouds first tinged blond, then salmon, then pink, then suddenly gray, silhouetted another moment against the slate-colored background of the sky, then entirely black: the pines, the vines, the earth over which they were crawling, the ditch, the straight road, and then the leap, the running, the headlights of the patrol car seen too late, the shots, and the running again, the fence scaled, the plowed field, the little woods, then a meadow, and still the shots, and more running, the flashlights already searching the little woods, and the light from a barn, and the man milking his cows who had stood up and simply said Quick. Over here. Follow me . . .

And now, in his bedroom in the vast building, as silent as it was dark, at the other end of which slept the two virginal old women, he groped for the switch, found it, the light instantly driving the shadows from the room where he pulled on his clothes with that cold calm, that glacial tranquility which now inhabited him, indifferent to the restored gaze of the unmasked woman and the remote ancestor with the elegant and useless hunting rifle, with his elegant powdered hair, his girlish neck, his pink cheeks, and that bloody spot which the scaling paint seemed to have opened in the temple, sliding down the cheek, the bare neck, soiling the casually open collar, as he must have been found, stretched out lifeless at the foot of the mantelpiece, staring with that same peaceful gaze, perhaps a little surprised, as though amazed himself by what he had just done, the servants (the unmasked woman too perhaps) having run in at the sound of the explosion which had echoed in the silence of the night between these same walls, the fingers curled round the trigger of the still-smoking saddle pistol with which, the evening of a lost battle, the elegant quail hunter had blown his brains out: bent over, busy now tying his shoelaces (and one of them broke, so that he had to take off one shoe, raise it in the light to thrust the frayed end in the eyelet, swearing between his teeth), still calm, cold, too absorbed by what was now concerning him even to think But I didn't remember so much blood. But maybe that damn painting has been chipped a little more, maybe it starts bleeding from time to time. Like those statues that saint where is it in Italy who bleeds and weeps on great occasions, thinking (or rather without even thinking, at least in words, but still with that same cold laugh): On anniversaries maybe. Of disasters, thinking again (now he had somehow managed by skipping two of the holes to knot the shortened ends of the lace): Only I haven't lost any battle, good God! I haven't even gone to war. Unless war consists in calmly riding in broad daylight on the back of a broken-down horse between two rows of burned cars and dead men waiting for one of those ambushed snipers behind a hedge to bother to make you a target. Good God! Just that. They hadn't left me a chance! A little stroll. But no doubt that idiot hadn't found any honorable way out except to get himself killed. Only he didn't have the right to . . . , still swearing between his teeth while standing now he pulled on the jacket that had become too big, not even bothering to tie his necktie, then turning out the light, leaving behind him the masked woman and the enigmatic suicide back in the shadows of the dim family mausoleum where past glories and lost honor continued to dialogue with the formidable marble general and their lineage of *rentiers,* of landowners, of amateur artists and ladies crowned with ringlets, now descending in silence the monumental staircase, crossing the courtyard, carefully closing behind him the small door in the vast portal, then walking (not running: walking, but rapidly) through the dim streets, passing in front of the dark terraces of the cafés: now and then he passed or met groups or couples, paying them no more attention than he would have given to vague shadows without real existence—in any case creatures belonging to another species than his own (he just managed to realize that they too were walking fast, muffled in overcoats with raised collars (he hadn't yet had time to buy himself one or rather it hadn't even occurred to him) which doubtless meant that it was cold—but he didn't feel it, any more than when he had arrived three days ago at the station, getting off the train shivering in his thin overalls), thinking vaguely (or rather remembering) without anger, without hostility or affection either, but with that same brief laugh: Cinemas!... But of course! Adventures... Why not? still walking fast, like those dogs you sometimes see trotting diligently along the house fronts or in the country without turning aside or letting themselves be distracted, guided by instinct or by some obscure direction of the memory toward the place where they can surely find the food, the female in heat, or the rubbish heap they must have. The two that he knew (where he had sometimes been in what now seemed to him a fantastically remote period of his life—or rather another life, a previous life so to speak, something (places—though these were the same, people—the same too though, where and among whom he remembered having existed) vaguely unreal, trivial, inconsequential) were closed: for a moment he stood there in front of the closed door, the façade with its blind windows, struggling now with a sentiment of unendurable rage, unendurable frustration, feeling something like panic swelling inside him, seeing again in the saucer that the waiter in the station buffet had set in front of him the two tiny tablets instead of sugar, wondering if during his absence they hadn't also passed a law or made a decree to close them, still furiously pressing on the doorbell then grabbing the knocker, knocking violently, hearing a noise like explosions echo in the silent street, the rain of blows, indifferent to the derision of two late passers-by, then beginning to knock again; nor did he look up again at the blinds of a window behind which a woman was shouting insults, already walking again, himself swearing between this teeth, following the tangle of narrow streets that rose toward the fortress, ready to start swearing again when the new door he knocked at opened.

This time it was slightly ajar, revealing a strip of pinkish light from inside, but a chain held it, so that even without paying attention to the bell, even without waiting for an answer to the first knock, he began to hammer with his fist on the panel that was not varnished (unlike the other one, it had no knocker of polished brass) but covered with a coat of ugly brown paint: it was a brothel of the second or even third class where he had never been, that he knew only the way you know a café or a hotel you have never gone to simply because you have often passed by, the kind of place frequented by the noncommissioned officers of the marines or traveling salesmen, and later he would remember this: the weary sound of footsteps (though the woman was wearing high heels she seemed to drag her feet as though in slippers), the strip of light blocked by something provided with eyes that examined him, the brief dialogue, the two voices equally harsh, without amenity, even hostile, hearing his own coming out of him with a kind of furious glee, that same sentiment of triumph, of

violence, and of invincibility still accompanied by that same
silent, peaceful laughter (thinking Drunk? . . . Well then:
drunk . . . Another thing I had forgotten . . .), which still
continued when the pinkish strip vanished and after a clatter made by the chain being unhooked the door opened
wide, revealing in the dim light inside a woman with an
exhausted face (the way, he thought, the face of a beaten
mule could look exhausted if it hadn't been alluringly
painted with carmine and decked out in a wig coming
uncurled) standing in the vestibule, continuing while she
stepped back to let him pass to repeat in a shrill voice
something about the noise and the late hour while staring
at him with an irritation under which, still shaken by that
same internal laughter, he recognized with a proud satisfaction (not out of any contempt for the woman and her
profession, finding himself on the contrary in a safe place,
delivered from that embarrassment he had been feeling
for the last three days, suddenly feeling for the mule's face
and the disagreeable voice coming out of it a kind of grat-
itude; everything was simple again, harsh, elementary, obvious) that same sentiment at once timid and hostile which
he had been able to discern in the eyes of the waiter at
the station buffet or, on the train that had brought him,
in those of the occupants of the compartment when he had
opened the door, shrinking so to speak at the sight of him,
huddling together, instinctively leaning away from the one
empty seat until he violently closed the door again, still
able to feel through the glass the glances of the nearest
passengers fixed on him looking him over from head to
foot while he stretched out on the linoleum of the corridor,
put the knapsack under his head, and went to sleep.

And he would still remember this (as he was still passing, moved by the same cold and attentive violence,
through a succession of obstacles and ordeals over which

he triumphed one after the other, appearing momentarily in his consciousness, then vanishing: the barbed wire, the thick ferns, the shots in the night): the station buffet, the bitter taste of the ersatz coffee steaming in the cup set before him while the waiter (an ageless man, short and stocky, with a round red face where nothing was missing but a mustache) stared at him, itemizing with that same aggressive and timid stare he remembered from the travelers huddled in the compartment the thin filthy overalls, the eight-day beard, the hand striped with a gash of dried blood, saying or rather howling: "Sugar? Su . . . You must be . . ." saying without even leaving him time to answer: "No there are no croissants!" And again: "Where do you think you . . ." Not even bothering to end his sentence, outraged, taking the change out of his trouser pocket (the change for the paper money which with a third-class ticket he had been given by the quartermaster sergeant at the demobilization center—another ageless man, well fed, wearing an impeccably brushed uniform and sitting under a chart with little pastel tags, pink, blue, yellow, green, behind a black-painted table, disgustedly leafing through his service record (or rather the rag of his service record) soaked with sweat and filth, then handing it to him, his expression severe, even reproachful, making him sign a receipt, then counting out the money), the coins ringing on the marble tabletop, joined by a filthy bill, the waiter already turning his back, walking away, crossing the empty room into which came from outside the noises of the clashing buffers: through the windows overlooking the platform you could see the reddish side of a freight train, the cars occasionally shaken by short shocks, alternately advancing and reversing a few yards while with a soft, almost somnambulistic gait a trainman carrying a lantern kept coming and going, stopping, in just as incomprehensible a way, as if by the light of several lamps under the smoky glass roof where the sounds of clashing metal spread in hollow reverberations were occurring some ceremony at once lugubrious, wretched, and absurd.

It was not yet daylight when he had entered the buffet, calculating that the two old women must still be asleep. His shirtsleeves rolled up, the waiter with apparent reluctance removed the chairs from the tabletop, then stood in front of him while he sat down, frowning, staring at him, waiting until he said "A coffee" (the same station, the same platform where almost day for day, fourteen months ago, in the heat of August, the crowd had surged in dark eddies against the sides of the cars, their faces alarmed, in tears, stamped with an incredulous consternation): now the waiter was sweeping a fringe of brown sawdust across the tiles; passing in front of the cashier's stool he said a few words to the woman sitting on it, checking little tabs of paper and impaling them on a metal stem and glancing briefly in her turn, frowning, in the direction of the table where the cup of coffee was still steaming, then going back to her work. The wall clock indicated only six forty-five. Gradually the glass panes in the roof began to grow pale: now the freight train had vanished, revealing the parallel steel rails which began to gleam (the cold and graying glass roof under which seemed to float, suspended in the void, a kind of inaudible and absurd protest, an inaudible murmur of sobs and farewells, the deserted platform where there continued to surge forward the invisible host of phantoms and where sitting in front of his empty cup, still shivering despite the illusory warmth of the illusory coffee, he now stared with a cold, hard, indifferent gaze, waiting until the yellowish lights gradually paled and the iron arches were silhouetted black against the blue sky dark at first, then gradually brightening). He cast a last glance at the clock, stood up, heading for the door, stopping, saying "What?" turning back toward the waiter who was repeating: "Your change!" (simply "your change," not "You're forgetting your change, monsieur"), then returning to the table, sweeping the filthy bill and the coins remaining on the marble with the back of his hand so that the coins scattered, rolled on the tiles, lost in the filthy scurf of sawdust, then walking out: outside, the avenue leading from the station stretched away, it too deserted, unreal, between the sleeping façades in the transparent and pearl-gray dawn where he was walking now, trembling no longer with cold but with rage, yet light, cheerful, with that body which for a long time no longer knew what fatigue was, filthy, covered with lice, feeling his wild beast's legs moving readily under him, passing in front of the warehouses, the gates of the palm-shaded gardens, the villas embellished with turrets and gables in which the rich wine merchants were sleeping, the shops with their shutters still closed. The first tram of the day passed him with a great clatter, heading toward the station, its windows still lit. Two men with shovels were working around a dust cart hitched to a horse. Each time the cart moved ahead, from one heap of garbage to the next, a little bell rang out in the silence. A woman opened a door, lugged out a trash can, and flung a pail of water on her doorstep which she then began to scrub. He walked on in that sort of triumph, continuing to swear between his teeth while that thing in him once again began to laugh, incoercibly, fiercely. At the end of the avenue, above the department store with the rococo roof, floated a little cloud with rounded edges, gradually tinged with pink by the first rays of the sun.

And now the faint smell of cooking, of leeks, of flat beer and cheap perfume, the inner door framed by red, green, and mauve stained glass, the central panel made of

one of those panes imitating frost through which the lights
gleaming on the other side disintegrated into shimmering
flakes, and once the woman let him in, not the usual salon
with the usual showy luxury: a marble-topped pedestal
table and its lace cloth, a stamped-velvet couch and armchairs, but (exactly as it should be, he thought, like the
crammed third-class compartment, like the filthy linoleum
in the train corridor) a bare, wan room lit by two wan
globes, like (the room) a nocturnal replica, implacable and
venereal, of the station buffet, just as lacking in warmth
and intimacy, with imitation-leather banquettes and café
tables, then (just as the glass of beer had appeared while
he watched without touching the dripping froth sliding
down the length of the glass, reaching the yellow wood
tray, and gradually spreading around the base of the glass),
there now materialized in the same way on the banquette,
not two women, not two whores, but the tangible presence
(perfume, breathing, warmth, patches of white flesh, density) of breasts and thighs and hips which with the same
glee, the same calm sentiment of victory, he had only to
stretch out his hand to touch, to feel under the thin kimonos, able to see in the wan light from the two bulbs the
jade-green shadow which ran like paint out of a tube from
the delicate turn of the neck down to where the lapels of
the kimono began to separate, widening, slipping over the
naked flesh made, apparently, of some translucent paste,
its sinuous and shifting contour changing with each breath,
insinuating itself like a liquid stream between the two parts
of the light garment decorated with leaves and fruits, apricot, red, orange, its bulging hems escaping from the carelessly knotted belt, revealing in a narrow interstice the
folds of the belly, then parting over the crossed thighs at
the hollow of which, between the apricots, the plums, and

the peaches, appeared a mossy nest the color of dry grass with bronze shadows.

And for a moment (or perhaps it only lasted a few seconds, for when he stood up neither of the two whores had had time to raise to her lips one of the two additional glasses overflowing with the same thick froth, merely concerned to ask him with the same insistent and docile lassitude (perhaps the woman with the mule's face had got them out of their beds, shameless, warm, and somnolent still) the same tempting and impatient question of the eternal and biblical Potiphar's wife), for a moment, then, nothing else, as if in a kind of torpor he was content to be sitting there, in the center of that priapic parody in cotton-flannel kimonos, not yet touching them, while the three pairs of painted eyes (those of the two young ones and of the mule who, after having served the beers, had withdrawn to the back of the room behind a sort of counter on one side of which a pile of folded napkins was paired with the pitch pine case of the gramophone which she had not even bothered to start up) examined him, though he was now, with the exception of the missing necktie, normally dressed (Only I don't have an overcoat, he thought: maybe that's it . . .), with that same suspicious mistrust, vaguely hostile, vaguely alarmed, peculiar not only to their profession but to something that doubtless now emanated from him (the mule apparently ready to press some button which would summon (perhaps she had also got him out of bed?) the person with plastered-down hair and dazzling alligator shoes—or more likely a pair of checked carpet slippers—who must be there in readiness). "Or maybe it's too obvious?" he thought, suddenly filled again by that rage, that unendurable indignation, thinking: "The fucking bastard, the . . . He couldn't just put a bullet through his

head? . . . Do us the favor of . . . ," then remembering that
at one moment (but was it before or after having paid for
those beers—or perhaps when he had noticed the disappearance of the two bicyclists?) he had turned toward them,
had said in his dry voice just tinged with irony, with contempt: "Well, shall we get on with it?" or perhaps nothing
but "And you guys? . . ." and the jockey—or perhaps himself in his somnolence, that state of imbecile semicon-
sciousness, of abdication, answering or rather stammering
something like "Yes, Colonel . . . ," then raising his head,
suddenly finding himself in one of the mirrors which ran
along the opposite wall above the empty banquettes: un-
framed mirrors, simply held in place by hooks, their
rounded tops making a series of arches, their beveled edges
reflecting shards of images, so that in the wan light he
could see himself several times: complete, then cut into
thin, rainbow-colored strips, with his round, almost shaven
skull, his inexpressive face where what he imagined to be
a smile barely tucked up one corner of his mouth, thinking:
"But maybe I don't know how to smile any more? . . . ,"
listening to the crude phrases the young redhead was whispering in his ear, thinking: "Yes. Good God, yes! The
fucking animal! We, I . . . ," but still not moving, relaxing,
for the first time back (surrounded by empty chairs, the
dreadful interior, listening to the obscene propositions) in
a universe now reassuring, trustworthy (as if since he had
left the guard post into which he had dashed five days
earlier, then discovered the spruce little town where the
quartermaster sergeant had given him a third-class ticket,
had climbed into that train full of passengers terrified at
the sight of him, had walked down the still-sleeping avenue
from the station at dawn, had traversed with mounting
indignation a scandalous and unendurable world which he
had a second time escaped by passing through the door

opened to him by the woman with the mule's face), the
enchanting and venal Circe gradually letting herself slide
down on the banquette, so that he could now see the
narrow strip of bare flesh between the two sides of the
bathrobe sliding apart like a theater curtain, the jade-green
shadow sliding at the same time, retracting, until between
the double pile of oranges, plums, and peaches accumulated in falling folds there no longer remained in the center
of the surface of smooth flesh anything but that tangle,
that tuft the color of dry grass and bronze, like some par-
asitical growth, a tawny bush where between the now
parted thighs two fingers with blood-red nails were opening something like a pale flower, and then standing, digging
in his pocket, taking out the bills, saying to the woman
with the mule face: "Yes: both. Together. Yes. What? How
much? Yes. Here . . . ,"then going up the narrow wooden
staircase in the wan light, following the rump which swayed
at each step under the petals of the broad poppies alternately distended and compressed, pulled in opposite directions and whose hairy stems he could now see twisting,
folding up like a fan, narrowing, then again spreading out
their dark hearts: a wide black band also bordered the
bottom of the robe, floating above the apricot heels, the
white calves phosphorescent in the wan light; then he no
longer saw them: as if suddenly all his faculties were abandoning him, withdrawing or rather concentrating in just
one, as if he was nothing more than a hand, a palm, fingers
moving up, feeling beneath them the silk of the thighs,
the muscles, and all that he remembered later about that
moment was that nest, that wild tangle, those folds, that
moisture, while without bothering about protestations,
without moving his hand from its place, as if he were
pushing, carrying the trembling body in front of him by
that crotch, he could hear his own laugh, his finally joyous

voice, perhaps a little hoarse saying: "No no, I won't let
you fall! . . . Get up! Good God, get up! Go on up! Get
up! . . . ," still laughing at the same time that he was insulting under his breath the sort of equestrian anachronism
brandishing his saber, the terrified passengers, the waiter
in the buffet, and the rich palm-shaded villas, then suddenly forgetting them, the external world suddenly done
away with, carried off, erased from his consciousness: falling on the two naked bodies, mingling with them or rather
drowning himself in the warm pools of flesh, and no longer
now those breasts, those bellies, those vulvas he had drawn
so many times, shaded with the tip of his pencil on the
pale sheets of paper, but something living, moving: hair,
membranes, lips, saliva, tongues, eyes, voices, breathing:
the flesh without falsehood, credible, docile in his hands,
moving, slipping, opening: solitude, death, doubt averted,
vanquished, then nothing more, nothing more than that
rush, that maelstrom while all the particles of his body
abandoned him, precipitated themselves, gathered in a
deafening racket at the pit of his stomach, out in front of
his stomach, exploded, flung themselves outward into
something burning bottomless endless . . . Then nothing
more: vacuum, peace: lying now on his back, panting still,
his bare chest with the protruding ribs rapidly rising and
falling, thinking only until his heart gradually recovered
its normal rhythm: Good God! Good God! Good God! . . .

Later he sent away the girl with the rough-cut face,
with the hard, black eyes, in the kimono decorated with
poppies, in whom he had emptied himself or rather had
exploded, finally lighting a cigarette, returning to lie down
on his back, one of his hands caressing the bare shoulders,
lifting from the head bent over him the bronze hair sweeping his gaunt belly, his thighs, while gradually the docile
hand, the docile mouth, again awakened in him, then gath-

ered up, then concentrated, then condensed, boiled, exploded, flung out of his depths not only that fountain, that sperm, but something like the very substance of those limbs, of that skinny and nervous body of which, still later, the light out, listening to the regular breathing beside him, still lying there, he could feel the muscles relaxed now, pacified, thinking again: Good God, good God, good God! thinking of the bodies stacked in the thick stench of the barracks, of the swarming lice, of the barbed wire, of the spindly silhouettes of the watchtowers with their raw pine poles, crudely planed, as if skinned, bristling here and there with tongues of bark.

He did not return there the next day, but the night afterwards. To the same one, with the same girl, the redhead. They knew him now. The mule with her still suspicious, mistrustful, rapacious stare, and the whore with whom he exchanged only a few obscene words or those stupid, distracted jokes which she listened to, watching him with that same intrigued, vaguely fearful expression, pensively following with her finger the enflamed flesh around the scabbed gash on the back of his hand, running her own hand over his head, saying: "Where did they give you that haircut?" He left her early, swallowed a bitter, harsh liquid in one of the first open cafés, went back to bed, slept again until noon, lunched with the two old women, went out to sit in the sun on a terrace shaded with palm trees where, sitting over the same bitter ersatz coffee, he watched sad-faced Jews offer people crossing the frontier the diamond fires of the tiny stones taken out of their tissue-paper wrappings which they furtively unfolded, terrified, grim, tragic. Every other night he returned to the brothel to spend the night in the same room with its hideous furnishings, nothing but the huge bed covered with some plushy, stained, faded pink cloth, a sink, a bidet, a chair, and two clothes hooks screwed into the wall on the hideous wallpaper with its vertical red and black stripes separated by a thin gold thread. In places mildew had loosened the paper, which buckled and pulled away from the wall. There was also a window, hidden by thick curtains of the same plush which he pulled open one morning to discover a sort of well of which the opposite wall, grayish and filthy, rose less than six feet away. Somewhere down below, a woman was singing to herself. At night he stayed in bed there, drained of everything, body and mind, in a vague well-being, breathing the congested odors of flesh, powder, and cheap perfume.

It seemed that nothing, neither captivity nor danger nor hunger, could spoil the replete placidity of the Oran pimp, a taciturn Jew with eyes like two pieces of coal between the heavy lids, at once companionable, incisive, and regal, who went to offer to their guards the naked and fornicating bodies patiently drawn each Sunday on the sheets of paper that he (the Oran pimp) obtained somehow in a courtyard surrounded with three rows of barbed wire and where every personal possession with the exception of a mess kit, a spoon, a nicked knife, and a piece of soap was fiercely forbidden; apparently one of the few (the Oran pimp) among all those imprisoned here (not only in the barracks but in the whole camp) to have fought (not that the others had seemed especially cowardly or timid: they had simply not had the occasion, taken or rather rounded up by men in green uniforms, helmeted, shouting and laughing, as they got off a train from their leaves or else peacefully sleeping in their barracks or in their stations thirty or forty kilometers behind the place where those who commanded them imagined the front to be): once (not twice: just once) he (the Oran pimp) told him about it: the commando corps for which he had volunteered, the

night patrol, the approach, the watch, the leap, and how
he had killed two Germans with cold steel; he made the
gesture, rapid, biblical, silent, bloodthirsty: left hand outstretched to gag the invisible enemy, fist closed over the
invisible dagger rapidly passing over his own throat, thick
lips pulled back showing the fierce teeth, tight-clenched,
and after that the five or six men who were there in the
stench of urine and excrement filling the vestible of the
barracks, puffing on the butts of butts, whispering, cursing,
or boasting in their remains of filthy uniforms, fell silent,
watching him calmly take out of his pocket a tobacco pouch
three-quarters full, a book of rice papers, and roll a cigarette which several hands reached out to light. And lying
in the dark beside the young and venal body between the
four walls covered with the hideous wallpaper (even in the
darkness he seemed to see it or rather to hear it, noisy,
violent, mildewed, naive, grim) he could remember that;
that is, that part of the barracks farthest away from the
door through which a guard could appear at any moment:
two tables and four benches around which a sort of aristocracy of Oran pimps surrounded by a respectful court
of little hooligans had organized a sort of club, a den where,
on the greasy filthy wood, with filthy cards, on Sundays or
after the evening meal (the fierce sharing with the help of
improvised scales of those loaves (those bars) of bread like
wet sawdust and over which he (the Oran pimp) presided,
always placid, biblical, regal) followed by no less fierce
poker games run by a sort of corpse (another Oran pimp)
with the head of a usurer, Portuguese, Jewish, or Spanish
(probably all three), with stakes consisting of cigarettes,
the camp money, or those same slices of agglutinated sawdust which had just been divided up. And he could still
remember this: the raising of the eyelids, the sharp glance,
the silent challenge which the Oran pimp had sent him

over the pitiless and expressionless faces of the boys the day when, straddling one of the benches, he had made so bold as to ask for some cards: for he (the Oran pimp) seemed to have adopted him, imposing on him as much as on the others, that is on his peers—or rather vassals, the cruel-faced brotherhood of weasels or bastards: and not (adopted) in the manner of a protector (he (the Oran pimp) had for that purpose an Arab, or rather a Kabyle, almost redheaded, with a broad peasant face, who did him little services such as washing his mess kit or his clothes: not a servant: rather a sort of dog he called "Raton" not out of malignity or scorn, simply because he knew no other name for an Arab, showing him an infinite solicitude and that visceral tenderness a man can feel for his dog, capable—he did it two or three times—of handing him under a circle of stupefied stares his still half-full mess kit, saying: "Here, I'm not hungry. Eat . . ."), not adopted then, but placed on the same footing, if not even slightly superior, and this not only because he was capable of representing with the help of a pencil certain naked bodies of men and women (or rather of nymphets), but showing him a sort of consideration, the kind, for instance, a brothelkeeper can show a fabulously rich or fabulously distinguished client frequenting his establishment, thinking (still surrounded by that invisible and hideous black cage on its red background): "And maybe that's why it's only here that I feel good. Maybe they—maybe I . . . ," incapable of formulating what he felt, leaving the town in the afternoon, walking alone in the countryside, at first just to walk, the way they had walked, covered more than forty kilometers during that first night after having escaped from the camp, following the roads where he sometimes passed a cart or two between the cypress-shaded kitchen gardens protected by laurel hedges. In the vaporous and reddish autumn twilights a faint wind made long bluish streaks of the smoke from the fragrant fires of dead leaves. The vines had just been stripped, revealing the earth again between the orangish-brown vinestocks sticking up everywhere. The roads were empty. Only an occasional truck passed by and you could hear the noise of it coming closer from a long ways off, then fading into silence. Everything was calm, intact, unchanged. He went to bed early: either he fell asleep right away or else, if sleep was too long in coming, he got up, dressed, silently left the house, and returned to the brothel. If the redhead was taken, he waited tranquilly, smoking cigarettes or exchanging a few words with one or another of the whores in their strangely reduced vocabulary (the same one he had used for fourteen months with the cavalrymen of his squadron or the prisoners in the barracks), sitting in front of the usual glass of beer whose froth overflowed, sliding slowly down the glass, without his ever touching it. One night he went into a movie theater which he left ten minutes later. He took the train (later he bought a bicycle) to go look at his vines, or rather the new bailiff (the old one—that is, the successor of the old slave-driver with the cap inveterately screwed onto his head—had been killed with half his regiment in the bombing of a station in Brittany, by the explosion of a munitions train halted beside theirs) who treated him with an exaggerated deference, as though he too were vaguely frightened, perplexed, servile, showed him the work done in the vines where he never knew just which were his and which those of the relatives who were in charge of their cultivation, and who had sent him regularly, since he had come of age, the quarterly checks they had continued to deposit in his bank account during the fourteen months that had passed, so that he could now spend the money that had been earned by the eight months during which he had ridden a horse first under snow and rain, then eight days under bombs, as well as five months digging trenches in the sandy soil of Saxony, pretending to install electric wires and drawing, after scenes of coitus or fellatio, portraits of *Feldwebeln*. He read nothing, not even a newspaper, stared coldly, quite indifferent when one of the old women showed him the headlines announcing bombardments, air battles, or torpedoings, merely glancing at news of local villages and sports events, all in not much more than five minutes, folding up the newspaper again and laying it on the table, One day, though, he bought a drawing board, some paper, and two clips and began copying with utmost exactitude the leaves of a branch, a reed, a tuft of grass, pebbles, neglecting no detail, no vein, notch, striation, or crack. The leaves still clinging to the vinestocks were an intense purple color, sometimes pink, sometimes still green along the veins. A yellow or brown rot attacked the edges and sometimes the interior, creating holes; he was particularly careful to reproduce the holes. He also drew the star-shaped leaves of the plane trees with white and ocellated trunks. Fallen to the ground and also turning brown, they took on a papery texture, drifting by the hundreds in the autumn gusts, leaping wildly, forming drifts against some wall or ditch. Gradually the only green things left in the whole countryside were the cypress hedges and the dark leaves of the laurels whose edges rippled like flames. One day when there was a high wind, he took the old tram to the beach, sat down in front of the row of half-timbered villas with their pretentious Normandy roofs, their pretentious turrets, their closed shutters and sanded doorways, and sat for a long time watching the yellow waves chasing each other over the sand that was the same color, collapsing in a vast and deafening roar. They kept coming in from the inexhaustible depths of the

horizon where sometimes he saw liquid explosions mounting toward the sky like geysers, rising one over the other,
tattered, galloping like horses, sliding down their own
slopes, rolling, tossing, struggling for speed, crushing each
other, spreading out finally in broad foamy sheets that the
sand drank down, sparkling as they vanished. This seemed
to have neither beginning nor end, like the sound or rather
the uproar—smooth, majestic, peaceable. Back in town,
where the lights were coming on, he passed the newspaper
office where each evening an employee chalked on a blackboard the figures representing the losses of the armies or
of the fleets. Winter came. The wind bent the pointed tips
of the cypresses, slowly swayed the branches of the huge
plane trees, blindingly white against the blue sky. One day
it knocked down seven, one after the next, that lay like
fabulous skeletons among the convulsive foliage of their
broken branches. He drew the mottled figures formed by
the peeling bark, grayish green with the sinuous shapes of
islands, gulfs, bays, tattered capes and peninsulas. Now he
no longer went to the brothel. The woman (the woman he
had married during a leave) had managed to cross that
frontier which now divided the country in two and had
joined him: the one who would undress, would patiently
pose for him, and had accompanied him fourteen months
earlier to the station, had packed in wax paper the sand-
wiches he had not managed to eat, and later on had sat
beside him in one of the armchairs of the *mairie* waiting
room in front of the table where a hurried deputy presided
over a sort of production-line ceremony—or rather an
administrative and funereal formality in a ridiculously
pompous setting, absurdly rhetorical, almost insulting to
the kind of couples who lined up at the door, composed
of women with strained faces (one was holding a baby in
her arms, another was accompanied by a little boy) and

men who had already lost the habit of wearing civilian
clothes, he in a suit bought the day before, she wearing
the ring with the solitaire diamond which he had gone to
the bank to get out of his vault that morning and had
abruptly thrust into her hand along with his will and the
key to the vault, joking until she began to cry. And now
he shared with her and the two old women the packages
of sausages, of chocolate and marzipan, which they had
sent him during the summer and which the quartermaster
sergeants of an army that was crushing cities under bombs,
killing human beings by the thousands, imperturbably returned to the sender, intact, only a little bruised, and
stamped "Unknown in the camp." It was too cold now,
except on a few sunny days and sheltered from the wind
that rattled the palms, to sit on the café terraces from which
the Jews with pathetic faces had gradually vanished. A
furious winter wind was cleaning the sky where, each night,
wheeled thousands of icy fires, silent and pitiless, a myriad
of stars like a dust of diamonds suspended and swept along
by some invisible and pitiless machine. In the library he
had inherited and which had been transported, along with
the enigmatic portraits of ancestors, the marquetry tables,
the damascened pistols, and the gold-framed mirrors, to
the part of the house he occupied, he found a few novels
by academicians of the early part of the century and a
broken set of the works of Rousseau, bound in pale leather,
the backs gilded, with panels of red morocco. Certain pages
bore marginal annotations in ink, written with a fine pen,
perhaps by the hunter with the womanish neck and the
bloody temple. At a bookseller's he bought the fifteen or
twenty volumes of the *Comédie Humaine* bound in reddish-
brown morocco, which he read patiently, without pleasure,
one after the other, not skipping one, listening to the wind
noisily rubbing against the roof, banging a shutter some-

where. Except for a few relatives, he knew only an old painter in town, a perpetual drunkard who endlessly repeated the same flowering peach trees and in whose house he met a few people stranded there like himself. Gradually he began to change. He began reading the newspapers again, looking at the maps they printed, the names of the cities, coasts, or deserts where battles were still being fought. One night he sat down at his desk in front of a sheet of blank paper. It was spring now. The bedroom window was open on the warm night. One of the branches of the big acacia growing in the garden almost touched the wall of the house, and he could see the closest fronds lit by his lamp, their leaves like feathers faintly palpitating against the darkness, the oval leaflets tinged a raw green by the electric light and occasionally stirring like aigrettes, as though suddenly animated with a movement of their own, as if the whole tree were waking, shaking itself, freeing itself, after which everything subsided and they became motionless again.

About the Author and Translator

Claude Simon won the Nobel Prize for literature in 1985. He fought in the Spanish Civil War, in World War II as a cavalryman, and later in the Resistance. After the Liberation, he returned to his ancestral home in the south of France, where he has cultivated vineyards and devoted himself to writing.

Richard Howard, who won the Pulitzer Prize for his own poetry, has translated from the French such acclaimed authors as Jean Cocteau, André Gide, Jean Giraudoux, and Alain Robbe-Grillet. He lives in New York City.